The Rules of Murder

The Rules of Murder

Rob Sinclair

CANELO

First published in the United Kingdom in 2020 by Canelo

This edition published in the United Kingdom in 2020 by

Canelo Digital Publishing Limited
Third Floor, 20 Mortimer Street
London W1T 3JW
United Kingdom

A CIP catalogue record for this book is available from the British Library.

Print ISBN 978 1 78863 778 7
Ebook ISBN 978 1 78863 776 3

This book is a work of fiction. Names, characters, businesses, organizations, places and events are either the product of the author's imagination or are used fictitiously. Any resemblance to actual persons, living or dead, events or locales is entirely coincidental.

Look for more great books at www.canelo.co

Printed and bound in Great Britain by Clays Ltd, Elcograf S.p.A.

For Nathan

Prologue

This is it, it's time.

I close my eyes. I try to block everything out. I know what I have to do, but I'm struggling to convince my body to move.

You have to go now. You won't have much time.

I shake my head in despair. What if I can't do it? What if I'm too scared? What if they find out what I'm doing and why? What if they stop me? What then?

They won't find out. Remember, we have this all planned. Nothing will go wrong if you stick to the plan.

I can't go back to that place. If I make a mistake, that's what will happen. I'd rather die than go back.

You won't go back. This is what we—

'Get out of my fucking head!' I scream.

Then silence.

I open my eyes and hold my breath. I hear nothing.

I thought I wanted the silence, but now it's thick and choking and my heart pummels my ribs as I begin to panic. I try to get up from the bed I'm sitting on, but my legs are weak and aching. I stumble from the room.

The silence doesn't last long. There was no respite, no pleasure in its emptiness, because I already know what comes next. A noise. A constant noise. Blaring, grating. Getting louder by the second. Like rats scratching across a hard floor. Hundreds of rats. Thousands, all crammed together, clawing and scratching and pushing and shoving. It's unbearable. My brain, my insides, vibrate from the din.

The rats are inside me. They're tearing around my body; their claws and their teeth scratch and scrape from the inside out…

I reach the bathroom. I virtually collapse onto the sink. My knee bangs the ground as my legs give way; my hands grasp the dirtied porcelain to keep me from smashing my head. I reach forward and turn the tap, splash cold water on my face.

But the noise is still there. Still growing. Disorientating. With immense effort I somehow manage to lift myself back to my feet. I catch a glimpse of my reflection in the murky glass of the mirror, but I look away.

I think about smashing my head against the glass. If I pummel my face into the mirror, the wall, over and over, the noise will stop. I might have some peace. I've done it before. I know it works. If only for a little while.

But no. Not this time. That's not why I dragged myself into this room. I prise open the cabinet. It takes enormous effort. My whole body is tense and contorted. I grab two pill bottles without looking at what they are. I discard the caps and chuck a handful from each bottle into my mouth. I crunch, I chew; I need just a little water to send the whole lot down into my stomach, where the rats are now screeching and screaming as they try to claw their way through flesh and bone, out of me and to freedom.

It's too much. My legs give way from under me again. I slump down against the wall. I think I bang my head – on a shelf? – but I'm not aware of any pain, just that my

2

head is now swimming and everything in front of me is blurred and spinning.

I close my eyes. I didn't think it possible, but the noises grow even louder and more all-consuming. It feels like my head is in a vice now, being slowly crushed. Just a few more turns and it will surely explode, and those rats will all surge free like lava from a volcano…

I roar with pain and desperation… And then…

When I think I can't possibly take any more, the rats are quietening down. Finally the pills are kicking in. The rats are becoming tired, sluggish. Not gone for good, they never leave me, but they're soon asleep, and before long I'm not aware of them at all, and that same eerie silence returns.

As ever, it's not for long.

That's good. You did it.

But what's better? The rats? Or this?

You did it. You have to stay strong. Stay strong for me now. We're so close.

I don't say anything in return. Instead I sit there on the floor, sobbing like an infant.

You need to get moving.

I do. Soon I'm on my feet and heading for the front door. I have no choice. I know I have to do this. This is my destiny.

And they all deserve to die.

Chapter One

She stepped off her bike and checked her watch. She was late. Too late. The drinks service was due to start in five minutes. She was supposed to arrive half an hour before that. Sophie slung her bike against the wall at the side of the ivy-covered mansion and hot-footed across to the main service entrance – perhaps the least grand aspect of the manor's exterior – where one of the cooks, a plump sweaty man in his thirties, who Sophie thought was called Greg but she wasn't quite sure, was standing vaping.

'Morning,' he said as Sophie tucked her bike up against the wall. 'You ready for this nonsense?'

'Nonsense?'

'Over two hundred guests. Food for five times that. Even more wine. They'll all be rolling on the floor pissed as twats by sunset. I'm just glad I get to go home once the food's out and the kitchen's clean.'

'Getting paid to watch a bunch of toffs getting sloshed? Can't be that bad surely,' Sophie said with a cheeky smile.

Greg, or whatever his name was, just rolled his eyes as though she really didn't get it.

She moved past him, in through the open service door and made her way through the original servants' quarters of the house. Well, they were *still* the servants' quarters really, even if the number of full-time staff at Drifford

House today was most likely considerably fewer than in years gone by.

Sophie soon found Pamela, a raven-haired woman in her fifties, whose face was stretched with curiously taut skin, and who was busily scanning through a list attached to her clipboard as she stood next to several crates of booze which had been plonked unceremoniously in a corridor.

'Morning, Pamela,' Sophie said as she approached.

Pamela looked up from the list the way an old schoolmistress might look at an unruly child while deciding whether or not to fetch the cane.

'You're late,' Pamela said without looking at her watch.

'I know. I'm sorry. It won't happen again.'

'That's what you said last time. I don't like making mistakes, but I'm beginning to wonder whether you might be one.'

'I said I'm sorry,' Sophie said, a little more sternly.

Pamela looked Sophie up and down, as if she were deciding whether or not she approved of what she saw.

'At least you've come ready,' she said after a long sigh. 'You'd better get into the gallery quick. Matilda is giving a final debrief. We're just about ready to start.'

Sophie nodded and turned and headed off for the gallery – a huge wood-panelled room that sat as something of a go-between, separating the servants' quarters and the main house. For smaller occasions, the gallery was used for dinners or drinks receptions, but today it was more like a store room with dozens of tables crammed with food, drinks, glasses, plates, cutlery, all waiting to be deployed to the gathering masses somewhere beyond.

Matilda, the most senior of the waitresses at Drifford House, who, like Pamela, was a full-time live-in employee, had already wrapped up by the time Sophie walked in, and the group of young men and women all dressed up in their suits and black dresses were busy getting trays of drinks ready.

Sophie slunk across the room, head down to avoid Matilda's watchful eye, heading for a familiar face. Maisie. Sophie had known her, loosely, for years. Maisie had been in the year above at primary school, but had moved on to a state-run comprehensive afterwards, rather than the expensive Highmount that Sophie's parents had splashed out on.

'What did I miss?' Sophie said.

Maisie gave a little smirk. Sophie wasn't sure why.

'Just what you'd expect. How privileged we should all feel to be here today. How we're about to meet the great and the good. How we get to keep any tips we're given, which can be very generous, particularly if your skirt is short enough and your smile wide enough, and your blouse unbuttoned just enough.'

Sophie's eyes wandered down. Maisie's blouse was buttoned up right to the neck.

'Keep them keen,' she said with a wink.

Sophie screwed her face up.

'Oh, come on,' Maisie said. 'The fact you're here at all suggests you know exactly what you can get out of an event like this. It's down to you how far you want to take things. How much you want to make from these cretins.'

Maisie thanked the pourer then carefully lifted the silver tray from the table and headed away.

—

Sophie didn't believe herself to be naive, at least no more naive than other eighteen-year-olds, and yes, she'd heard plenty of rumours about the Redfearnes' notorious summer balls. Of course, such rumours had to be taken for what they were; little more than tabloid stories. But still, Sophie realised there had to be some truth to it all.

Yet she'd still willingly signed up for this. What did that say about her?

What it said was: where else could an eighteen-year-old expect to make two hundred pounds a day in salary, plus however many hundreds more from the punters just by smiling and flirting a little every now and then?

Determined to make the most of it all, Sophie had taken the first arse-pinch in her stride. Hadn't even bothered to turn around and glare at whoever had done it. The second one too. She'd not flinched when a guy who must have been in his seventies stuffed a twenty pound note into her bra strap just above her breast.

The third arse-pinch though, the guy went for a longer squeeze, as she was busy refilling his champagne glass for the umpteenth time. She squirmed to try and release his grip and when that didn't work she 'accidentally' sloshed champagne down his suit arm.

That got him to let go.

The guy, a pot-bellied and heavily tanned balding man in his forties, stepped back and was clearly gritting his teeth ready to give her some grief.

'I'm so sorry,' Sophie said. 'Let me fetch you a cloth.'

She turned and hurried off before he said anything. She glanced at the clock on the wall as she went. Not even six p.m. What the hell were these wankers going to be like in a few hours' time?

She didn't bother to go back with a cloth. Instead she headed into the library with her bottle and for the next hour went to the gallery and back each time, rather than to the ballroom where the arse-grabber had been. Matilda wouldn't be impressed if she saw, but Sophie needed some respite, and she was happy that the guests in the library seemed a notch or two lower on the loutish stakes.

But then later, as Sophie was heading along the portrait-covered corridor to the gallery for a new bottle, she saw the arse-grabber up ahead, on his own and sauntering her way.

His eyes pinched when he spotted her, before he gave a ridiculously smug look.

'You get the cloth yet?' he said.

'So sorry, sir. I was asked to come serve in the library. I can get it for you now?'

She made to head past him, but he came to a stop, his frame wide enough to halt her in her tracks unless she wanted to barge past him.

'What's your name?' he said.

'Sophie. Sorry, do you think I could get past?'

She went to duck to the side, but he put his hand out onto the wall to block her.

'Well, Sophie, my clothes are still sopping. Is there somewhere you could help me get out of them do you think?'

The look he gave her made her insides curdle; his stale alcohol breath made her wince.

'Hey, Arnold, do you think I could squeeze past you there, chap?'

Sophie recognised the voice. Oscar Redfearne.

The letch known as Arnold looked somewhat despondently over Sophie's shoulder and took his hand from the wall.

'Oscar,' he said, 'I've been meaning to come and talk to you. Your father mentioned about your plans for next summer.'

Oh, so not only was he a letch, but he was a kiss-ass too.

'Of course,' Oscar said. 'But if I may, I just need to steal this young lady away. Pamela was looking for her.'

Arnold's face soured. 'Not a problem. I was just looking for Raf and the others.'

'I think I saw them in the drawing room last,' Oscar said.

Arnold nodded and grumbled something as he glared at Sophie before he turned on his heel and headed off in the opposite direction. Sophie spun to face Oscar who had a knowing grin plastered on his youthful and handsome face.

'Don't worry,' he said, 'he'll be fast asleep on the sofa before long. Last year his wife had him hauled out of here before ten o'clock. He's an arrogant sod, and a hopeless drinker, but he's harmless.'

'Harmless? When was the last time he grabbed your arse and then propositioned you in a quiet hallway?'

'Well...' Oscar's face turned from playful to serious in a flash. 'Sorry, I'm sensing you wouldn't appreciate me joking about it.'

Sophie shrugged. Oscar looked at his watch.

'When's your next break?' he asked.

'It was an hour ago. I missed it.'

'Does Matilda know?' His face full of concern now.

Sophie shrugged again.

'You guys get scheduled breaks for a reason,' he said, as though he was an expert on workers' rights, and a voice of the people. 'You've got a long night ahead. Come on, why don't we get some fresh air?'

Sophie knew exactly what answer she should give to that, but she found herself reaching for the exact opposite.

'Yeah, why not?'

Oscar smiled and grabbed the empty champagne bottle from her hand and plonked it down onto a heavily polished side table. The simple gesture made Sophie wince. If her boss had seen her discard a bottle onto the furniture like that…

Oscar was soon heading off back towards the library. Sophie somewhat tentatively followed. He bounded ahead and back into the melee and reappeared a moment later with another bottle in his hand.

'Just in case,' he said with that same cheeky smile back on his face, before he moved to the side and pulled down on the handle of a set of patio doors that led out.

Sophie looked over her shoulder, as if checking the coast was clear, then despite herself, she followed him out, at the last moment getting a glimpse inside the bustling library up ahead and noticing Maisie, empty-handed, heading towards her. Sophie was sure her colleague gave her a questioning look.

–

'Come on, follow me,' Oscar said when Sophie stepped out into the warmth of the sunny summer afternoon. He beckoned her over before taking a swig from the nearly full bottle. 'You want some?'

Actually, she really did, but she politely declined. No point in sealing her own fate with Pamela so foolhardily, she decided.

What was she talking about? Like taking a 'break' outside with her employer's son was an otherwise sensible thing to do...

They walked side by side away from the house, heading for a thicket of trees across the other side of an expansive lawn. There were no other guests out here, at this side of the house, and Sophie was glad for the respite from it all even if she was uncomfortable about what she was doing.

'You look really beautiful today,' Oscar said.

Sophie looked over and caught his eye and he coyly looked away.

'I know you're not like the other girls here,' he added.

Sophie laughed, a little sarcastically. 'I have no idea what you mean by that.'

He pulled her to a stop. 'Of course you do. You're special, Sophie. You know I've always liked you.'

He'd said pretty much the same thing last time he'd been drunk in her presence, except that time she'd been drunk too, and they'd both been in the VIP lounge of a nightclub in Birmingham. She'd also been within the safety of a group of friends then.

She'd kissed him that night, and they'd swapped phone numbers. They'd messaged each other plenty since, and she was well aware that he'd had his watchful eyes on her all day today. Yet alone together at his parents' home, he in his Savile Row suit, she in her waitress outfit, the dynamic felt so very different to at school or in a club.

Not exactly dangerous, but certainly... wrong.

But perhaps in a good way.

Oscar was still talking as they carried on meandering away from the house, but her mind had wandered to all of the rich owners the house had belonged to, all of the many servants who'd worked here. Wasn't it by now a ridiculous cliche? It was almost like a scene from one of those bloody awful outdated period dramas that her mum and gran were so into. The shy but pretty, poor young woman being wooed by the wealthy and handsome bachelor. In days gone by, young women in Sophie's position would have had little ability to say no.

Could *she* say no to Oscar, and whatever it was he had planned as he led her away from the house to this secluded spot?

Did she want to say no?

They soon reached the end of the lawn and Sophie stopped. She looked back to the house.

'I'll need to get back soon.'

'I know, I know. But let me just show you something first. You've never been down here, have you?'

She shook her head.

'It's really amazing. I promise you.'

He took another long glug from the bottle then grabbed her hand and pulled her into the trees.

The next time she glanced over her shoulder, she couldn't see the house at all beyond the thick of green. But she could hear running water.

Her hand slipped from Oscar's and she looked back to see him heading off away from her, able to move far more easily without two-inch heels.

He pushed his way past bushes and undergrowth and moments later he was out of sight.

'Oscar!'

She stopped and listened. All she could hear was the running water and the gentle rustle of the trees all around. She knew the best thing to do was to turn and head for the house. She was here to work, not to screw around with Oscar.

Instead, she carried on.

She came to a small clearing; the sound of water was even louder now than before. She sighed in relief when up ahead she saw Oscar, calmly standing by the edge of a stream, frothing as the water cascaded down across jagged rocks.

'What did I tell you?' he said, turning back to her with an impressed look on his face. 'Not many people know of this spot. I come down here all the time, just to get away from it all.'

She moved up to his side and looked around. There was no denying it was a beautiful spot. The trees here opened out and the sun's rays seeped through, making the water glisten. Across the other side of the stream was a thicket of wild flowers, all manner of colours, lustrous in the warm summer light.

She squirmed, but only because it was unexpected, when he wrapped his arm around her waist.

She looked at him, sure he was about to lean forward to kiss her.

'Wait there, just one moment.' He put the champagne bottle on the ground next to her feet. 'There's something else I really want you to see.'

She opened her mouth to speak but he was already trudging away. Soon he was out of sight. What the hell?

Several minutes passed, each one becoming more uncomfortable and more eerie than the last. No sign of

Oscar, and the rushing water right next to her drowned out the sound of anything else around.

She picked up the champagne and took a long gulp. Then another. Then looked around again.

'Oscar!' Sophie shouted.

She couldn't make out any response. What the hell was he playing at?

'Oscar!'

Still nothing. She was about to take another swig when she thought she saw something moving off to the right, the direction Oscar had headed off in. But when she looked, she could see nothing but gently swaying branches.

No, she didn't like this.

The sound of voices got her attention. She whipped her head around, left and right, but could see nothing. Yet she was certain she'd heard people laughing.

Had Oscar brought his mates down here too?

Sophie shivered now as ominous thoughts wormed into her mind.

Then came the sound of a snapping twig, right behind her.

Her heart lurched as she spun in the direction it'd come from.

It burst in a panic when she saw the figure right there next to her.

Open-mouthed, she stepped back, as scared as she was confused.

'What the—?'

They were the only words she managed to get out before the blow to her head knocked her to the ground.

Chapter Two

The presence of the marked police car at the grand wrought-iron entrance gates to Drifford House meant there were already several nosy bystanders gathering on the street outside when Dani arrived a little past ten a.m., despite it being a Sunday morning. She showed the officers her ID and they opened the gates and let her through, and she drove her Ford Focus up the dead straight driveway towards the house.

In front of her, magnificent Drifford House sat prominently within its glorious ten acre plot of land like a jewel-encrusted ring on a perfectly manicured finger. Lying within the wealthy South Staffordshire enclave of Little Aston, the early-nineteenth-century manor house wasn't just another of the myriad expensive executive homes in the area, it was *the* home. The very reason for the existence of the enclave at all.

The rows of sycamores and oaks in full summer bloom either side of the long tree-lined approach framed the glimpse Dani had of the mansion as she headed along. She wasn't sure if she was in awe of the place or if she detested every ounce of it and the extravagant wealth of the few that it represented.

In truth, she knew little of the family who owned it, even if she'd already built up plenty of preconceptions about them on her way here.

As she came out of the tree-lined drive the house came into full view for the first time and Dani did a double-take at the scale and beauty of what she saw.

The initial awestruck reaction didn't last long though. Largely because of the cluster of police cars and the two ambulances that were all hastily parked up on the gravel drive. Despite the grandeur of the mansion, this place was a crime scene now, the same as any other, and Dani would treat it as such.

She parked her car, but as she looked out of the window, past the police cars and up to the sweeping mansion, a wave of dizziness washed over her. She grabbed her bag and took a pill and flung it into her mouth. Yet another backward step in her recent attempts at weaning herself off the medication. She stepped out of the car, the sudden burst of heat outside of the air-conditioned cabin taking her breath away for a moment. Out of the corner of her eye she noticed the figure heading her way. DS Easton. He had a curious look on his face. Had he seen her popping the pill?

'Aaron,' she said as he approached. 'You beat me to it.'

'I only live the other side of the park. I was still at home, about to get outside in the sunshine, when we got the call.'

She'd come from HQ in central Birmingham. Yes it was Sunday morning, but for weeks now there'd been nothing she could do to keep her mind off the trial – even the pills couldn't do that – so she'd thought she may as well try and do something useful over the weekend, and anyway, Jason was off playing golf.

One of them knew how to relax at least.

'But I only got here two minutes ago,' Easton added, 'so I've not seen anything yet.'

Dani nodded and looked over at the entrance to the house: two wide oak doors, which were both currently opened. A bleary-eyed man in corduroy trousers and a messy shirt was standing in the doorway chatting with a uniformed police officer.

'He's the owner?' Dani said to Easton.

'Yeah. House belongs to Henry and Caroline Redfearne. That's Henry. I believe his wife is somewhere inside.'

'You haven't spoken to either of them yet?'

'No. I was about to introduce myself when I saw your car coming up the drive. You want to do it now?'

The police officer put his hand on Henry Redfearne's shoulder and, heads bowed, the two of them disappeared inside.

'No. There's no rush. They're not going anywhere. Let's see what we've got first.'

They grabbed some gear and then Dani followed Easton around the side of the house and across a lawn to a wooded area. Easton stopped at the edge.

'It's just through here,' he said. 'We should get suited up.'

Dani nodded and they each slipped on some blue plastic coverings for their shoes, white overalls, and latex gloves then headed on their way through the trees.

'The body was found just after nine by one of the groundskeepers,' Easton said. 'There was some sort of party last night, which went on well into the early hours, apparently. Potentially explains why the alarm wasn't raised sooner. Mr and Mrs R were still tucked up in bed recovering when the 999 call was made.'

Dani glanced over at Easton. 'According to?'

'According to the PC I spoke to before you arrived. Who I guess took it from either the groundsman or the Redfearnes.'

'Something we'll need to clear up properly then.'

'Of course. Just giving you the little I've got so far.'

They carried on through the woods, the shade from the tree canopy providing welcome relief from the fierce sun. It was already approaching thirty degrees outside and there was talk of records being broken once again. The heat was oppressive enough, but the rising humidity was worse, and Dani was already damp with sweat even after just a few minutes out of the car. They followed a path through the trees, instinctively closing in on the glimpses of white they could see moving through the foliage, and the sound of water which was drawing them in all the time. They soon came to a small clearing where two white-clothed Forensic Scene Investigators were busy prepping a tent to cover the... well, Dani didn't really quite know how to describe what she found herself looking at on the ground by the stream.

She caught Easton's eye, and noticed he shared the same look of disquiet that she was feeling. Despite her reticence, her eyes soon fell back upon the bloody, pulpy mess on the ground.

One of the two FSIs strode over.

'You're DI Stephens?'

Dani nodded. 'I am. This is DS Easton.'

'Saad Tariq.' Dani didn't know him and assumed he was new to the forensics team as she by now unfortunately knew pretty much everyone they had. There was no offer of a handshake: who knew what he'd been touching already? Though she did spot the tell tale glance up to the scar above her ear; the only visible permanent reminder of an attack that had nearly claimed her life. Even though she'd found a way of styling her hair to more or less hide the lumpy bald patch of skin to casual observers, it was still common for people who knew of her past to flick their eyes there – voyeurism, or something like it. 'We were just getting the… er, the remains covered. It's not yet clear where the rest is, but this is what we've got.'

Dani simply nodded at the loaded words, trying her best to remain calm and in control as she stepped forward, her eyes never leaving the mushy heap of blood and sinew and flesh and bone and innards that frankly looked like discarded set pieces from a cheap horror movie, and nothing at all like the remains of a human being. Except for the partially attached head, which was almost surreally untouched, the eyes looking to the sky in a twisted and pained death stare.

Dani's mind whirred with thoughts about the effect the high temperature would have on decomposition. How long before rot infestation would set in when the weather was like this?

'What did the groundskeeper say?' Dani asked Easton, trying to push the putrid thoughts away as she came to a stop three yards away from the corpse. As used to dead bodies as Dani was, that was plenty close enough for now.

'This is second hand,' Easton said. 'So I'd suggest we make him our first call once we're done down here, before the Redfearnes, even.'

'Not least because we'll need to rule him out one way or another.'

'Absolutely. From what I gather he's the only person from the house who's seen the body so far, so we need to arrange something more formal, but basically the guy has worked here his whole adult life. Over twenty years. He reckons he knows every single person who works and lives here.'

'So if anybody knows who this is, he should.'

'Indeed. And he's absolutely convinced that we're looking at what's left of the owners' son. Oscar Redfearne.'

Chapter Three

Dani managed to pull her eyes away from Oscar Redfearne's remains for a moment. 'What can you tell me so far?' she asked Tariq.

He sighed before answering. 'Have you asked Ledford to come down?'

'I called him on my way over, based on what I'd already heard.'

Although a pathologist wasn't always required to attend a murder scene, Dani could see that this young man's death was particularly horrific and unusual, and she was glad she'd called, as she felt she'd need the extra help not just in determining cause of death – which would be properly concluded in post-mortem – but what on earth had happened to the poor sod leading up to his demise. Jack Ledford, despite his many oddities, was the best pathologist Dani knew.

'Any sign of a murder weapon?' Dani asked.

'We're still to finish our searches of the area, but there's nothing obvious within sight. Obviously you'll need Ledford to get you the detail at a later date, but my own inclination would be you're looking for probably more than one weapon here, given we've got massive lacerations to the skin, consistent with a blade, but also obvious gouges more in line with something like a machete or a hatchet or even an axe.'

Dani tried her best not to flinch at the thoughts bubbling in her mind.

'Like I said, that's my conjecture though, so please don't write it down.'

Easton looked up and stopped scribbling in his notepad. 'Just for my own benefit,' he said.

'We're just prepping the scene still,' Tariq said, 'but you can see the state he's in. It shouldn't be long before I start going over the body to record what I can and collect samples. We'll do a full sweep of the nearby scene too but...'

Tariq looked off, first to the body, then around the woods, which Dani could well imagine was normally a spot of pleasant serenity. Not today.

'You might want to think about doing a wider search, but we'll need more personnel. And I really think we should get this body moved as soon as we can, given the heat.'

Dani had to fight back the rising bile as the thought of decomposing flesh rushed through her mind once more.

'OK, leave it with me,' she said.

Tariq turned back to the body and carried on with his work.

'Ledford'll love you,' Easton said with a smirk. 'Waking him up on a Sunday morning for this.'

'I'm not sure I see another choice,' Dani said, sounding blunter than she'd intended; but she knew she was struggling to keep calm and focussed today, for more than one reason, and even despite the extra pills.

She glanced to Easton and saw the smirk drop away.

'Sorry,' Easton said. 'I meant… you know.'

Dani kind of did. Ledford could be a stuck-up prat sometimes, and he certainly wouldn't welcome being disturbed without justification, but he was also a damn good pathologist and he'd never shirk his responsibilities.

For the next few minutes Dani and Easton watched in silence as the two FSIs finished preparing the tent to protect the remains from the elements. It was a hot, sunny morning, but thunder and rain were due later – which would hopefully clear the air – and as much as Tariq probably wanted to scoop up what was left of Oscar Redfearne sooner rather than later, he wouldn't do so until he was certain he'd done every bit of analysis at the scene that he could.

With one side of the tent left open, Dani continued to watch as Tariq got to work with a pair of tweezers going over the body – that was still partially clothed, albeit the clothes were torn and ragged – looking for fibres and whatever else stuck out to him. The other FSI was now busy photographing the scene from every conceivable angle.

'Do you know much about the Redfearnes?' Easton asked, snapping Dani from her thoughts as to the manner of Oscar's violent end.

'Nothing. You?'

'Henry Redfearne is a top investment manager for a pensions provider, though he also has a sizeable stake in various finance companies and commercial properties. Apparently he's worth hundreds of millions, though he was born into money, so he's not exactly self-made.'

'You knew all this already?' Dani asked.

Easton shrugged. 'You hear things. It's not exactly an inconspicuous house, is it? They're among the wealthiest people in the entire West Midlands. Plus, I know a couple of lads who grew up nearby. People talk.'

'And his wife?'

'Caroline? Don't know much. I'm not sure if she works.'

'Kids?'

'Just Oscar. Eighteen years old. Still lived at home. Recently finished sixth form at Highmount College and was planning on attending London School of Economics in September.'

Dani shook her head. Whatever the reason for Oscar's death, it was such a sad waste.

'Have the Redfearnes been told we think it's their son?' she asked, thinking back to when she'd arrived at the house not long ago. Henry Redfearne had looked tired and ragged but not exactly distraught.

'No,' Easton said.

She raised an eyebrow. 'So the groundskeeper stumbled over the body, called the police and then just sat tight-lipped from then until now?'

Easton shrugged. 'From what I gather the first response was here in less than five minutes. Maybe after making the call he went to the gates or something to wait for them. And, like I said, the Redfearnes were fast asleep still at that point.'

'Then why didn't he bloody knock on their bedroom door?'

Easton looked a little taken aback by Dani's abruptness, but he once again didn't rise to it. Apparently he'd long ago learned to ignore Dani's unconscious curtness, even though she felt that people ignoring her problems was hardly the best way of helping her.

'Maybe he doesn't have access to the house. Or maybe he did try to wake them but couldn't. Remember I said there was a party here last night. And when I say party... have you really heard nothing of the Redfearnes?'

'Nothing.'

Why was that really so hard to believe? They weren't exactly the Kardashians. In fact, even if they were, Dani wouldn't know much because she had no interest whatsoever in that kind of thing.

'They hold an annual summer party for the great and good,' Easton said. 'They get all sorts coming here. The last few years there's always been a few pictures in the press the day after. Minor royalty, TV personalities, sports stars, lords, MPs, plus a hell of a lot of plain old rich folk. They raise money for charities, but really it's just an excuse for a huge piss-up from what I gather. But...'

Easton trailed off.

'But what?'

'Remember that story in the national press about the Presidents Club charity dinner?'

'What, where agency models were hired as hostesses and plied with alcohol so that slimy old men could ogle them and grope them and hopefully take them to their suites to screw them after?'

'All vindictive allegations according to the organisers. Anyway, I've heard the Redfearnes' event is kind of like the West Midlands' equivalent.'

Dani cringed at the thought of what that meant. In fact she was now wondering how exactly she'd never heard any of this.

'Back to the point, though,' she said, 'the parents don't know Oscar is down here?'

'Not that I'm aware of.'

Dani shook her head in despair. The parents, or some other family member, would have to do a formal identification at the morgue at some stage, and while she really didn't want the Redfearnes seeing their son out here like this, it felt wrong to Dani that they were stuck back up at the house not even knowing it was their son who'd been found dead in their garden.

'Why was the groundskeeper down here anyway?' Dani asked.

'How do you mean?'

'Look around you. It's not exactly an ornamental lawn here, is it? There're no trimmed hedges or flowerbeds or rows of vegetables. So why was he down here?'

Easton just shrugged yet again. She made a mental note of the unanswered question. The conversation paused. With her brain absorbed, Dani continued to stare at the two FSIs who were now deep in conversation about something.

'Is there a problem?' Dani said when she noticed the quizzical look on what she could see of Tariq's face, given his hood and mask.

He looked up at her and sighed. 'Come and take a look.'

But before Dani moved, his eyes flicked to behind her shoulder, a split second before there was a blood-curdling scream.

Dani flinched and spun around, sinking down as though prepping herself to attack whatever threat was there.

She didn't attack. Instead she straightened up to see a woman a few yards away, mouth and eyes wide in horror. Wearing grey sweatpants and matching hoody, she had dyed blonde hair, which was all mussy, remnants of make-up from the night before still around her eyes.

'No!' she screamed. 'Oscar!'

She fell to her knees. A uniformed police officer came darting up from behind her.

'What the hell?' Easton shouted as he stepped forward, towards the PC.

'I'm… sorry,' the young PC said, out of breath, his face as white as Caroline Redfearne's now was.

'Come, on, Mrs Redfearne,' Easton said, as he crouched down and gently tried to prise Caroline back to her feet. 'You don't need to see this.'

She was sobbing as she shakily got back up. Easton was doing a good job of standing between her and the body a few yards behind him. But then her face turned to determination in a flash, and she shoved Easton out of the way and took another step towards her son before she screamed again, even louder and more pained this time.

'Oscar!'

The PC reached out for her and strangely his touch seemed to calm her for an instant, before she turned and hunched over and spewed thick red vomit all down the crotch of his uniform.

'Bloody hell!' He shouted as he stepped back in disgust, but when his eyes found Dani's hard glare, his outburst was short-lived. Comeuppance, she thought.

Dani moved up to them and held back her gag reflex at the sight and stench of the thick, chunky vomit as she gently put her arm on Caroline's shoulder.

'I'm so sorry, Mrs Redfearne. I can't imagine what you're feeling. But please, you don't need to see this. And we need to work here. If you go back to the house, we'll come to speak with you very shortly.'

Caroline looked to Dani and gave a kind of glare that she couldn't quite read. The next moment the vomit-covered PC had managed to coerce her into moving and they were slowly heading away without any more words spoken.

'Great,' Tariq said, coming up to Dani's side. 'And now the crime scene is bloody contaminated with the remnants of late-night cocktails and whatever the hell she was eating at two a.m.'

'At least now we know they know,' Easton said.

Strangely, Dani kind of agreed. If anything, the surprising thing was that it had taken them so long to find out. 'You said you'd found something,' she said to Tariq.

She moved over to him and he bent down and indicated a small bloody object in the dirt a few feet away from the body.

'An earring?' Dani asked after she'd studied it for a few seconds.

'Looks like it,' Tariq said, picking the silvery object up with tweezers before dangling it in the air while he and Dani stared.

'I'm guessing Oscar Redfearne wasn't wearing that,' Dani said.

'Neither of his ears is pierced.'

'Could he have had it in a pocket or something and dropped it?' Easton asked, who was now hovering over Dani.

'Possibly,' Tariq said. 'Though it is covered in blood, even if it's not clear whose blood it is. But look closely at the pin.'

Dani edged her head further forward a couple of inches. 'That's not dirt, is it?' she said.

'We'll test, but I don't think so. It looks more like a small clump of flesh to me.'

'So it was torn out?' Easton said.

'Could have been.'

'You think he did it?' Easton said, indicating Oscar Redfearne.

'Maybe he did.'

'So there was a struggle with a woman—' Easton said.

'No. Just someone wearing an earring—' Dani interjected.

'Oscar rips out the earring but then... comes off worse... much worse.'

'Possibly,' Dani said, deep in thought as Tariq placed the earring into an evidence bag. 'Either that, or perhaps worse... we have another victim.'

Chapter Four

By the time Dani made her way back up to the house with Easton, she was already feeling mentally fatigued from the time spent witnessing the grim crime scene. Tariq and his team, which had now been expanded in order to undertake a more thorough sweep of the area, would be on site for some time yet, as would Jack Ledford, who'd arrived less than an hour ago. Dani, too, was unsure exactly how long she'd be at Drifford House today, though she'd already made clear to Easton that he should scrub any plans he'd had for the day. She'd texted Jason to let him know the position too, and he'd called more than once while Dani had been in the woods.

Before heading into the house, she wandered over to her car and took the chance to call him back and explain the situation to him. Not just the fact she would be likely tied up for the rest of the day, but the basics of what they were looking at with the Redfearne crime scene too. Jason might not be an active police officer any more, but he remained Dani's main sounding board for every facet of her life, from her ongoing recovery from the traumatic brain injury which had nearly ended her life almost three years ago, and everything that brought with it, to her thoughts and requests for advice on cases.

Would her boss, DCI McNair, approve of that? Dani really didn't know, and she wouldn't let on to McNair that she used Jason in that manner, but she did know that she trusted Jason's integrity implicitly.

Though that didn't mean she liked or agreed with everything he said.

'Just take it easy,' Jason said, not for the first time during the brief conversation. 'You've got a big day tomorrow.'

The Clarkson trial. He didn't need to remind her of that. It was the very reason she'd been so on edge for weeks now. Yet, in a strange way, it wasn't thoughts of the trial itself which were bothering her right now, it was thoughts of how she'd manage to keep on top of this new case and still find the time to ensure she was in court. She'd promised she'd be there. She couldn't break that.

'You need to be ready,' Jason said.

'I will be ready.'

'What have you taken today?' he asked.

'I've got to go,' she said.

She gritted her teeth as she ended the call and turned back to Easton, who was standing ten yards away fiddling with his phone. He put the mobile away as she walked up to him. He had a questioning look, though he said nothing as they turned and approached the uniformed officer who was standing guard at the closed main doors to the house. Not the same officer who'd been vomited on earlier, Dani noted, and she wasn't clear if this officer was there now to keep people in or out.

'Now for the worst part,' Easton said.

'Indeed,' Dani said. 'But you can be damn sure it's going to be a lot worse for them than it is for us.'

The room they eventually settled in was a library, a room nearly as big as the entire downstairs of most standard family homes. The walls on two sides of the room had dark wood, floor-to-ceiling bookshelves crammed with all manner of works. Leather sofas, armchairs, and reading tables filled the middle of the room. On one wall were three huge sash windows with original internal shutters, the tall panes looking out over rolling lawns and huge beech and oak trees in full greenery. It was like something out of a movie. And this was just one of a multitude of rooms on the ground floor.

And then there were the servants… or staff, or whatever it was the illustrious owners called the hired help. In the intervening half hour since Dani and Easton had walked through the front doors of the mansion, they'd already been introduced to several members of the team. Pamela Longbridge, the overall head of staff and something of an assistant to the Redfearnes it seemed; Matilda Fraser, head of domestic services, which Dani took to mean she was in charge of those responsible for cooking and cleaning; Clive Pichon, the groundskeeper who'd found the body, and there was also a cluster of cleaners busily removing debris from the night before. Excepting the cleaners perhaps, they'd all have to be formally interviewed, some of them several times over, and Dani had already set in motion the order for a team of DCs and DSs to start the process of gathering initial statements from the people still on site.

But for her and Easton it was the thankless task of Henry and Caroline Redfearne up first.

The Redfearnes were sitting next to each other on brown leather armchairs, Easton and Dani opposite on a cream sofa. Caroline Redfearne had tidied herself up some since she'd spewed her guts up outside. She was now wearing jeans and a smart red blouse, her make-up was fully removed, and her hair was tied back. Henry looked as though he might be going to the office, dressed in smart grey trousers and a salmon-pink shirt. Despite their tidy attire, both were red-eyed, their features droopy and lifeless. How much of that was from the night before, and how much because of their son, Dani couldn't tell, though she was certain the latter weighed far more heavily, no matter how horrendous their hangovers were.

'I'm very sorry for your loss,' Dani said, knowing how lame those words were, though she felt they had to be said.

Henry shook his head solemnly. Caroline blew her nose into a hanky which she left scrunched in her hand for further use.

'We're going to need to ask you a few questions about your son. About what happened to him. I can't imagine your pain right now, but I promise you we'll do everything we can to find the truth, and who did this.'

A couple of nods.

'When did you last see Oscar?' Dani asked. 'Alive, I mean.'

The couple looked at each other for a few moments as if searching for the answer. Caroline motioned for her husband to go for it.

'I can only say for certain that it was some time yesterday afternoon,' he said.

'Do you know what time roughly?'

'Four o'clock? Maybe five? But... when did this happen? Do you know?'

'I'm afraid we aren't able to say yet. The alarm was raised at just after nine a.m. this morning. We're very keen to narrow the window as much as we can, which is why it'd be very helpful to know when you last saw him.'

The couple shared a look again. 'I'm sorry,' Henry said. 'He was here at the party, but... I honestly don't know what time I last saw him.'

'What was the party? Was it a special occasion?' Easton asked.

'It was just an informal gathering,' Henry said. 'Friends, acquaintances.'

That didn't much sound like what Easton had referred to.

'There must have been a fair few people here if you didn't see Oscar at all for several hours?' Easton said.

Henry glared at him, and Dani gave her colleague a look which she hoped he'd recognise as *tone it down a little, will you*. His question had been innocent enough, but Dani had sensed the scepticism in his tone.

'How many guests were here?' Dani asked.

'I mean... exact numbers? I don't know. Over two hundred. Plus we had a lot of extra hired help for the day. A couple dozen. Pamela could give you names and details for all of the staff.'

'And the guests?' Easton asked. 'We'll need a full list. It'll be very important for our enquiries.'

Henry looked as though he was about to argue against that for a moment. 'You're going to be speaking to all of them?' he asked, sounding deflated. 'You can imagine this is an incredibly private matter.'

'We understand,' Dani said, 'and we always act as discreetly as possible in matters of this nature, but it's going to be essential that we follow up with anyone who was here yesterday. I hope that makes sense? We just want to find out what happened to Oscar.'

Henry shut his eyes. His wife reached out and put her hand on his lap. Dani thought she understood, at least from the Redfearnes' point of view, why they might be reticent for the police to speak to the party-goers. As traumatised as they clearly were about their son's death, Henry was a man who, in his own eyes, was rich and powerful and who had a reputation to uphold. His natural will to keep that reputation intact was there, right beneath the surface, despite the horrific circumstances.

For one thing, the great and good, as Easton had put it, would certainly be thinking twice about attending next year's party, if there even was one, given what had happened.

'Of course,' Caroline said when it was clear her husband was saying nothing. 'We'll give you everything you need.'

Henry opened his eyes again and nodded resolutely.

'So you think the last time you saw Oscar was around four or five p.m.?' Dani asked.

'Something like that,' Henry said. 'But I really don't know for sure.'

'Who was he with?' Easton asked.

'When?'

'When you last saw him.'

'I already said I can't really recall exactly when I last saw him.'

He looked to his wife again for reassurance, but she said nothing.

'Did he have any friends with him yesterday?' Dani asked.

'A couple of close friends of his were here, yes.'

'Did you see him with them?'

'Of course, at various points, but Oscar knew a lot of the guests and he liked to mingle.'

'What time did the party end?' Easton asked.

The couple looked at one another again. 'Officially it was until one in the morning,' Caroline said, 'but some of our close friends stayed well past that. I went to bed a little after two. Henry?'

Another puzzled look. 'Probably after four. Something like that.'

'And you'd no indication at that point that anything untoward had happened?' Easton asked.

'Do you really think I'd have been sipping brandy and talking crap if I had!' Henry snapped in a sudden outburst.

The room fell into a momentary silence. Dani gave Henry the time to defuse. There was no point in getting him hot and bothered. Though it seemed Easton was intent on toeing a different line.

'And there was no point in, what, that twelve hours, when you wondered where Oscar had got to?' he asked.

'He's eighteen,' Henry said, glaring. 'He gets on with things. We're not his babysitters.'

Henry was now getting riled, Dani could see, and she wasn't sure she wanted that, but then it did seem odd to her that over such a long period, Oscar's parents had not once considered where their son might be and had simply carried on partying.

'What about Oscar's friends?' Easton asked.

'What about them?'

'You mentioned he had a couple of friends here. Did you see them at all through the rest of the day and night?'

'I've no idea when I last saw them. I wasn't keeping a fucking rota of where and when I saw every single person.'

Caroline put her hand on her husband's thigh again and rubbed gently, though it did nothing to soothe his bubbling tension, which was now clear on his tensed-up face.

'I appreciate that, Mr Redfearne,' Easton said, and Dani was torn as to whether she wanted him to carry on pushing. 'But can either of you recall specifically whether you saw Oscar's friends during the evening? Or, like Oscar, was the last time you saw them during the afternoon?'

'I'm pretty sure Alex was here later on,' Caroline said, looking to Henry for confirmation.

He nodded slightly.

'Alex?' Dani said.

'Alex Acaster,' Caroline said. 'But then his parents were here too, probably until midnightish I'd say.'

'Perhaps we could move on?' Dani said. 'Hopefully, the timeline will become clearer once we've spoken to the other guests. Now, I know this is a difficult question, but can you think of any reason why someone would want to hurt Oscar?'

'No,' Henry said after barely a second's thought.

'No,' Caroline echoed a moment later.

'He's never been in any kind of trouble? Gangs? Drugs?' Easton asked.

'Of course not,' Henry said, his heckles once again raised by Easton, even though the question had been perfectly reasonable in Dani's mind. 'That's a ridiculous and baseless thing to suggest.'

'And you can't think of anyone in particular who's got a grudge against your son?' Dani said.

'He's a popular kid.'

'So that's a no?' Easton said.

'Yes, it's a bloody no.'

'What about you?' Dani said, and for a few moments the room fell deathly silent as Henry glared defiantly at Dani, then at Easton, then back to Dani.

'How do you mean?'

'Is there anyone you've had a falling out with?' Dani said. 'Either personally or professionally? Anyone who might harbour a grudge against you or your family who could have done this in order to punish you.'

'Detectives, this is getting out of hand,' Henry said through clenched teeth. 'If you're going to interrogate us then perhaps I should be asking my lawyer to attend.'

'We can, of course, halt this and carry on more formally with your lawyer if you wish,' Dani said.

She left the invitation dangling. She certainly didn't want to do that so early in the investigation, when all she was trying to do was understand the lay of the land. This was no interrogation as far as she was concerned, even if their questions were making the couple uncomfortable.

'Honey, come on,' Caroline said to her husband quietly, 'we don't have anything to hide. We should carry on.'

A sigh, then the slightest of nods from Henry.

'Did you have any security personnel on site yesterday?' Dani asked.

'No,' Henry said. 'We've never had security personnel here. This is our home, not a fort.'

'But you had a lot of guests, and some of them are quite prominent people. Lord Hastings. Andrew Lawrence, the local MP here. Weren't Michael Whyte and his wife here too? I thought he played in Spain now.'

'Yes, he was here. His agent is a very good friend of mine. What's your point?'

'How did you ensure no one came onto the property who shouldn't have been here?'

'The front gates are electronically controlled. One of Pamela's team was responsible for recording who came through. And we had a guest list at the door to mark who came into the house.'

That was kind of what Dani had been asking about. So there weren't professional security guards, but there were still measures in place by the house staff to make sure only invited guests were admitted.

'Other than the gates, are there any other means of entry to the grounds?' she asked.

'Any old idiot can climb over a wall, I guess, but there's no other proper route, no.'

'But we do have CCTV cameras too,' Caroline said. 'They cover right around the outside of the house, and there's a few in the gardens too.'

Dani already knew this. In fact she'd already set up one of the DCs to look over the footage from the previous day, and was keen to make that her next stop.

The room went silent. The natural detective in Dani was telling her to continue to probe. For more than one reason she was a little uncomfortable about the party that had taken place the night before. Between the

Redfearnes and the guests who'd been there, why had no one noticed that Oscar had disappeared? And how had a killer managed to not only get on and off the grounds of Drifford House, leaving barely a trace, as far as Dani was aware, but also to kill Oscar Redfearne quite horrifically without any of the more than two hundred other people around being any the wiser?

The most obvious answer was that the killer was already on the grounds. One of the guests, or one of the staff, though so early in the investigation Dani had no way of knowing why that would be the case.

She didn't have to keep pushing these two here and now, though. They were consumed by grief and they deserved Dani's and Easton's patience and respect. There was a time and place for pushing and this wasn't it.

'OK, thank you very much for your time. I think we probably have enough for now.' Dani got to her feet. Easton followed suit. 'I really am very sorry for you both. We're going to be on site for a good deal longer yet, so if you need anything from us at all, please do just ask.'

Caroline nodded but said nothing. Henry looked away, out of the window.

Dani and Easton made their way to the door.

'When can I see my son?' Henry asked.

Dani paused. She closed her eyes as the gory images of Oscar's corpse flashed in her mind once more. She pushed them away as best she could as she turned back to Henry.

'There's currently a team of forensics scrutinising the scene. I'm afraid it'd only hamper their efforts right now to have anyone who's not working with them to go down there. I'm so sorry, Mr Redfearne, I do hope you understand?'

He said nothing.

'Of course, you'll be able to come and see Oscar once his body has been removed.'

'In the morgue. You're saying I'm not able to see my son until he's in the morgue.'

'I'm very sorry, Mr Redfearne.'

He said nothing more, and neither did anyone else. Feeling about as shitty as she could imagine, Dani turned and opened the door to leave.

Chapter Five

'You OK?' Easton asked as he and Dani headed away from the library down a corridor that was plastered with various oil-painted portraits. Past members of the Redfearne family?

'You were pretty close to the line back there,' she said, sounding more agitated than she'd intended.

'Good cop, bad cop,' Easton said. 'I thought you'd be happy that it was me pushing and not you.'

'Time and place, Aaron. The mutilated body of their only son is lying in a pool of blood and guts in their garden.'

Though she was hardly one to talk. It was far more usual for her to be the bad cop in such a situation. In a way, she was glad Easton had taken on that mantle, in what had been one of the hardest conversations with a victim's family she could recall.

'Yeah,' Easton said, 'and he was killed out there while his parents were busy getting pissed, and no one gave a damn. In fact, they apparently had no inkling at all that anything was untoward until we arrived this morning.'

'You're saying you think they're lying to us?'

'I'm saying regardless of the fact their son is dead, I don't like them. I don't like their attitude to life, the—'

'You don't like the fact they're worth millions and live in this huge mansion and drive expensive cars and throw big bash parties with celebrities. Sounds more like envy to me.'

Easton was now sour-faced. 'That's not it at all. You can be rich and humble. I got the opposite impression from him.'

Dani wouldn't necessarily disagree with him on that, but still…

Easton's buzzing phone distracted them both from the conversation. They stopped walking as he answered.

'Yeah,' he said. 'Got it. We're coming now.' He pulled the phone from his ear and turned to Dani. 'Constable found something on the CCTV.'

DC Constable was one of several DCs in the homicide team. He was a close friend of Easton's, and a good worker, though even having known him for coming up to a year, the humour of his surname still tickled Dani, particularly when she saw the questioning looks whenever he was introduced to someone for the first time.

'Then let's go,' she said.

—

They carried on their way, through a room that had been introduced to them as the gallery, and deep into the old servants' wing of the house, past the kitchen, pantry, a utility room, eventually coming to a cluster of basic square rooms that in years gone by may have been bedrooms for the live-in workers.

Today the rooms were mostly used for storage, although one of the rooms, a ten by ten foot square with a single, small barred window with frosted glass, was now

43

some sort of security suite with a desk and chair and computer with two widescreen monitors.

Constable was sitting at the chair by the desk, busily scrolling through colour video footage from the night before. Pamela Longbridge, the stony-faced head of staff, was standing over his shoulder, still sullen. Dani couldn't tell if it was her natural demeanour or the toll of the day's events.

'I've scoured the footage and I'm pretty sure I've found the last glimpse of Oscar Redfearne,' Constable said.

Dani moved closer to the screen. Unlike the grainy green CCTV of years gone by, this was full colour and the image clear and vibrant high definition, albeit the people on screen were still small and Dani found herself squinting a little to really focus.

'Just here,' Constable said, and he paused the image as a man stepped out from an open side door. Dani thought she recognised the spot the camera was picking up: the doors that led out from the corridor by the library where they'd been moments before.

'That's definitely Oscar,' Pamela said.

'Six-zero-nine p.m.,' Dani said.

So a little later than Oscar's parents had recalled last seeing him.

Constable hit play again, and as Oscar took another step from the house, his right hand trailed behind him and the next second he'd pulled a young woman in a black dress outside with him. The two walked off to the left and were soon out of the camera's view.

'Who is that?' Dani asked.

Pamela sighed. 'Sophie Blackwood. A member of the serving team. She's only been with us a couple of weeks, mainly helping to cover staff summer holidays. And she was supposed to be working yesterday, not cavorting with her employers' son.'

Dani ignored that comment.

'Is there a camera that picks up where they went?' she asked, to neither Pamela nor Constable in particular.

'Only barely,' Constable said.

He typed away and pulled the mouse across the desk here and there and moments later another screen popped up. He spent a few moments getting to the right point in time. This camera was once again angled so that much of what it picked up was an area immediately along the outside wall of the house, but as Constable found the right time and clicked play, sure enough in the top corner, heading in and then out of the screen in the space of a couple of seconds, were four legs.

'We can't see their faces?' Dani said.

'Unfortunately not,' Constable said. 'But the time works. Perhaps if you wanted to be absolutely certain you could map the exact route outside, but there's no other logical explanation other than this being them.'

'Heading away from the house, towards the woods,' Dani said, thinking through the orientation of the outside of the mansion.

'I just can't believe this,' Pamela said, angry more than anything else. 'She was supposed to be working. What the hell was she thinking?'

Dani once again ignored the comment. 'And there's nothing at all picking out Oscar coming back to the house after that?'

'I've been through once,' Constable said. 'I can do it again to be sure.'

'Please. And Sophie?'

'I wasn't looking out for her in particular the first time, so I'll do that on the next run, but I'm pretty sure I didn't pick up anyone else at all coming back past these two cameras. It's not the main entrance after all.'

'What time was Sophie supposed to be working until?' Easton asked Pamela.

'The whole night. Until two a.m., to give time after the last guests left to start the clean-up.'

'So?' Dani asked.

'So what?'

'Was she still here working until two a.m. or not?'

Pamela looked worried now, as though the issue at hand was finally dawning on her.

'I can't be sure. We had dozens of staff yesterday, and as you can surely imagine it's a hectic day and night to say the least. Matilda might be able to be more definitive.'

'OK. Well I suggest you go and find her. And we'll need Sophie's contact details.'

Pamela nodded and went to move away.

'What about the cameras inside the house?' Dani said.

Pamela paused.

'What cameras?' Constable said.

'There's one in the main hallway,' Dani said. 'One in the corridor out here, and another just outside the corridor by the gallery? I spotted them as we walked through.'

Constable looked to Pamela.

'They're on a different system,' she said.

'How do we get access?' Dani asked.

Pamela looked a little flustered now. 'Yes they're for security, but those cameras cover movements of the family

46

and their guests within the sanctity of their own home. I just...'

'And they might provide us with more clues as to what happened to Oscar. And Sophie,' Dani said.

Pamela's face had gone pale. 'I'd have to check with Henry.'

'I'm sure he'll understand,' Dani said.

Pamela said nothing as she stepped out of the room, and Easton's earlier words about the Redfearnes' party being the equivalent of the Presidents Club dinner bounced in Dani's mind. Pamela hadn't mentioned those cameras to Constable before now, and was clearly hesitant to provide access. Was that because she knew *exactly* what took place at these parties and was intent on sparing her employers' blushes? Was it more than blushes she was sparing?

Dani cringed at the thought.

Regardless, with or without the Redfearnes' permission, they'd get hold of those tapes. This was a murder investigation.

Dani was glad that Henry Redfearne quickly came to that conclusion too. Less than ten minutes later Pamela returned with his blessing and the details and access codes for Constable to pull the recordings up, though it was notable that there were no cameras from the main living rooms downstairs, where most of the guests would have been, and nothing at all covering the upstairs of the house and its multitude of bedrooms.

'Find the one from the corridor by the gallery,' Dani said. 'That might show Oscar's last movements before he left the house.'

Constable nodded and after a bit of trial and error he found the right one. He opened up the recording and began to scroll through; the image on the screen moved rapidly through the day, people ebbing and flowing at speed.

'Stop there!' Dani said.

Constable hit the pause button. Dani's eyes flicked to the time stamp. Five fifteen. Too early.

'That's Oscar, isn't it?' Dani said. The clothing was certainly the same, but the view was only of the back of him as he headed along the corridor.

'Yes,' Pamela said.

'But it's too early,' Constable said.

'Perhaps he was just heading into the library,' Pamela said.

Which made sense. 'OK, keep going,' Dani said, 'but more slowly.'

Constable nodded, and Oscar had soon moved away and out of sight of the camera. People continued to come and go as the time in the corner of the screen sped towards six p.m., but no sign of Oscar now. In the intervening time Sophie had gone back and forth, presumably from the gallery to the library, to get fresh bottles of champagne, but there was no sign of her interacting with Oscar, or anyone else.

There was a knock on the door. Dani turned to see the matronly Matilda standing there with a piece of A4 paper in her hand. She looked to Pamela before catching Dani's eye.

'You wanted Sophie's details?' Matilda said. 'This is what we have. It's the CV she gave us. It has her home address, email, mobile.'

'Thank you.'

Dani took the paper; Matilda was already turning to head away.

'Do you know where Sophie is?' Dani asked.

Matilda paused and turned, looking a little more worried now.

'I've not seen her since yesterday,' she said.

'But when yesterday? Pamela said she was due to be working through the night. Was she?'

'I'm sorry, I really can't say. It was a busy night. You know?'

Dani didn't really, though it seemed like everyone else thought that she should. What exactly had gone on last night when it was accepted that a young waitress would just disappear for most of her shift?

'So when did you last see her?' Dani asked.

'Boss?' Constable said.

Matilda seemed glad of the intervention. Dani turned back. Her eyes first looked down to the time on the screen. Just after six p.m. She looked at the image to see the back end of a short, plump man swaying down the corridor.

'Who's that?' Dani asked, to no response.

A moment later, at the top of the screen, two bare legs appeared. Sophie Blackwood came into view, heading away from the library, champagne bottle in hand. The man slowed in his step and seemed to deliberately move into Sophie's path. He put his hand out onto the wall when Sophie tried to edge past. It was clear by the scowl on her face that she was less than impressed.

'Who is he?' Dani asked again.

She turned to Matilda who was playing with her phone. She looked up and shrugged. Dani looked to Pamela who was staring at the screen, lips pursed.

'Pamela?'

'I can't see his face, but… I think it's Arnold Davenport.'

'Davenport?' Easton said. 'As in Davenport Associates?'

'I believe so.'

Dani looked to Easton, her baffled face indicating she had no idea what he was talking about.

'Davenport Associates,' he said. 'An accountancy firm. They're the shirt sponsors for Walsall FC. I think he owns the club now. He's loaded.'

Of course, if it was football related, Easton would know.

'Here we go,' Constable said, grabbing Dani's attention back.

She looked to the screen again and in the top corner, from behind Sophie, the legs of Oscar Redfearne appeared. He stopped, his shoulders at the top of the screen, his neck and face out of view.

'That's definitely Oscar, isn't it?' Dani asked.

'Unless someone else with the same frame and clothing was in that corridor at the exact same time,' Constable said.

Davenport's demeanour changed with Oscar's arrival, and not long after, the older man finally turned and wobbled away, something of an angry sneer on his face once he was turned from Sophie and Oscar.

'This is it,' Constable said. 'Just a few seconds before we picked up Sophie and Oscar heading outside.'

'Pause it,' Dani said.

Constable did so, and Dani froze as she stared at Sophie's image on the screen as the young woman went to turn around.

'Can you zoom in?'

'I think so, give me a sec.'

'It's not even ringing?' Matilda said.

Dani turned to her. Matilda was staring at her phone quizzically. 'I've got full bars, it's not the signal.'

'Sophie?' Dani asked.

Matilda nodded. 'Her phone's going straight to voice-mail.'

'Boss?' Constable said. 'What did you see?'

Dani looked back to the screen. Her heart was beating several notches more quickly now than a few seconds before. She didn't like this at all.

'Is that as far as you can go?' Dani said, as she stared unblinking at Sophie's face.

'I think so.'

It was enough anyway, she realised. The image was clear and crisp.

'What do you think, Aaron?' Dani asked.

Easton said nothing, just nodded.

'What's going on?' Pamela said.

'Please, could we have a moment?' Dani said, to her and Matilda.

They looked at each other questioningly before Pamela nodded and she and Matilda shuffled confusedly towards the door. Once they were outside Dani shut the door and turned back to her officers.

'Boss?' Constable said once again.

'Those earrings.' Dani pointed to the image on the screen. 'One of them was found at the crime scene. Yanked out of her ear, by the looks of it.'

'And now no one can get hold of her,' Easton added.

'She killed Oscar?' Constable said.

'Whether she did or didn't, whether she's alive or dead, we need to find her, and fast.'

Easton nodded. 'On it.'

Dani's eyes narrowed as she thought, 'And make a priority on tracking down Arnold Davenport too. Right now, he's one of the last people to have seen Oscar and Sophie alive.'

Chapter Six

Thick drops of rain had already started falling by the time Dani and Easton made it back outside, though the air remained stifling hot and even more sticky than before, making Dani's head spin within just a few seconds as they traipsed away from the house.

With the help of others from the homicide team, initial statements had now been taken, or were in the process of being taken, from the various staff within Drifford House. Plans were also being drawn up to get in touch with each and every one of the guests who'd been present at the party the previous night, with the Redfearnes now having furnished the police with a full guest list. A guest list which was eye-opening to say the least.

Perhaps most strange to Dani, was the disparate nature of the party's attendees, from Michael Whyte, a twenty-something England international footballer who now played for Atletico Madrid, through to Jasper Patrick, a sixty-something billionaire investor from South Africa who, after a bit of highly publicised short selling of stocks, was now one of the richest people in the world. Admittedly, plenty of names on the list Dani had never heard of, but the one and only similarity that she could see between them was that all of the guests were universally loaded, one way or another.

Or did they share common interests that Dani simply wasn't seeing?

The idea of getting to the bottom of that, to the truth that sat behind the lives of the wealthy and privileged, was already making Dani's head spin. Whether any of the guests were involved in the murder, or any other nefarious activities, their prominent nature only heaped added pressure on Dani to solve the case, and quickly, before the press and top brass started breathing down her neck.

Regardless, her immediate focus was on Sophie Blackwood. Was she a victim or a suspect? If the former, was she still alive and in need of help? Either way, Dani would make tracking her whereabouts a priority, and had already arranged for two officers to go and speak to Sophie's parents at their home, a little under two miles away from Drifford House, where Sophie still lived.

'Do you know what's bugging me?' Easton said, as he and Dani walked along the gravel drive, and onwards towards the side of the house where Sophie and Oscar had come from to take them to the woods.

'What?'

'Well—'

'Wait a sec.'

Dani paused in her step, thinking, as she looked off into the near distance.

'Go and get Pamela for me.'

Easton raised an eyebrow.

'Please?' Dani said.

'Sure.'

Easton trudged off leaving Dani in the rain as the bubbling thoughts continued. When the rain ratcheted up a couple of notches she finally decided to pull out her umbrella. Easton was back within two minutes with a curious-looking Pamela by his side, huddled down into her suit jacket.

'Detective?' she said when they reached Dani.

'How does Sophie Blackwood get here?'

Pamela looked at her as if to say, *that's all you wanted?*

'On her bike usually,' she said. 'She doesn't live that far away.'

'Where does she leave it?'

The look on Pamela's face changed as though she'd just had a eureka moment.

'Follow me.'

Pamela led them around the house, past the patio doors by the library and onwards to a much grubbier side of the building, where there were industrial bins, large chrome pipes sticking out of walls, and the constant whir of extractor fans from the kitchen and from the building's air conditioning. This side of the house reminded Dani more of a hotel, than a family home.

'This is the main service entrance,' Pamela said. 'We don't really have a bike park as such, and I told her more than once not to just leave that thing lying about, but...'

She trailed off as she stared over to the closed service door in front of them. Dani realised what she'd seen. Tucked to the side of the door, wedged between the house and a hedge, a shiny handlebar was visible. Dani walked over.

'This is hers?' she asked Pamela.

'I think so, yes.'

'OK, thank you.'

Pamela paused for a moment, as if unsure whether she should say or do anything more, before she half nodded and turned and headed back the way they'd just come.

'We could get Constable to confirm she definitely did arrive on this thing and what time,' Easton said.

'Yes, we should,' Dani said. 'But the most important thing is that she definitely didn't leave on it.'

'Which was kind of the point I was about to make before.'

'It was?'

'How did the killer get inside in the first place? We've got nothing on the cameras of anyone sneaking around. It can't be random that they got onto and off the property and avoided every camera in the process.'

'But we do still need to get the cameras mapped out to determine any black spots.'

'Even so. If the killer knew the exact position of black spots, doesn't that tell you something?'

'It tells me that they were well prepared.'

'Well prepared. And possibly...' Easton's face changed to a look of concern as he looked back to Drifford House, 'possibly they were already on the property.'

'Already on the property when?'

'As in, this *was* someone who came into the house through the front door, and they left the exact same way. You saw yourself on the CCTV that people were milling outside at the back of the house all through the night. It wouldn't have been too hard for someone to slip by the cameras. We can't rule out that Oscar was killed by xsomeone from the house.'

It was certainly possible, as that had already crossed Dani's mind much earlier.

'I agree this wasn't random,' Dani said. 'It was planned, not just in terms of location, but timing too. Last night was the perfect opportunity. So the big question is why Oscar?'

'And Sophie.'

'There is one hitch to all of that, though.'

'There's more than one, to be honest,' Easton said. 'That's why I said it's bugging me.'

'Wait a minute,' Dani said as a thought hit her.

'What is it?'

'Come on, you'll see.'

Dani headed off back towards the crime scene. As they moved off the grass and into the wood, the ground underfoot, bone dry before, was now covered by a surface layer of sloppy water, the dusty liquid unable to penetrate the hard surface, and her feet splashed away as she traipsed along, soaking through her shoes and the bottom of her trousers.

–

The tent over Oscar's body was now fully closed up. Several bodies moved about around it, all dressed in white, most of them on their haunches, searching, recording. One of the figures bobbed up, sensing Dani and Easton's arrival. Tariq.

'Detectives, you're back.'

'Is Ledford inside?' Dani asked.

'He is. You want to speak?'

'Please. With you too.'

The four of them were soon assembled inside the tent, out of the rain at least, though not exactly comfortable with the corpse among them. The smell in the tent was far more noxious than earlier.

'I have to say, DI Stephens, this really is a mess,' Ledford said.

She assumed he was referring to the state of Oscar Redfearne, rather than to the fledgling investigation into his death.

'These are just my preliminary observations, but our victim has suffered horrendous injuries, internal and external, together with what look like obvious defensive wounds to his arms and torso; I imagine this was a brutal and frenzied attack.'

Dani said nothing as she took it all in. Ledford crouched down and with a gloved hand he gently pushed Oscar's head up.

'And there's this,' he said.

Dani frowned. 'A bite?'

'Definitely teeth marks. And human teeth at that. Cut right into the skin.'

Everything she'd seen so far had indicated that this killer was well rehearsed and clever. But if the killer had bitten Oscar, that potentially left a clear route to identification.

'I'm guessing you've already swabbed for saliva?'

'We have. Fingers crossed we'll be able to get a DNA trace. And, of course, the bite marks could be matched to a dental profile later down the line.'

Dani didn't know what to say. Had the killer really been so careless?

'Any idea on the weapon we're looking for?' she said.

'My first impression is an axe, possibly combined with a machete or a katana, something that's made for slicing.'

'So more than one weapon?'

'Almost certainly, given the variety of wounds.'

'Carried out at the same time?'

'Hard to say which wounds came first.'

'Are you saying it's possible there was more than one attacker?' Easton said.

'Possible? Of course, DS Easton. There are many possibilities.'

'Sorry, Jack,' Dani said, 'but I was actually more interested in discussing the wider scene, rather than the body.'

He looked a little put out. 'I've not been here long, and it's the body that I've concentrated on so far. I am a pathologist, not an FSI.'

'Of course, Jack. I understand.' She turned to Tariq. 'Did you find the rest of him?'

'Yes and no,' Tariq said. 'We've found most of what's been hacked off, but unfortunately it's… a bit chewed up. Foxes most likely. They're all over the place around here. Apparently.'

Dani tried not to wince at the thought.

'Does that suggest anything about time of death?' she asked Ledford.

'Not really,' he said. 'Foxes will generally hunt at night, of course, but I think we knew the window of death was during the night anyway, didn't we?'

'And no murder weapon?'

'I'm afraid not,' Tariq said. 'We've plenty of fibres around the body and a few around the wider scene. There was a blood trail, which is more or less gone now because of the rain; it suggests he was possibly first attacked a few yards from here.'

'Does it?' Dani asked.

'How do you mean?'

'Couldn't a blood trail indicate the killer getting away?'

Tariq looked to Ledford who nodded.

'Of course it *could*, depending on what you mean by trail,' Tariq said. 'By which I mean, how much blood there is at either end; is there an explanation for termination? Where does each direction lead? Plus, in some cases, you can tell the direction of travel from the spatter pattern.'

'In this case?' Dani asked.

'We'll have to show you on camera now, due to the weather, but the pattern of blood, and the amount of it, suggested to me, at least, that that was the initial point of attack, as opposed to the killer fleeing to that point, blood dripping.'

'Of course, there's no indication the killer was bleeding, is there?' Ledford said.

'Actually there possibly is. That earring you found earlier?' Dani said, catching Tariq's eye. 'It belonged to a young woman who was captured on CCTV heading down here with Oscar, a little past six p.m. last night.'

Ledford looked to Tariq as though the earring was something he wasn't aware of.

'You're telling me this young woman is your suspect?' Ledford asked.

'That's possible, yes. Regardless, she *was* bleeding. And now she's missing. So whether she's the killer or another victim, I would expect a trail of where she went, because it definitely wasn't back to the house.'

Ledford stared, or more like glared, at Tariq for a few seconds.

'Let's take a walk,' he said. 'I think we all need to get on the same page here.'

They all headed back outside, where the rain was in a momentary lull. Tariq moved off along the edge of the water before coming to a stop not far from the tent, just past a young cherry tree whose fruit was traipsed into the mud around its trunk.

'You can still see some of the red here,' Tariq said, pointing to the now-increasingly muddy ground.

'But what about the rest of the area?' Dani asked. 'Have your team finished scouring yet?'

'We've done a first pass,' Tariq said. 'We found no other obvious signs of blood, if that's what you're asking. We've bagged plenty of items which may be relevant, or may be completely useless; rubbish, small bits of fabric and hair. Certainly, nothing that represents a viable trail though.'

'But we have a young woman, bleeding, who managed to get away from here,' Ledford said.

'What about the other side of the water?' Dani asked.

'We checked there too,' Tariq said, sounding defensive now. 'I already said, we didn't find any obvious trail.'

'But where does it lead, over that side?' Easton asked.

'You can't see from this spot because of the under-growth but there's a redbrick wall about ten yards back from the water. It leads onto a private lane which connects the closest neighbouring property about a mile away, I've been told. We checked all along the inside of the wall too. We found nothing to indicate the girl or anyone else went that way.'

The foursome fell into an awkward silence. Dani's mind rumbled away. She looked down to the spot on the ground where Tariq had indicated before. Sure enough, among the expanding puddles of rain, it was still possible to make out the thin swirls of red. Dani followed one of the swirls as the water drained away into...

'The stream,' she said.

The three all looked to her. 'The killer used the water to mask their movements.'

Before anyone said a word Dani was striding along by the water's edge. At a narrow point she hopped over, just managing to reach the other side as she stumbled forward. She carried on, taking a few scratches and scrapes to her legs from the overgrown verge. Pushing her way through the undergrowth she soon came to the ancient-looking but handsome seven foot tall redbrick wall, capped with Staffordshire blue apex stones. The stream passed through an archway at the bottom of the wall that was covered by a metal grate, where twigs and other debris was gathered.

'Bag it all,' Dani said to Tariq when he reached her. She turned to Easton. 'Give me a leg up.'

Easton nodded and crouched down by the wall and laced his fingers together at waist height. Dani put a hand to his shoulder and pushed her foot into his hands then hauled herself up and grasped the top of the blue stones. Easton pushed and Dani clambered to the top. She glanced over, satisfying herself there was no danger on the other side, then swivelled and dropped down.

She landed in a cluster of nettles but with her trousers on she wasn't stung at all. She stepped out from the verge and onto a shoddy-looking single-track tarmac road. She looked up and down it. The lane curved off out of sight in both directions, and she was unable to see either the main road or the house the private road connected to from where she was. Twenty yards in the distance though, there was a small bare verge where no nettles or weeds or grass grew – a passing point on the narrow lane? Was that where the killer had parked? They surely had to have had a vehicle?

'Boss, what have you got?' Easton shouted over.

'Come and take a look.'

'Are you sure that's wise, DI Stephens?' Ledford shouted over.

'Easton, just come over the same spot I did.'

She could hear Ledford grumbling about something but seconds later there was shuffling the other side and then two hands appeared at the top of the wall. Easton grunted as he hauled his body to the top, likely with the help of Tariq, before he jumped down and stumbled out into the road next to Dani. He brushed himself down, doing a lousy job of removing the damp green mould that had rubbed off the wall onto his clothes.

'Just there,' Dani said, pointing to a spot by the edge of the wall, about a yard away from where she'd climbed over, almost directly in line with where the stream passed under. It looked as though the weeds and grass had been flattened.

Easton's eyes narrowed as he stepped closer. Dani went with him and both were soon crouching down as they stared at the ground in front of them. Easton slipped on a glove and put his hand forward to push the nettles and other weeds aside.

He looked to Dani then pulled his hand back. Dani stared at the red smudge on his fingers.

'Send your team over here, now,' Dani shouted to Ledford and Tariq.

'We know Sophie was bleeding,' Easton said. 'And we've now got a blood trail to follow. Does that mean she's the killer?'

'No,' Dani said. 'I'm pretty sure she isn't.'

'I know she was slight, from what we've seen,' Easton said, 'but I struggled to get over that wall on my own, never mind carrying another person. So if you're saying she was kidnapped by our killer, who the hell is he? Arnie?'

'No,' Dani said. 'But like you said yourself, he is someone who is well planned, and who had plenty of time on his hands last night.' Dani straightened up and looked up to the edge of the blue stones on top of the wall. 'Do you see it?'

Easton squinted again as he stood up straight. He reached up with one gloved finger and touched the wall as gently as Dani imagined he could, right at the spot where there looked to be a faint scuff mark on the lower edge of one of the coping stones. He pulled his finger back and Dani stared at the tiny and thin piece of brown fabric that was now stuck to the end of the glove.

'Rope?' he said.

'Looks like it. What if he hoisted Sophie over the wall?'

'So she is a victim?'

'A victim, yes. And unless our culprit likes collecting corpses, it's very possible that she's still alive.'

64

Chapter Seven

I drive my knuckle into the side of my head, as though I'm trying to bore right through my skull and into my brain. It's a pathetic attempt to try and erase the noise of the rats. My eyes are squeezed shut as they tear around me, the thoughts of what I've already done, the smell and taste of blood, the sight of flesh parting, consuming my senses and only making the rats' movements more frantic.

I roar in desperation and, finally, with my knuckles digging into my temples so hard it feels like I've burrowed right through bone, the noise begins to die down.

You did it, you took the first step. I'm so proud of you.

I close my eyes. I'm not sure whether or not the words are congratulatory. I'm not sure whether I should feel happiness right now, or if I've sealed my own doom through my actions.

But Oscar was just the start. You can't stop now. You have to keep going. Go and get the list.

I'm soon back in the bedroom. I open the drawer.

Take the list. Take it. You're doing well, but there's plenty more still to come.

The list is in my hands now. The list.

That's good. You know what comes next. Make sure you're ready.

'I will be ready.'

I have to be.

—

Later, I'm kneeling on the cold metal floor as I stare at her. She's so pretty it makes my eyes sting and my head pound with confusion. Even with her dirty and torn clothes. Even with her skin all scraped and red raw and bleeding in places from where I dragged her away. Even with the black streaks underneath her teary eyes.

I'm still not sure why she's here. I know it's not the plan. Did I feel sorry for her? Am I trying to prove to myself that I'm not all bad, that I'm not here to hurt innocent people? Or is it the look in her eyes, the look I saw then, the look I see still, a look which has somehow touched me and convinced me that I—

I thought you were ready. You must see this is a mistake?

I try to block out the voice, even though I know my disobedience will not be ignored.

'You need to drink,' I say as I push the plastic cup along the floor of the van towards her. 'Move forwards and I'll take the tape off.'

She glares at me defiantly and doesn't move from the back of the van at all. She hates me. She hates me even more than she's scared of me. I see that. But I'm not the monster she thinks I am.

'Please, you have to drink.'

Stop this! You can't do this. You have to kill her. You'll ruin everything.

I shake my head. 'No. No, I won't. Not like this.'

Now she looks at me curiously as her chest heaves in and out. She doesn't understand. How could she?

She's seen your face. There's no going back. Finish this. We have to move on to the next.

I grind my teeth as I try to block out the demand. My jaw is clenched so tightly that it feels like my teeth will shatter. The front of my head begins to stab in pain.

'You need to drink,' I say to her. I sound angry, but it's not with her. I want to be calm. I want to be nice. But I'm being pushed closer and closer.

I'm on my feet. I grab the water and stomp towards her. She cowers back, as best she can with her wrists cuffed to the railing on the side of the van. Her legs writhe about to try and fend me off, but I crouch down and dig my knees into the flesh on her thighs and it's enough to halt her protest.

I rip the tape from her mouth. She cries. Pain? Then screams. I slap her across the face to try to quieten her, then grab her hair and yank it back to tilt her head. She purses her lips as I tip the water towards her mouth.

'Drink.'

Her mouth is closed.

'Drink!'

The water goes everywhere. She opens her lips for barely a second. She takes some in – I can see that she swallows. But the cup is empty now. She's blown it for herself.

'That was stupid. You shouldn't fight me.'

'Why?' she stammers as tears begin to roll. 'Why... are you doing this?'

It doesn't matter why. Kill her!

'Please. Just let me go.'

She's sobbing now. It's a horrible sound. Together with the voice in my head, I'm not sure I can take it.

I thought you were stronger than this.

'Please. I want go home.'

I thought you could see this through.

'I won't tell anyone. I just want my mum.'

She's nothing. Get rid of her. We have to keep going! Kill her! Kill her now!

'JUST SHUT UP! SHUT THE FUCK UP!'

Spittle flies from my mouth as I bark. Sophie, that's her name, she scrambles back until she's pressed up against the far end of the van. She looks even more petrified now, even if my words weren't directed at her.

Then... the inevitable. Silence.

I close my eyes. I begin to tremble. I can already hear the rats beginning to move.

'No, no, no!' I say. My words are shaky, pleading and desperate.

I lurch forwards and push the tape back onto her mouth, then turn and more or less fall out of the open back doors of the van onto the mottled concrete outside. I slam the doors shut.

The noise inside me is already growing, already unbearable. I push my palms against my temples and squeeze.

When I open my eyes again I'm sure I see a tiny little grey figure darting across the floor of the dank space in front of me. A rat. Just one. Nothing like the thousands that are now devouring my insides.

My hands still to my head, I stumble across the floor for the loading doors. I need to go. I have to get home. I need my fix. Despite my words, my actions, I can't operate like this. I have to follow through. I have to keep going.

More than anything though, as the rats take over, as they begin to consume me, I'm just desperate to have the voice – a voice of reason and control – back in my head once more.

Despite everything, I simply can't function without *her*.

Chapter Eight

'Do you want another?' Dani asked Jason, pointing to his empty glass.

'Better not,' he said as Dani beckoned the waiter over.

She looked back at him, disappointed. She ordered two Diet Cokes. She'd really wanted another large merlot, but trust Jason to see sense. She had to love his control.

As the waiter walked away, Jason was staring at her. Trying to read her, no doubt.

'Good golf?' Dani asked.

Jason forced a laugh. His contemplative mood was beginning to irk her.

'I've had worse,' he said, 'but I'm sure you've other things on your mind than that.'

Dani scoffed. She looked away, around the half-empty restaurant. Giovanni's was one of their locals, just five minutes' walk from their house near Harborne High Street. Near closing time on a Sunday night it was pretty much dead, and she was sure the staff couldn't wait for them to leave. Really Dani should have been tucked up in bed by now, yet she knew she wouldn't be able to sleep.

'I don't have to go away tomorrow, if you don't want me to,' he said.

Dani thought about that one for a moment. In many ways she'd enjoyed their recent new routine. For the past month he'd been away pretty much the whole time Monday to Friday, and she'd enjoyed having some space to herself, knowing that he was only on the other end of the phone, and that he'd be back by the weekend. It was certainly true that she was still getting used to the idea of being shacked up with someone. Not that this was the first time they'd lived together, but after coming out of hospital following her brain injury, Jason had been more a carer than a lover, and their relationship had soon broken down – something which Dani knew she was almost entirely to blame for. This time though, their living together felt all the more permanent, not least because they'd actually bought this house together, joint mortgage and all, and there was little doubt that she was madly in love with him.

'You don't have to do that,' Dani said. 'I'll be fine.'

Jason looked at her as though he didn't believe a word of it. He'd left the police force barely a year ago, and his inner policeman was still brimming away right near the surface. His leaving the force had been a joint decision, of sorts, in no small part due to the trauma – mental and physical – that both of them had suffered as they'd brought a demented mother and son killing team to justice. Well, technically, they'd put them both six feet under, which as far as Dani was concerned, was justice enough. That case was Jason's last for West Midlands Police, and his first real taste of personal trauma. But not Dani's.

What did it say about her that she was still fighting away, still determined to prove to everyone that she could be a good copper, even after all that she'd suffered?

Jason meanwhile was already rapidly making another life for himself as a freelance management consultant, following in his father's footsteps. She admired his ability to get on and get ahead, even if she worried that part of him was in denial about everything.

She was hardly one to talk about such things.

Jason sighed. 'It's not a problem,' he said. 'My clients will understand.'

'There's nothing to understand,' Dani snapped. 'I already said I'll be fine on my own.'

She was about to add, 'I don't need my hand held constantly,' but she really didn't want to hurt him, and she wasn't even sure if that statement was true any more, despite her bullishness.

'Why don't we just get back to the house?' she said.

Jason said nothing to that. Just nodded his head before he held his hand up to ask for the bill.

–

Dani was badly in need of coffee when she headed into HQ, a little before seven a.m. the following morning. After fixing herself a strong black coffee, she headed to her desk, hoping to have at least a half hour on her own to get her thoughts together before everyone else arrived.

Actually she got more than forty-five minutes before the next person walked through the doors – her boss, DCI McNair – though Dani by then had made little headway, such was the commotion taking place inside her head.

'Morning, DI Stephens,' McNair said as she came to a stop by Dani's desk.

'Morning, ma'am.'

In many ways McNair was a strange creature to Dani. Stuck somewhere between the old school and the new in virtually every aspect of her job, she'd just recently started to occasionally use the first names of those who worked under her, rather than their titles, when speaking to them or about them, but always looked seriously put out if any of those same people reciprocated in kind. It seemed she'd forgotten about that change today.

'Big day, eh?' McNair said.

Was McNair referring to the Clarkson trial or the Redfearne investigation?

'Something like that,' Dani said.

'Anything else I should know beforehand?'

OK, so this was about Redfearne, and the team briefing due to take place in just a few minutes. Dani had already briefed McNair a couple of times from Drifford House yesterday, so there probably wasn't much need, particularly given she was still trying her best to work through a million different thoughts herself.

'No. I think we're all good.'

'Very well. And good luck later. I'm sure it'll turn out exactly as we hoped.'

Dani nodded but said nothing, and McNair took a step away, then paused. When she turned back around she had an uncomfortable look on her face. Dani was sure she wasn't going to like this.

'I don't get to see you on your own very often,' McNair said, looking around the otherwise empty office space. 'But how's everything now?'

Dani shrugged. 'It's all good, thanks.'

What did McNair really expect her to say? It wasn't as if they'd ever been close confidantes.

'I know the Clarkson trial has been heavy for you. Especially coming directly after the Grant case.'

'This is my job. I don't get to pick and choose my cases.'

'No, you don't. But you have an unfortunate habit of getting the worst ones. Your efforts don't go unappreciated, though. As long as you know that.'

That was about as big a compliment as McNair had ever dished out. What did it even mean, though? At more than one point over the past few years it had been suggested that Dani was a spent force, so it wasn't as though McNair and the other top dogs felt she was infallible. Yet Dani kept on delivering, despite it all, and even if McNair's praise was fleeting, it did still carry a lot of weight.

'And DI Barnes?' McNair said. 'You know, I've not heard anything from him since his leaving party.'

'He's just Jason now, ma'am.'

McNair laughed. Or was it a scoff? Perhaps something in between.

'I guess he'll always be DI Barnes to me. It really was a shame to lose him like we did.'

'He's not lost, ma'am. If anything, I think he's found his true self now.'

That scoff again. 'That's good to hear. I'm very pleased for you both.'

Although she sounded anything but. Would McNair have preferred it if Jason had been the one still on the team and Dani the one who'd sacked it in to chase an alternative career, and to give the other the space to flourish?

'Tell him I said hi,' McNair said.

'Of course. When I see him. He's away all this week trying to woo some new clients.'

'He always was a charmer,' McNair said with a strange look of pride. She turned and walked away, leaving Dani with an uneasy feeling. McNair and Jason? Dani quivered at the thought.

–

At eight o'clock the meeting room was filled with over a dozen weary-looking detectives, most of whom had been working until late the previous night. Dani and Easton stood at the front of the room and Dani began her opening spiel. McNair was sitting off to the side, away from the others, the only one who looked fresh, although a heavy frown had soon found its way onto her face and Dani wasn't sure if it was because she was deep in thought or because she disapproved of something. If the latter, Dani was sure she'd hear about it sooner or later.

'We need to put every effort we can into finding what's happened to Sophie Blackwood,' Dani said, coming to the end of her initial briefing. 'She remains out of contact. From what we've been told her family have heard nothing from her at all. If there's even a tiny chance she's still alive, we need to find her before it's too late.'

A hand went up towards the back of the room.

'Yes, Claire?' Dani said to DC Grayling. Usually her long blonde hair was flowing, and she would have neat make-up over her blemish-free skin. Today her face was puffy, and her hair was messily tied back.

'Has triangulation given any clues as to what happened to Sophie?' Grayling asked.

'The phone was turned off just before eight p.m., or the battery ran dry. We can't trace its movements since that point, but we know it was still on the property then. It's not been found by the forensics team, so we have to assume it went with Sophie.'

'And that's consistent with the time of the attack,' Easton said. 'We know Oscar and Sophie must have first been at the murder scene around six fifteen. Whether the attack took place immediately or sometime after, it's not clear; but we know for sure that the killer was on the premises for a good while.'

'How do you mean?' McNair said.

'Whatever the sequence of events, it would have taken the killer some time after attacking Oscar to carry Sophie and winch her over that wall. Did he already have the rope to do that? If so, why? Was Sophie, her kidnapping, the real purpose here, perhaps? We need to be mindful of every possibility right now.'

'It doesn't go dark until after nine,' McNair said. 'You honestly believe the killer did all this in daylight?'

'It's possible,' Easton said. 'Unless Oscar and Sophie spent a few hours down by the stream on their own before the attack happened. Or unless, after attacking them, the killer sat waiting for darkness before he cleaned up and took Sophie. We don't have much evidence to point in either direction right now.'

'But it does seem unlikely,' McNair said. 'That a killer would be so brazen, in daylight, when all those other people are nearby.'

'Or just that our killer is extremely confident,' Dani said. 'Everything about this attack shows a good deal of planning.' Except for biting Oscar, Dani thought but didn't say. 'Taking place on a day when the parents and everyone else was so pre-occupied by the party. The neighbours, too, were away, and still are. This meant the private lane behind Drifford House, which heads up to their nearest neighbours at Hawthorne Cottage, was deserted that day, even in the early evening. Yes it was daylight, but there was no one to see the killer there.'

'What about cameras on the main street?' DC Grayling asked.

'There are cameras on the nearest main road, Drifford Road,' Easton said. 'But none that captures the entrance to that lane. We're going to have to scour through movements on the cameras on Drifford Road, but we could be looking at a hundred or more vehicles that passed near to Drifford House within our window of time.'

Another hand went up. DC Constable. Dani nodded to him. 'If we look outside the window of time, we can narrow down vehicles of interest by identifying those seen more than once. You said yourself this killer must have pre-planned the attack. He knew the location and the layout of Drifford House, so he must have been before.'

'It's not the A1,' Easton said, 'but Drifford Road gets a fair bit of traffic. You're going to have a whole host of vehicles captured multiple times on the street cameras. Neighbours, et cetera, but I agree it's worth having a look to see what sticks out.'

'And throw into that a wider search of the cameras at the gates to Drifford House,' Dani said. 'If the killer is so familiar with the inside of the grounds, it's possible they came in through a more legitimate route at one point or another. You can lead on all things CCTV, OK?'

Constable nodded, and looked a little flattered with the responsibility he'd been given, but Dani had already surmised from his quick work the previous day that he was in a good position to quickly pull results in that area.

'We also need to do a thorough check on all of the staff at Drifford House. Who were these people; how did they get the job; what links did they have to the Redfearnes? Could any of them be our perp? Same for the guests. We need to forget about their celebrity status. This is about finding a killer, and a kidnapped eighteen-year-old.'

DC Grayling had her hand up again.

'Yes?' Dani said.

'Are we going to go public? For Sophie's benefit.'

Dani looked to McNair who now stood from her chair. 'Before this briefing I wasn't sure that was necessary, but the more I hear, the more I think we need to set up a press conference as soon as we can. We won't give details of Oscar Redfearne's murder, nor of the party that took place, as we don't want this to turn into a media frenzy, focusing only on the guests, but we will issue a plea for help in identifying what's happened to Sophie Blackwood.' McNair looked back to Dani. 'You let me handle that.'

Dani nodded, a little relieved in honesty. She wasn't a fan of having her face plastered over TV or in newspapers. Not after what had happened in the past. McNair seemed to get that. Or at the very least, didn't trust Dani to do a good enough job of it, given her history.

Either way, that was fine by Dani. She knew where her strengths lay, and she certainly knew her weaknesses, as did plenty of other people.

'Anything else, Dani?' McNair said.

Dani shook her head. McNair turned back to the room.

'Good. Then let's get to it,' McNair said. 'The teams taking statements, you're going to come up against some resistance here. I've already seen the guest list from the Redfearnes' party, and I can only imagine how reluctant some of these people will be about our desire to speak to them, particularly once they realise what the case is about and that it's at least partly in the public domain. Expect pushback; expect prattish lawyers trying to play games. If anyone obstructs unnecessarily, you have my permission to haul them in.'

A few nods and half smiles from around the room. It was certainly a refreshing take from McNair.

Dani looked at her watch. Her heart drummed a little harder in her chest when she saw the time. When she looked back to the DCI, she was giving Dani the eye. She nodded, as though she'd sensed what Dani was thinking and was giving her approval.

'A young woman's life hangs in the balance,' Dani said. 'And a killer is out there. We need to find them both, as soon as we can. I'll let DS Easton wrap things up here.'

Dani gave a meek smile to Easton, then McNair, then took a deep breath to calm her bubbling nerves before she headed for the door.

Chapter Nine

The courtroom was already filling up by the time Dani arrived. She headed straight over to the seats where the prosecution team were gathered, all of them in sombre moods.

'How are you?' Dani asked as she took a seat a few rows behind the CPS team, next to Larissa who was sitting with her head bowed, as she had for much of the entire four-week trial thus far.

'Nervous,' Larissa said.

'Me too,' Dani said. 'But I have faith. We've done everything we can.'

Larissa looked up. Her eyes were bloodshot. Crying? Or was it a lack of sleep? Dani knew one of the many after-effects of Larissa's ordeal was a case of chronic insomnia. She herself had suffered similarly more than once. Alcohol and pills, for months at a time, had been Dani's best route to a good night's sleep. Luckily those darkest of days were now well and truly behind her, even if they would never be forgotten. Larissa was still in a much earlier stage of recovery. Dani had questioned more than once whether Larissa should be in the courtroom at all, but the seventeen-year-old had insisted over and over again that she couldn't be anywhere else. Not until she was certain that her father was locked away for good, and could do no more harm to her or what remained of her family.

Dani knew better than most that Larissa's troubles wouldn't end today, even if they got the result they needed, but she wasn't about to go into that with her now.

Before long, the judge and jury were in place and the defendant, Campbell Clarkson, was brought to the dock, his hands cuffed in front of him. Larissa remained with her head bowed, but Dani watched him the whole way, and was sure he was watching her right back. They'd first met the day Dani, with Easton's help, had cornered and subdued him after he'd fled his friend's house on the outskirts of Coventry, where he'd been hiding for the best part of three weeks following his rampage.

That day he'd been full of fight and had had plenty to say. Throughout this trial he'd been quite the different man. His plain face was now passive, as always, no hint of emotion – anger, sadness or regret – as it had been throughout the last few weeks. What was really going on in his head? The man had been accused of three murders: his mother-in-law, his wife and his son. He'd also tried to kill Larissa, his daughter, in one frenzied and jealousy-fuelled attack. Allegedly. Yet now he was entirely detached from the goings-on. Did that point more to his innocence or his guilt?

Not that there was any doubt in Dani's mind. Campbell Clarkson was a murderer. He'd covered his tracks well, all things considered, and DNA evidence wasn't anywhere near as conclusive as the prosecution had hoped it would be, yet Dani knew he was the killer.

Today was Clarkson's day of reckoning.

The judge summoned the foreman of the jury. Larissa, head still down, placed her hand onto Dani's lap. Dani put her hand over the top and squeezed gently.

Larissa was sobbing, almost silently. Dani closed her eyes as her mind took her back in time. She saw so much of herself in this young lady sitting by her side. Not in who she was as a person, but what she'd been through. How one person, one person who should have been there for her, had taken so much away, had tried to kill her. Unlike Larissa though, Dani hadn't made it to court. She'd still been in hospital when her brother had been found guilty.

'Has the jury reached a verdict?' the judge asked.

'Yes.'

'On the charge of the murder of Tobias Clarkson, how do you find the defendant?'

'Guilty.'

There were a few whoops from behind in the public gallery, more than one groan too – Clarkson did still have allies. Larissa turned her hand over and squeezed Dani's even harder. The judge read out the next charge.

'Guilty,' came the foreman's reply once more.

Then the third charge was read. Same result. The final charge was the attempted murder of Larissa Clarkson.

Larissa finally lifted her head as the judge spoke her name. She took her hand back.

'He didn't kill me,' she whispered, just loud enough for Dani to hear. 'But I wish he had.'

Dani shivered at the all too familiar words; her heart ached. Tears welled and she struggled to fight them off. A moment later, for the fourth time that morning, the foreman repeated the same word.

'Guilty.'

In the court's anteroom, the CPS team were relieved more than jubilant. Dani was conscious of time ticking by, but so far she'd been unable to draw herself away from Larissa who seemed attached to her side. There was no air of victory from the young woman at all. If anything, her sadness and contemplation seemed to have ramped up even more than before, as though she couldn't work out why she wasn't yet feeling any better. Dani felt better, even if she didn't want to egregiously show it. Campbell Clarkson was a despicable and cowardly human being – not just a killer, but a killer who didn't have the guts to admit to what he'd done, to come to terms with the damage he'd caused to the people who loved him the most – and he would now rightly serve the rest of his life behind bars.

Dani's phone buzzed in her bag for the umpteenth time.

'I don't mind,' Larissa said, looking up at her. 'I know you're busy, and you've done everything you can for me now.'

Dani said nothing as she smiled and pulled the phone from her bag. It was Katherine Wyatt, one of the team's PAs.

'Dani, we had an urgent call for you. I've been trying to reach you for ages.'

Dani got to her feet. 'About the case?' she said, expectantly.

'No. It's… a private matter.'

She said the last two words more quietly, as though she was worried someone on her end was listening in. Dani frowned, as a whole host of unwelcome thoughts crashed in her mind. Had something happened to Jason?

'What is it?' Dani asked.

'I thought I recognised the number when it came through. It was from Long Lartin.'

Dani's heart thudded in her chest now. She turned away from Larissa. Of course she knew exactly who might want to speak to her from Long Lartin prison, even before Katherine helpfully clarified.

'It's your brother,' she said.

Which Dani had already guessed. What she didn't know, and why she was so tense all of a sudden, was why?

Chapter Ten

Dani was surprised when the guard opened the door and she was left staring only at her brother, all alone in the prison interview room. It had transpired back at court that in fact Ben hadn't been the person on the other end of the urgent phone call for Dani, but rather his lawyer, Gregory Daley, and subsequently, naturally, she'd been expecting both Daley and Ben to be meeting with her.

So where was the lawyer now? Would Dani have even bothered to drop everything and make the impromptu trip to Worcestershire if she'd known?

'Long time no see,' Ben said with a wry smile.

Dani said nothing as she stepped into the plain room that had dirtied white-painted walls, lino floor and a single buzzing and flickering strip light above the simple desk and two chairs. The thick door was closed behind her with a loud thunk before locks were clicked into place.

'Where's Daley?' Dani asked.

'It's just you and me.'

Dani remained standing as she looked over to the large mirror on one of the walls, then back to Ben. He shook his head, obviously picking up on her thought. 'There's no one there,' he said. 'It's just you and me, honestly.'

'Daley said we needed to speak urgently,' Dani said, already riled not just by the false pretence but by Ben's apparent nonchalance to it. 'He said you had confidential information you would pass only to me.'

'Dani, I've not seen you for the best part of – what? twenty months. Not since—'

'I'm well aware how long it's been.'

Ben paused for a few moments as he held Dani's eye. Was this just all him playing with her? But then, if that was the case, how had he got Daley, a respected lawyer, generally speaking at least, to play along too? Unless it hadn't been Daley she'd spoken to at all. Was that possible?

No, surely there was more to Dani being here than Ben wanting a bit of fun at her expense.

'Why don't you sit down,' Ben said.

'Why don't you tell me what this is really about?'

'I think Gregory already did that.'

'Not really.'

Ben sat back in his chair. Despite the handcuffs on his wrists, his prison garb, he looked relaxed and confident. 'We think we have an offer that will appeal to you.'

'What could you possibly have to offer me?' Dani said. 'Ben, you're the one person who's taken so much *from* me.'

An image of Larissa, teary-eyed and defeated, flashed in Dani's mind. A kindred spirit of sorts. Campbell Clarkson had killed three members of his own family, had failed in killing his only daughter. Ben had similarly killed or attempted to kill those closest to him. Dani, along with his second wife Gemma, were the ones who got away. The ones who would never recover.

'Oh, here we go, poor old Dani,' Ben sneered. 'So bloody traumatised, damaged frontal lobes, traumatic brain injury, blah blah fucking blah. Poor little thing. She only gets to carry on her nice little life on the outside, job, boyfriend, time with *my* kids, the works, while her twin brother stews in jail for the rest of his life.'

'Because you're a bloody murderer, Ben! You tried to kill *me*! Yes I'm fucking traumatised, however long it's been since I last saw you.'

Ben's eyes were now pinched as though he'd taken offence at Dani calling him a murderer. Was he really still in denial about that?

'I heard what happened to you,' he said.

'What happened to me *which* time?'

Ben laughed. 'The Grant case. Mother and son.'

'That was months ago,' Dani said. 'Nearly two years in fact.'

'Seems like you don't have much luck.'

'I'm a murder detective. I come up against the scum of the earth on the regular.'

She could tell that one annoyed him.

'How long have you been back at work now?'

'This time? Long enough.'

'And Jason?'

Dani hesitated. She'd never talked to Ben about their relationship, but of course he knew about her and Jason – most likely because of what had happened to them both the autumn before last in their hunt for Mary and Ethan Grant, the mother and son killing duo whose reign of terror she and Jason had brought to a close. Both detectives had suffered horrible injuries in the process, particularly Jason who still bore grim-looking scars over one whole side of his body from the acid that had eaten through skin and flesh as he'd fought to apprehend the killers.

After recovering physically, if not mentally, from that latest trauma, Dani had gone back to work a few months later. Jason had ultimately packed it all in for good. Ben wouldn't know all that, but he would have read the basics of the Grant case from the papers.

'Jason's fine,' Dani said.

'And you?'

'I'm like a bloody Duracell bunny. I never stop.' She winked at him, though her tone had been cold.

The outsides of Ben's mouth twitched as if he was about to smile, but he didn't.

'How does it feel?' he asked.

'What?'

'You know.'

'Do I?'

'How does it feel, killing someone?'

The smile did break out on his face now. Dani shut her eyes for a beat. In that brief moment, sounds and smells and sensations flashed through her mind from that fateful night the year before last. The night she'd taken Ethan Grant's life. She opened her eyes again and it was all gone.

She said nothing.

'Dani. You still really don't see it, do you? We're *exactly* the same. We always were. Whereas I got locked up in here for what I did, you get a damn slap on the back and a medal for your services.'

'The man I killed was a vile murderer,' she said. 'And I didn't do it out of revenge or hatred or anything other than my own survival instinct. I had no choice.'

'I would say exactly the same thing for myself,' Ben said, through clenched teeth now. 'But who would listen?'

Dani had had enough. She wasn't here for his sob story, or to hear how wronged he felt. She pushed back on her chair and went to get up.

'Sorry, Ben. When Daley said this was urgent, I foolishly believed him. But I really don't have time for this. Whatever *this* is.'

'I need your help,' Ben said.

Dani was already on her feet.

'You help me, I help you,' he said.

'What could you possibly have to offer me?'

Confidence and arrogance had returned to Ben now. So many different and clashing personalities and emotions were on display, Dani could scarcely keep up with it all.

'You're a homicide detective, aren't you?' he said.

Dani didn't respond. Though the fact she remained standing and looking over at him likely showed him he still had her attention.

'So go figure,' he said.

'You have information about a crime? A murder? Murders?'

A petulant flick of his eyebrows.

'Give me more,' she said.

'I will. When you've agreed to help me.'

'Why me?'

'Because you're in a unique position to reciprocate.'

'How?'

'You may or may not know that Gregory's working on my appeal, but as a backstop he's also exploring other options. Like he's suggesting a quid pro quo to increase my chances of a successful parole. I help the authorities if they help me.'

'Then why isn't Daley here? And if you're asking for some sort of immunity or reduction in sentence, I'm not a judge or a prosecutor. I can't do that, Ben. And I probably wouldn't, for you, even if I could.'

'Fair enough, but it all starts with you, Dani.'

'What are you talking about?'

'Like I said, you're in a unique position to help. You're right, you're not a judge or a prosecutor, but you have links to them. But you also have links to my family.'

'Gemma? The kids? What—?'

'You need to help me, Dani.'

'I don't *need* to do anything for you.'

'I have to see them. I have to be a part of their lives.'

'You honestly believe that?'

'I'm Harry and Chloe's dad.'

'Then maybe you should have thought twice about killing Harry's mother, and trying to kill Chloe's.'

Ben looked angered again now.

'You can try, Dani. Try to talk to them. I *have* to see them.'

'I could try. But I won't.'

'You'd see people die instead of helping me?' he said, incredulous now.

Dani tensed up. What did that mean?

'No, I wouldn't want that,' she said. 'But you need to give me something first, to show me this isn't some ridiculous fantasy.'

'Actually, no. I don't think I do. If you don't want to talk, then fine. Perhaps you'll figure it out sooner or later. But if more people die before then, don't come blaming me.'

A smug look had returned to his face. It pissed Dani off more than she would care to admit.

'Ben, tell me what the hell is going on. What do you know?'

He turned his head away from her, his lips firmly shut.

'So you'll give me nothing?' she said, her own anger rising now.

Ben still didn't say a word. Just flicked his eyebrows once again. Dani wouldn't waste any more of her time. She had far more pressing matters. She turned for the door, knocked on it and heard locks clicking. The door opened with a whoomph of air.

'I expect I'll see you very soon, sis,' Ben said with oily confidence. 'Oh, and how was the party at the Redfearnes'?'

Dani paused now, her whole body rigid, but she didn't turn back to face him.

'Quite the place they have, I hear.'

Dani cringed and clenched her fists as tightly as she could as she stepped out of the room, slamming the door behind her.

–

'I need to see Cartwright, now,' Dani said to the guard standing outside.

The guard looked a little taken aback by Dani's abruptness, but he nodded and they plodded off along corridors and through security doors until they came to the Deputy Governor's out-of-date office.

The guard knocked and opened the door when prompted. Dani stormed in past him without waiting for any sort of introduction.

'Where's Gregory Daley?'

'DI Stephens,' Cartwright said, getting to her feet from behind her desk, clearly perturbed by the sudden intrusion, even if her words didn't show it. 'I heard you were here—'

'I need to see Daley, now.'

Cartwright huffed. She nodded to the guard in the doorway, who grumbled as he moved away, shutting the door behind him.

'Perhaps you'd like to take a minute to calm down. I'm sure I've not done anything to warrant your animosity.'

It was a fair point, and Cartwright's level tone took the edge off Dani's bubbling anger. A little.

'Is he still here?'

'I believe so,' Cartwright said. 'I was told he'd want to see your brother again once you were finished.'

'Well we're finished. But I need to see Daley first.'

'Is there a problem? I was told you were coming here on police business? As you know from past experience, you can only make personal visits through the formal—'

'Yes there's a problem. The problem is I need to see Daley, and I need to see him now. And yes, this is official business.'

Cartwright considered this for a few moments before she sighed and turned and picked up her desk phone and had a hushed conversation with someone on the other end. When she put the phone down a few moments later Dani was still on edge, though the edge was continuing to dull.

'I'll take you to him,' Cartwright said.

'Thank you,' Dani said, trying to sound sincere, though she really wasn't feeling it, even if she realised that Cartwright had done nothing wrong here. If anything, she was being accommodating to Dani.

Cartwright led them back along the same bland corridors as before, and they soon passed the room where minutes earlier Dani had been speaking to Ben. Two doors further along and Cartwright stopped. Dani presumed the door in between here and the room she'd met with Ben led to a listening room. Had Daley been in there earlier when she was with Ben, despite what Ben had said?

Cartwright knocked and opened the door and said a few words while Dani held back, trying to compose herself, trying to stay calm. Cartwright stepped out of the doorway.

'Go ahead,' Cartwright said. 'I'll send a guard down to escort you out when you're done.'

Dani nodded and stepped inside.

–

She tried to hold back, she really did. Was it the situation and the thoughts of Ben messing with her head that had her so riled, or was it her own mental problems haunting her once again, as they still did even after all this time, ever since Ben had attacked and tried to kill her?

Perhaps it was even because she detested Gregory Daley about as much as she detested anyone else she'd ever met.

'What the fuck are you playing at, you piece of shit?' Dani slammed as she stepped into the room and banged the door shut behind her.

Daley just sat in his chair and stared at her. In his mid-forties, he had thinning dark brown hair, all mussy on top, designer thick-rimmed glasses, and he wore an immaculate dark blue suit. Everything about him screamed lawyer. Everything about him screamed arrogance and a know-it-all attitude. He'd been Ben's lawyer from day one after his arrest, and had a string of incredible defences under his belt prior to that. As far as Dani could see, he'd only taken Ben's case, at a vastly reduced fee, to further his public career. Although ultimately Ben's case was considered by many to be Daley's biggest humiliation, he was still beavering away to gain whatever advantages he could for his murderous client.

'Were you listening?' Dani said.

'Would you care to take a seat?'

'No. Were you listening?'

'Very well. No is the answer,' Daley said, cupping his hands together, elbows on the desk. 'My client asked me not to. He wanted a private discussion with his sister.'

'Yeah, but you know exactly what it was about, don't you?'

'What I do and don't know about your brother is irrelevant.'

'Tell me what's going on.'

'What's going on?'

He asked the question as though it was the most complex question to mankind, as though the answer was infinite.

'*You* called me to get me here, so don't play dumb, however much it suits you.' Dani was perversely pleased to see the look of offence at that. 'What does Ben know about murder cases? Active or otherwise. He says he has information. I need that information.'

'Ms Stephens—'

'DI Stephens. I'm here in a professional capacity.'

'DI Stephens, what I discuss with your brother, my client, is protected by privilege, as you are very much aware.'

'Really? You want to play that game? From what I gather my brother has information pertinent to the

94

homicide team at West Midlands Police. That's what I'm here for. Information he'll only divulge if his demands are met. *You* know that, because *you* called me—'

'Well I really—'

'You're happy to have blood on your hands, if it comes to that?'

'Detective, my conscience is clear,' Daley said, now sounding uptight as he went on the defensive. 'Your brother has a right to representation, and I assist my client in *his* best interests. I'm aware he has stated to you that he has information which may be of benefit to the West Midlands Police. And I'm also aware that as part of my work with him, he'll be willing to divulge this information if the right guarantees are met by you, and by the CPS. It's for you to decide how you wish to proceed with that. My client is not trying or wanting to be difficult here, and neither am I—'

'You're scum. You really are.'

'I'm afraid personal insults are lost on me, Detective.'

His words belied the fact that he by now looked seriously pissed off by Dani's aggression towards him. Sod it. He was lucky she wasn't launching herself over the desk to throttle him into telling her the truth, the whole truth, and nothing but the damn truth.

'I'm done,' Dani said turning for the door. 'I want nothing to do with this sick deal, whatever the hell it is.'

'Very well, DI Stephens.'

Dani felt ready to explode. It took everything she had not to turn around and lay into Daley some more. Verbally. Physically. She just needed to go, before she lost it. She knew she'd only regret it if she did.

Her body tingling with surging adrenaline, she reached out with a shaky hand and opened the door.

'I shall inform my client of your decision,' Daley said, calm and in control, which only made Dani all the more angry. 'Though he assures me you'll change your mind soon enough.'

Dani cringed as she stepped out of the room and slammed the door shut behind her.

Chapter Eleven

A handful of pills and a drive back to Birmingham later, Dani was finally feeling as though she could operate on an even keel once again, though she felt horrible knowing that the only way for her to even attempt to feel 'normal' lately was through chemical inducement.

Had she really fallen back into this?

She could hear with crystal clarity Jason's nagging tone, warning her of the pitfalls of upping her meds. As much as that nagging tone irked, she also knew he was damn right.

Still, tomorrow would be a new day, right?

The others were already waiting for Dani when she arrived back at HQ. Her first action as soon as she'd reached her car on leaving the prison – after necking her pills that is – was to call DCI McNair to explain what had happened with Ben. Dani had no choice. She really didn't know how else to deal with what Ben had said. Did he really have information relevant to the homicide team? About the Redfearne case? Regardless, she couldn't keep something so potentially significant to herself.

Needless to say, McNair had taken the revelation, as lacking in supporting evidence as it was, very seriously indeed, and had set up a meeting for her and Dani with Chief Superintendent Eric Baxter plus a senior lawyer from the Crown Prosecution Service – Ahmad Hussein – who Dani hadn't met before.

Dani walked into the room full of senior personnel expecting a grilling. She almost fainted when what she actually received wasn't far short of a bloody standing ovation.

'I hear congratulations are in order,' Baxter, a silver fox, said as he headed over to Dani, all smiles, and shook her hand and patted her shoulder like a proud dad might.

'You really helped us to put a watertight case together,' Hussein said. In his forties, he was pot-bellied and had a shiny bald head, a warming smile to go with it. He too came around to shake Dani's hand. 'I've heard good things about you, DI Stephens, and the whole team on the Clarkson case is very grateful for your hard and meticulous work.'

Dani was lost for words.

'Well done, Dani,' McNair said, beaming with pride. 'Clarkson got what he deserved.'

What the hell was all this? Had she stepped into an alternate universe? Or maybe this was all a pill-induced hallucination. Perhaps her car was lying in a ditch somewhere off the A435.

The overt pleasantries were thankfully soon over with, even if the praise had been a brief and welcome diversion. The room took on a more hushed and contemplative tone as Dani explained, as succinctly and with as little emotion as she could, what had transpired at Long Lartin earlier.

'How on earth would he know about the Redfearnes' party?' Baxter asked, his eyes sweeping the room as if the question was directed at each one of them.

Dani had no answer.

'We should look at what relationships he's made on the inside,' Dani said. 'If he really does know anything about any crimes that have taken place or are about to take place that has to be his source.'

'Possibly,' Hussein said. 'Unless this is information he's held since before he was jailed. He mentioned the Redfearnes' party but that doesn't mean his information is related to that case. He could have information on a cold case from years ago.'

'Or he could have nothing at all,' McNair said.

The room fell silent for a few moments.

'The key question is,' Dani said, 'regardless of what he knows, how do we get him to tell us?'

'If he doesn't tell us then can we not just hit him, and his lawyer, with a charge of obstruction?' Baxter said, looking to Hussein.

Hussein sighed and thought about that one for a few moments. 'It's not so easy to answer based on the little we know.'

'But it's possible?'

'It's possible. Whether the simple threat of that would be enough to get what we want… who knows?'

Dani wasn't so sure. Would such a charge even sway Ben, given he was already currently staring at a life in prison? And Daley certainly wasn't one to be pressured easily.

She glanced at her watch. Not for the first time, and the move didn't go unnoticed by McNair.

'DI Stephens?'

'Sorry, it's just… I was supposed to be at an interview. For the Redfearne case.'

McNair looked over to Baxter and Hussein.

'It's fine,' Baxter said. 'Don't let us keep you from your duty. We've got plenty more to discuss here but McNair can fill you in later.'

Dani nodded and was soon out of the room, feeling relief more than anything. Coming out of the prison, Ben's ultimatum had felt like a huge and personal burden, but with the senior team taking ownership of the problem, Dani could at least try and forget all about Ben, however hard that was.

As she strode through the corridors of HQ, she checked her watch again. If she was quick, she'd just about make it on time.

–

'Do you make a habit of harassing teenage girls... Mr Davenport?'

The interview room fell silent. Dani could sense Easton shuffling quietly next to her, perhaps as taken aback by her abrupt change of pace and tone as the others in the room. Dani didn't look to her colleague. Instead she maintained eye contact with Arnold Davenport, the portly businessman sitting opposite the table to her, next to his no doubt ridiculously expensive solicitor, Amanda Johansson. Perhaps the question, out of the blue, was a bit strong, and a bit unwarranted, but Dani really didn't care much.

'Mr Davenport?' Dani said.

'Detective, I'm not sure of the relevance of the question,' Johansson said, cutting off her client as he opened his mouth to retort.

'Mr Davenport?' Dani said again, not interested in Johansson's view.

'No of course I don't,' he said. 'What a ridiculous and baseless question.'

He looked to Johansson as if to question why she wasn't pushing back more strongly, but then Dani's change of pace had very deliberately been intended to catch them both off-guard. They'd already gone through his version of events as to what he'd seen and done at the Redfearnes' party on Saturday night in excruciatingly boring detail. His version being bland, to say the least. As though the whole thing had just been a small group of friends sitting around a table quaffing fine wine and chatting about who had more money than whom. There was more to that party than that. More sleaze, certainly. Crimes? Dani wasn't sure. Now was the perfect time to turn things around and try and find out.

'You're unmarried?' Dani asked.

'Divorced. Twice.'

'So you're single?'

'Unattached.'

'Do you engage in the use of escorts?'

Davenport looked to his lawyer.

'He doesn't have to answer that,' Johansson said, a steely glare now fixed on Dani.

'How about prostitutes? I understand—'

'Detective Stephens, that is enough!' Johansson shouted. 'You—'

'How dare you?' Davenport said to Dani, as if unwilling to let his lawyer do his defending on her own.

His interruption of his counsel gave Dani the opportunity to go again. She wouldn't let up.

'From what I understand, you *do* engage in the use of paid escorts, or whatever you want to call them, Mr Davenport.'

His cheeks were now red with fury; he turned to his lawyer again.

'This is completely unacceptable,' Davenport said to her.

'I agree,' Johansson said, facing Dani. 'This line of questioning is of absolutely no relevance to the events that took place at Drifford House on Saturday, and I'm as surprised as I am appalled that it appears you've coaxed us here under false pretences today, DI Stephens. You can be sure I'll be—'

'False pretences?' Dani said.

'My client is here of his own volition to provide the police with his witness statement as to his actions and movements on the night of—'

'Mrs Johansson, I'm afraid it's not for you to decide who *the police* determine to be witness and suspect.'

Another short silence. Davenport looked seriously uncomfortable now.

'Are you saying you're treating my client as a suspect now?' Johansson said, her almost sarcastic tone conveying exactly how preposterous she found that prospect. 'If you are, then I'm afraid we'll have to halt this meeting until you have properly put forward under what grounds you consider Mr Davenport to be a suspect in a criminal action. And, more specifically, exactly what criminal action you are suggesting he was party to.'

'Thank you, Mrs Johansson. But as I already stated, it's for the police to decide who is witness and suspect, and of course we don't have to state our case against your client or anybody else at this stage of the investigation. This is not a court.'

'This is utter nonsense,' Johansson said. 'On what grounds could you possibly be suggesting my client is a suspect in your case?'

'I'll leave aside the vagaries of what you mean by *my case*, but the grounds under which we are asking these questions is pertinent in relation to the murder of Oscar Redfearne, and the disappearance and/or murder of Sophie Blackwood. At present, we believe Mr Davenport was one of the last people to see Oscar Redfearne and Sophie Blackwood alive.'

This seemed to be news to Johansson who couldn't resist a glance to her client to seek his confirmation.

'Of course, if you have nothing to hide, Mr Davenport, then I really don't see why we can't carry on with this line of questioning,' Dani said. 'Do you?'

He turned to Johansson again who leaned over to him. He reciprocated and the two of them had a brief whispered exchange. Dani could see from Johansson's increasing exasperation that she was losing whatever debate they were having. When they were done Davenport faced back to Dani.

'We can carry on,' he said to her, ever confident. Perhaps a less arrogant man would have heeded his lawyer's advice. 'I told you already I spoke to Oscar, briefly, in the hallway, around about six p.m.'

'After he interrupted you harassing Sophie Blackwood,' Dani said.

'No,' he said, his tone displaying just a hint of anger. 'After he interrupted me having a *chat* with her.'

'How many of the female waiting staff did you grope this year, Mr Davenport?'

'Detective, I—'

Davenport cut Johansson off once more with an angry wave of his hand. A pleasing sight for Dani. Regardless of whether Davenport was involved in Oscar's death and Sophie's disappearance, Dani knew one thing for sure: Davenport was an entitled creep, and Dani despised him, and was more than happy to haul him over the coals for his unscrupulous behaviour if she could.

'I did not grope anyone,' Davenport said.

'That's not what we've heard,' Easton butted in, finally joining the conversation for the first time since Dani's change of course. His decision to speak up seemed to throw the two on the other side of the desk for a second.

'Then what have you heard?' Davenport asked.

Easton shuffled the papers on the desk in front of him, though Dani believed it was likely more for effect than anything. He'd know the answer. Dani certainly did.

Easton's eyes were on the papers in his hands as he spoke. 'We have three statements from female staff at Drifford House that you groped their... buttocks at various points on Saturday.' Easton's cheeks blushed a little at his momentary stumble over trying to find the right word. Dani would forgive him for it. 'One of those three women also alleges you also put your hand up her skirt and squeezed her inner thigh. Another staff member, male, I might add, so I think he got away with the squeezing by the sounds of it, claims he saw you grab Sophie Black-wood more than once too.'

Easton looked up from the papers now. Dani glared at Davenport who looked as though he was about ready to breathe fire. Johansson was sullen-faced as she glared at her client. Was that because she too was shocked by what she'd just heard, and was happy to see how he'd try to worm his way out of his obnoxious behaviour? Or just because she was perturbed that he'd overridden her advice to call time on this meeting?

'You do understand, Mr Davenport, that sexual harassment is a crime, as covered in detail in the Protection from Harassment Act 1997?' Easton said. 'These young women were simply going about their jobs, and unless you're going to suggest otherwise, they did nothing to encourage or to warrant your unwanted sexual advances.'

Davenport was now tight-lipped.

'Mr Davenport, do you accept what these witnesses have said about you?' Dani asked.

'You can answer no comment if you prefer,' Easton said after a short silence. 'It'd help our notes to show that you did give a response, of sorts.'

Nothing.

'Mr Davenport, do you accept what these witnesses have said about you?' Dani asked again.

'No comment.'

'Have you ever had sexual intercourse or engaged in a sex act during any of your visits to Drifford House?' Dani asked.

'No comment.'

'Have you ever had sexual intercourse or engaged in a sex act with one of the house staff, current or former, at Drifford House?'

'No comment.'

'Detective, I'm presuming you're now referring to consensual sexual contact?' Johansson asked.

'Consensual or otherwise?' Dani asked. 'Paid for or otherwise?'

'No comment,' Davenport said through clenched teeth.

'Was your intention to try and have sexual intercourse or engage in a sex act with Sophie Blackwood at the party at Drifford House last Saturday night?'

'No,' Davenport said, now baring his teeth like a dog.

Quite a telling answer, Dani thought. Could she take it from that rebuttal that the answer to all the previous questions was actually *yes* then?

'She was a pretty young woman,' Davenport said. 'I was merely interested and intrigued by her, and my intentions were perfectly respectable, however vulgar you're trying to portray my actions.'

Dani said nothing to that, even though she really wanted to. Did this man honestly believe he was in anyway respectable?

'Mr Davenport, how long have you known the Redfearnes?' Dani asked.

'More than ten years. I met Henry in a professional capacity, but we've socialised together for years.'

'So you've known Oscar Redfearne for years too?'

'Yes.'

'Can you tell us about him?'

'I'm sure I could.'

'Did you like him?'

'He was savvy.'

'Did you ever have disagreements with him?'

'About what?'

'About anything.'

'Not that I can recall.'

'Mr Davenport, did you attack Oscar Redfearne?' Easton asked.

'No.'

'Did you become involved in a quarrel with him that turned physical?'

'Not at all. The last time I saw him was in the hallway, as we've already established.'

'Do you know who killed him?' Dani asked.

'No.'

'Do you have any knowledge as to *why* someone would kill him?'

'None whatsoever.'

'Did you kill Sophie Blackwood?'

'I wasn't aware that she had been killed?' Johansson said, quite unnecessarily, Dani felt. Perhaps she was determined to show everyone she was still there.

'The question stands, Mr Davenport,' Dani said.

Johansson mumbled something under her breath.

'No,' Davenport said.

'Did you kidnap Sophie Blackwood?'

'No.'

'Do you know where Sophie Blackwood is now?'

'No.'

Dani looked to Easton. He shook his head gently.

'OK. Then I think we're done here. For now. Though you might want to think some more about what we've talked about here today. Thank you both for your time.'

–

Ten minutes later Dani was waiting by the lifts for Easton to return. He'd gladly offered to show Davenport and Johansson out of the building, leaving Dani to stew on the meeting they'd just had. Did she believe Davenport was somehow involved in Oscar's death and Sophie's disappearance? In all truth, having put him through the wringer over the last two hours, she now felt it highly unlikely, but that didn't mean he was in the clear. Not yet. Although he'd given a very clear and articulate account of his movements on Saturday, both at Drifford House and thereafter, Dani would make sure they cross-referenced his statement against whatever other evidence they could. If anything looked off...

The lift to Dani's left pinged, shaking away her thoughts. The doors slid open and Easton strolled out. He smiled and raised his hand as he came up to Dani. She smiled back and high-fived him.

'Well we sure showed him,' Easton said, sounding as smug as he looked.

'Not really,' Dani said.

The smile on his face dropped a little.

'Perhaps you've never been on the receiving end of men like him—'

'Hey, don't get me started. I was a barman on ladies' night at our local nightclub. I've had my arse squeezed without my consent plenty.'

Dani rolled her eyes at that. She wanted to argue that it wasn't the same thing at all, but then, was she right about that?

'The point is,' she said, 'however despicable we think his behaviour was and is, it's never going to amount to much, in court.'

'Don't be so negative. Just because no prosecutor would likely take a case like that on in criminal court, don't think he can't get some comeuppance. If the tabloids got wind of what any of those waitresses have said...'

He left that one dangling. Dani knew fine well what he meant. If anything, the ruin of Davenport's business career through sexual scandal was probably more of a punishment to a man like him than a few months of jail time. Still, it wasn't her place to start that process.

She wanted to catch a killer.

Chapter Twelve

It was once again dark by the time Dani made it home, a few minutes after ten p.m. Monday had been as gruelling as the previous day, if for very different reasons. Having lost much of the morning with her visit to Long Lartin prison and the meeting at HQ afterwards, then a good chunk of the afternoon interviewing Davenport, Dani had felt under pressure the rest of the day, and had worked at a hundred miles an hour to try to keep on top of the Redfearne case, which likely explained why she was now so drained, her mind foggy and her body lethargic as she stepped out of the car and shut the door.

She headed off the road and onto the small and narrow tarmac drive of the terraced house she and Jason had bought in the spring in trendy Harborne. So close to the bustling high street, all of the houses on the road, largely Victorian and often head-achingly expensive given their modest sizes, were crammed tightly together on thin plots. Their drive barely fitted Jason's car alone, which remained parked up safe and sound with him having headed off to Manchester on the train first thing in the morning. She wouldn't see him again until Friday, and despite usually being glad of the space, she wasn't so sure she was feeling it tonight.

The security light at the front of the house flicked on as Dani approached the front door, bathing the area in bright white light. Dani stuck the key in the lock and opened the door. She expected the alarm to blip, but it didn't.

Odd. Because she was sure she'd set it that morning before she left for work. But then she'd pretty much been a zombie all those hours ago, just like she was again now.

She flipped the hall light on, then as she shut the door, she heard a creaking somewhere across the downstairs. The lounge? She paused. Listened again. Nothing.

She hated this. She knew her anxiety levels today weren't helped by her fatigue, even if she had earlier taken extra pills to get her through the day.

She shook her head, as if trying to shake away the irrational thoughts that were building. After all, the house was built over a hundred years ago, it was always creaking and straining.

She took two steps down the hall when she heard the noise again.

No. That wasn't a creak.

'Hello?'

Nothing.

Her body tensed and primed, but her mind trying its best to convince her this was nothing, she moved towards the closed lounge door as quietly as she could. She couldn't see any light seeping out from underneath, but she was sure she'd heard something, someone, in there.

Her heart, already thudding in her chest, nearly exploded when the lounge door swung open and a dark figure stepped out.

Dani was ready to leap forwards and attack—

'Jesus fu… Jason? What the bloody hell!'

'Dani? I didn't hear you come in.'

'Jason, what are you doing?'

He looked at her as though she was a crazed idiot. Perhaps she was.

'You know you can't scare me like that!' she said, as exasperated as she was embarrassed. 'I was about to tear your face off!'

He smirked. Apparently there was a funny side to this. 'I wanted to surprise you. I ditched the meetings today. I'll go tomorrow. I wanted to congratulate you… But I fell asleep on the sofa waiting for you. Do you know what time it is?'

He glanced at his watch then rubbed the back of his head, as though he realised the funny side wasn't quite so funny to Dani.

'It was definitely a surprise,' she said.

'So… congratulations?' he said, his face unable to hide his awkwardness. He grabbed her and squeezed her, and his touch helped to take away a good chunk of her anxiety in just a few seconds. He released her and stepped back into the lounge. He came back out clutching a bottle of Moet with a red bow attached.

'For you,' he said. 'Now that the Clarkson case is done and dusted.'

'Thanks.'

She took the bottle from him. His smile faltered.

'You look shattered,' he said.

'Tell me about it.'

'Ready for bed?'

She put the bottle onto the side table. 'Ready for sleep, yes.'

—

Though an hour later, both were still awake, and Dani had her head on his chest as they lay in bed talking.

'Ben is just looking for a way to suck you back in,' Jason said.

'So you don't think he knows anything?'

'I really don't know. But even if he does, if he's heard something on the prison rumour merry-go-round, you know he's only looking out for himself. And he hates that you detached yourself from him again, so he'll play you as much as he can. Everyone else has disowned him. He probably thought before when you started going to see him during the Grant investigation that he had a pal for life. Then...'

He didn't finish the sentence. Dani wasn't sure why. She thought what he'd been trying to say was *then you and I were caught up in tracking down two horrible murderers, who attacked us and horribly injured us. But they came off worse and are both now dead, and afterwards you only wanted to get your life with me back on track, and it's not been easy for either of us, and because of those struggles you've tried your hardest to push your worthless brother out of your life for good.*

Or something like that.

'What annoys me more than anything is that I *do* still feel drawn to him,' Dani said. 'Not in a positive way. Not in a sisterly way. I can't even explain it, but I feel compelled to see him.'

'Which is exactly what he wants.'

'I'll have to wait and see what Baxter and the CPS come back with.'

'If I were you, I wouldn't even think about it. Carry on with the Redfearne case.'

On which she'd already explained the salient points of the day to Jason. As ever, he took it all in his stride, and offered sound advice in return. Not only was Jason an ex-copper, but he was a bloody good sounding board, even if her confiding in him was professionally questionable.

'You know the most likely answer is that it was someone at the party,' Jason said. 'One of the guests, or one of the staff.'

'I know. But even that's over two hundred people. We've not even made contact with them all yet.'

'But you know who they all are. That's the main thing.'

'It still doesn't make sense. Why Oscar? Why Sophie?'

'We're talking about murder, Dani. When does it ever make sense? Go through each of them. Treat them all as suspects until you're positive they're not. It's the only way.'

'And if the killer is someone else entirely?'

'It'll come out. Follow what you've got. The bite marks, fibres, whatever. You're only two days in.'

'Two days will feel like a lifetime for Sophie Black-wood.'

Jason said nothing to that.

'I worry sometimes,' Dani said. 'No, not sometimes. Every fricking day. Did we make the right choice?'

Jason sighed. He'd clearly understood the vague question.

'Dani, you were born to be in the police.'

'I reckon McNair would say the same about you. She's got a real soft spot for you still.'

Jason huffed. 'I can talk the talk, but you're the one that goes the extra mile to get results. You always get results, Dani. Maybe you don't see it, but McNair is a fan of yours too. And yes, we made the right choice. We made a choice for *us*. It's not just about what one or the other wants.'

His words didn't really help to ease her tension. Was he saying that he did regret leaving the police? But that he'd done it for her? In a way, it made her feel all the worse: the thought that she was the cause of him cutting short the career he'd loved.

'I just don't want you to resent me,' she said. 'Or to resent this life.'

'Dani, learn when to shut up and move on. I love this life, and I love you more than anything.'

And this time, his words meant everything.

Chapter Thirteen

I look at my watch. It's nearly midnight. I'm starting to get worried now. Where is she? Is she coming back tonight at all?

I glance to the bed across from where I'm sitting in a plush velvet-covered armchair. There are no lights on in the bedroom, but the one in the en suite is on, just as it was when I arrived, and with the door partially open, there's an arc of orange light stretching out across the bedroom, across the bed, across his face.

The blood dribbling from the wound in his hair glistens. Streaks of red are running down his cheeks, onto the white bedsheets – at least I think they're white. Every now and then there's a tiny splattering sound as another drop falls from the bed and onto the growing patch of red on the thick carpet below.

He's slumped on his side, facing me. His eyes remain closed, though he's still breathing. I can tell because of the rise and fall of his body under the sheet.

I only hit him once. The strange little stone ornament I used is back on the bedside table next to me.

I've been staring at that ornament for minutes, and I can't work out what it's supposed to be. Perhaps two figures hugging, though their limbs and their heads are moulded together, and the more I stare, the more

116

disturbing I find it. Like conjoined twins, except they're facing each other. That might be it. They're not hugging. They're facing each other, trying to pull away, but they can't because their skin and their flesh is knitted together.

Now as I stare, I can hear the creak and strain as they pull. The figures seem to be moving apart from one another ever so slightly. The skin is straining, beginning to tear. The sound it makes is sickening yet strangely curious, even as it intensifies.

They're screaming now. But they don't stop pulling, they just keep on going, pushing through the pain. Pulling for freedom, whatever the cost. Their screams get louder and louder, the sounds of their skin tearing, the blood-curdling squelch, gets louder and louder...

Stay focussed.

Her voice snaps the visions and the sounds away.

I realise there's a thin film of sweat on my brow.

No mistakes.

I wipe the droplets away with my sleeve.

'I know.'

As I look back now, the figures are statuesque – and quiet – once more. My eyes fall to the bottom of the ornament. I think a small chunk is missing from the corner of the base.

Did I do that? Did the chunk fall away, or is it now wedged in the man's skull?

Thoughts of blood and bone and flesh come to the fore once more...

Stop. I said to stay focussed.

'I am focussed.'

Perhaps you should give him the shot.

I look at him, lying on the bed. Peaceful. Is he dreaming? I wonder what about.

'He doesn't need the shot.'

If he wakes up I'll just hit him again.

If he wakes up. Perhaps he never will.

I hear a car engine outside, somewhere not far away. The low-pitched rumble drifts through the partially open bedroom window. Then a car door opens. And closes. Footsteps. Hard-soled shoes — heels — on compacted gravel.

I get up from the chair and walk around the bed and pull one curtain aside an inch to peek out.

She's here. Finally.

Get ready.

I am ready. Sometimes I wish I was trusted more.

I do trust you.

Sometimes I wish I could at least think without you listening!

Silence now.

I creep across the room towards the bedroom door which is open a few inches. Down below I hear the front door opening and closing. A few small bangs downstairs. Softer footsteps padding about. I think she's drunk. I saw how she was wobbling up the drive and I know she likes these nights out with her friends. A tap goes on in the kitchen. Yeah, she's pissed as a fart. Wants some water to stop her waking up tomorrow with a screaming headache. Poor thing. If only she knew.

At least she's had some fun on her last night on earth.

She's on the stairs now. I turn back to look at the bed. He's still out of it. He hasn't a clue what's going on.

I retreat to the armchair by his side. It's within the band of light coming from the en suite. That's good. I want her to see my face.

My breathing is getting quicker by the second, in line with my now racing heart. But I'm not scared. I'm not nervous. I'm perfectly ready.

I *want* this.

She's on the landing now. The bedroom door opens slowly. She's trying to be quiet and discreet. I suddenly realise, when she steps in she'll see my face, but on the dark side of the room, I won't see hers.

It's not important.

I want to see her face.

I lean across and press the switch on the wall above the bedside table. The main light in the centre of the room flicks on. The bedroom is lit up brightly.

There she is, right in the open doorway.

She freezes. She's looking at him, rather than me. I slowly get to my feet as her gaze sweeps across.

Oh, this is so perfect!

She sees me now. And even though she can say nothing, she's so paralysed by fear, I know she recognises me.

The whole moment probably lasts only a second or two, but I savour it as her eyes glance down to my hand. Down to the six-pound axe that I'm grasping.

And now finally she screams.

But it's too late for her.

I'm already lurching forward, the newly sharpened blade swinging wildly through the air.

Chapter Fourteen

Bright and early on Tuesday morning, Dani was waiting outside Easton's house in Sutton Coldfield with the engine running. He stormed out of the front door of his modest semidetached, sullen-faced, and stepped into the car with a grumbled greeting.

'Run out of cornflakes again?' Dani said.

Easton huffed. 'Very funny. No. Claire's back.'

'Oh.'

Dani was looking at him, but he was glaring out of the windscreen, clearly not wanting to engage.

'Just drive,' he said.

Dani put her foot down.

'You don't owe her anything,' Dani said as she came to a stop at the end of the street and took the turn onto Chester Road.

'She's my sister.'

Yet another family relationship gone wrong. Did it make Dani feel better to know that pretty much every family she knew was fucked up, one way or another? Not really. Though in Easton's case, his problem sister really shouldn't have been such a big problem for him personally, if he actually just told her straight to go and get herself sorted out.

'Kids with her?' Dani asked.

'Where else would they be?'

'So you two and four kids in your two-bedroom house. Sounds ideal.'

'It's gonna be chaos.'

'What about school? Bit of a trek over to Rugeley each morning.'

'School holidays, isn't it. Another month before they go back.'

'So what are you going to do?'

'What can I do? She's my sister. I can't just turn her away.'

No. Apparently not. And apparently not many other men could either. Which was why at the age of twenty-six she had four kids from three dads.

'At least you get some time with your nieces and nephews.'

'Don't get me started. They're the devil's spawn.'

Dani tried to hold back her laugh at that, but couldn't manage it, and when she glanced over she saw Easton now had a wry smile too.

'Enough about her,' he said. 'She'll probably go crawling back to Andre soon enough. And if she doesn't I'll get her into a flat somewhere before school starts again.'

'Somewhere far, far away?'

'Not far enough. Anyway, what's new?'

'Since I last saw you all of ten hours ago? Nothing really. Certainly not compared to you at least.'

Easton rolled his eyes, but the conversation about his sister was over, and when they arrived outside the gates to Drifford House not long after, he had a focussed look back on his face.

Pamela Longbridge answered the intercom, and they were soon heading up the driveway to the house. Easton had spoken on the phone to Caroline Redfearne late in the afternoon the previous day, and although she'd pushed back on the homicide team returning to their home for what would be a third day in a row, Easton had eventually persuaded her that it was in the best interests of the investigation.

The grounds immediately around the house, without the myriad of police vehicles and ambulances, were quite the contrast to when Dani had last been, and although there was an overarching stifled mood about the place, the charm of the house and its carefully kept gardens was plainly evident.

Dani parked the car on the gravel drive and a second later the hefty oak door to the house opened and there stood the head of staff, Pamela Longbridge. Her long face was sullen and suspicious. Dani didn't believe that was because of grieving any more, she just felt it was Pamela's naturally stern demeanour.

As Dani and Easton stepped from the car, Dani glanced across the side of the house to the woods. No sign at all of the crime scene from here. Although the body had been, by now, long removed, and the forensic scour complete, Dani would make sure they took a wander down there before they left today. She could always hope for a flash of inspiration.

Dani turned her gaze back to the house, and as she did so her eyes swept over the other two parked cars on the gravel. One was a gleaming black Bentley Continental GT, which Dani recognised as belonging to the Redfearnes, the other was a garishly yellow Porsche.

'Good morning,' Dani said as she and Easton approached Pamela, trying to sound warm and friendly.

'Detectives,' Pamela said. Her face remained sour. 'I'm afraid there's not much good around here right now.'

Dani let the comment slide. Pamela showed them in.

'What can I do for you today?' Pamela asked, as though it were her house. 'I thought after the last of you left yesterday that the Redfearnes would be given some time alone to grieve.'

'I'm very sorry, Mrs—'

'Ms.'

'Sorry, Ms Longbridge, but until we get to the bottom of Oscar's death, and Sophie Blackwood's disappearance, we may need to make frequent trips back here. I hope you can appreciate that?'

Pamela humphed.

'Are Mr and Mrs Redfearne available?' Easton asked.

They should be, Dani thought, given this was the time Easton had arranged to meet with them yesterday.

'I'll take you to them,' Pamela said before turning and heading off.

'Do you have some free time this morning as well, Ms Longbridge?' Dani said as they walked across the expansive, wood-panelled main entrance hall. 'We'd really like to speak with you too.'

'About what?'

'About the case.'

'I've already given a statement to some of your colleagues.'

'Which we've both read. But it'd be very helpful to ask you some follow-up questions.'

Pamela turned to glare at Dani. 'Very well. But I am very busy. This house doesn't run itself, you know.'

When Pamela faced back the other way, Dani looked over to Easton and saw he was smirking. Just as well Pamela didn't see.

They headed on down a corridor that Dani hadn't seen before but was much like the rest of the house, with unnecessarily tall ceilings complete with elaborate decorative mouldings, huge chandelier light fittings, side tables with expensive-looking ornaments, and large, framed oil paintings dotted here, there and everywhere. They arrived at a closed door, and Pamela knocked and waited for a response before she opened it and stuck her head inside.

There was a muffled exchange before she pulled her head back.

'You can go in,' she said to Dani. 'I'll get someone to come and take a drinks order.'

With that Pamela turned and strode off.

Dani pushed the door open fully, then did a double-take when she saw who was inside, and tried her best not to show any reaction.

Amanda Johansson, the same lawyer who'd been with Arnold Davenport, was sitting on her own behind a desk in a room that Dani would have described simply as a smaller version of the library they'd been in on their previous visit. Was this the Redfearnes' home office?

'Good morning, detectives,' Johansson said, with something of a snide smile. 'The Redfearnes will be with us shortly, but first I wanted to make sure I understood exactly what it is you'd like to talk to them about *this* time.'

Dani glanced at Easton. The unimpressed raised eyebrow showed he was thinking exactly the same thing as she was.

–

Despite Johansson's best efforts, Dani was determined to ask the questions they'd come to ask. In fact, it was likely because of Johansson, fully prepared and in overly bullish mood, that Dani was happy to steer the meeting towards more uncomfortable subjects once it was clear, after forty minutes, that they were otherwise going nowhere.

'Mr and Mrs Redfearne, what is the purpose of your summer party?' Dani asked.

'Purpose?' Henry said, a deep scowl on his face.

'Well, is every person you invite a genuine close friend, or—?'

'Many of them are close friends, yes. But it's also a fundraising exercise. We help raise tens of thousands of pounds for charities through the activities we undertake during the day.'

Tens of thousands? Wasn't that pocket change for billionaires?

'Activities?' Dani said. 'Would those include sexual activities with the waitresses?'

'Detective, please,' Johansson said. 'Not this again.'

'Not what again?' Dani turned from Johansson back to Henry. 'We've taken multiple witness statements now that include allegations of sexual harassment. Are you saying these people are all lying?'

'I didn't say that,' Henry said.

'Are you saying you were aware of these activities, then? In fact, isn't that all part and parcel of the *fun*?'

'You're supposed to be catching our son's killer,' Caroline said. 'Not dredging up lurid claims.'

'But are the two connected?' Dani asked.

'Connected?' Henry said.

'What other nefarious activities are being covered up here?'

'OK, Ms Stephens,' Johansson said, getting to her feet. 'I think you're done here. And you can be sure I'll be passing a complaint to your superiors about your behaviour.'

Dani and Easton remained seated, though Dani could feel her colleague's unease.

'Our behaviour?' Dani said. 'I'm sorry, but we're neck-deep in a murder investigation here, and at every avenue we're hitting brick walls whenever we ask questions about what exactly happened at this so-called party on Saturday night. A party at which one man lost his life, and a young lady has gone missing. Now, on what basis are you suggesting that details of that party, who was here, what they did, are not relevant to that investigation?'

'On the basis that—'

'Oh, and it's interesting that you're here today, Ms Johansson. What is it that you and your clients are trying to hide about what happened here on Saturday night?'

Johansson didn't even attempt to answer that. Neither did either of the Redfearnes.

'Now would be a good time for you to speak up,' Dani said. 'I'm simply trying to understand what happened on Saturday night. Why is it so difficult for anyone to tell me straight?'

Not one word in response. Henry folded his arms in defiance.

Whatever. Dani had had enough.

'Thank you all for your time. We'll be in touch.'

Dani rose to her feet. Easton tentatively followed her out of the room.

'Well that was a waste of time,' he said as Dani stormed away, back towards the entrance hallway.

'Kind of,' Dani said. 'But it did tell me one thing.'

'Yeah?'

'They're not telling us everything, are they? The Redfearnes. Davenport. That damn lawyer.'

'Yeah. Talk about a coincidence with her being here.'

'It's no coincidence, though, is it?'

'Not from what I can see.'

'So what are they not telling us and why?'

'Could be these people just don't want their reputations ruined. I can't speak for the mega rich.'

'Are their reputations really worth more than finding their son's killer?'

Easton shrugged.

'We need to find out more,' Dani said.

'We do. And I think I might know what you're thinking.'

Dani stopped and turned to face Easton.

'You do?'

'We're not leaving, are we?'

'No. Not yet we're not. Come on, this way.'

Chapter Fifteen

Pamela was sitting tapping away on an iPad in the library when they found her.

'Detectives. You're done?' she said, looking up and pushing her glasses further up her nose. 'Shall I show you out?'

'Actually, if you had a few minutes spare?' Dani said.

Pamela sighed. 'Not really...' She held Dani's eye for a couple of seconds before she reached forwards and placed the iPad on the coffee table in front of her. 'But if it's just a few minutes I guess I can humour you. You'll be eating into my relaxation time later this evening because of it though.'

Dani tried to avoid an eye roll to that. 'Thank you. We appreciate it, really.'

Dani and Easton took up seats in the armchairs opposite Pamela and soon the conversation got started. Pamela, like all of the other house staff, had already given her formal witness statement in relation to the events of Saturday night and Sunday morning, but Dani wanted to find out more about *her*. And with it, more about what the Redfearnes were really about. As head of staff, Dani had already sensed that Pamela was omnipresent at Drifford House. If anyone knew of untoward happenings, it would be her.

'How long have you worked here?' Easton asked.

'Twenty-six years this autumn.'

'Blimey, so you mustn't have been very old when you started.'

Dani stifled a snort. Was Easton seriously trying to flatter her or was it a genuine comment?

'Thank you, Detective,' Pamela said, unmoved. 'I was thirty-one when I started working here. I was made head of staff the same year I turned forty.'

'What happened to your predecessor?' Dani asked.

Pamela locked her hard stare on Dani. 'She died of a stroke. In the gallery. I found her body.'

'Oh…' Dani said, rather lamely. 'I'm sorry.'

'She was only fifty-three. Everyone thought she was fit as a fiddle. But, this job, it's not as easy or as glamorous as you might think.'

'How do you mean?' Easton said.

Now it was Easton's turn to receive the death glare.

'I mean it's demanding,' Pamela said. 'There's nothing sinister about it, before you start going down that line. I work upwards of fourteen hours a day, often seven days a week.'

That kind of talk was lost on Dani. It wasn't like her job was a nine to five.

'So you were working here even before Oscar was born?' Dani asked.

At the mention of his name, or perhaps the flash of memories that were induced in Pamela at the thought of Oscar's birth and childhood, her face softened slightly for the first time.

'That's right,' she said. 'I'd known Oscar his whole life.'

'How would you describe him?' Easton said.

'He was a lovely boy. Warm, lively, personable. He was confident and bright.' She was speaking with genuine affection now. How much of his upbringing was down to Pamela and the other staff as compared to mother and father, Dani wondered?

'But he was also hopelessly arrogant,' Pamela said. 'Like his father, really. Taking his positives into account, too, Oscar would have gone far in life, there's absolutely no doubt about that.'

The last sentence was a little choked and Dani paused for a few seconds to see if Pamela would add anything to the heartfelt statement. She didn't.

'Did he get in trouble much?' Easton asked.

'What kind of trouble?'

Easton shrugged. 'Kid stuff. Being naughty. Not listening. Arguing. Fighting.'

'Why is that relevant? Why is any of this relevant?'

'It's all relevant to us understanding who Oscar was,' Dani said. 'We never had the chance to meet him. It's very helpful to build up a picture of who he was so we can try to figure out why on earth he was killed like he was, and by who.'

'Oscar was no saint,' Pamela said. 'But then which children are?'

Dani agreed, though neither she nor Pamela were mothers, so they weren't necessarily the best barometers.

'Did he fight with his parents?' Easton asked.

'I guess so.'

'With the house staff?'

'Not so much.'

'Was that when he was younger, or more recently as a teenager?'

'Of course, as a teenager and then a young man, the arguments and the strains took on a different shape. He had such a clear vision of who he thought he was, and what he wanted from life, and it wasn't always what others saw for his future. Like any child, though, it's the voice of authority that they rebel against most, whether it's overtly or otherwise.'

'So he butted heads with his dad?' Easton said.

'Henry? No, I meant his mother. She was the one he fell out with most.'

Dani made a mental note of that. Caroline Redfearne was the voice of authority in the house?

'Did Oscar ever talk to you about any problems he had?' Easton asked. 'At home, at school, with friends. Did he have any enemies?'

'Detective, please, I've been through all this before. You said you'd read my witness statement, and I made it quite clear then that I have no idea who killed Oscar, nor do I know of anyone who would want to.'

'That's fine,' Dani said. 'We can move on.'

Pamela checked her watch and sighed. That wasn't a good sign. If they didn't keep her relaxed and talking she was going to call quits sooner rather than later, and the whole bloody morning would have been a waste of time.

'I bet the house has changed a lot since you first worked here?' Dani asked.

'In what way?' Pamela asked.

'The coming and going of staff. Updating and renovating. If you've worked here twenty-six years, didn't the Redfearnes buy it just before that?'

'They'd had it two years. And yes, it was a state, to say the least. For the first few years I was here they were confined to the East wing while the main house was gutted and refurbished. I worked closely with the architects and project managers to see a lot of that work completed. I didn't train as a housemaid, I was a design project manager for a hotel chain before I came here.'

'What do you know about the history of the house?' Easton asked.

'If you're genuinely interested, there's a book about it. In fact, it's on the shelf right behind you. It was written by a local historian and takes you right up to five years after the Redfearnes moved in.'

Easton nodded and looked over his shoulder to the bookshelf. 'Sounds like my kind of read,' he said, which Dani knew was a lie. 'What's the long and short?'

Pamela sighed again. 'It was built by Baron Theodore Gray in 1745, after he was granted a large parcel of land here following some war or other. The Gray family held the house for well over two hundred years, though successive generations, from what I know, became less and less wealthy, until in 1976 Jeremiah Gray died leaving his widow, Eliza, living here alone. Needless to say, one widow here on her own, with minimal funds and few family members who gave a damn, the house suffered some.'

'Until the Redfearnes came along,' Dani said.

'Indeed. They bought it from what was left of the Grays' estate when Eliza died.'

'I guess the Redfearnes, in a way, share a similar story to the Grays,' Easton said.

'How do you mean?' Pamela said.

'In that their wealth has passed through a few generations now too.'

'Except their wealth is far from dwindling,' Pamela said, quite defensively. 'Henry has worked tirelessly for years to ensure that was not the case. And I'm sure Oscar would have taken on the family mantle more than capably too, eventually.'

'What do you know of Henry's main business activities now?' Dani asked.

'I'm head of staff, not his accountant.'

'Yes, sorry—'

'But he's an investor mostly. Property, start-up businesses, hedge funds. He's a businessman in every sense of the word.'

'And he saw the same for Oscar's future?'

'Actually no,' Pamela said. 'Oscar wanted to be a lawyer, believe it or not, and his father was happy to go along with that desire. Caroline was more inclined to have him take over Henry's work.'

Another intriguing comment about the dynamic between Oscar and his parents.

'You went to school with Caroline, didn't you?' Easton asked.

The question, or was it a statement, seemed to stump Pamela for a moment.

'How did you know that?' she asked.

Easton glanced at Dani, looking a little sheepish. 'It was in your records. And hers.'

'But why are you delving into my past like that? And Caroline's too?'

She sounded seriously pissed off now.

'Ms Longbridge, I assure you it's nothing more than routine background work,' Dani said, trying to sound amenable.

Pamela said nothing for a few moments, as though weighing up whether or not she was happy to carry on. Why was she so uptight all of a sudden?

'Were you friends back then?' Easton asked.

'We were friends, yes. Best friends? Not really, but we've known each other on and off since we were eight.'

'Were you still in contact with her as an adult?' Easton asked. 'Before you came to work here, I mean.'

Pamela remained put out by the questioning, Dani could tell.

'Yes. We were.'

'She helped you get the job?' Dani asked.

'I got the job because of my skill set and experience.'

'Oh, I have no doubt,' Dani said. 'But—'

'There's no but to it. There was no favour granted, no backhander or dirty dealings. I knew Caroline, I knew there was a job opening, and I knew I was perfectly suited for it. That's it.'

Though the way she was talking suggested that wasn't it at all.

'How would you describe Caroline?' Dani asked.

'In what sense?'

'You've known her for years. What's she like? What are her motivations?'

'I'm really not sure what you're getting at here,' Pamela said. 'But I've nothing to hide, and I'm sure she doesn't either. As teenagers, Caroline was so… what I'm trying to say is she knew what she wanted, and there wasn't a cat in hell's chance that she wasn't going to get it.'

'And she wanted?'

'Well look where she ended up,' Pamela said. 'And I don't mean any of this disrespectfully, because she's an incredibly strong woman, but Caroline has never *worked* a day in her life. Not in paid employment anyway, nor do I ever think she intended to. She met and married a rich man, she had a child with that man, and has spent years moulding her family unit, and pushing her husband to continue growing his business. She's no gold digger though, and neither is she a shrinking violet. If there's one person who's made this family, this house, and everything that goes with it tick over more than any other over the last three decades, then it's Caroline Redfearne. She's a true matriarch, and I mean that with the utmost affection and respect.'

Dani found herself nodding at Pamela's outspoken words. In the two times she'd met the Redfearnes, she certainly hadn't seen Caroline in quite that light. Was that because of the devastation of losing her only son, or was she as good an actor as she was a leader of a rich and powerful family?

'What are your thoughts on the summer parties held here?' Easton asked.

Pamela returned her glare to him. 'It doesn't matter what I think.'

'Did you approve?'

'Of what exactly?'

'We've heard all sorts of rumours of inappropriate behaviour. Sexual encounters between guests; I guess the more technical term is swinging or dogging, but also groping and inappropriate touching of some of the waitresses.'

'I've never been a part of anything like that,' Pamela said, and she sounded truly disgusted.

'But have you heard of these things? The waitresses in question would, technically, be under your watch after all?'

'The house staff here are paid more than healthily for their services. Everything is above board.'

'Then why are some of the waitresses claiming they were groped?' Dani said. 'That's not above board. That's sexual harassment. Sexual assault even.'

Pamela was backed into a corner now, and the look of concern on her face showed it. She certainly wasn't the perpetrator of any of the wretched behaviour, but as the manager of those young women, she had a duty of care. On the other hand, this wasn't an investigation into sexual harassment in the workplace – not yet anyway – and Dani didn't want Pamela closing down on her.

'Did the Redfearnes ever engage in this overt sexual behaviour?' Easton asked, clearly not on the same wavelength as Dani.

'You'd have to ask them,' Pamela said with a sneer. 'This is really disgusting, what the two of you are doing. They haven't even buried their son and you're trying to whip up nonsense sensationalist stories.'

'What do you know about Arnold Davenport?' Dani said, deciding Easton had left the door open, so she may as well step inside. The writing was on the wall for this interview anyway, so she may as well try one last gasp effort at eking something of use from it.

'Davenport?' Pamela said, her eyes pinching in disdain.

'He was a regular at these parties?'

'He and Henry are good friends.'

'Do you know how?'

'I've no idea. Their paths crossed, businesswise, some years ago.'

'What do you know of him?'

'Not much.'

'What do you think of him?'

'Not much.'

'We know he was one of the men, though there were certainly others, who saw your waitresses as fair game. Pinching bums, hands up their skirts.'

Pamela winced.

'Ms Longbridge?' Dani said.

'It doesn't surprise me, and that's all I've got to say on the matter.' She looked at her watch and got to her feet. 'Detectives, this hasn't exactly been a pleasure, but I really do have things I need to get to.'

Dani and Easton both got to their feet too. Then Easton held a hand up. 'Just one more question, if that's OK?'

Pamela sighed.

'Are you aware of either Henry or Caroline having an affair? Now or in the past?'

Pamela looked as though she was about to explode.

'I'm done humouring you two,' she said through clenched teeth. 'I'll show you out.'

Pamela did show them out, though Dani just about managed to persuade her that they needed a few minutes to go into the woods to take a look around. They didn't spend long there though. Other than the lines of police tape which had been left around the scene, providing little defence against the elements or intruders of whatever sort, there was no sign of what had taken place there at all. Neither Dani nor Easton came up with anything, though Dani at least felt that going back had refreshed her memory of the lay of the land, which wasn't a bad thing.

As they reached the house once more, they found Pamela standing, arms folded, by the open front door.

'Have a nice day,' she said.

'You too,' Dani said before she and Easton climbed into the car.

Dani reversed out, just as Pamela headed inside and shut the door. Dani noticed the yellow Porsche – Johansson's? – was gone now. She'd served her purpose. Though Dani was almost tempted to go back to the house and see if she could get some time alone with either of the Redfearnes without their lawyer.

No. There were plenty other things to be doing.

As Dani stuck the car into first, she looked back up to the house. Her eyes fell on an upstairs window where a straight-faced Caroline Redfearne was standing, staring down. Dani stared right back, and a few beats later Caroline back-stepped and disappeared into the darkness beyond.

'What was that?' Easton asked as Dani turned back and put her foot down.

'Nothing,' Dani said.

'So what next, boss?'

Dani looked at her watch. It was approaching eleven. McNair would have finished the press conference she'd arranged for first thing by now. Sophie's name and face would be everywhere. Hopefully, it would kickstart their efforts in finding her.

'Let's go and see who's back at the ranch,' Dani said.

-

With the light post-rush-hour traffic, they were soon back in central Birmingham and inside HQ, and they headed side by side to the homicide team's open-plan space. It turned out there was virtually nobody in. Which was kind of a good thing, Dani decided. It meant the team were mostly out and about working the case. After all, there were tens of statements still to be taken, not to mention all of the supplemental work on CCTV and the like. McNair wasn't around either though, which Dani was disappointed about, as she'd wanted to catch-up with the DCI both about the press con and the frustrating yet intriguing meetings she and Easton had just had at Drifford House.

Instead, she and Easton went to their respective desks and Dani was soon scouring the HOLMES 2 system to identify and review any new case documents that had been uploaded.

Across the way, Dani heard McNair's desk phone ringing through her open office door. After a few seconds, the call stopped, unanswered. Seconds later the phone was ringing again.

Dani and Easton shared a look across the room. Where was Katherine Wyatt, anyway? Dani got up from her desk and strode over and into McNair's office. She glanced at the phone. She recognised the number. Or at least the organisation it was coming from.

'DCI McNair's phone, DI Stephens speaking?'

A short pause.

'DCI Halliday from West Mercia. Is DCI McNair available?'

'I'm afraid not. Can I help?'

'It's about McNair's case. The Redfearnes.'

Dani's heartbeat ramped up a little with expectation. 'Go for it.'

'My officers attended the scene of a murder this morning near Bridgnorth… To put it simply, we think you're going to want to come and see this one.'

Chapter Sixteen

After a failed call to McNair's mobile to update her, Dani and Easton were soon in Dani's car en route to Shropshire. She finally managed to get hold of McNair while they were closing in on the quaint riverside town of Bridgnorth. Thankfully, McNair agreed with Dani's course of action. Strangely to Dani, it felt almost surreal to have so many of her recent decisions backed by her superior. When had that last been the case? She was far more used to opposition from the top brass.

The house they arrived at, a little over a mile before Bridgnorth, was found off a twisting single track that was lined with thick hawthorn bushes, farmers' fields beyond. A cluster of three large detached houses sat in a small valley where a ford flowed across the road. The rural setting was a far cry from the metropolis that Dani was more used to policing. The houses, mock-Tudor with white rendered walls interspersed with black-painted timber, were each a different size and shape, and each bore their own name, rather than number. Dani found the one they were looking for, Eastmeade, even before she'd spotted the neat little sign – the blue and white police tape rolled across the front gates clearly marked the scene.

Dani parked up outside the wooden gates and she and Easton headed in on foot, up a short incline to the house, where two marked police cars from West Mercia Police, a van belonging to their forensics team, and another unmarked car were parked.

A uniformed officer was standing by the closed front door. Dani introduced herself and Easton, and they were soon greeted by DI Leyland, a short and dishevelled man in his mid-thirties.

'I wasn't expecting you so soon,' he said as he took off his latex glove to shake Dani's hand. 'You'll need to cover your feet, if you don't mind. Although forensics are just about done.'

Dani and Easton both put on shoe covers and gloves before Leyland showed them inside.

'The victim's name is Mary Deville,' Leyland started as they stood in the dark hallway. 'She was a Crown Court judge, worked in Birmingham for the last couple of decades until she retired a couple of months ago.'

Her work location was apparently one of various factors which had tipped West Mercia to the possible link to the Redfearne case.

'She'd been out to a local pub in Bridgnorth with some female friends until closing time last night. Husband was asleep before she arrived home.'

'How is he?' Dani asked.

'In serious shock, to say the least. He's in hospital under guard.'

'Under guard?'

'We don't think he did this, but the guard is there just in case. Both to stop him leaving, and to stop our killer coming back to finish him off.'

'You think the killer wanted him dead too?' Easton asked.

'Hard to say, but he's got a pretty nasty head wound. It could quite easily have killed him. Was that the intent? I'm not sure, but we won't rule it out.'

Dani noticed Leyland's gaze flick up to the scar above her ear. Her own reminder of an attack similar to what Mr Deville had endured last night. Her attacker, her own brother, had thought her dead. Perhaps Mary Deville's killer had made the same mistake, or perhaps her husband simply wasn't the target.

Leyland's words, though, and that glance to Dani's scar did make her curious as to how much he knew of her own brush with death. Within the West Midlands she often felt notorious, as though everyone knew of her dark past, including her mental and physical struggles to get herself back on the force, but did the notoriety stretch as far as here?

'So you haven't completely ruled him out?' Dani asked, trying to push thoughts of her brother and her troubles away.

'As the suspect in his wife's murder?' Leyland said. 'I wouldn't say we've ruled him out conclusively, not until we've taken a formal statement and have forensics results back. But what he says fits. He was asleep. He was bludgeoned, which explains his wound and the fact he wasn't woken during the attack on her.'

'Have you got a sense of the sequence of events?'

'My theory is that the killer lay in wait until Mary arrived home, then attacked her when she reached the bedroom. You'll see for yourself when we go upstairs, but if the blood on the bed is his and only his, and the blood around elsewhere in the room is hers and only hers, it seems to make sense. Likewise, we believe the blood on the stairs is his.' Leyland pointed off to the stairs on his right where there were several spots of dark red on the floral wallpaper, on the worn carpet below too. 'Mr Deville was found wandering around downstairs like a zombie when the uniforms arrived, so we think those splatters came from him.'

The forensic results would help to validate the theory, though Dani would keep an open mind. What if Mary had hit him first, as he lay in bed, and then he retaliated and killed her?

'Any sign of forced entry?' Easton asked.

'Not forced, as such. Come this way.'

Leyland walked off to the end of the hallway, where there was a glorious country-style kitchen. Not particularly big, but certainly put together with love and care and attention and a decent amount of money. A single wide window provided views of the luscious garden beyond.

'The back door was unlocked,' Leyland said, moving over to it. He pulled the handle down and opened it. 'The husband swears he would have locked it before going to bed. There are plenty of scuffs and scratches to the outside of the lock, which could just be from years of use, but we're thinking the killer possibly picked his way in through here. We've dusted the floors for footprints, the doors and frames for fingerprints, but as you know it'll take a while to decipher everything. We'll have forensics take a closer look at the marks on the lock too, inside and out.'

Dani felt a faint shiver as she stared at the lock. The killer could pick his way in. But was last night his first visit or had he been before?

'No house alarm?' Easton asked.

Leyland looked at him as though it was a strange question. 'I guess people around here don't think they need much security. This is proper old school English countryside. You can see yourself, the locks on the doors and windows are basic at best. Any old idiot could crash through this one in seconds if they weren't bothered about making noise. It's generally only when people have fallen foul that they realise it's time to upgrade. That's just the way it is around here.'

To be honest, although the degrees were different, it was like that virtually anywhere, Dani pondered. The people with the best security tended to be those who'd been burned in the past.

'Shall we go upstairs?' Dani suggested.

Leyland led the way up to the first floor, where the blood specks on the landing carpet and wall quickly turned to huge pools of red and maroon past the threshold of the master bedroom. There were wide streaks of blood on the walls too. Some of the patches on the carpet were turning black around the edges where the blood was coagulating and drying. Dani could do nothing but gulp at the sight of so much red, which reminded her of the excessive gore of a Hollywood B-movie from the 1980s.

'The body was found just over by the en suite door,' Leyland said, 'but I'm thinking most likely she was attacked as she came in through the door, then either struggled that way or was dragged.' He pointed away at the blood spots in the various locations as he spoke. 'The husband claims to have woken up sometime after one a.m. with a gash on his head and covered in blood.'

'Who made the connection to the Redfearne case?' Dani asked.

'I did. Without wanting to sound like some back-water operation, we don't get many deaths like this out here. Yes, we get a few domestics, but they're normally more… straightforward. This is the first time I've ever seen anything so vicious.'

Though strangely he didn't seem too moved by that. Perhaps he was still running on adrenaline and the horrors would come back to him at some later point.

'I know of the Devilles. She was quite prominent in the town, getting involved in charities and such. And I know she has links to some powerful people. Councillors, politicians, that sort of thing. But I also remember her doing a fundraiser with the Redfearnes. I was already working the scene here when I heard about your press con, and after reading the case notes on HOLMES about Oscar Redfearne's death… well, there's the link. Not just the manner of her death, but the fact I know she knows that family. I have to say it all sounds horribly similar. Obviously, Mary Deville's body has been moved now, but I can show you the crime scene photos if it'll help you to see what I mean.'

Dani really didn't want to see them, but she knew she'd have to at some point. 'Thanks. We'll definitely do that,' she said.

'There weren't any bite marks found on her body, were there?' Easton asked.

Leyland looked at him quizzically.

'No,' Leyland said, frowning. 'Not that were brought to my attention anyway, but I can put a note for the pathologist to check at the PM.'

'That would be helpful,' Dani said. 'Thank you.'

'Shall I leave you two to take a look around, gather your thoughts?' Leyland said.

'Please,' Dani said.

Leyland nodded and was soon heading away.

–

Dani and Easton spent another half hour at the Devilles' home, talking to the police, the FSIs who were still on site, and mooching. Dani's head was swimming. On the one hand, the link to the Redfearne case seemed so tenuous. Killed in a similar manner? A huge proportion of murder cases she'd worked on were a frenzied attack, one way or another, and there was nothing in particular about the crime scenes which screamed to her this was the same murderer. For starters, what was with the bite marks on Oscar, but not here? At the Redfearnes, Sophie Blackwood, the witness, had been taken, but here Mr Deville, the witness, had been bludgeoned but then left.

Yet the personal link between the Devilles and the Redfearnes? That tied the two cases together firmly in Dani's mind, and with it the similarities between the two crime scenes had to be properly considered.

They were walking down the drive towards Dani's car in silence when her phone pinged with an incoming call. She didn't recognise the number.

'DI Stephens, it's Saad Tariq.' She hoped she knew what this was about. 'We've had some preliminary DNA results.'

'From which sample?'

'The bite mark on Oscar Redfearne. We've hit a match in the DNA database.'

'Go on.'

They reached Dani's car and both of them remained standing on the outside, Easton looking at her expectantly.

'Damian Curtis,' Tariq said. 'I'm just about to hit send on an email to you with the details... should be with you now.'

Dani took the phone away from her ear and opened up her inbox app and the email sprang onto the top of the page from the ether. She pulled the phone back up again.

'I'll let you know as soon as we have anything more,' Tariq said.

'Thank you.'

Dani ended the call and clicked Tariq's email open.

'We got something?' Easton said as he came to hover over her shoulder.

'A DNA match on the saliva taken from the bite on Oscar's shoulder.'

'Seriously? Bullseye. Name?'

'Damian Curtis.'

Dani glanced at Easton. She understood the look on his face easy enough. He knew the name too. Of course he did.

'Shit,' was all Easton could say.

Which was pretty much what Dani had thought herself.

She finished typing into her phone and held it up to her ear.

'DI Stephens, West Midlands Police,' she said when the call was answered. 'I need to speak to Deputy Governor Cartwright. Now.'

Chapter Seventeen

Once again the big dogs at West Midlands Police had pulled through with their rubber-stamping of Dani's plans, and with the time approaching six p.m., less than three hours after Dani and Easton had left Eastmeade, they were sitting in her car outside a row of terraces in Perry Barr, not far from central Birmingham. Small commercial units – predominantly takeaways of various forms – took up the ground floor of each of the terraces, though it was 181b, a flat above a downtrodden-looking convenience store, that Dani had her eyes on.

With the engine and the air conditioning off, so as to not draw attention, and the early evening sun beating down on them, the inside of the car was sweltering and sweat was forming big globules all across Dani's face, not to mention running down her back.

'No sign that anyone's home,' Easton said as he wiped his brow with his arm and craned his neck to look out of the windscreen and across to the windows of 181b, about twenty yards from where they were parked.

'We'll find out soon enough,' Dani said.

She checked her watch. Two minutes to go. Up ahead, around the corner of an adjacent street, she saw a white van pull up. No police insignia or lights or sirens, but Dani knew who was inside. She flicked her gaze into the rear-view mirror. Three cars back from hers was a smaller van. A hundred yards further away up the street was the only marked police car in sight, though it was parked up and drawing no attention.

Dani looked at her watch again. Each second took an age.

Finally the minute hand ticked over to twelve.

Bang on time Dani heard the metal doors of the vans clunking open. There was a rush of heavy footsteps up ahead. Dani watched the gang of six hefty policeman – each with thick stab vests on, bulking out their high-vis jackets, riot helmets with their visors down – come jogging around the corner in front. Behind her, by the smaller van, two more officers were now out on foot, each holding back a hulking Alsatian, the beasts tugging on their leads enthusiastically. The one or two pedestrians inside the shops in front of Dani and on the street were caught in two minds all of a sudden. Stand and watch goggle-eyed, or make themselves scarce. Most chose the former, perhaps already aware they weren't the targets.

The troop of officers arrived at the door, shouting.

'This is the police!'

'Stand back from the door!'

One of the officers stepped forward, holding the thirty-five-pound enforcer – a one man battering ram, affectionately known as the Big Red Key.

Dani had her hand to her car door as the officer swung the enforcer forwards with venom. The paint-peeling front door to flat 181b burst open at the first thrust, splintering around the lock. Barely a second later three of the officers had disappeared up the stairs. By the time Dani was outside with the car door shut, they were all inside.

The marked police car that had been behind her moments before now had its siren blaring, its lights flashing and it screeched to a halt in the road right by Dani, blocking oncoming traffic. Another did the same from the other side.

There was shouting and banging from inside the building. Dani knew there was also a team at the back of the terraces where there was a crude metal fire escape, just in case anyone inside decided to make a run for it. The dogs, right next to her now, would give chase if so.

A few moments later all the shouting and banging inside had stopped. Dani held her breath in anticipation as she listened to the sounds of the boots descending the stairs, full of hope that she would see the officers dragging Damian Curtis out of the front door with them.

But one by one the officers came out empty-handed. Dani deflated a little more with each one.

One of the officers idled over to Dani, himself looking seriously fed up.

'Empty,' was all he said.

'Empty abandoned, or just no one home?' Dani asked.

'Looks like someone's been there recent enough. Go and take a look. It's all yours.'

Dani sighed as she tried to push away her frustration.

'OK. You're good to go,' she said to him. She turned to the dog handlers. 'And you.' Then to Easton. 'Get the officers in the cars to stay. They can roll some tape out and keep the scene.'

Easton nodded. Though it was hardly a scene. Dani made a quick call to confirm the forensics team were good to come and do their thing. A couple of minutes later she and Easton, shoe covers and gloves on, were heading up the creaky and bare stairs.

'Well they were a miserable lot,' Easton said.

'I think they wanted some action,' Dani said. So had she, to be honest.

'You're disappointed,' Easton said, picking up on Dani's flat mood.

'Of course I am.'

They reached the top of the stairs where a grubby-looking internal door – white paint well and truly yellow now – led into a cramped one-bedroom flat that was in serious need of repair and love. At least with the makeshift curtains – bedsheets, essentially – drawn across the windows, the flat hadn't received any sunlight for some time and was far cooler than outside.

'You ever fancied being in the thick of it?' Easton asked Dani as he came to her side.

'A raid? Have you?' she said, eyebrow raised.

'Did it once, when I was a bobby. Not my cup of tea.'

'What happened?'

Easton caught her eye. He looked like he was about to wave the question away. Embarrassment?

'Let me guess—'

'I fell over.'

Dani smirked. She'd been about to suggest something similar.

'I was the guy with the enforcer,' Easton said. 'I insisted. You know you have to take training to use those things? I thought I was the dog's bollocks. But it took me three goes, and then when the door finally opened I lost my balance and fell face first. I was dazed and blocking the door. The rest of the team were scrambling over me.

The guy we were after legged it out the back door in the melee.'

Dani was still smiling at Easton's misfortune. On the first case they'd worked together he'd had a similar haphazard moment. Although it hadn't had a happy ending. A young man had lost his life later that afternoon in a foot-chase with Dani and Easton.

She wiped her smile away.

'What happened to the perp?' she asked.

'Oh, the dogs got him within a minute or so, so it wasn't all bad. But I was never trusted with that blasted enforcer again. Plus, I had to live with the nickname Twinkletoes for a good while after that.'

Dani found herself smiling again.

'Yeah, yeah, lap it up,' Easton said.

'You've got to admit, you are a bit of a klutz. And I think the name suits you actually. We might have to bring that back.'

'I'm a detective for my brain, not my poise and balance.'

'Fair point. Come on, let's get to it.'

Dani focussed again, and they each spent the next few minutes rummaging around the sparse flat. The truth was, despite her jovial chat with Easton, she wasn't just disappointed that the raid had been fruitless, but hugely concerned about Curtis's whereabouts.

It didn't take her long to come to the same conclusion as the officer from the raid team; the flat certainly wasn't abandoned. Among the basic furniture inside there were clothes, including some freshly washed in the rusting washing machine. There was a half-full bottle of milk in the fridge, butter, ham, cheese and it was all in date.

'He's going to come back,' Easton said.

'Unless he already saw us smashing our way in.'

Her mind immediately took her back to the moments before the raid, to the pedestrians she'd been closely watching, among other reasons for the very purpose of looking out for their suspect returning home and being spooked. She'd seen nothing to suggest that was the case at all.

'No sign of Sophie Blackwood,' Easton said. 'Clothes and stuff, I mean.'

'No,' Dani said. 'Nor blood or anything obvious like that. No computer, no pictures, no knick-knacks or correspondence even. This isn't a home. More a place to crash. But forensics will do a full sweep for prints, hair, whatever else.'

'So we're done?'

Dani slumped. 'Yeah, we're done.'

'What next?'

'Time to go rally the troops once more.'

Chapter Eighteen

The detectives crammed into the meeting room at HQ looked a lot less bleary-eyed and jaded than they had on Monday morning, despite them all having worked all the hours under the sun since then. Dani guessed that's what the adrenaline and focus from a key finding could do for a case, even if, for now, their main suspect was nowhere to be found.

'Perhaps, DI Stephens, you can explain what we know about Damian Curtis so far,' McNair said, as always sitting at the front and side of the room, a perfect position for overseeing both Dani and Easton up front, but also the rest of the crew.

'As you'll recall, the FSIs at Drifford House found a single large bite mark on Oscar Redfearne's shoulder,' Dani said, pointing to the picture on the whiteboard. 'Forensics swabbed the wound in the hope of pulling any saliva left there. Having run DNA tests on the sample, and excluded Redfearne's DNA from the analysis, we were left with one other identifiable DNA sequence. That sequence was matched with the highest probability to Damian Curtis.'

Dani pointed to the mugshot picture of Curtis now – a plain-looking man with a thin face, mussy brown hair, droopy green eyes.

'Curtis is twenty-nine years old,' Dani said. 'He's lived in the West Midlands his whole life, has a string of petty offences starting from when he was fifteen. He first served time when he was nineteen for theft. At the age of twenty-one, with the help of his probation worker, he found regular employment for the first time in his life, as an apprentice mechanic. But coming up for four years ago now, he was involved in a fatal car crash. He was driving and high on drugs. His on-off girlfriend and her five-year-old son were both killed. He survived.'

Another picture on the board that Dani pointed to now. This one of the wrecked Vauxhall Corsa that had smashed head-on into a parked van.

'Curtis was ultimately convicted of manslaughter. He was only recently released on probation, coming up for four weeks ago, having served half of his eight-year sentence.'

For now Dani left out the part about which prison he'd been held in, and who his most recent cellmate had been. A fact she herself had discovered through her own digging following her previous meeting with McNair, Baxter and Hussein.

'This afternoon we attended a raid at an address on Wade Road in Perry Barr: the address Curtis has registered with the probation service. Unfortunately, he wasn't there. We need to find him. Let's track down anyone we can from his past who could be harbouring him. Friends, family. Easton?'

Easton nodded before facing the room. 'Curtis's mother is dead. She died of cancer two years ago. She was divorced from his father and lived in Northumberland, and we've already asked our friends up there to look into who she knew in the area. Curtis's father is a retired factory worker who lives in Derbyshire. Again, we've got the local constabulary there to help in tracking him down. Curtis has no siblings and no grandparents who are alive, but we'll need to widen the search for other family members. DC Mutambe, perhaps you can lead?'

Mutambe, a recently promoted and conscientious DC, nodded.

'Is there a link between Curtis and Redfearne?' DC Constable asked.

'Not that we're aware of at the moment,' Easton said. 'Nor do we know of any link between Curtis and Sophie Blackwood.'

DC Grayling put her hand up.

'Yes,' Dani said to her.

'The bite marks don't make sense,' Grayling said.

'How do you mean?'

'I know we've only been working this for a couple of days, but you have to admit, everything else about our suspect suggests he was highly planned. The lack of direct witnesses, lack of CCTV. We haven't a weapon, or a vehicle or a motive or anything. He was calculated. But he leaves those bite marks? It doesn't make sense. To me, at least.'

Grayling sank in her seat a little with her last few words, now that she had several sets of questioning eyes on her. Though Dani didn't believe that the others disagreed with her, but more likely, as Dani was, they were busy trying to think through the implications.

'Your instincts are sound,' Dani said to Grayling. 'And we know that, although we believe this killer to be well planned and rehearsed in some respects, the attacks themselves were frenzied. The answer could be as simple as a momentary loss of control.'

'Once again, a fair point. Though the post-mortem confirmed the bite marks were inflicted very close to death, and we see no other reason why Curtis would have been at Drifford House at that point in time. At the very least he attacked Oscar Redfearne in the moments before death, and most likely Curtis is our killer. Until we have an alternative theory, I suggest we all maintain the focus on Curtis as our sole suspect in Redfearne's murder, and in Sophie's disappearance. Remember, finding her, alive, remains an absolute priority. Although let's all keep an open mind here, because it's fair to say we *don't* yet know why Redfearne was targeted at all, nor Sophie Black-wood.'

'Thank you, DI Stephens,' McNair said. 'Perhaps we can move on.'

'Certainly.'

Dani took a couple of moments to get her thoughts back on track. Easton was looking at her as though asking whether she wanted him to carry on for her. She shook her head and he looked back into the room. 'DS Easton and I also attended a crime scene earlier today in Shrop-shire, at the request of West Mercia Police. They believe that the murder there yesterday of fifty-eight-year-old Mary Deville bore similarities to the Redfearne case.'

Dani indicated the gory crime scene photos of Mary Deville's mangled body as Easton pinned them up on the board. There were a few murmurs of disquiet from the team.

'Mary's husband was also attacked, though he survived and is currently in hospital under guard. The West Mercia team believed the killer had stealthily broken into the home at night, subdued the husband by force, and lay in wait for Mary Deville to return home.'

'That doesn't sound anything like what happened to Redfearne,' interrupted one of the DSs at the back of the room.

'Well it does and it doesn't,' Dani said. 'The nature of the attack itself, frenzied and savage, is similar, as is the fact that no weapon was recovered, and on the face of it we have very little clear indication of motive for either.'

'Those aren't similarities,' Constable said. 'That's simply a lack of evidence. Just because two murders have a lack of evidence doesn't mean they're connected.'

'I agree,' Dani said, getting a little exasperated now. 'And I'm certainly not one hundred per cent telling you we have a double murderer here. I'm simply pointing out progress. It's too early for us to say how Curtis specifically could be linked to the Deville murder, and we'll keep on top of the forensics results from the scene as and when they become available. But we do believe there's a link between Mary Deville and the Redfearnes. We've heard they were involved in charitable fundraising together. She also had links to councillors, politicians, as we know the Redfearnes do. We need to focus on that link as a matter of priority. How well do the Redfearnes know the Devilles? Were the Devilles ever guests at Drifford House? Had they ever attended the summer parties there—'

'Er, boss?'

Grayling's hand was up again, although she was staring down at the papers in her hand.

'Yes?'

'There is another link.'

'Go on?'

Grayling held the papers up almost victoriously.

'Mary Deville was a Crown Court judge in Birmingham,' Grayling said. 'And she was the judge who oversaw Damian Curtis's manslaughter trial.'

For the first time in the meeting, Dani was rendered truly speechless.

—

'I'm surprised you hadn't spotted that link yourself,' McNair said as Dani stepped out of the toilet. McNair was standing, arms folded, by the lifts. Had she followed Dani out from the office floor just to accost her?

'We'd only known about Curtis a few hours,' Dani said, trying not to sound too defensive. 'I haven't even fully read his case history yet. I focussed on getting the raid organised so we could try and bring him into custody.'

McNair held a hand up. 'I'm not saying you should have known.'

Then why did you bother saying it at all, Dani thought.

'At least be glad that we have a switched-on team,' Dani said.

'They are indeed. And you're doing a good job leading them on this.'

Dani had no idea how to take that flattery. It certainly wasn't a common occurrence from McNair. What was going on?

'Though I also noted with interest that you left out details of Curtis's time in incarceration.'

Dani didn't say anything to that. Of course she'd told her boss all about the link to Ben. Following the meeting yesterday with McNair, Baxter and Hussein, Dani had done what she could to find out basic information about who Ben had spent time with in prison, who could be the source of the apparent knowledge he now had. Curtis's was the first name that came up. Ben's cellmate for the majority of his time inside, until Curtis was released a few weeks ago. But the whole team didn't need to know that. Not yet anyway.

'You have to admit this doesn't look good, Dani,' McNair said, her face screwed in concern. 'Yesterday your brother calls you in to the prison for a private meeting, spouting he's got relevant information for us. Referencing the Redfearne party. Today we find out the key suspect in one, possibly two murders over the last three days was, until a few weeks ago, your brother's cellmate.'

'Ma'am, the connection is all too clear to me, you don't need to spell it out.'

'Perhaps. Perhaps not. But I'm sure you can see this puts you in a particularly vulnerable position.'

Dani tried to remain strong on the outside, but inside she was all over the place. Her brother's words from the day before echoed in her mind. He'd warned her people could die if she didn't get him what he wanted. Was Dani to blame for Mary Deville's murder? Could the police have been in a position to prevent her death if Dani had been more accommodating to Ben's demands?

She could almost hear McNair's next words.

Sorry, Dani, but you can't lead this case.

And Dani could see the point. Almost.

'I have every confidence in your ability to see this one through...'

Here it was. The big *but*...

'But… we're going to have to put some safeguards in place.'

OK. That wasn't quite as bad as Dani had expected.

'You can continue as SIO on the Redfearne case. And I know as part of that you're going to have to go back to Long Lartin.'

'We've already arranged to go there first thing tomorrow. I spoke with Cartwright earlier.'

'I'm aware of that,' McNair said. 'But you're not to make any unaccompanied personal visits to your brother until this case is over. Do you understand?'

'I do.'

'Every interaction with your brother needs to be on record. Everything needs to be above board. Don't get yourself into a position where you're compromising your integrity, or more importantly, the lives of other people.'

Dani was nodding, even though McNair's words felt double-edged. If more people died, would she get the blame? The thought made her insides curdle.

'I'll speak to Baxter about organising another press con,' McNair said. 'There's a tough choice here as to whether or not we publicly name Curtis.'

'Better to have his face in the press and send him underground, than to let him feel he's got the upper hand and risk him killing again,' Dani said.

'I'll let you know,' McNair said. She turned and pressed the button for the lift. 'Go home and get some rest, Dani. It's been a crazy few days.'

Dani couldn't agree more with that. And yes, she would go home. But how could she possibly get rest? There was no time for complacency now. She had to act, and fast, otherwise as far as she was concerned, the next blood that flowed would well and truly be on her hands.

–

Darkness had once again descended by the time Dani arrived home, though the temperature had barely dropped from the earlier highs, and as Dani stepped from her car into the street, she could already imagine how uncomfortable the coming stuffy night in bed – alone – was going to be.

As with the previous night, her weariness got the better of her as she headed towards her front gate, and when the hooded figure stepped out from the shadows into an arc of light from the streetlight overhead, Dani was entirely unprepared.

Her body twitched, her brain in two minds as to whether she should rush forwards to attack, or make a hasty exit.

She was erring towards the former when the figure pulled the hood down.

'Larissa?'

The young girl said nothing.

'What are you doing here?'

Dani's tone was far more off than she'd intended, and the look of hurt in the girl's eyes only echoed this.

'I… I didn't know where else to go,' she stammered.

'But…' But what? Dani really didn't know. Yes she'd felt close to Larissa, in more ways than one, over recent weeks, but… well… Dani didn't even know how to explain it, but it felt wrong. How had Larissa even found out where Dani lived?

'When you left court yesterday...' a tear rolled down Larissa's cheek, 'I thought you'd be coming back. I thought you'd get in touch. I just... I just needed someone to talk to.'

'How did you find me here?' Dani said, immediately angered at herself that those had been her choice of words, rather than offering any kind of comfort. But this wasn't right. Something was off here.

'I've no one else,' Larissa said, sobbing now. 'They're all dead. I don't know what to do.'

Dani moved up to her and put her arm around her shoulder, and Larissa dug her face into Dani.

'Come on, don't talk like that. It's going to take time to adjust. You've focussed so much effort on the trial. But that's finished now. It's time to forget all about it.'

'And do what?'

Dani didn't answer that straight away, her mind was too muddled as she tried to distinguish her own anguish from Larissa's. Plenty of times Dani had felt entirely worthless and like there was no point in carrying on. But she had. Was it different, even more severe, for Larissa who'd not just been attacked herself but had lost her closest family members? Ever since her dad had been arrested, she'd been under the care of social services. She had no other direct family in the UK at all. Her only surviving grandparents, and the rest of their family, were still in Jamaica. At seventeen, she was so close to finishing her education that everyone involved had been determined to keep her in the Midlands, at least until after next summer. Could she take another year here, alone, though?

'It's going to be OK,' Dani said. 'You're so young still. You've got a good, long life ahead of you. You just need to—'

Larissa lifted her head and shoved Dani away. Shocked, Dani stumbled back, even more concerned when she saw the screwed and angry look now on Larissa's face. She'd never seen that before.

'I just need to what?' Larissa said, her voice lower and harder, raspier than before. 'Just need to move on? Just need to forget about what *he* did. Except I can't, can I? How the fuck can I ever move on? I thought *you* of all people would understand that.'

'Larissa, please—'

Larissa lurched forwards and Dani tensed again as she barged past and strode off down the dark street.

Should she chase after her?

'Larissa!'

But she didn't look back, and Dani remained rooted to the spot, and moments later Larissa was out of sight.

After a few seconds in the darkness, each more eerie than the last, Dani spun back and forth and looked up and down the street.

She was all alone.

Feeling more rattled than she'd care to admit, she hurried towards her gate, up the drive, and through her front door, and she only exhaled in relief once the door to her darkened house was closed and locked behind her.

Chapter Nineteen

'It's been three days. You need to eat something.'

She doesn't respond to me at all. She's crumpled in a heap in the corner of the van. Her head is bowed, her cuffed hands dangle uselessly above her, her arms suspended by the chain attached to her wrists which connects to the rail at the top of the van wall.

Is she asleep or unconscious or just ignoring me?

'You need to eat,' I say again.

Hunched down in the van, I take a tentative step closer to her, holding out one of the sandwiches I've bought from the pack of two.

Still nothing. Not even a murmur from her.

It's a strange connection, but I have a sudden flash of a memory from many years ago. When I was a young child, maybe only three or four years old. We were at a petting zoo; I was holding out some pellets in my hand for the goats, through the gaps between the slats of a wooden fence. The little bastards on the other side all scrambled towards me, bashing the fence and shaking it trying to get to my hand. My tiny brain was terrified. I thought the little beasts were going to snatch my arm off. I whipped my hand back to safety just in time. My dad thought it was hilarious. My mum was shouting at me for being so stupid. She grabbed my wrist and dragged me back to the fence and forced my hand into position. I screamed and grimaced and looked away and imagined my fingers being chewed off and the blood and the pain and the anguish and the life of torment without my hand…

When mum let go and I pulled back and saw my hand entirely intact but covered in thick greasy goat slobber, I really didn't know what to think. Relief? Embarrassment? Satisfaction?

'Don't worry, we'll make a man of you yet, son,' my dad said to me.

To this day I still don't understand his intention in those words. Were they supposed to be confidence-boosting, or was it his way of showing his disappointment in me?

'Sophie, you need to eat this.'

I take another step forwards, outstretch my hand a little more. The edge of the sandwich is only about a foot from her lips now. She must be able to smell it. She must be hungry. Since I brought her here on Saturday night, all she's had from me are dribbles of water. She needs to eat to live.

As I wait for movement, I stare at her face. At her lips. Not so red now as they were two days ago, and the skin looks dry and cracked. She was so pretty on Sunday, now she's changing. It's almost as though she's falling apart, her natural prettiness disintegrating. I guess beneath the skin of any human being, whatever shape or size or colour, we're all just the same ugly mass of flesh and blood and bone.

As I stare, a nagging worry begins to take hold…

Is she breathing at all?

So what if she isn't? She needs to die anyway.

'Sophie? Can you hear me? Sophie?'

I pull back the sandwich. I put my free hand onto her shoulder and gently shake her. Her head slumps further forwards.

'No, no, no.'

I drop the sandwich now. I kneel down and lift up her head.

'Sophie?'

I didn't want her to die. She didn't deserve it.

What did I do wrong?

Then her eyelids spring open suddenly. She launches herself forwards, thrusts her head up. Her skull cracks into my chin and sends my head snapping back. Before I know it she's snarling like a dog and she comes at me and opens her mouth and I see what's coming just in time. I lift my arm up and cower back and she gnashes down. Her jaw clenches onto my bare upper arm and her teeth sink into my flesh.

'Fuck! You stupid—'

I ball my other fist and slam it down on the top of her head. It does nothing. She doesn't release the grip on my arm at all. She's a crazed beast all of a sudden. It's amazing what a human can do when running on adrenaline and survival instinct.

I know that only too well…

I raise my elbow and slam that down on the same spot at the top of her head.

Look what happens when you don't listen to me.

Her voice, her condemnation of me, is all I need to summon an inner hate and strength. I roar and push up from my heels and rise to my feet, and I easily take Sophie's weight as I lurch forwards and slam her against the side wall. Sophie groans as the van rocks on its suspension. I slam her against the metal a second time and hear the burst of air squeezed from her lungs. Finally her teeth release from my flesh and she crumples onto the bench.

I don't give her the chance to come back at me.

I lift my foot back and drive it into her stomach, and she groans in pain again. I kick her again. And again. I'm seething now. I'm growling. I lift my heel and hammer it down onto her face, and her nose and mouth erupt with blood.

I get back down onto my knees and grab a handful of hair and yank back so I'm looking into her bleary and panicked eyes.

I want to say something to her. I want to warn her that she shouldn't fight with me, that I was only trying to be nice.

Instead I'm thinking about punching her in the face. Over and over.

Do it.

In my head I'm hitting her again and again. Blood is pouring out of her. Her mouth is a dark mess of broken teeth and open wounds. Her eyes sink into her skull; her nose all but disappears as her face caves in from the relentless attack…

Do it!

I roar with rage and ball my fists and get ready to strike. Kill her. Then we move on to the next.

But Sophie isn't one of them. She isn't part of this.

The strength of *her* voice grows in my head, but I try to push it away. It doesn't really work. All that happens is that I open the door to the blaring noise of the rats. Now it's all there, inside my head, at the same time. Her voice, the rats. The scratching, the screaming, the shouting, the nagging, the criticising. It's unbearable. The walls close in, my head spins, it feels like it's about to explode.

Kill her!

'NO!'

I throw my fist forwards, but it doesn't hit Sophie. Instead it slams into the wall of the van. I let go of Sophie and I fall back, panting, chest heaving.

Silence.

Except for the throbbing of my heart. And the suck and splutter of blood as Sophie breathes through her bloodied nose and mouth. But she is still breathing.

I look down at my shaking hands. My knuckles are on fire and covered in blood from ramming the van wall. The sandwich lies between me and Sophie, squashed almost beyond recognition from the ruckus.

'I only... wanted you... to eat,' I say through laboured breaths.

Sophie says nothing now. Just like before. She doesn't even attempt to. She's slumped in a pathetic heap on the floor, her arms still dangling above her. I was thinking of releasing one of her hands so she could eat the sandwich herself. More dignified than me passing her food mouthful by mouthful. But she blew it.

The food is right there for her; she can bend down and eat it face down to the floor like an animal whenever she wants. This was her choice.

'You need to eat,' I say.

I get to my feet and open the van doors. I step down to the warehouse floor and take one last look at Sophie, blood pouring from her once pretty face, the small pool of red reaching out to the flattened sandwich in front of her.

I slam the doors shut and walk away.

Chapter Twenty

Dani knew that somewhere outside the windowless interview room it was yet another hot and gloriously sunny summer's day in Worcestershire, and across pretty much every inch of the country too. Deep inside Long Lartin prison, it may as well have been bleakest winter. The mood in the room – or was it just in Dani's head? – certainly felt like that would have been more appropriate.

Dani simply couldn't shake her irritability and feeling of despair as her brother pulled her deeper and deeper back into his dark mind, opening up the space for her own demons to come to the fore at the same time – which certainly hadn't been helped by her nonstop thoughts about Larissa Clarkson and what she was now going through so soon into her own recovery. Dani really thought – hoped – she'd moved on from this, but was now beginning to wonder if she ever could, despite her words to Larissa. The fact she'd had to delve even deeper into her stash of antidepressants that morning was evidence enough of how far Ben had already got under her skin these last few days.

'How long did you share a cell with Damian Curtis?' Easton asked. At least Easton was focussed this morning, despite the fact that his sister was still causing him problems and he'd had barely any sleep because of the house full of restless kids.

Join the club on that one, Dani thought – she'd barely slept for three hours.

Ben looked to Gregory Daley who gave a slight nod.

'About ten months,' Ben said.

Dani did her best to ride over the little exchange between client and lawyer, though she remained irritated by whatever play the two of them were concocting. The interview had only been going for ten minutes, though Ben hadn't answered even the simplest of questions without first looking for assurance from his hired help. So far Easton had taken the lead, at Dani's request, and she was simply fighting to stay focussed.

McNair's words from the day before swam in Dani's mind once more. Yes her boss had said she could still be on this case, had made it clear that it was OK for Dani to be interviewing – investigating? – her brother even, as long as she was accompanied to any meetings with him. But now that she was here with Ben, she wasn't so sure she agreed with her boss. Which Dani really didn't want to admit to anyone. Put simply, though, Dani *was* conflicted here, and she wasn't sure she could keep her cool when she knew Ben was doing little more than toying with the police, and her in particular.

'Tell me about him,' Easton said, thankfully sounding way more calm than Dani was feeling.

'Tell you about him?' Ben said, rather smugly Dani thought. 'That's pretty open-ended.'

'What was he like as a cellmate?'

'I only have two others to compare him to,' Ben said. 'And I have to say none of them were exactly easy-going.

You do realise this is a maximum-security prison, right? You're a policeman, I'm sure you can imagine the characters we get in here.'

'So he was violent? Aggressive?'

Ben looked to Daley who gave the slightest shrug.

'I didn't say that,' Ben said.

'So that's a no?'

'He was never violent to me.'

'OK,' Easton said, sounding like that straight answer was something of a breakthrough, even if Ben hadn't really fully answered the question at all. Perhaps Easton was being deliberately sarcastic. 'So coming back to my first question then. What was Curtis like? Did you chat much? Did you fight, either verbally or physically? Was he tidy or messy? Did he fart a lot?'

'You want me to answer all of those at once?'

'Ben, stop being an idiot,' Dani said. 'You know fine well what DS Easton is asking for.'

Ben gave a little snort of discontent, likely because Dani had used her tone of authority with him. He'd always hated her doing that.

'Maybe you don't know what life is like in a place like this,' Ben said, looking from Dani and back to Easton.

'Damn right we don't,' Dani said.

Ben's eyes narrowed now as he glared at her.

'It's not exactly a holiday club,' he said. 'And the men I've had to share a cell with aren't exactly the type of blokes you'd want to have a beer with down the pub.'

He paused as though waiting for another snide comment from Dani. She managed to hold back this time.

'But Curtis…' Another shared look between Ben and Daley. 'Curtis is seriously damaged.'

'Damaged?' Dani said.

'Messed up in the head. I'm not going to pretend to know the technical terms, but he's crazy. Properly crazy.'

Ben paused.

'That's it?' Dani said. 'He's *crazy*? Crazy how?'

'I think you'll be well aware that my client is not trained in psychiatry or psychoanalysis or any related subject,' Daley said.

Dani glared at him now.

'That's fair enough,' Easton said. 'But what behaviours did he exhibit to lead you to think he was *crazy*?'

'It was just... the way he talked. The way he acted. He's got a few screws loose. Honestly, I don't know how else to explain it to you.'

'Did he rant?' Easton said.

'Not really.'

'Talk to himself?'

'No.'

'Did he display anger or aggressiveness?'

'All the time.'

'Towards you?'

'Sometimes.'

'But you said he was never violent to you.'

'I did.'

'Just angry?'

'I guess so.'

'About what?'

'About whatever. There wasn't always a catalyst. But I have to say again, don't forget where we are. This place is a pressure cooker. Everyone's on edge, all the time. You're more likely to be concerned about the people who aren't angry and aggressive, who sit by themselves in a corner all quiet.'

'What did you know about Curtis's crimes?' Easton asked. 'His reason for being here?'

Ben looked to Daley again. For the first time the lawyer shook his head.

'Excuse me?' Dani said, feeling her anger rising further. She realised Easton was looking at her now too, but she ignored whatever prompt he was trying to give her.

'Sorry?' Ben said.

'What does that head shake mean?' Dani said to Daley.

'It means he doesn't have to answer that question,' Daley said.

'Why not?'

'Because I'm his lawyer and I advised him not to.'

'What do you know about Curtis's crimes?' Dani asked again, now glaring at her brother. 'Those he committed that led to his imprisonment here.'

'No comment,' Ben said.

'No comment?'

'I think you heard him just fine, Detective,' Daley said.

'I understand he was involved in a fatal car crash,' Dani said, still holding Ben's eye. 'Two people died. Is that your understanding too?'

'No comment.'

'He was convicted of manslaughter, correct?'

'No comment.'

'Did he ever talk to you about that night?'

'No comment.'

What the hell was Ben playing at now? What did he not want Dani and the police to know?

'Did Curtis ever talk to you about the Redfearne family?' Easton asked.

Another silent exchange between client and lawyer.

'No comment,' Ben said.

'Specifically Oscar Redfearne?'

'No comment.'

'Or Sophie Blackwood.'

'No comment.'

Dani let out a long sigh. Was there even any point in carrying on if he was only going to do this?

The meeting fell into an uneasy silence. Dani's brain raced with conflicting thoughts. Could they steer Ben back to ground he'd talk about? But then, why *wouldn't* he talk now? All Easton had asked about was the crime Curtis had committed that led to his imprisonment. That was public record.

'On Monday night a woman by the name of Mary Deville was murdered in her home,' Easton said. 'She was a retired judge. In fact, she was the judge who presided over Curtis's manslaughter trial. Did he ever mention her to you?'

'No comment.'

'Do you have any knowledge of Curtis's involvement in the murders of Oscar Redfearne or Mary Deville?' Dani asked.

'No comment.'

'Is Curtis going to kill again?'

'I think you probably get the gist of my client's position by now in relation to this line of questioning,' Daley said.

'Well, to be honest, not really,' Dani said. 'What exactly *is* his position?'

'I can still help you,' Ben said, fixing his gaze on Dani.

'Me? Or the police? Or people out there who are potential murder victims?'

'You do realise we could charge you as an accessory to murder,' Easton said, for the first time sounding agitated. 'If you were aware beforehand of Curtis's planned actions and did nothing to help us, then that's what you are.'

'If you recall, it was actually at my client's behest that we first asked DI Stephens here,' Daley said. 'So please don't try to turn this onto him. He *wants* to help, but it has to be a reciprocal arrangement, and I really don't understand why that is so hard for the police to understand.'

'What do you want, Ben?' Dani asked.

'I believe he's told you that already,' Daley said.

'I asked him, not you,' Dani said to Daley before looking back to her brother again, who now looked amused by the whole thing.

Dani hated him so much…

Stay focussed.

'Are more people going to die?' she asked.

No answer at all this time.

'Is that actually what you want? What does that say about you, Ben?'

'DI Stephens, please,' Daley said. 'Our position is clear. If we are given assurances over my client's legal position in relation to the information he has, and if progress is made on his personal familial matters, then he will tell you everything he knows. Any questions you have around the subject of his knowledge of crimes, past or present, will not be answered until then.'

'Mr Daley, you surely understand we're not in a position to give you any kind of legal assurances,' Easton said. 'We're conducting a murder inquiry. I'd strongly suggest you take your client's legal demands through the appropriate channels, but to withhold information which could allow us to save lives—'

'He is not withholding,' Daley said. 'It's Wednesday today. It was *two* days ago, Monday, when my client advised DI Stephens of his position on this matter. And what progress has been made thus far in achieving what he has asked for? Any negative repercussions from here are not flowing from my client's behaviour, but from the lack of action taken by the police and the CPS.'

Now it was Dani's turn to be silent. Of course, she'd met with McNair, Baxter and the CPS lawyer the very day Ben had first asked her here to discuss his messed-up deal. What actions had resulted subsequent to that meeting? Apparently nothing. Regardless, she had nothing to say to Daley about the steps she had taken.

'You'd better hope that no one else dies,' Easton said. 'Or I'll do my best to see both of you charged.'

Fighting talk from Easton, and Dani loved to see just a sliver of confidence taken from Daley's icy exterior by Easton's coolly delivered threat.

'Next time I only want to speak to Dani,' Ben said, giving Easton a sly look that Dani would have loved to wipe off his face for good.

The room fell silent for a few moments.

'Sorry,' Dani said, 'but you're not in a position to dictate—'

'I'll speak to *you*, and only you,' Ben said, cutting her off. 'I don't want to see *him* again.'

'I'm afraid that's really not for you to decide,' Easton said, though his protest sounded weak.

Dani said nothing more, but how the hell was she going to explain that to McNair?

'Ben, what are you doing?' Dani said. '*Why* are you doing this?'

She hadn't intended to, but she sounded desperate, and she saw the power in Ben's demeanour grow as a result. He didn't bother to answer the question.

'Detectives,' Daley said, 'unless you have anything else to add, I think this meeting is over.'

Dani slumped. She had nothing.

–

'Talk to me,' Easton said.

'It's nothing,' Dani said as she pulled the phone from her ear and deleted the voicemail. The message had been from Larissa's foster carer. They'd spoken earlier, at Dani's prompting, only for Dani to discover that Larissa hadn't returned home the previous night. Both of them had been in a fret about that, after Larissa's late-night trip to Harborne, but Poppy had called back half an hour ago to confirm that Larissa was back home now, and seemed fine, even if she wouldn't explain where she'd been.

'I meant talk to me about that meeting, not your voice message,' Easton said.

'Oh.'

Dani sighed and started the engine and pulled the car out of its spot and towards the security gate.

They drove on for several minutes as Dani tried to gather her thoughts. By that point she wasn't even sure if she was angry any more. She was simply dumbfounded. She really didn't know what to say or do next, either about Ben, or Larissa.

'So?' Easton said.

'Well what do you think?' Dani responded.

'That Ben pretty much admitted that he knew what was going on.'

'Not really.'

'What? All that *no comment* crap? You can probably exchange every one of those answers for a *yes*.'

'You know it doesn't work like that, however obvious it might be to us. For the CPS to even consider a charge against him we'd have to prove Ben knew about Curtis's plans. Whatever the hell his plans are. And we can only do that if either Ben or Curtis admits it. And it's not even the most important thing. The most important thing is finding Curtis. Stopping anyone else from dying, not sticking another charge on Ben.'

'The fact we're having the conversation with him at all shows he knows something.'

'I agree,' Dani said. 'But it could be he knows something small and insignificant.'

'No. No way.'

'I know. I don't believe that either. But like I said, right now we can't *prove* otherwise.'

'But you agree it sounds as though more people are going to die?'

Dani clenched the steering wheel tightly as she tried to channel her confusion and frustration. Her knuckles turned white.

'We don't even know for sure that Curtis killed both Oscar and Mary,' she said. 'It's just our theory.'

'But it's the only explanation we have so far. And your brother's games are likely going to lead to more people getting killed unless we find Curtis first.'

Dani was about to bite back at Easton's reference to her sibling relationship with Ben. The way he'd said it was almost accusatory against her. She held her tongue.

'I'll brief McNair on the interview,' Dani said. 'And after that I suggest we leave the lawyers to it. We need to get on with the investigation. McNair is holding a press con later. Curtis's face will be out there soon enough. We're closing the net.'

Easton sighed, suggesting he wasn't particularly satisfied with her response. Neither was she, really. She was both desperate and determined to find out what Ben knew. If she could, she'd have him strung up and every effort made to force the information out of him however they could. But she couldn't. The only solution now was for the police to play to their strengths and for her and the investigation team to keep on top of what they could control.

A thought struck her.

'Do you remember what question his first no comment answer was in response to?' she asked.

She glanced to Easton who was looking quizzically out of the window as though trying to wrack his brain. He didn't get there and was soon poring over his notepad. He tapped the paper with his finger when he found the right spot.

'It was something along the lines of what did Ben know about why Curtis was in Long Lartin.'

Dani chewed on that for a few seconds. Why was that so controversial a question? Ben had been answering questions about Curtis on the inside by that point, albeit in an obtuse manner, so why the sudden change with that question?

'We need to dig more deeply into Curtis's trial,' Dani said.

'In what sense?'

'We've already posed the hypothesis that Curtis was out for revenge. How else do we explain the death of his trial judge?'

'And Oscar Redfearne?'

'I don't know.' Which was a glaring hole in their already paper-thin theory.

'There has to be more at play than simple revenge,' Easton said.

'Maybe. Or maybe not. But we should start there still. We need to find out everything we can about that trial. Who the barristers were. Which witnesses were called. How the verdict was reached. There'll be a clue somewhere.'

There *has* to be, Dani thought, as hopeful as she was desperate.

Chapter Twenty-One

Never had Dani been so glad for modern airflow technology as when she entered the morgue on a hot summer's day. Already somewhat flustered from the earlier visit to the prison, she was sweating just from walking from her car to the front entrance of the building, and unhelpfully, her churning mind was pre-infused with thoughts of the smell of stinking, rotting, maggot-infested flesh of cadavers in the sun.

Nice.

Luckily, as she opened the doors, and felt the waft of supercooled air-conditioned air, those smells and thoughts all but disappeared.

In fact, as she continued along the corridor to the theatre room, she shivered from the chilly air, which was strangely a welcome relief.

Though the smell of death remained. It was something that never left a morgue, no matter how much bleach was used.

She knocked on the doors to the theatre and a moment later Jack Ledford, in his white robes, opened up and beckoned her inside. He had a deep frown on his already normally furrowed brow.

'Everything OK, Jack?' Dani asked as he led her through the clinical room to the silvery gurney in the centre, upon which sat an unidentifiable bundle under a white sheet.

'Not really,' he said, before grabbing a pile of papers from a side table. 'It's one thing trying to draw conclusions from two dead bodies within my own theatre, but asking me to do so with one body of my own and just a pile of notes from another pathologist fifty miles away is quite something else.'

She'd had word from Ledford earlier that not only had he completed the post-mortem of Oscar Redfearne, but that he'd also received the results of the post-mortem of Mary Deville, which had been carried out by a pathologist in Shropshire.

'Is it someone you know?' Dani asked, not ignoring his grumble exactly, but hoping she could gloss over it.

'What?' he said, glancing up from the papers in his hand. 'Yes. Yes, I do know her. She's perfectly good, as you can probably imagine from her speed in getting this back, but still, we all have different techniques and methods of reporting and you appreciate I've only had this to review since this morning.'

Though it was he who'd called Dani, not the other way around, so any lack of understanding of the Deville report was surely down to him having not taken long enough to familiarise himself with it. Not that Dani would point that out to him.

'I understand,' Dani said. 'And I'll make sure I spend plenty of time comparing the two sets of notes myself, to see what conclusions I can draw, but you know how much I value your opinion on these matters.'

Her flattery seemed to do the trick. Ledford sighed and caught her eye and then fished some glasses from the top pocket of his white coat which he dropped onto the end of his nose.

'Very well,' he said. 'Let's start with Deville.' He paused a few moments as he rifled through the papers. 'You're going to have to wait for full forensics results for the scene analysis, but there are some intriguing finds here.'

'Such as?'

'Nothing to indicate any kind of sexual penetration prior to death. No foreign fluids recovered from her orifices.' Dani clenched her teeth at the images conveyed by the clinical words. At least it was positive news, of sorts. 'But they did identify metallic slivers in more than one of the wounds.'

Dani frowned. 'What does that mean?'

'Often two reasons in relation to stab victims. One could be a rusted blade, though I don't think that's what we're seeing here as the wounds are so neat, and the slivers, from what I can see in the notes, were not obviously rusted.'

'So the other?'

'The other reason is a newly sharpened blade. In the process of sharpening you're essentially cutting the outer edge off the blade, and you naturally get residue because of that. Unless you clean the thing to perfection you can get tiny fragments stuck to the metal which get transferred on subsequent use.'

'Did you see similar traces in Redfearne's wounds?'

'We did.'

'So you can potentially match the same weapon to both cases?'

'We'll have to request the metallic sample from West Mercia, but of course we can try to match them.'

'Please.'

And such a conclusion would be of huge importance in a court of law in order to prove the same weapon had been used in both murders, and if they found a potential murder weapon, in proving that said weapon was the one used. Although to Dani, even without that forensic conclusion, the fact the slivers were there on both bodies in the first place didn't sound like a feasible coincidence. Not when put together with other factors. The evidence was pointing more and more to supporting the theory that both Oscar and Mary were killed by the same person, and to that person being Damian Curtis.

'And the wounds themselves, would you say they're of a similar nature?' Dani asked.

'You're asking if it looks as though the same weapons were used by the same person?'

'Weapons?'

'There's definitely more than one for each victim. I think I suggested that to you at Drifford House.'

'You did. You said perhaps an axe, together with something that had a longer blade. A katana or machete.'

'And it's the same for Mary Deville.'

Yet another fact that was unlikely to be a coincidence.

'Two weapons,' Dani said as a strange thought struck her.

'Yes. That's what I said.'

'I assumed until now it was one person with two weapons. But an axe and a machete? How on earth do you wield both at the same time?'

'I'm not sure I suggested—'

'No, I know you didn't say that. But just thinking through logically... why two weapons? Could it be that there were two attackers?'

Ledford stared at Dani for a few seconds.

'I really can't answer that,' he said. 'Based on what I can see, two attackers is no more or less likely than one attacker with two weapons.'

Did it make sense to Dani? No one had really put the idea of two attackers forward as a theory yet, but could it be the case?

'Clearly both victims died in frenzied attacks,' Ledford said. 'They suffered multiple horrendous and hugely destructive injuries. Yes, it's possible two people inflicted those injuries, but it's not at all impossible that one person wielding two weapons could have done this, or even that it was one person who switched weapons during the attack, for whatever reason.'

Dani really didn't know which of those scenarios was the most likely, or even what any of the scenarios told her about the attacks.

'No bite marks on Mary Deville?'

'None.'

'Any indication she fought back?'

'Not really. Nothing under her nails or anything like that which you could use to identify the attacker. Really no obvious signs of defensive wounds as such, though it's hard to define exactly what would be a defensive wound when you have so many injuries like this, all inflicted with such brutality. I'd suggest from what I've read in the report that the injury to the left side of her head – likely caused by an axe or similar object – rendered her incapacitated and the other wounds followed subsequently, though you'd have a hard time proving that conclusively, even if it does follow in terms of the pattern of injuries being largely to the front and one side of her body. By which I mean she was very possibly on the ground when many of those wounds were inflicted.'

'And cause of death was the head trauma?' Dani said.

'That's the pathologist's conclusion. The head wound caused massive damage to the brain tissue. Intracranial bleeding is the likely fatal result.'

'And Redfearne?'

'There wasn't an equivalent penetrative wound to the head, but there was blunt force trauma. Perhaps he was hit with something or he fell and hit his head.'

Ledford put the pile of papers down and moved to the gurney. He peeled back the white sheet and Dani held her breath for a second as she stared at the stitched-up remains of Oscar Redfearne. Strangely, he almost seemed to be in better shape now than the mangled mess she'd first seen at Drifford House.

'But the head wound didn't kill him?'

'No. It did cause a lot of internal damage. You've heard of a coup and contrecoup injury?'

'Yes,' Dani said. She knew more than she wished about those. A coup injury was exactly what she'd suffered when Ben had tried to kill her. She was a traumatic brain injury survivor, though the damage to her brain, her frontal lobes, was permanent, as was her resultant new and more anxious, more angry personality.

Ledford decided to explain it to her regardless, such was his manner. 'A coup injury occurs where the brain is damaged at the site of impact on the head. So when a moving object hits a stationary head, most usually. The opposite would be a contrecoup, where a moving head hits something stationary, causing the brain to bounce to the other side of the head and thus causing injury at the side opposite to initial impact. You can of course have an impact where you get both injuries, if the force is sufficient, and in fact that is what we have with Oscar Redfearne.'

'Why the difference, I wonder?' Dani asked.

'The difference?'

'Mary was hit in the head with an axe, you suggested. But not Oscar. In fact, you're suggesting the blow to his head was very possibly from a fall, if I'm not mistaken?'

'Him falling and banging his head would be consistent with the brain injury, yes. And I do have a possible explanation for the differences in head wounds between the victims, although it's a theory, not a provable fact.'

'Go on?' It was most unlike Ledford to offer theories, so Dani wouldn't pass up on the opportunity.

'Height,' he said, then paused as if waiting for Dani to get it. She did get it; she was just a bit disappointed that this was his theory.

'Oscar was six foot three,' Dani said.

'And Mary Deville was five foot five. Quite a difference in height. The attacker, assuming they're the same person for each victim, had no issue swinging an axe at Mary's head height, but he perhaps struggled to wield it high enough to connect with Oscar's head with force.'

'So we're looking for an attacker who's smaller than Oscar but taller than Mary?'

Ledford shrugged. 'Possibly. But if the wounds are explained in that context, it does give more weight to the theory that both victims were attacked by the same person, in a roundabout way at least.'

Dani thought for a moment as she continued to stare at Oscar's youthful, though ghostly, face.

'From what I can see, and remember of the scene, Oscar had far more injuries around his body than Mary Deville?' Dani said, pulling her eyes from the corpse.

'I'd say so. My own conclusion is that there was something of a struggle here. Perhaps in Oscar's case he was attacked with the blade first. He was able to defend himself to some extent, which resulted in the slashes to his limbs. I'd say the head injury likely did incapacitate him, and that theory would accord with the similarities in the attack on Mary Deville, but Oscar died of blood loss from his wounds. It's hard to pinpoint exactly which was the fatal blow given they all happened within such a short space of time, and there are several which on their own could have killed him.'

'Are you able to conclude when the bite marks were inflicted?'

'There was no evidence of healing, and no significant levels of blood coagulation as compared to any of the other wounds, which would suggest to me he was bitten during this attack. But it could have been the first wound, it could even have been the last. I really can't say which is most likely with any conviction.'

Which unfortunately didn't really help Dani at all. Why had the killer – Curtis? – made such a seemingly obvious mistake as biting the victim, and hence leaving behind his DNA?

Dani noticed Ledford glance at his watch. The second time he'd done so now.

'I appreciate your time,' Dani said, deciding she was perfectly happy to leave the place anyway. There was only so long she could stand being in a room so filled with death. 'You'll keep me updated with further results? Toxicology?'

'Of course. Both PM reports should be in your inbox now. Give me another twenty-four hours on tox; hopefully I'll have something by then.'

Dani thanked him and was soon on her way out.

–

As she stepped into the sunshine and took a welcome breath of fresh but stiflingly hot air, she felt more frustrated than anything else. Although cause of death in both murders was relatively clear-cut, and the post mortems had thrown up no unexpected surprises, Dani remained hugely confused as to the circumstances of Oscar Redfearne's and Mary Deville's deaths. Not because it appeared anything other than that both people had been killed by the same person, but because the biggest question remained: Why? What linked the two victims? The connection between Curtis and Mary Deville was apparently clear-cut. And Mary Deville, apparently, knew the Redfearnes in some manner or other. But what was the connection between Curtis and Oscar Redfearne?

As she reached her car she pulled out her phone. She sat down into her seat – the air in the car was barely breathable and she fired up the engine and turned the air-con to full blast.

She had a missed call and text message from Jason, plus a missed call and voicemail from Easton. She called Jason back first. When he answered he sounded surprised that she'd called back so quickly – it certainly wasn't to form. What did that say about her current state of mind that she was seeking comfort in him sooner than she'd call her colleague back to update him on the case? There was no doubt she was feeling far more rattled these last couple of days without Jason than she normally did, particularly after the day she'd had – Larissa, Ben, and then the visit to the morgue. She really needed a pick-me-up.

The brief chat didn't really help much, but perhaps that was more due to Dani than Jason.

As soon as the conversation was over, she called Easton back.

'All done in the morgue?' Easton said.

'Thankfully,' Dani replied. With the car still far from cool, she had sweat droplets on her forehead and in the small of her back. With the images of corpses still on her mind, a flash of nausea washed over her.

'Anything to report?' Easton asked.

Dani thought about that one for a moment, but really she couldn't think of much that she felt she hadn't already known, only adding to her sense of frustration. 'Not really. You?'

'Yes actually,' Easton said, and Dani was about to get her hopes up before he let out a long sigh. 'I've started going through Curtis's trial documentation. First up, this is going to take a bloody age. It was anything but straightforward. And if you're talking about us considering everyone involved in this trial as a potential victim, from witnesses to jury members to legal teams… there's no way we can find the resource to offer them all protection.'

Dani and Easton had posed that question, and the problem, to McNair on the phone earlier, on their way back from Long Lartin. The DCI had at that point recon-firmed her belief that there was insufficient cause to provide personal protection for anyone at this stage, but that she'd speak to Baxter about the possibility, and also discuss with him whether an advisory notice of some sort needed to go out to anyone. It was better than nothing, Dani guessed.

'Let's hope we don't have to get to that point,' she said.

'Indeed. But there is something I spotted… and I'm not sure you're going to like it much.'

'Spit it out.'

Another sigh from Easton. Dani took a long inhale of air to prepare herself. At least now the air was cooling down and almost breathable.

'I don't get the ins and outs of all this, I have to admit,' Easton said, 'but one of the witnesses on Curtis's defence was a psychiatrist. She was trying to suggest Curtis was acting with diminished responsibility the night he caused the crash that killed his girlfriend and her kid.'

'But that wasn't the trial conclusion?' Dani said.

'I've not fully understood why, but I don't think so, no.'

'So what's the finding?'

'It's who the psychiatrist is,' he said. 'Helen Collins. The same—'

'The same psychiatrist who tried to convince everyone Ben was insane, so that he wouldn't be convicted of murder.'

She said the words monotone.

'That's the one. What do you think?'

What did she think? About yet another link back to her brother? Dani really didn't know. She was simply stunned.

'We need to find Dr Collins,' Dani said. 'Now.'

Chapter Twenty-Two

I can't make this too easy for them. The police, I mean. If I'm to keep going and complete my work, I have to keep them off my back as long as I can. I need to think more cleverly. I've seen my name, my face in the paper, so I have to keep my wits about me and my head low, although with two weeks' stubble and a different hairstyle from what's been plastered on the local news, and given the fact I'm not exactly hanging out in busy public places day in, day out, will anybody really notice me if I'm careful?

That's not the point. They shouldn't have found out about you so quickly.

They shouldn't have, but they have.

You see, I'm wanted in relation to Oscar Redfearne's murder—

You must have made a mistake.

Regardless, the key now is to be as careful as I possibly can.

Sophie was a mistake too.

Sophie isn't my concern right now. If she plays things right, then when this is all over she'll walk away.

With her scars and forever living in fear from the trauma you've caused. She'll suffer even more.

I shake my head to try and focus. I don't need to think about any of this right now.

I close my eyes for a few seconds and think through my plan for being here.

Yes, everything is in place.

I open my eyes again and look around. The road I'm parked on is quiet. I haven't been to this place much before, but I wonder now why not. It's nicer than the city. There are a few parked cars dotted about on the road I'm on, which leads up into the hills, but very few people about. Houses line only one side of this street, off to my left, though they're each on wide plots and there's only six on the whole street. To my right are farmers' fields stretching away into the distance.

Satisfied, I step from the car and throw the backpack with my tools and equipment over my shoulders then casually walk away.

Today has been another hot and sunny day, and even though it's early evening now, the sun is still fierce in the blue sky and I have a baseball cap to shield my face both from the sun's rays and from anyone who might be looking for me. Not that anyone around here will recognise me. All of the police alerts I've seen have focussed on the Midlands. I'm certainly not national news. Yet. I plan to keep it that way.

You'll keep it that way so long as you listen to me.

I take a glance over my shoulder. No one there. Then I turn sharply off the pavement and up the drive of a house I know from my earlier drive past is derelict and up for sale. It's the only one on the street that's obviously unoccupied. No doubt someone will soon make a mint turning it around so that it's as handsome as the others on the street. For now, its disrepair and neglect provide me with an opportunity.

I head to the side gate to the left of what is a traditional limestone house – a style that remains so prevalent in this area. The dilapidated gate is unlocked, and I carefully swing it open, trying not to make any noise that might arouse the interest of the neighbours, although as I traipse down the weed-filled side passage, I don't hear anybody about in their gardens on either side.

The back garden of the house is a mess. Old furniture and rubbish heaped together, grass and weeds three feet high all over. I clamber across. My heart rate is quickening now as, despite the mess surrounding me, I feel exposed. Anyone looking out the back windows of the neighbours' houses will see me. But I still think it's the safest way, and even if I'm spotted would anyone really care that much?

I think about glancing over my shoulder to look back to the houses. I'd rather know if there's a problem.

No, just keep going. You're almost there.

I reach the crumbling fence at the end of the garden and clamber over far more ungracefully than I'd imagined. The damn thing nearly collapses under my weight, but I'm safe still and unscathed.

I land among a neatly planted border that leads onto a manicured lawn. The small block of flats is just in front of me now.

Of course, I could have approached the front entrance of the block from the road it sits on, but on my drive-by a little earlier, I spotted the unmarked car across the street with the bored-looking chap in the driver's seat. I can't say one hundred per cent, but I'm sure he's a policeman. It makes some sense that they would try to find me here.

I'm soon at the back entrance to the block. I've recently perfected this new skill and I'm genuinely pumped when it takes me only a couple of minutes to pick the lock with the small torsion wrench and pins I've brought with me. I push open the door and step inside into the overly warm interior.

The block of flats is perhaps twenty years old and is far from a shithole, but it's not particularly modern or upmarket either, and clearly it doesn't have air conditioning or anything like that. On a hot day like today it's like a tin can in a microwave.

The other thing I notice is the smell. The musty smell of old people. Although not a retirement home, this place may as well be as I can't imagine there's a single resident in this type of accommodation, in this location, who's under seventy.

I pass no one as I move up the stairs to the first floor. When I reach apartment fourteen I stop and stare at the door for a moment. I think about knocking but then I recall that unmarked car out front again. If I knock, I give him the opportunity to alert someone.

I need to remain stealthy as long as I can.

This lock is more tricky than the first, or perhaps it's just that I'm more nervous now, the closer I get. It takes a few minutes but finally I'm there, and I ever so gently push down on the handle and inch the door open. As expected, it catches on the chain. Not a problem. The gap is easily big enough to slip my hand through, and with the small screwdriver clasped in my fingers, I begin to work on the screws for the panel holding the chain in place. Far easier and less noisy than trying to snap the thing, or even crunching through it with bolt cutters.

I deftly catch the first screw in my hand when it falls loose. The second falls to the floor and makes a small clatter when it hits the thin carpet below, but after holding my breath for a few seconds I'm pretty sure I'm still in the clear. I put the screwdriver away and open the door fully then step inside.

I've been here before, though not for a few years. Although familiar, there's nothing particularly warming or welcoming about my return, no happy memories or anything like that.

I can hear the TV is on. Some shitty talk show, by the sound of it. I reach the doorway to the open-plan lounge and stare inside.

There he is. Slumped on the sofa, cider can in his hand. What a pathetic life his has become. He must have sensed my presence because he turns his head to look up at me, confused more than anything. Perhaps he's too pissed to do anything else.

No. There's the surprise. Then the fear. He goes to get to his feet.

No chance. I'm on him in a flash. I jump on top of him on the sofa, pinning him in place. The cider can flies from his grasp and the sticky liquid glugs out onto the carpet as I slam my head into his. For a couple of seconds I see stars. But when clarity returns I see the damage to him is far worse than to me. There's a gash on the bridge of his nose and blood is already dribbling out. His eyes are rolling; he's dazed and nearly out of it.

I headbutt him again, with even more ferocity and venom this time. His head slumps and his arms flop uselessly to his side.

Honestly, that was easier than I'd thought. I'm almost disappointed he didn't put up more of a fight.

I lift his chin up. His eyes are barely open.

'Dad,' I say. 'Dad, stay awake, please.'

He groans and there's just a little shuffle from him, but it's not an impending fight-back.

'I only have one question for you,' I say. I wait a moment until I know he's listening. I duck my head just a little and our eyes connect. Yes, he's listening. 'Dad, am I man enough for you now?'

He doesn't answer, although I guess I don't give him much of a chance because I thrust the knife into the side of his neck just a second later. The blade is so sharp, and the blow is so forceful that the tip of the sharpened metal pierces out the other side, just underneath his ear.

I withdraw the knife and blood surges.

Just one blow and he's already drifting to nothingness, his lifeblood draining. He simply has nothing to offer in return.

But I'm not done.

I lift the knife and plunge it into his chest. I do it again and again and again. His eyes are connected to mine the whole time. It's curious to watch as his life force ebbs away.

I keep going. The knife goes in and out in a blur of motion. I can't even count how many strikes; it's too quick and too prolonged, and I'm not focussed on counting, but on watching. Watching.

–

Darkness has long since arrived when I'm finally back in my car heading home. It was one thing entering the block of flats during daylight, but leaving that way was never an option, not carrying my dad, no matter how many pieces he's in now.

It wasn't easy lugging the suitcase and holdall back over the fence and to my car, but I got there in the end. Weighed down with a few large stones once I get to the river, I'm sure those bags won't be found anytime soon. Even if they are, I've bought myself some time this way. He doesn't get visitors. He barely leaves that apartment. In fact, I probably could have just left him in there, his bloody corpse quickly becoming putrefied in the heat of summer. The maggots would have seen through him soon enough, though the stench would have alerted the neighbours before long.

No, cutting him up and taking him out of there and dumping him was the best way.

You did good. That can't have been easy for you.

Yet the most surprising thing is that it was *so* easy for me.

And as I head back from that place I'm on a high. That man had been a noose around my neck for so many years. Now that noose is gone, I feel free. I'm elated. Truly happy.

This moment is mine, and no one is going to stop me now.

Chapter Twenty-Three

With a meeting arranged at the central Birmingham office of Dr Helen Collins at eleven a.m., Dani had some rare spare time come Thursday morning. While she could quite usefully have used that time in the office checking over the various strands of the Redfearne/Deville murder investigations, she'd instead made arrangements to go and see her sister-in-law, Gemma, at her home in Sutton Coldfield. It was a visit Dani continued to make too infrequently, however much she cherished any time she got to spend with her niece and nephew, and it was with a heavy heart that she knew on this occasion she wouldn't even get a chance to see the children, who were both already at a holiday club at their school, but in reality it was probably best that they weren't around for this conversation.

'No way. Absolutely not,' Gemma said, with an angry wave.

It wasn't the first time she'd said that to Dani today, as they sat in the lounge of Gemma's modest family home drinking coffee.

'Gemma, please, I—'

'No. My kids need to forget all about Ben, not rekindle anything with him. That's it.'

'He's their father.'

'He's a bloody killer! He tried to kill *you*! And me! Come on, Dani, take your detective hat off for a second and think about what you're asking me here.'

Dani sighed. The fact was, Ben's 'offer' had been directed to Dani for very considered reasons. Yes, he was hoping for some leniency from the justice system, one way or another, for his divulgence of whatever it was he knew, and that was undoubtedly the biggest play in his and his lawyer's book, but he'd also been very specific with Dani that she was to persuade Gemma to make familial visits to the prison. He'd not seen the kids since he'd been locked up. Dani could understand his anguish, even if she didn't feel sorry for him. And, the reality was, this was the only part of Ben's offer that Dani felt she could try and sway.

'I'm not here as a detective,' Dani said.

'That's crap and you know it. As a sister, as an aunt, would you still be here asking me this?'

Dani didn't respond to that. Gemma had her. The answer was no. Of course as an aunt or sister to Ben, she would never be suggesting to Gemma that she and the kids needed to revive contact with Ben. Dani had barely managed to drag herself to see her brother until the year before last, and that had only been because it was something she'd wanted to try out to help her in her mental recovery as a result of the damage he'd caused. His kids really didn't need that.

But innocent people's lives were on the line here, and Dani was seriously struggling with reconciling the conflicting positions of private life and public duty.

'It's possible that Ben really does have information that can help us catch this killer,' Dani said. 'I'm not asking for you to maintain visits to him forever, but if you just tried now, one time, two times, see if that's enough to satisfy him so that he begins to talk to the police.'

'Dani, you're not listening to me. I said no.'

'Will you even think about it? I can come back and chat again tomorrow? Talk to the kids about it tonight.'

'I'm at work tomorrow.'

Dani sighed. The conversation took a pause. Dani's brain was firing away as she tried in vain to think of a way to try and persuade Gemma to change her position. She came up with nothing much.

'So the job's going OK?' Dani asked.

Gemma raised an eyebrow as if to say, *do you really care?* She took a gulp of her coffee before setting the cup back down again on a coffee table that was mostly piled high with comics and football cards.

'Gemma?'

Gemma sighed. 'Changing the subject isn't going to get me to change my mind.'

'I'm asking because I'm genuinely interested.'

Gemma paused for a few moments as though trying to decide whether she believed Dani.

'I'll be going full-time in a few weeks. First time since… you know.'

She didn't sound at all excited by the prospect, in fact she remained downright sullen, but Dani guessed that was more likely because the mood of the conversation had already been irrevocably tarnished because of the talk of Ben.

'I'm really pleased for you,' Dani said. 'You deserve it.'

'I need a life outside of these walls.'

'And you're still seeing…?'

'Paul?' Gemma looked away now. Not sadness, more like embarrassment. 'No. Why would anyone take this mess of a family on?'

'Gemma, I've never heard such nonsense. You're a fantastic mum, you're a loving, caring person, and you're bloody gorgeous.'

Gemma scoffed but said nothing, yet Dani's heart ached to hear her talk like that. Knowing that the happiness of Gemma and the kids – Dani's own blood – had been so tainted by her brother. Yes, life wasn't exactly a walk in the park for Dani either, but she had Jason, and she certainly didn't have the added complication of kids to the mess that Ben had made. Dani really couldn't imagine how much harder life was for Gemma than it was for her.

And yet here was Dani in Gemma's home, trying to persuade her that she and the kids needed to spend time with Ben, the very man who had caused all this misery and pain in the first place.

Dani looked at her watch.

'I'd better get going,' she said, getting to her feet. 'But please, Gemma, just think about what I said. You're right, I've come here with my detective hat on today, but perhaps you need to think about this without your mother's hat on. You understand exactly the pain and misery that can be caused by a killer. You can help stop other families being torn apart like that.'

Gemma said nothing, though the way her face was now screwed suggested she was more angry than anything with Dani's parting comment, which really hadn't been her intention at all.

'I'll let myself out.' Dani said.

It was five to eleven when Dani and Easton arrived outside the building which housed Dr Helen Collins's office. Not even ten minutes' walk from HQ, the office was located in an odd-looking and narrow five-storey stone building that was crammed between two much larger and more prestigious neighbours.

The intercom on the wall had at least a dozen different buttons for the various companies that took up the space beyond.

Dani pressed the button for Collins Psychiatry Limited and waited. There was a brief silence before a smooth female voice came out of the box. Moments later Dani and Easton were steadily climbing the bare stone stairs to the fourth floor, where they found several closed and locked doors, each with a small plaque identifying the modest-sized business beyond.

Dr Helen Collins, a short and smartly dressed woman in her mid-thirties, with strawberry blonde hair pulled tightly back and a lightly freckled nose, was standing in the open doorway of her rented space.

'Come on in,' she said, eyeing Dani quizzically.

Of course the two of them had never met before, Dani had still been in hospital throughout Ben's trial, but Collins would know exactly who Dani was. Dani would come to that later anyway.

She and Easton stepped through. Beyond the door was a small waiting area with a single armchair and a basic reception desk, though there was no one working there. Collins led them through a narrow corridor that had just two doors: one a kitchenette with a toilet off it, the other

Collins's office, which was far more plush than Dani had been expecting, given what had come before it.

'Can I offer you tea, coffee?' Collins asked as she indicated for Dani and Easton to sit at the two seats in front of the sturdy-looking oak desk.

Dani and Easton both declined, and Collins was soon seated as Dani spied around the room. She'd come to expect a certain style of office for people in Collins's field of work. She'd certainly seen the inside of plenty of such places herself the last few years, and this one had all the trappings she expected, from the comfy chairs in one corner, to the bookcase crammed with medical books and literature on mental health and the like, to the abstract art on the walls and the abundance of houseplants – everything designed to create a professional yet relaxed ambience, however forced it might be.

'We need to discuss Damian Curtis with you,' Dani said.

Collins sighed and sat back in her chair. Dani half expected her to come back with some bullshit about patient confidentiality.

'What is it you want to know?' Collins asked.

'We want to understand more about the work you did with him,' Dani said. 'You spent many hours interviewing and talking to him as part of his trial a few years ago.'

'I did indeed. And I've seen him plenty of times since then too.'

'You have?' That was news to Dani. She looked to Easton who shrugged.

'Damian's defence team tried for years both for an appeal, and for him to be moved out of Long Lartin on medical grounds, but neither was ever granted.'

Dani played that one over in her head. She'd come back to it.

'At trial, his defence team claimed that the night he was involved in the fatal car crash, he was acting with diminished responsibility.'

'I believe they did,' Collins said.

'And that defence was in a large part as a result of evidence you gave on the witness stand.'

Collins shuffled a little uncomfortably in her seat now.

'Is that right?' Dani said.

'Yes, that's right.'

'But the jury didn't buy it.'

'I'm not sure I'd put it quite so simply,' Collins said.

'Then how would you put it?'

Collins sighed. 'Have you spoken to his defence team?'

'Not yet.'

'Then I'd suggest you do, as I can't speak for everything that happened in that trial, or the decisions that were made either in the court room or thereafter. I wasn't *part* of the defence team, you have to realise; I was appointed as an expert witness. I didn't testify to their position, I testified in relation to my medical expertise.'

'But you must have been party to their strategy, to their intentions for proving that Curtis was... well, what was it exactly that you concluded?'

'Once again, I'm not sure I'm the right person to say exactly what their strategy or intentions were. From what I gather about the legal process, there were various possible outcomes from Curtis's trial in relation to what he could be convicted for, and what sentencing would follow. You know he was originally charged with murder?'

Dani didn't, but found herself nodding.

'In fact, much of the CPS's case continued based on that charge during the trial,' Collins said. 'Yes, I understand Curtis's defence were arguing diminished responsibility. You'd have to speak to the lawyers to better understand this, but under such circumstances you cannot convict someone of murder.'

'But in the end neither verdict was returned. He was convicted of manslaughter?'

'I believe that's what he plead guilty to ultimately, though at one stage his team were even talking about a death by dangerous driving conviction, which would perhaps have been the most lenient outcome, sentence-wise. There were a lot of possibilities. You can see it wasn't such a simple case of the jury believing or not believing what I said about him.'

'Then for my benefit, could you explain exactly what your position was in relation to Damian Curtis's mental state?'

'My position?'

'Do you think he's crazy?' Easton asked, cutting to the chase.

Collins stared at him for a few moments.

'Crazy?' she said. 'That's certainly not a legal or clinical definition. Do I think Curtis was acting with diminished responsibility that night? Absolutely I do. I testified to that effect, and I'd continue to do so if pressed.'

'Can you explain that more clearly, please, Dr Collins?' Dani said. 'What is wrong with Damian Curtis?'

'What's wrong with him?' Collins sighed again and sat back in her chair. 'Perhaps we should start from the beginning. Because this isn't a simple case at all. But to try to put it in simple terms for you, based on my own experiences… Damian Curtis is one of the most disturbed people I have ever met.'

Chapter Twenty-Four

Collins's words sent a shrill shiver down Dani's spine.

'So you're saying Damian Curtis was mentally ill?' Dani said.

'Oh absolutely,' Collins said. 'I hadn't realised that was ever under any real doubt? Even at trial the prosecution did little to counter anything I said, and they didn't call their own expert on the matter to dispute anything.'

'But he wasn't convicted of—'

'Please, DI Stephens, if it's analysis of the legal case for and against Curtis, and how the court reached its decision, then I'm really not the best person for you to speak to.'

Dani paused as she thought how to better rephrase what she was asking.

'Can you tell us more specifically about your time with Curtis?' Easton asked, before Dani got there. 'What behavioural problems did he exhibit?'

'Where to start? It must be coming up for four years ago that I first met Curtis. By that point he'd already been charged with murder, and was in the midst of preparing for his trial. How much that pressure had already affected him I really can't say, but certainly he was already exhibiting strong signs of psychosis at that point.'

'In what manner?' Dani asked.

'Such that I often failed to have any rational or logical contact with him. Sometimes he barely seemed to comprehend where he was or why. And when he did, he believed people were trying to frame him, that there was some big conspiracy, which as far as I could see, was all nonsensical. But I also got the distinct impression that… basically he was hearing things.'

'Voices?'

'It's a very judgemental thing to analyse,' Collins said. 'People in his position often have a hard time explaining it themselves. Is it really a voice or just their conscience? Or just an internal monologue? We've all heard someone in our minds, in some way or another. A friend, a family member. Does that mean we're all psychotic?'

'But you did believe he was suffering from psychosis?' Easton said. 'You said that already?'

'On balance, yes. And he'd suffered mental health problems for a large portion of his life.'

'Really?' Dani said. 'Like what?'

'Perhaps you really should speak to his QC,' Collins said, looking a little vexed now.

'I assure you, we will be doing that,' Dani said. 'And I have read your witness statement too, but this is your area of expertise and we really want to understand everything we can from your point of view, in your words.'

Plus, Dani hadn't even started on the apparent coincidence that Collins was also the expert witness for Ben, who would later become Curtis's cellmate. What was that all about?

'I can only attest to this second hand—'

'Noted, and that's fine.'

'Curtis didn't come from a bad family, there was no broken home, no drunk or abusive parent, or nothing more extreme than ninety-nine per cent of us experience in family life. So there was no violent or stressful trigger in that sense that could explain his deterioration in mental health. The fact is, some people are simply predisposed to these issues. Curtis's father suffered depression for many years, which I understand eventually led to his separation from Curtis's mother. Curtis had been estranged from his father for years because of that. Perhaps Curtis had been suffering mentally for years too, maybe since early childhood, but if I recall correctly it wasn't until he was nearly twenty that he first spoke to a doctor about it. Did his parents not care about him enough to have sought help sooner? Or did they simply not understand what they were dealing with? I'd say the latter is the most common reason why mental health issues go untreated. Most of us simply aren't aware of, and hence ignore, or at the very least gloss over the warning signs.'

Dani would say Collins was spot on with that one. She herself had never even really thought about depression or other related issues, either in herself or in people around her, until depression had hit her like a freight train after her brother tried to kill her.

'But if his father had depression, how did the parents not recognise the warning signs?' Easton asked.

'Clearly I can't answer for them,' Collins said. 'But depression comes in many forms and people show it differently. And the very fact that the marriage broke down because of the father's depression shows that perhaps they weren't dealing with it constructively, so it's not really that much of a surprise if the mother also didn't recognise the problems with her son.'

'But depression is a long way from psychosis and from killing people?' Easton said. 'So how do you explain what happened?'

'As I was unable to assess Curtis until after the event, I really can't say how much things changed for him over the years, or whether his symptoms had been the same for some time.'

Which sounded a bit like a cop out to Dani, though she didn't bring Collins up on it.

'I understand he wasn't close to either of his parents, and his mother died when he was in jail, which I believe hit him hard.'

'Even though they weren't close?'

'Her death meant there was a lack of closure.'

'Going back to the start though,' Dani said. 'The doctors he saw initially when he was younger, are you saying they got their diagnosis wrong?'

'I don't think I said that at all. From what I gather, Damian saw his GP initially. Actually, over the years he saw different GPs at different points in time, starting from when he was nineteen. More than once he was referred to a specialist, but he rarely kept up with his appointments for any period of time. I'm not going to either criticise or make apologies for any doctor in particular, but this was all care provided under the NHS, and... quite frankly, to say they're overstretched is an understatement. If a patient frequently misses appointments then eventually... that's it. The matter just gets closed. You can only help someone who wants to be helped.'

Dani really didn't know what to say to that. Was it brutal and simple honesty?

'It would seem to me,' Collins continued, 'based on my experience of these matters, that Damian favoured the quick fix of prescription drugs over psychotherapy, which itself is not at all uncommon.'

Dani found herself shaking her head to that, even though she had come to rely on drugs, and still did regularly. But her problems were surely on a different level altogether than Curtis's? Was it really so easy for someone with a lifetime of mental health issues to fall through the cracks, repeatedly, year after year?

'What about my brother?' Dani asked.

Collins's face screwed up as she caught Dani's eye. 'Why is that relevant here?'

'Were you aware Curtis and Ben were cellmates?' Dani asked.

'Yes,' was all she said.

'You've spent a lot of time with both Ben and with Curtis. How would you characterise their positions in relation to each other?' Dani asked.

'I'm really not sure what you're getting at.'

'You were an expert witness for the defence at Ben's trial too. If I remember rightly, you claimed he too was acting under severe pressure when he killed, that it was your belief that his actions were carried out with diminished responsibility. Correct?'

'Yes.'

'So it's a very similar case to Curtis's, surely?'

'Actually they're miles apart.'

'Could you explain?'

'Ben did not have anything like the same history as Damian.' Collins sighed now and took a deep breath. 'If you've the time I can try and explain.'

Dani looked at Easton who nodded. 'We have all the time you need,' Dani said.

'There are four legal tests to consider in determining whether someone who committed a criminal act was acting with diminished responsibility. And remember these are *legal* points, but an expert in the medical field must attest to them. Firstly, it has to be shown that the defendant suffered an abnormality of mental functioning. Secondly, that abnormality must arise from a recognised medical condition. Thirdly, it must have substantially impaired the defendant's ability either to understand the nature of their conduct, or to form a rational judgement over it. Lastly, you have to decide whether all of that is an explanation for the conduct itself.'

It sounded almost like she was reading from a legal textbook. How many times had she had to regurgitate those lines?

'But you attested that Ben met all four criteria, the same as Curtis?' Dani said. 'The jury didn't buy it, but how is the defence any different, and how are the positions any different?'

'I did attest to that, yes, but even that doesn't mean their cases were in any way related. You need to understand that there are countless circumstances in which a person's actions could be put to this test, and there's a huge degree of judgement required for each stage. At Damian's trial, the prosecution didn't have their own expert, and I honestly don't know why. But for Ben's trial, there was an opposing expert witness who testified that Ben didn't meet the first two criteria. Yes his judgement was impaired, but they argued it was through what would be termed loss of control, rather than because of a medically recognised condition. Basically, Ben was under pressure in his life, he lost it and killed people.'

Dani winced at the words. 'You didn't believe that though,' she said.

'No. *I* didn't. I believed Ben had more deep-rooted problems, but just because I believed both he and Damian passed those four legal tests, it didn't mean Ben's and Damian's positions were in any way the same either.'

'Do you think it's a coincidence that Ben Stephens and Damian Curtis, both of whom you helped to defend, and, I guess, you could say whom you failed to defend, wound up in the same cell?' Easton asked.

Now it was Collins's turn to wince. How did it make her feel to know that two men she'd tried to defend ended up in jail rather than in hospital? Guilt? Shame? Anguish?

'What does that even mean?' Collins said. 'Are you suggesting there's an alternative explanation, other than it being pure coincidence? You realise there are plenty of other cases where I've testified in court too? Have you analysed every one of those defendants to identify any subsequent interaction within or without the prison system?'

Dani looked to Easton and could tell he was chewing on that response, not quite sure where to take the line of questioning next. The answer was, they hadn't done that research. Should they?

'When was the last time you saw Curtis?' Dani asked.

Collins sighed and reached forwards for her mouse and clicked away for a few seconds as she stared at her computer screen.

'Just over two months ago,' she said. 'At that point, his legal team were beginning preparations for his parole hearing. The fact that went so well obviously meant that they had no more need for my services.'

'It wasn't required as part of his parole that he continue seeing a psychiatrist?' Dani said.

'I don't know,' Collins said. 'He wasn't seeing me for reasons of psychotherapy but in relation to his legal case. I have no idea what the terms of his parole were.'

'And that was OK by you?'

'How do you mean?'

'You've just spent some time explaining to us how this man has suffered mentally for years, and you were aware that he was to be released on parole, yet rather than check what safeguarding conditions were put in place in relation to his ongoing mental health, you just walked away?'

'I'm not sure that's fair, DI Stephens, I—'

'Even after his actions had caused the death of his girlfriend and her son? Do you not have a professional duty to—'

'I'd appreciate it if you didn't bring my professionalism into this,' Collins said, her face reddening with anger. 'Whatever you might think, I did my best by Damian Curtis.'

'Except you knew he was psychotic and you washed your hands of him the moment he was released into the public.'

'Detective, this is ridiculous. How dare you—'

'Did you believe Damian Curtis represented an ongoing threat to the public?' Dani asked.

'That's not a question I was ever asked to consider.'

'I'm asking you to consider it now.'

'But it's not a question I can answer off the cuff.'

'Of course it is. Though it's quite telling that you won't.'

Collins was now fuming. Dani didn't care. Against her better judgement, Dani had come to this meeting with a chip on her shoulder. This woman, after all, had tried to defend her brother's actions in court, and rightly or wrongly, Dani did feel bitter about that.

'OK. Then I will answer it for you,' Collins said. 'Yes, I believed Damian Curtis's psychosis was an ongoing problem that, if left untreated, could lead to a further degradation in his mental wellbeing.'

'What the hell does that even mean?' Dani said. 'So you're saying he *was* a risk?'

'I've given you my answer.'

'So why didn't you do anything to help him?'

'I've done everything I can to help him,' Collins said, sounding more and more irate.

'Except now we have a recently paroled offender with a history of mental health issues who in the last week we have linked to two very serious and extremely violent murders.'

Collins shook her head and opened her mouth but said nothing. Her face went a shade paler.

'Do you have any knowledge of *why* Damian Curtis would kill Oscar Redfearne or Mary Deville?'

'I… I don't even know those people.'

'Mary Deville was the judge at Curtis's trial. So you *do* know her.'

Her face was even paler now.

'Had Curtis ever talked to you about wanting to kill people?' Dani asked.

'No. Not at all.' She was shaking her head again. She looked shocked now. Were the ramifications of her lack of action hitting home?

'Did he ever talk about wanting to get revenge?'

'Revenge? On whom?'

'On anyone. You said he believed people were after him. How about them, whoever *they* are?'

'He was paranoid, yes, but... I have no explanation for what you're suggesting.'

'So, in your professional opinion, you can't correlate Curtis's actions in allegedly killing two people this week to the mental health problems you know he was suffering from?'

'That's... that's not an easy question to answer. But on the face of it... look, *if* Damian Curtis is responsible for those two murders, then there must be some other trigger still.'

'Could he have been faking it?' Easton asked.

'Faking what?'

'Everything you've just talked about. The depression, the psychosis, the voices?'

'You realise how ludicrous that sounds?'

'But possible?'

'And isn't that basically what the prosecution witness said at my brother's trial?' Dani said.

'I thought we'd moved on from Ben? And to come back to DS Easton's question: is it possible Damian was faking it? Yes, it's possible. Feasible? Not at all.'

'But you do agree it's possible,' Easton said again. 'That perhaps he made up all the mental health crap to try and get off a murder charge. He's not suffering psychosis. He's not a paranoid schizophrenic. He's an out and out sociopath.'

Collins glared at Easton for a few seconds but said nothing.

'Dr Collins?' Dani prompted.

'That theory is as outlandish as it is unlikely. Quite frankly I'm surprised you think it warrants a response from me.'

'So you don't think Curtis is a sociopath?' Dani asked.

'I think I'm just about done with these baseless questions now.'

'Can you answer the question?' Dani said.

'Detectives, it's time for you to leave.'

Chapter Twenty-Five

'I can't work out if she's lying about something or if she's just trying to protect her own skin,' Easton said as he and Dani strode back down Colmore Row heading for HQ. The sun blazed down on them and even with just a cotton blouse and thin linen trousers on, Dani was sweating as they headed along. What she needed was a long, iced drink. Perhaps with vodka in it. All the talk of mental health and Ben had exhausted her.

'I can't see any reason for her to lie about anything we asked about,' Dani said.

'You can't?' Easton said. 'How about because she doesn't even believe half the stuff she testifies about? How much do you reckon she gets paid for one of those gigs? Talk about a bloody conflict of interest. She said it herself. Curtis and Ben are nothing alike in their circumstances, yet she testified in court for both of them that the cause of their actions was basically the same. When it all boils down, she said what the people who employed her wanted to hear.'

Dani didn't say anything to that. Was that a likely explanation for Collins's apparent unease at some of the questions she was asked? She guessed it would be interesting to see how much Collins was paid for each case. Curtis's defence was covered by Legal Aid, so Collins's remuneration for that case would have been limited some-what by statutory guidelines, but Ben's case was funded by that slimeball Daley, who'd only charged Ben a pittance because of his desire for publicity, and who knew how much had been ploughed into that? Not that it had paid off, in the end, but Daley's clout was a possible expla-nation for why the CPS had themselves put up a bigger counterargument in Ben's case, with contradictory expert testimony.

'She didn't really help much, did she?' Easton said, sounding disheartened now.

'Help what? Us?'

'Yeah. This investigation.'

'No. But we do have a better idea now of Curtis's history at least.'

'Except Collins basically said she can't reconcile what she knows of him to these murders. That he never talked about killing. Even after opening by saying how disturbed he was.'

'True.'

'So what are we missing about Curtis?'

'I really don't know.'

And that was perhaps what worried her the most.

–

By two p.m., the third team meeting of the week was well underway. As always, Dani had opened up by discussing the key findings of the case, though there really wasn't much since the last time they'd all met. McNair was absent this time. Was that because she felt the lack of tangible progress meant it was a waste of her time?

'How many more witnesses are there to track down from the Redfearnes' party?' Dani asked.

'Less than ten,' DC Grayling responded. 'We haven't managed to speak to them all in person, but we do have signed statements through the lawyers for those that we couldn't get to see.'

Dani shook her head, but she believed for now that was sufficient. As far as she was concerned, Curtis was Oscar's killer. She didn't know why Curtis had done it, but insisting on hauling in an international footballer, a lord, or whoever else was on the guest list, to make a likely blank statement saying they knew nothing, was probably unnecessary given there was no other evidence that any of the guests was involved in Oscar's death.

Of course the question remained as to what other less than salubrious activities had taken place at the Redfearnes' party, but for now that wasn't Dani's priority.

'All the statements we've taken should be uploaded to HOLMES by the end of tomorrow,' Grayling said, 'but on the face of it, the gist is that no one saw or heard anything untoward.'

Which was really pretty damn useless, Dani thought, but they'd had to cross everyone off, one way or another.

'What about the link between the Devilles and the Redfearnes?'

'There really isn't much,' Grayling said. 'Yes, we've found some evidence that Mary Deville had provided some support for charitable activities that Caroline Redfearne ran in the past, so the two must have met, but I've spoken to both Caroline Redfearne and Pamela Longbridge and neither of them say they knew the Devilles socially.'

'So the Devilles weren't ever at one of these parties?'

'Not according to what I've been told.'

Would the Redfearnes lie about that? Dani would have a think about that. The link between the two families, however small, was still there.

'And the follow-up with Sophie Blackwood's friends and family?'

'It's not turned up anything at all,' said DS Kitsch, looking glum about that fact. 'And there's been no movement in her bank accounts, no access to her email or social media accounts or anything like that.'

Dani was increasingly coming to the conclusion that she was already dead. Why would Curtis be keeping her alive after all? But she wouldn't stop in the efforts to find her. Not until they were absolutely certain.

'And on Curtis?' Dani asked.

'Similar,' Kitsch said. 'Father hasn't seen him since his release, and actually not since his imprisonment. We've still got an unmarked car outside his father's home just in case, but this morning I've been fielding some pushback from Derbyshire who are unhappy with the waste of their resources.'

'I couldn't give a toss,' Dani said. 'Until we find Curtis tell them to keep on it.'

Kitsch nodded though didn't look impressed that he'd have to do the pushback.

'What about prison visits?' Dani asked.

'He never had any, apart from his lawyer and his psychiatrist.'

Which Dani already knew about. So who was helping Curtis, and how, and why?

'You were also going to speak to his parole officer?' Dani said.

'I did,' Kitsch said. 'Nothing to tell. The address we raided was the only one on file. Curtis had kept up his scheduled appointments, and was last seen a couple of weeks ago. The phone number on file for him was a burner phone that's now run out of battery, or credits or both. Not sure where else we go with that one.'

No, and neither was Dani, much to her increasing frustration.

'He must be staying somewhere. And he must be getting cash from somewhere?'

The room remained silent.

'His face is all over the bloody news,' Dani said. 'How can we not find one man?'

No attempt at an answer from anyone in the room, even though she hadn't meant it as rhetorical.

Not long after, Dani closed the meeting down and came out of the room after everyone else, feeling about as demoralised as ever.

—

The rest of the day passed by in growing frustration, and by the time she made it home that night, a little after six p.m., she'd already decided she needed a stiff drink or two to take the edge off her bad mood. The house was eerily empty as she stepped inside. Together with the lack of progress on the murder case, the emptiness at home left her feeling isolated and alone and downright miserable. When her phone vibrated with an incoming call, even seeing who was calling did little to lift her mood.

'Hey,' Dani said.

'You OK?' Jason said.

'Not really.'

'Talk to me.'

Dani did so. At length.

'You're doing everything right,' Jason said. 'You need to stop beating yourself up.'

'They why does none of this make sense?' Dani said.

'It doesn't even need to. All you have to do is find Curtis.'

Which was true. Jason always saw these things with such black and white clarity. Yet his simple answer really didn't sit easily with Dani. She had to know why. She had to understand how Ben was involved. It wasn't good enough to Dani to just find Curtis and congratulate themselves for taking a killer off the streets.

But why not?

'I'll be back tomorrow night,' Jason said. 'I'll take you out somewhere. Where do you fancy?'

'Somewhere we can get gallons of cocktails,' Dani said.

Jason sighed. 'Dani, you're not—'

'I've got to go,' she said, before hitting the red button to kill the call.

She didn't need his advice on what was and wasn't good for her. She'd heard it all before. She went to fix herself another drink. Half an hour later, when it was clear the vodka wasn't doing the job of making her feel better on its own, Dani knew there was only one other solution. The medicine cabinet. As miserable as that in itself made her feel.

For hours afterward, Dani sat in silence in the lounge, steadily drinking as she stared out of the window to their overgrown garden. How the hell were she and Jason supposed to find the time to deal with that on top of everything else?

Front of mind for Dani was not just Damian Curtis and what else the police could do to catch him, but the many elements of her own life that were still so far from perfect; Ben, Gemma, the kids, her own mental health. Her home life?

It certainly hadn't escaped her attention during the meeting with Dr Collins that morning that Dani herself had been seeing a psychiatrist ever since she'd suffered her brain injury. Her fall into mental health anguish had a clear trigger at least. What about Curtis? Dani simply couldn't reconcile Collins's mixed responses about Curtis to the two killings they were investigating, nor to Ben's claim that he had information about Curtis that could help the police.

What was she not seeing?

More importantly, what was the *truth* about the situation, because there were so many conflicting possibilities and explanations?

Dani had no clue.

But she did have a very clear idea of how she could get to the bottom of it all. Ben. Somehow or other, she had to do everything she could to get him to talk.

Chapter Twenty-Six

It's still light outside when I arrive at the warehouse at nearly nine p.m., and it doesn't feel like night time is near, but it's been a long day and my body aches and my head is fuzzy and I want nothing more than to take the edge off with some whisky, and then pass out for a few hours. Alcohol is the best way of me achieving undisturbed sleep – no voices, no rats, no nightmares – even if I often regret it come morning.

But I'm not going to get the chance to sleep just yet.

I look around me. There's no one in sight in the derelict back alley, and I slide the loading door open a couple of feet, having to use all of my strength to move it on its rusted and misshapen sliders.

Once inside, I close the door behind me and I'm plunged into near darkness, the only illumination coming from the grimy Perspex panels high up in the roof. I'm sure I hear her murmuring from inside the van, likely triggered by the sound of my entrance.

I flick the main lights on and head over to the van. I unlock the back doors and stare inside. Sophie, as always, has pushed her body into the far corner. But she's not slumped this time. She's sitting straight up on the bench and her eyes are open – as much as they can be with the swelling from when I booted her in the face – and she's looking right at me.

'Hi,' I say.

She says nothing in response, but there's something about the way she's looking at me. Almost like she's been waiting for my return. It's Thursday now. She's been here since Saturday night, so I guess we're getting into something of a routine. There's no sobbing or pleading or screaming to leave the van any more. Maybe she saves all that for when I'm not here. Not that anyone would hear her, so she can scream all she wants.

Don't trust her. Remember what happened last time.

I look down at the van floor. Nothing is left of the food I put there last night. She wants to survive, I see that, and it warms my heart to know that I'm the one who's keeping her safe and alive right now.

'I brought you something a little different today,' I say, holding up the fried rice from a takeaway shop half a mile away, which as far as I'm concerned is a vast improvement on the limp pre-made sandwiches she's had the last two days. 'But first, let me take a look at that face.'

She still says nothing, barely even flinches as I step into the van, and crouch down and move over to her. I sit next to her on the bench. Her hands remain cuffed and secured, but I'm only a foot away from her, and if she wanted she could launch herself at me again and try to tear my face off.

She doesn't. I think she's learned her lesson.

I unzip my backpack and take out the medical supplies I've brought: some wipes, antiseptic cream, plasters.

'Open your mouth,' I say.

She does so first time of asking, and I use a pocket torch to light up the inside. It's still bloody in there. Her bottom lip is fat and purple and there's an open cut to the gum on the inside, but I see no signs of infection.

'I'm going to take a look at the cut above your eye,' I say. She closes her mouth and nods. 'You know what will happen if you try anything stupid.'

I tentatively reach out. She doesn't move at all. Not until I grab the end of the tape holding the gauze in place and tug gently, which causes her to flinch. I pull the tape off. The wound remains open and is a big pulpy mess of red and purple and black.

'You should let me stitch it,' I say. 'Please.'

'No,' she says, shaking her head fearfully. I see her left eye, the least swollen of the two, well with tears.

'There's only so much I can do without stitches.'

'No,' she says again.

I sigh but it's her choice. I spend a few minutes doing what I can to repair her. When I press around her ribs, I'm certain something is broken there because she cries out and writhes in agony, but she won't let me look under her dirtied clothes. If I even attempt to she bucks and screams.

Whatever. Her choice. Not that I'm sure how exactly I could help her broken ribs. But it pisses me off that she doesn't see that I'm only trying to help. As pretty as she is, I'm not some fucking sex freak. That is not why she is here.

Then why is she here?

She's here because she was in the wrong place at the wrong time, and this is a better outcome for her than if I'd slit her throat.

Says you. And what about the Deville husband? You let him live. You didn't take him. Come on, think about it, why is Sophie here?

But he didn't see my face. It's different.

Yes. It's different. That's why you look at her the way you do. Why you think about her all the time.

When I'm finished tending her wounds I reach into the bag for the food—

You could fuck her. Who would know? Who would care?

'Shut up!'

I slam the heel of my hand into my head. Sophie grimaces. My head pounds from the blow, but I think it does the trick of pushing her away.

I pull out the carton of rice and the plastic fork. My belly grumbles. I haven't eaten in hours. I begin to feed her, forkful by forkful. I can see she's in pain with each mouthful she takes, and with each swallow.

'Perhaps soup would have been better,' I say with a chuckle.

She doesn't laugh back, and I squirm a little with embarrassment.

You're pathetic.

I ignore the heckle.

'It's too... much,' Sophie says as a tear escapes.

Her words are slurred and garbled. I send another fork of steaming rice her way, but she purses her lips and shakes her head.

'Please?' I say.

'If you... leave it... later... I'll eat.'

I stare at her as I process her words. Her gaze never leaves mine.

You're so weak. You're going to screw everything up.

'I'll un-cuff one hand,' I say. 'That's it. But you try to fight back… I won't stop this time. I'll batter your fucking head until it's a pile of mush.'

Sophie whimpers and nods.

I reach into my pocket for the key.

Don't do it.

I slide across the bench a little closer to her. I can feel the warmth of her body now. I try to push away the thoughts that are forming at the back of my mind.

I was right. You want her. You filthy cretin.

I reach up with the key, but as I do so, I realise my hand is shaking.

Listen to me. She has to die. Don't do this.

Her voice continues in my head. Over and over. Heckling me. Criticising me.

'Stop,' I say, under my breath.

But she doesn't. She carries on.

Fool. Imbecile. Loser.

She goes on and on and I'm losing my focus.

'Stop!' I say louder.

Sophie is whimpering more loudly now. It's as though she already understands me. That she can see the signs of what is to come.

I manage to get the key into the lock, but the barrage of abuse continues, my heart is pounding in my chest, blood is surging through my veins, and I know I'm only seconds away from an explosion.

You're going to fuck everything up, you worthless bastard.

I grit my teeth in determination. My head pounds. My legs begin to shake as adrenaline surges.

I fight to control it, but I can't.

I begin to growl. I catch Sophie's eye. She's terrified of me when I'm like this. I want to stop, but it's impossible. I don't want her to see this, but the abuse continues and I know it's only a matter of time...

Kill her! Kill her now!

Here it comes...

I roar and slam my head against the wall of the van. Sophie sobs and blubbers now. I ball my fists and pummel the metal. I gnash my teeth and pound my head against the van again, then again, over and over.

The van rocks from side to side on its suspension, such is the force of the hits. Before long, my vision is blurred and red from the blood that's dripping down my face.

Still I keep going.

Until...

Serene yet foreboding silence.

I wipe the blood away from my eyes with my forearms. *She's* gone. I know she is. I know exactly how to stop her. But I also know what's coming next. In fact, I can already feel them inside me.

My hands are trembling so badly I can barely pick the key up from the blood-spattered floor. Sophie continues to whimper and moan. Her anguish, which is not what I intended at all, is enough to cause a moment of rage to surge again, but I fight it off this time.

The cuffs are undone. Sophie whips one hand down to her side. She helpfully and willingly leaves the other in place, and I've soon reattached the chain. I shorten the slack just a little to stop her free hand reaching too far.

But the rats are moving more quickly now. I don't know how long I can take this before I'll be lying on the floor, a quivering useless wreck.

'I'll be… back… tomorrow,' I slur as I push the rice and the fork closer to Sophie.

Blinking to try to keep focus, I stumble out of the van, slam the doors shut. As I stumble towards the exit, I hold a hand to my throbbing skull, and pray I can make it back to the flat in time before my insides explode and the rats break free.

Chapter Twenty-Seven

Dani had been sitting staring at the forensics reports from the Drifford House crime scene for more than two hours, trying her damnedest to eke out anything of use, any tiny lead, from the bland words. Toxicology results were now back for Oscar Redfearne, but the results showed nothing of note, other than the fact he was likely drunk when he was hacked to death.

Nothing. That's what she had.

'You fancy a break?'

Dani jumped at the unexpected voice and her head shot up. Easton was hovering over her desk.

'Not just yet.'

'You look like you need one.'

Dani sighed. 'We need a breakthrough here,' she said.

'To find Curtis?'

'Yes, but...' Of course that was exactly where all their efforts should be, and indeed there were tens of officers assigned to help track Curtis down, yet that wasn't where Dani's head was at. She still wanted to know *why*. Having that answer could not only help to find Curtis, but could stop him killing again. And wouldn't it explain why and how Ben was involved?

'I'm not sure you're going to find any of the answers you need just by staring at that same page over and over,' Easton said.

Dani flashed him a glare, even though she knew he was right.

'We still haven't found any link between Curtis and either Oscar Redfearne or Sophie Blackwood,' Dani said. Was it a statement or a question?

'No, we haven't,' Easton said. 'Nothing in phone or email or social media records at least.'

'Maybe the link isn't quite so direct,' Dani said.

'Why does there have to be a link at all? What we need is to get Curtis. What if you're searching for something that simply isn't there?'

'No,' Dani said with absolute certainty. 'The attack on Oscar wasn't random. We've said that right from the start. It was planned and absolutely deliberate. Which means there has to be a reason why Curtis had Oscar on his radar.'

Easton held Dani's gaze for a few moments as if weighing up a response, though in the end he didn't offer anything.

'So did you want to go for a coffee or not?' he said.

'We only have one other option,' Dani said.

'One option other than coffee?'

'No, Aaron, one other option to figure out why Curtis targeted Oscar. Or, more specifically, why he targeted the Redfearnes.'

Easton's eyes narrowed a little as though he was starting to see where Dani was going.

'McNair will never buy it,' he said.

'Why not?'

'I'm just saying.'

'Well, thanks for the encouragement. But I guess there's only one way to find out. Come on.'

Dani got to her feet and headed over to the DCI's office.

–

'Not a goddamn chance!' McNair shouted, throwing her hands up in the air in exasperation.

'But, ma'am—'

'DI Stephens, this is a murder investigation, not an opportunity to look for dirt on one of the region's most wealthy families.'

'That's not what I'm suggesting we do, or what I want to do at all.'

'Then I'm a bit lost. What exactly are you suggesting? And this time explain it to me in a manner which makes sense in terms of catching our killer, rather than satisfying any personal agenda you may have.'

Dani ignored the barbed comment. 'Damian Curtis specifically targeted Oscar Redfearne. Everyone agrees on that, right? But we've found no link whatsoever between them. And please, bear with me, but like you said yourself, the Redfearnes are a wealthy and prominent family. Perhaps it's the family that Curtis was targeting rather than Oscar specifically. If Curtis is out for revenge, then that starts to make some sense. And that family… there's things happening there under the surface that we're just not seeing.'

'*Things happening*,' McNair said with genuine disgust in her tone, her face screwed for further effect. 'Bloody hell, is this the level of explanation we get these days from an SIO on a murder investigation?'

'Fine,' Dani said. 'Then let me be clearer. I don't trust the Redfearnes. I don't like them at all actually. I don't like what they represent—'

'So now you're admitting that you're letting personal prejudices get in the way of proper procedure.'

'No! I—'

'Don't you think I've already had discussions with Baxter and others about the Redfearnes? Don't you think we haven't already been hearing from lawyers, warning us about their clients' names being linked to this investigation—'

'So that's it? The top brass have skulked off into a corner because they're scared of a libel case if the papers say their clients were at that party? Why? Why are a bunch of celebrities and rich people so bothered about being associated with that party? If they were there, then that's a bloody cold, hard fact!'

'It's nothing to do with the goddamn party. It's to do with the fact that there was a gruesome murder at that party, which I think even you would agree had nothing to do with some spray-tanned sports star.'

'Ma'am, if I may?' Easton said, and Dani was more than happy for his interjection. She sat back in her seat, frustrated and flustered, largely because of her own inability to clearly explain what she was thinking, rather than because of McNair's negative reaction.

'I know Dani understands the sensitivity involved here, but we believe Curtis killed his trial judge,' Easton said. 'The motive for that one would appear pretty damn clear-cut. We also believe he killed Oscar, and even if we can prove forensically that he was the culprit, the CPS is going to seriously question our work if we pass this case to them without any idea of a motive for that killing.'

'Other than he's an unhinged sociopath,' McNair said. 'Isn't that what you were trying to tell me earlier?'

She glanced at Dani who said nothing.

'Unhinged, yes,' Easton said. 'Sociopath, possibly. But still someone who takes time to plan. Figuring out why Curtis killed Oscar won't just help to put a watertight case forward to the CPS, it could help us in stopping him killing anyone else, and most importantly, in finding him, which is what we all want more than anything right now.'

The room fell silent. Dani wasn't sure whether she was pleased or agitated that Easton had managed to break through to McNair in a way which she hadn't.

'I can see the sense in that,' McNair said. 'But what are you asking for here? The Redfearnes' legal team will be all over any request we make for access to their personal records.'

'I was hoping we could avoid that,' Dani said. 'That we could gain access to their financial records—'

'DI Stephens, don't even go there. That is not going to happen. We're not a spy agency, and on the paper-thin *evidence* of what you think these people have done wrong, no judge would ever give the go-ahead for any kind of covert fishing expedition.'

McNair's forceful rebuke caused Dani to take pause. What else could she say?

'The best I can offer you here is that we request a court order for access to the Redfearnes' personal and financial records,' McNair said. 'But I have to stress to you both that it's highly likely it will get rejected, unless you have something more concrete that we can use to help our case.'

'Then why don't we dress it up as an investigation into the sexual harassment allegations?' Dani said. 'I know that's not *our* investigation, but there's no reason why it shouldn't be a valid route of inquiry for the West Midlands Police. It's certainly serious enough to warrant further investigation, and what if those allegations are just the start of it? And you have to admit that the only reason an investigation isn't already underway in relation to the allegations is for the very fact that we're talking about a revered family who've got political and legal clout to stop it. Personally, that only makes me even more determined to find the truth, not less.'

The fact McNair didn't shoot the proposal down outright suggested she was at least contemplating it.

'We do have a wealth of evidence in relation to the harassment claims,' Easton said.

'The very point that they are revered is why we need to tread so carefully,' McNair said. 'As unfortunate or unfair as it may be, we can't get away from that point. The Redfearnes will cry foul, and you have to realise that, and be prepared for it. Their legal team will be onto us like hounds smelling a steak.'

'None of which are good enough reasons to prevent us seeking justice,' Dani said. 'We'll just have to deal with whatever they throw back our way.'

'We. Interesting choice of word, as more than likely it'll be me who has to deflect all the crap that they shoot at us.'

McNair sighed deeply. Dani realised she was clenching her fists in anticipation.

'I'll run it through Baxter today,' McNair said, 'and if he's in agreement we'll be onto a judge before close of play.'

'Thank you, ma'am,' Dani and Easton chorused.

'You won't be thanking me later,' McNair said. 'Now go and catch our killer.'

—

'That could have gone worse,' Dani said without taking her eyes off the road ahead. She was driving them once again, this time on their way to a scheduled appointment with Kenneth Feathers, the QC who'd represented Curtis at trial.

'She agreed to the proposal,' Easton said, 'so you'd have to say it was a success, even if our request is only likely to get some serious kickback from their lawyers.'

'An unavoidable sideshow.'

'I hope you didn't mind that I butted in back there,' Easton said.

'We're a team. You don't have to ask for my permission to speak.'

'But still…' Dani could feel his eyes burning into her. She resisted the urge to look over to him. 'I sensed I got your back up a bit.'

'Not exactly,' Dani said. 'I just feel as though she still doesn't trust me properly. A few days ago she was congratulating me on the Clarkson case, now I can't get her to see my point of view at all.'

'Of course she trusts you,' Easton said. 'Sometimes I think it's just a style thing.'

'You mean you think I'm too bullish and aggressive,' Dani said.

Which she knew to be the case, even if she couldn't control it. But was that really her fault, if it was caused by her brain's permanently damaged wiring?

'I didn't say that,' Easton said.

Dani waited for a further explanation from Easton, but he said nothing more, which didn't make Dani feel any better at all.

Easton sighed. 'I get what you're trying to achieve here, Dani, but I just… the Redfearnes lost their son. I mean… don't you feel even a little bit bad about what we're trying to do?'

Dani grit her teeth before answering. So was Easton not even on the same wavelength as her? The last few days he'd repeatedly helped her out of tricky points in their various meetings and interviews, but was that out of some sort of loyalty to her rather than because he actually agreed with her and *got* her?

'I don't feel bad in the least,' Dani said.

An entirely true statement that made Dani feel cold inside. Why did she care so little about these people?

The awkward conversation ended on that less than satisfactory note. They carried on their journey mostly in silence for the few short miles to an upmarket leafy street in Edgbaston that was lined with classical Georgian detached homes – largely boxy structures with an array of tall windows and rendered white walls. They came to a set of wrought-iron gates and Dani pulled the car to a stop, looking for an intercom on the wall that ran off from the gate. There wasn't one. She looked over to Easton.

'I'll go and take a look,' he said.

The gates were indeed locked, but there was a pedestrian gate just off from the driveway that wasn't, so Dani parked up by the roadside and the two of them headed on through and up to the green–painted front door of the expansive and handsome property.

'Not quite up to the Redfearnes' standards, but I wouldn't say no,' Easton said.

It certainly wasn't a property that would come cheap. None of those on the street were. Dani rang the bell then turned to take a look around. The various tall and dense trees lining all sides of the property meant that it was well secluded from the neighbouring houses, and the Feathers' home could well have been in the middle of the countryside rather than a short hop to the centre of England's second largest city.

'No one home?' Easton said.

Dani turned back around and pressed on the bell again, sticking her head closer to the door this time. It definitely rang.

They waited a few more seconds but there was no indication of movement from inside. Easton's face was already showing a hint of concern. He hunched over and pushed the letterbox open to peek inside as Dani pulled her phone out. She dialled the number for Feathers. No answer.

'You see anything?' Dani asked.

'Nothing,' Easton said, still looking in.

Dani rang again. No answer. She was about to leave a voicemail…

'Wait a second,' Easton said. 'Call again.'

Dani did so. Still no answer. Easton craned his neck to look up to her.

'I can hear it ringing,' he said.

Dani pulled the phone away from her ear as Easton straightened up.

'I don't like this,' Dani said as the niggling ominous thoughts in the back of her mind continued to take shape and grow.

'No, me neither.'

Easton banged on the door with his fist. The first thump made Dani jump.

'Police! Please, open the door.'

Dani hunched down to look through the letterbox. No sign, or sound, of movement from within. Dani came back up.

'Take a look around that way,' she said. 'I'll go the other.'

Easton nodded and they set off in opposite directions. Dani peered through each window as she went. All were locked shut, and she saw no signs of life from the glimpses inside. In fact, the house was immaculate, both in its decor and cleanliness.

Dani and Easton soon congregated by a set of patio doors at the back of the house that led from a country-style kitchen.

'Anything?' Dani asked.

'No,' Easton said. 'But this'll be the easiest way in.'

'Go ahead then,' Dani said.

Easton hesitated, as though unsure whether Dani's instruction was serious. Once he'd realised it was, it only took two whacks of his elbow to break through one of the small glass squares in the patio door to allow him to reach in and unlock the door.

Dani stepped inside first. No alarm. She inhaled deeply. Nothing of note. What was she expecting?

'This is the police!' Dani shouted. 'Mr Feathers? Mrs Feathers? Are you home?'

No answer.

Dani was part way through the kitchen when she heard a shuffling noise from out in the hall. She whipped her eyes to Easton. She could see from the determined look on his face that he'd heard the noise too.

Dani indicated that she would go first, and Easton nodded as she stepped forwards. As much as she tried to stay calm, her heart was throbbing and her hands were clammy with sweat as she moved forwards. She reached the doorway and peered into the hall. She could see nothing but then came that shuffling noise again. It sounded like it was coming from the adjacent room; the entrance was five yards away.

Dani crept out into the hall, her feet soft and silent on the polished oak floor. She was two yards from the doorway to the next room when there was a blur of movement from beyond the threshold. Dani gulped in shock. She stumbled backwards.

'Dani!' Easton shouted.

He raced in front of her as Dani lost her footing and fell to the floor with a thud. Easton burst into the room, then…

'Fuck's sake,' he shouted. He stopped and turned back to face Dani, half smiling. A moment later a cat bounded between his legs and out of the room and scooted past Dani into the kitchen and out of sight.

Dani put her head to her hand, embarrassed as much as anything else.

She wiped at her brow that was damp with sweat.

No. She wasn't sweating *that* much. She looked at her hand.

'Shit.'

She clambered to her feet and stared at the smudge of red on the dark floor. As her gaze moved up she spotted the line of thick dark liquid running down the bannister. A drop forming at the end of the wood broke free and fell to the floor.

'Upstairs,' Dani said.

She and Easton were both soon striding up. It wasn't hard to find the master suite. The trail of still glistening blood only got thicker and larger with each step they took.

Dani stopped when she reached the doorway.

'Shit,' was all Easton said as he stopped by her side. 'Is that Feathers?'

From the little Dani could see of the bloodied face, she really couldn't be sure. In truth it didn't matter much, because there was absolutely no doubt: whoever was lying on the floor in front of them was already dead.

Chapter Twenty-Eight

I've already showered and changed – discarding my soiled clothes – before I head to the warehouse, yet I can still smell the blood. I can taste it in fact, and I move the flavour around my mouth with my tongue, up and down, between my gums. The taste doesn't disturb me at all; in fact, quite satisfyingly, it helps me to linger a little longer on my progress and the day's deeds, though I do have to keep checking and rechecking my reflection in shop windows as I walk along to make sure that no red remains on my face.

Although I know I'm making good, efficient progress, there's still a way to go, and I know that some of the hardest tasks remain. I won't be deterred. The police are hunting for me now, but if I'm careful and consistent, I'll stay one step ahead and continue to evade them. Once my mission is complete... well, I still don't know what comes next for me after this is done. In many ways, it's not even important.

I glance around before I head off the main road and on to the side street, then a few yards later I do the same again before I move onto the even quieter alley. It's quite strange but my heart rate is steadily rising as I walk along towards the loading doors, and I feel a slight bubble of something building in my stomach. Not anxiousness, more anticipation.

Yearning. Like a fucking puppy dog.

The bubble pops and I feel anger rising now. My body becomes more tense as I idle along.

OK, so I'll admit, I like Sophie, and I enjoy the interaction I have with her. It's... real.

She hates you. She's petrified of you. There's nothing real about it.

I take care of her. She knows that. Perhaps if we hadn't met in the way we did...

Regardless, I'm at the doors now, and I won't hide from the fact that I'm feeling excited to see her. It's been a long night and day, another tick on the long list, and I'm glad to now have this much-needed respite before I go again.

I reach forwards and pull open the doors. It upsets me that the first thing that hits me as I step inside is the smell. Urine. Faeces. Sophie's. She doesn't deserve this indignity, but what else can I do? I can't give her a plumbed-in toilet in the van.

By the time I've moved a few yards inside the warehouse, I'm already accustomed to the smell, and I'm pleased that at the back of my nostrils there's still that tingling metallic twang of blood.

I reach the van door and push down on the handle.

I freeze when I look inside.

The van is empty.

You fool. Look at what you've—

'SHUT UP!'

I don't need to hear it. I can see the problem with my own eyes, and my instantly bursting rage is the only response I can muster right now.

248

I trusted Sophie. After the last time, I thought she trusted me. But she never wanted to be here. She never wanted anything to do with me. I gave her the benefit of the doubt and she wrenched it from my hand and tore it up and threw it into the fire.

And now she's gone.

But that fire is still burning. Fierce and unrelenting. I'm a long way from finished, and I pray only that I get the chance to face her one more time, to show her what a mistake she's made in betraying me like this.

Chapter Twenty-Nine

The FSIs in their white suits had soon descended on Edgbaston, and Dani and Easton became little more than bystanders as the experts got on with their jobs. Dani had already satisfied herself that the hacked-apart dead man in the bedroom was indeed Kenneth Feathers, though a formal identification would still need to take place. He was alone in the house, which was some sort of consolation, Dani figured, with his wife having travelled away from home that morning to visit their daughter in Worcestershire. Easton had had the horrific task of calling her to inform her of her husband's death, and given that call was the best part of an hour ago, Dani was expecting she'd be home any minute now.

Since they'd called the cavalry, Dani and Easton had both spent some time rummaging around the house. They found nothing of note. Of course they'd never been to this home before, so they didn't know what it *should* look like, but other than the dead body in the bedroom, and the blood, there was no evidence of anything untoward. No obvious sign of broken entry – other than the damage Easton had caused – and the house was spick and span.

'It has to be him,' Easton said as he and Dani re-gathered outside the bedroom, where the FSIs were still busy poring over the body. 'Curtis, I mean.'

Dani didn't answer him, though there was surely no other explanation, under the circumstances.

Dani's phone buzzed in her pocket and she lifted it out. McNair. About time.

'Ma'am,' Dani said.

'Give me the short version,' McNair said. 'I'm still not nearly finished pushing through your earlier request, even. I was hoping to get an early finish today but that's all been blown to crap now.'

Not the most sympathetic of statements given they now had another murder victim, though Dani didn't say anything about it.

'That court order is still important, and necessary,' Dani said, 'but I'm not sure it's even the priority right now.'

A sigh from McNair. 'Dani, I really—'

'Curtis has now killed both his barrister and the trial judge. Who knows why Oscar Redfearne was targeted, and I do still want to figure that out, but it's blindingly obvious that anyone associated with his trial is potentially the next victim.'

A short silence. 'What are you asking for now?'

'There's only one thing we can do. We have to provide protection for *everyone*. Lawyers, on both sides, jurors, witnesses.'

There was a longer silence this time.

'I really don't see any other way,' Dani said.

'This morning you were telling me the best way to help find Curtis was to dig up dirt on the Redfearnes.'

'That's not what I said at all,' Dani said, sounding as irritated as she felt. 'Digging into the Redfearnes is necessary. It could provide answers as to why Oscar was a target, and it could help any court case against Curtis, which we have to hope we're going to get. But the priority was and still is stopping him before he kills again.'

'And look where that got us.'

Dani didn't like how McNair said that. As though it was Dani's inaction, or wayward action, that had led to Feathers's death. What about the police's inaction in helping to get Ben to talk?

'Which is exactly why I'm now saying we have to provide protection for anyone else involved in Curtis's trial,' Dani said. 'Is that heavy-handed? Possibly? Is it really necessary? I don't know any better than you do. But can we afford to take the risk of not doing so? Absolutely not.'

'I agree,' McNair said before another long sigh. 'God knows how we're going to organise it, but we have to somehow. Leave it with me.'

McNair ended the call, and Dani stuffed the phone away then glanced back into the bedroom where one of the FSIs was busy prodding an open wound on the dead man's chest with a swab. The mass of bone and flesh looked like a rack of ribs in a butcher's shop. Dani pushed the rush of bile back down her throat and looked away.

'She said yes?' Easton asked.

'Surprisingly, she did.'

'Told you she trusted you.'

Dani still wasn't so sure, otherwise why had McNair opened up the conversation with a rebuke?

'You're still wondering about Oscar Redfearne?' Easton asked.

'I can't help it. It still makes no sense.'

'Yeah, but none of it makes sense really.'

'It doesn't?'

'Sure, we think Curtis is doing this for revenge, but that still doesn't explain *why* he feels the need to kill these people, like *this*.'

Easton indicated into the bedroom. Dani took only a cursory look. She was truly sick of seeing similar gory sights now.

'What I'm saying is, this was a guy with some mental health issues, right?'

'Apparently,' Dani said.

'But it wasn't a guy who'd been on a killing spree before. He spent a few years in jail, fair enough, but he's just got out after barely four years. Would he really feel so disgruntled about that? Yeah, OK, why not, but it's not like his whole life was taken away from him in those years. He's still in his twenties, for Christ's sake. So how did he go from a guy with depression, or whatever it was, before he was sent down, to a bloody crazed but pretty damn calculated killer a few years later? And without any warning signs either, apparently.'

Easton had hit the nail bang on the head with that one. Revenge was such a simple answer to explain Curtis's actions, yet really it didn't explain much at all. Yes Curtis was killing these people in a blood-soaked rampage, yet there remained a certain degree of calculation and planning in each attack.

'We'll find the answers,' Dani said. 'But first, we have to find Curtis. Let's redouble efforts on his friends and family. Can you see where the other forces are at with that?'

'Of course.'

'He's got to be getting help from somewhere, even if it's just a roof over his head.'

Easton nodded. 'I'm on it.'

'And get someone to look back through phone history, bank records, whatever we can get. There has to be a clue somewhere.'

Dani's phone buzzed again. She immediately suspected it was McNair, passing on bad news about one of the two fronts she was now working on. But no, it was DC Grayling.

Dani felt a pang of optimism for once as she answered.

'Boss, you're needed right away.'

'What is it?'

'Sophie Blackwood. We found her. Alive.'

Chapter Thirty

Talk about a quandary. Dani's first instinct was to jump in her car and race as fast as she could the short distance to Birmingham City Hospital, where Sophie Blackwood was now in a private ward under armed police guard.

But no. Dani had to think more strategically than that. From the information relayed by Grayling, she knew that Sophie was in a confused, gibbering state when she'd been found collapsed outside a shop on a main road a couple of miles from central Birmingham, and had already been heavily sedated by the medical staff at the hospital once she'd arrived there. She'd come around sooner or later, and Dani would absolutely be at the hospital before long, but she could make better use of her time rather than sitting and waiting.

Instead, she and Easton were travelling to Butler Street in Winson Green, an ethnic enclave that was the scene of one of numerous riots that spread through England in August 2011, kicked off by racial tension in London, but which culminated in the deaths of three men in Winson Green following a devastating hit and run. Years later, tensions remained high in the area, and Dani felt it was only ever a spark away from a repeat of those events. Why had Curtis taken Sophie there?

Dani parked up on double yellow lines outside a row of shops that ranged from an Indian grocery store with an array of fresh fruit, vegetables and spices on display outside, to a nail bar, to a barber, to a Caribbean fast food takeaway. There was still a marked police car here, and a few onlookers keen to see if there would be any further action today.

As Dani and Easton stepped out, a uniformed PC idled over.

'DI Stephens and DS Easton,' Dani said as she shook the officer's hand.

'PC Khan,' she said.

'Sophie was found here?' Dani asked.

'She was wandering down the street from over that way,' Khan said, pointing the opposite way to which Dani and Easton had arrived. 'She collapsed outside here. Mr Ali called the police.' Khan indicated the grocery store behind her.

'He's inside?'

'Yeah,' Khan said.

'Easton, you go and speak to him. Khan, you can come with me.'

Khan beamed at that.

'Do you know the area well?' Dani said as they began to walk.

'Kind of,' Khan said. 'We were first response because we'd just been to another call at the prison, but I'm based at Smethwick.'

Which was a bit of a shame. Someone who knew the area inside out might have been better able to quickly pinpoint where Sophie had likely come from.

'OK, that's not a problem,' Dani said. 'We'll have to use our instincts.'

Dani kept her eyes busy as they slowly walked. 'CCTV up there,' she said, pointing to the cameras high up on a pole. 'And another further down.'

'Yeah. I spotted those,' Khan said. 'I advised DC Grayling when we spoke on the phone earlier.'

Which was helpful; if they could at least narrow down where Sophie had entered Butler Street, they could begin to trace where she'd come from. And could they even get images of Curtis coming and going?

They'd soon walked past the shops and found themselves with a row of terraced houses either side of them that stretched away into the near distance. Farther up ahead was a large roundabout connecting to the Birmingham ring road. The multiple lanes there were clogged with heavy traffic.

'Surely she couldn't have come this far,' Dani said. 'A young woman in broad daylight, shoeless, face bruised, grimy clothes, covered in filth. Someone else would have stopped her, would have alerted the police, before she'd got to the shops. And how would she have got across that carriageway without anyone raising the alarm?'

'I think you're right,' Khan said.

Dani stopped and turned around.

'Which means she came from one of the roads between here and the shops.'

Khan nodded. Dani began to walk back. At each side street they passed, she stopped and peered down. The first street was residential with small terraced houses on both sides, running in a straight line as far as the eye could see. Cars were jammed together on both sides of the road, providing just enough space for traffic to move in between. As on Butler Street, Dani spotted a CCTV tower on the pavement a hundred yards down. That wasn't the street they were looking for.

They kept on going. The next street was much the same as the previous one, but the third street was markedly different. The terraces on this one continued only for half a dozen houses before commercial properties took over: small offices, warehouses.

'She's more likely to have been kept somewhere big and quiet, than in one of the terraces,' Khan said.

Dani agreed. Plus, as they headed down, Dani noticed there was no CCTV here on the street itself, albeit some of the businesses had their own systems installed to keep watch over their premises.

The buildings they passed were a concoction of different businesses, in various states of repair. More than one property was decrepit and clearly abandoned. Some looked abandoned but were in fact in full use. Some looked new and fresh, even.

'Do you think it's one of these closed-down places?' Khan asked.

'Not one we've passed yet,' Dani said. 'All the ones I've seen have security fences, padlocked gates. From what I've heard of the state of Sophie, do you think she could have made it past obstacles like that?'

'She was running for her life, so who knows?' Khan said. 'Or there could be back entrances?'

A fair point, and one which made a bit more of an impression when they came to another side street that was nothing more than an alleyway between two rows of commercial properties. With no through road, it appeared its only use was for access and dumping rubbish, judging by the lack of anything other than industrial bins.

Dani paused at the entrance to the alleyway and looked all around. In years gone by this was an area thriving with industry, and even today, despite huge changes in the economic landscape within the Midlands and further afield, the businesses here had good access to the ring road and out of the city – yet it was also incredibly quiet. A perfect place for keeping out of sight and out of mind.

Dani was about to move off down the alley to further investigate when she spotted something on the ground. She bent down and took a plastic glove from one pocket and a small evidence bag from another. She reached out with her gloved hand and picked up the loose strands of dyed blonde hair, dark brown near the roots. Dani rubbed her finger across the hair and then stared at the red residue on her fingers.

She placed the hairs in the bag then looked up to Khan who seemed far more anxious now than moments before.

'Come on,' Dani said.

She straightened up and the two of them headed down the alley. Distant banging, music from tinny radios, the whir of machinery wafted over from nearby buildings, but there was no sign of anyone at all within the alley. They came to a set of rusted loading doors that were open several inches. Not a particularly secure way to leave a building, whether it was in use or otherwise. Dani tried to open the doors further, but they were wedged in position, the sliding mechanism all but failed for good.

'What is that smell?' Khan said, holding her nose.

Dani already knew, and the thoughts running through her mind now made her insides curdle.

She slipped in through the gap, and spotted the van, back doors open, a few yards away in the darkened space. Dani reached for her phone.

Chapter Thirty-One

'I'm going to have to start charging you for call outs,' Tariq said when he arrived suited and booted with his team of FSIs.

'Believe me, I'd call you less if I could,' Dani said.

'At least there's no body this time, I suppose.'

Dani didn't say anything to that. However positive it was that Sophie was alive, she wasn't sure this was a time to feel lighthearted, though she certainly understood why others tried to make light of horrible situations like this. It wasn't as though anybody actually enjoyed prodding and cataloguing dead bodies and bloody crime scenes.

Not anyone Dani knew on the right side of the law, anyhow.

With the situation under control, Dani didn't stay at the warehouse much longer. She'd already seen enough. The FSIs would once again do their painstaking work, and hopefully find the evidence to allow the police to tie Curtis to the scene. Dani had no real use there.

She re-congregated with Easton by the grocery store. He was already standing by her car waiting for her and had learned nothing much of interest from the shopkeeper. They were soon on their way to the hospital where word had come through that Sophie was able to take visitors, but at nearly five p.m. on a Friday afternoon, the traffic, so close to the city centre, was grinding to a halt in nearly every direction.

'Don't look so glum,' Easton said, breaking what had been an increasingly uncomfortable silence as they sat at a standstill with less than half a mile to go to their destination.

Dani hadn't thought she was looking glum, more pensive.

'We're closing in on him,' Easton said. 'He knows that too.'

'Which could just make him more ruthless. Or disappear altogether.'

'No. We're going to corner him.'

She hoped he was right, though she wasn't feeling quite so confident herself any more.

'Do you think he was staying there, at the warehouse?' Easton asked.

'I saw nothing to suggest that. No clothes, no food waste other than in the van. No mattresses or anything like that.'

'We need to figure out who owns that building and how it links to Curtis.'

'Yeah, but it looked pretty damn abandoned to me. Most likely he was simply squatting there.'

Another silence followed as they finally started to crawl forwards. Dani's mind wouldn't rest at all.

'I can't help but think about what Sophie's been through,' Dani said.

'She's still alive. That's the main thing.'

'But you didn't see that place,' Dani said, as another wave of bile rose up inside her. 'He had her chained in there. There was filth and blood everywhere. What on earth was he doing?'

Dani really didn't want to think about Sophie's ordeal, about how terrified she must have been, yet it was the *only* thing that she was now thinking about. Why had Curtis done that to her? He could have left her at Drifford House. He could have killed her at any point. Why did he keep her alive but imprisoned like that?

The dashboard on Dani's car lit up with an incoming call. Jason.

'Aren't you going to answer that?' Easton said after a few seconds.

Dani shook her head.

'Don't worry about me,' Easton said. 'I'll close my ears if you two want to say sweet nothings to each other.'

Easton smirked.

Dani really wasn't in the mood. The call, just like the last Jason had made twenty minutes ago, went unanswered. She expected he was home from his business trip by now, and that was the reason he was calling, to check where she was. After the abrupt end to their call last night, Jason had confirmed via text their plans to go to a newly opened bistro after work. Dani hadn't seen him all week, and until a few hours ago she'd been longing for him to return. But she felt jaded now, and as much as she wanted Jason to be there with her, to hold her and hug her, she really wasn't sure she was in the mood for nice food and wine tonight any more.

They arrived at the horrendously busy hospital and spent several minutes navigating their way around until eventually they found the corridor off from A&E where Sophie was being kept. Along the way they'd passed by a waiting area where Dani had spotted Sophie's parents huddled together on a bench, hands entwined as they stared at the floor. Both of them looked shell-shocked, relief not yet properly taking hold. Dani and Easton spent a couple of minutes talking to them. They'd been allowed to see Sophie earlier, but their poor daughter had been too drugged up at that point to enter into any kind of coherent conversation with them.

Despite the earlier call, Dani and Easton had to wait for nearly an hour before they finally got the go-ahead to see Sophie from the consultant in charge of the ward.

'She's only been awake a few minutes,' he said, as they stood outside the door to Sophie's room. His trepidation was apparent, but it'd also been made quite clear to him how serious the investigation was, and how urgent it was for the police to speak to Sophie in order to help catch the man who'd kidnapped her. 'She's likely to be confused, incoherent. If you need me at all, I'll be right outside.'

Easton thanked him before he and Dani stepped into the room and Dani closed the door softly behind her. As she looked over to the figure in the bed she had to hold back a gasp. Dani had seen plenty of pictures of Sophie these last few days. One in particular, which had been splashed all over the media, was ingrained in Dani's brain, and showed a smiley, carefree teenage girl, flowing blonde hair, lovely skin, bright and vibrant eyes. The young woman in the bed was unrecognisable. Her hair was matted and bushy. Her face was pulpy and swollen; her skin was blotchy; one eye was nearly closed it was so bruised.

'Sophie?' Dani said as she stepped forward. Sophie was upright in the bed, eyes closed, though she stirred at the sound of Dani's voice. 'My name's DI Stephens, from the police.'

Sophie groaned as she forced open her eyes a little. Dani sat in the plastic chair next to the bed. Easton remained standing and went over to the window where the curtains were open, letting in a swathe of natural light.

Dani was trying really hard to keep her emotions in check. Not just because of the thoughts of what Sophie had been through, but because of the rush of raw memories that were now filling Dani's head as she recalled her own period of hospitalisation following Ben's attack. Just the smell of the place, the sound of the machines and monitors, was enough to take her back to that dark time.

'Sophie, I know you've been through hell,' Dani said. 'We only need a few moments of your time today.'

Sophie's better eye opened a little further. She shuffled in the bed and grimaced in pain.

'I want... my... mum. Dad.'

'They're here,' Dani said. She wondered whether she should reach out for Sophie's hand. Would that give her more comfort and strength to talk? She didn't. 'We'll get them to come back in as soon as we're finished. Is that OK?'

Sophie nodded. Kind of.

'You wouldn't believe how much they've missed you,' Dani said.

A tear escaped Sophie's eye.

'Sophie, do you know what happened to you? Who took you?'

Her face quivered in terror, though she shook her head.

'You didn't know him?'

Another more definite shake this time. She wasn't lying, and this was what the police had always thought. There was no prior link between Sophie and Curtis. Nor between Oscar and Curtis. What the hell was going on?

'But you would recognise him?'

A nod. Easton came over and pulled out his phone. He held it out, the screen showing an image of Damian Curtis.

'Is this him?' Dani asked.

Sophie's face trembled now. She glanced at the picture then looked down, but she said nothing.

'Is that the man who took you?' Dani asked.

'Y-Yes,' Sophie said.

'His name is Damian Curtis. Do you know that name?'

A head shake.

'Do you know why he took you? What did he want?'

'He... wants to kill them. He wants to kill them all.'

Dani's heart skipped a beat at the connotations of that statement. What had Curtis told her?

'But he didn't kill you, Sophie. Why?'

She was sobbing now. Dani's phone vibrated in her pocket. She didn't bother to take it out. Was it Jason again?

'Sophie? He killed Oscar,' Easton said. 'You were there. Do you know why he did that?'

Sophie looked even more shocked now. Did she not know that Oscar was dead?

A few minutes of awkward and confused conversation followed. Dani had hundreds of questions for Sophie, mostly revolving around what she knew of Curtis's plans, where he now was, how they could find him and stop him from killing again. But it was clear enough that Sophie wasn't up to all of that yet. She'd been punished enough.

'Sophie?' Easton said.

Dani's phone was ringing again. She resisted the urge to take it out.

'I… just want… my mum.'

'OK, Sophie. We'll go and get your parents,' Dani said. 'Thank you for your time. You're one hell of a brave woman.'

For the first time Sophie's eyes met Dani's. She really wasn't sure what the look meant, but it was far from positive.

Dani got to her feet and she and Easton headed out. Dani took a deep breath as soon as she stepped out into the corridor, as though she'd just been through an ordeal herself.

'Go and get her parents,' she said to Easton.

He scooted off as Dani took her phone out. The last calls hadn't been from Jason at all but from DC Constable. He'd left a message too. Dani didn't bother to listen to it, just phoned him straight back as she watched Easton wander off down the corridor.

'Did you get my message?' Constable asked.

'I've not listened to it.'

'McNair gave me the list for witness protection to sort through.'

'You're hitting some roadblocks?'

'Yes and no, but with McNair's help I'm dealing with it.'

'So what was it then?'

'We identified all of the people from Curtis's trial, but McNair suggested we also look over his other records, including his arrest records, to see which other people are in there who could be relevant.'

'Sounds sensible.'

'Did you already know, then?'

Dani frowned. 'Know what?'

'The arresting officer the night of the car crash…' Dani held her breath as her brain whirred. 'It was Jason.'

Chapter Thirty-Two

I'm still angry as I sit in my van outside the house in Harborne. Angry at Sophie, angry at myself, angry at the police. I watched them outside the warehouse. Like cockroaches clustering and roaming and invading. That was my space. Mine and Sophie's. Now she's gone, and that place is gone too. The police have taken over, and I can never go back.

All because I trusted her.

When I saw the empty van, I knew I didn't have time to clean that place up. I had to believe that as soon as Sophie was found, the police would descend. And I was right.

Now it's time to get my own back on them all. The police think they're running the show here. I'm about to show them how wrong they are.

I watch him walking away from me. He didn't even glance at my van as he walked past. This might be my biggest challenge yet, quite literally, I realise. The guy is tall and muscled and in his prime, so I need to be careful, yet I remain confident that he'll be no match when the time comes. He turns a corner further down the road and heads away towards the high street. Fetching bread and milk, or some wine to share with his loved one tonight perhaps. Will she be back before or after the show I wonder?

This time the phrase the *more the merrier* really might be apt after all.

I check in the side mirror. The pavement outside is quiet. I open the van door and step into the sun-drenched street. I backtrack away from the van and just a few houses further along the road I open the gate and head up the drive. This could well be my easiest entry yet. The front door is aged and has two locks, but I know he didn't use the deadbolt, just the far easier to pick mortice lock. But I don't need to even do that this time. This house is on a busier street than the others I've been to recently, so I've made sure I'm even more prepared. Of course I always scope out beforehand; I like to roam around the homes of my tormenters when they're not there. It gives me a great sense of power. For this house, I've gone a step further still.

Anyone watching from their windows might see me as suspicious if they're familiar with the homeowners, but I act with such calmness that I'm counting on not drawing the eye. I head right up to the door with the key in my hand and within seconds I'm stepping inside. I shut the door behind me without once looking back.

Preparedness. It's the be-all and end-all for me. The owners have no clue that three days ago, after coming in the hard way, so to speak, I took a little souvenir for myself in the form of their spare key. Their spare key which is now back where I left it on my second visit to this house yesterday. The newly cut key in my pocket is my very own.

I take a deep breath and listen. The house is silent, just as I knew it would be. For now no one is home, but me.

I smile to myself then set off to find the perfect place to hide.

That perfect place to hide, I decide, is the kitchen. I'm sure he's gone to the shops. Perhaps the first thing he'll do when he comes back is to take a piss in the toilet under the stairs, but after that he'll be coming in here with whatever goodies he's just bought. I'm excited to find out what kind of night he had planned.

And I don't have to wait too long. A little over twelve minutes, to be precise, before I hear the clump, clump of footsteps coming up the drive outside, and then the slide and click as the key is pushed into the lock on the front door...

Chapter Thirty-Three

Dani's car had no flashing blue lights, no blaring sirens, but that didn't stop her racing through the streets from City Hospital and across to Harborne. At least the Friday evening traffic, with the time now approaching seven p.m., had died down some.

'He's still not answering,' Dani said, as yet another call went through to voicemail.

'What do you want to do?' Easton asked. 'We could get the blue lights there before us easily.'

Dani hadn't yet made that call. Yes it was possible, based on what Constable had found, that Jason was on whatever kill list Curtis had concocted, but he surely wasn't the most obvious next target, was he? He was the arresting officer all those years ago, not someone who'd been instrumental in the trial which had seen Curtis sentenced for manslaughter.

At least that's how she kept trying to reassure herself, yet she was still in a state of panic and didn't let up on her rapid drive across Birmingham.

She fiddled with the buttons in the centre console to ring Jason again. It rang through twice before it was finally answered.

Dani heaved a sigh of relief, but then two long seconds passed where all she could hear was heavy breathing and grim thoughts quickly took over once more.

'Jason?'

Her voice was high-pitched and panicked.

'Jason!'

'Dani? You OK?' Jason finally said.

'Where are you?' Dani asked.

'I've just walked in the door. Sorry, babe, I had a load of shopping, I couldn't get to my phone.'

'But you're OK?' Dani asked.

'Yeah?' he said, a little unsure. 'But you don't sound it?'

'I'll be home in a few mins. Jason, listen to me very carefully—'

There was a blip from the dashboard and the phone call disconnected.

'What the hell?' Dani shouted. 'Grab the phone, it's in my bag.'

Easton dug into the bag by his feet. 'Battery must have gone,' he said as he came back up with the phone in his hand.

'Got to be kidding me,' Dani said, hitting the steering wheel in frustration. 'Can you call him for me?'

'Dani, he's fine. Just try and relax, we'll be there in two minutes.'

But Dani couldn't relax, not even slightly. 'We can still call for back-up,' she said.

'Back-up for what? To help him put the cornflakes in the cupboard?' Easton said with a smile.

Dani knew Easton was only trying to lighten the mood, but his jibe only pissed her off.

'Jesus, Dani, stop!'

Dani thumped the brake. Tyres screeched and she weaved the car left and right, trying to keep control as the wheels lost traction. The car behind her honked as it nearly rammed them. The cyclist in front who'd pulled out on her stopped and stepped from his bike, pure nonchalance, as Dani's car jolted to a halt next to him.

'Are you blind or something!' he yelled at her.

'You bloody pulled out on me, you idiot!'

'Dani, let's just go.'

Dani was het up, and really wanted to give the guy a piece of her mind, but she relented and put her foot down to pull away. She checked in her mirror to see the cyclist disappear into the distance behind them.

If anything, the unwanted interlude had taken just a fleck of her anxiety away, and they made it to her road two minutes later, unscathed. Dani parked up in the spot directly outside her house. She looked up at her home as she stepped from the car. All was quiet and… normal.

'You want me to come in?' Easton asked as he got out.

'No, it's fine, wait here. I'll only be a couple of minutes, then I'll drop you off back at the ranch.'

'I can get the bus from here.'

'It's not a problem. Just give me two minutes.'

Dani left Easton hanging off her car and she headed up the drive. She unlocked and opened the front door and stepped inside.

'Jason?'

There was a bang from across the hall, somewhere in the kitchen.

'Dani!'

It was Jason. His voice was rushed and muffled.

'Dani. Run!'

The panic in his voice was clear. A muted thud followed. Dani stood frozen to the spot as the figure stepped into the doorway in front of her, blood dripping from the tip of the axe in his hand.

Damian Curtis.

Chapter Thirty-Four

Dani had no idea how long the moment lasted as her eyes locked with Curtis's. One second? Two? It felt like several minutes. And after the initial shock of what she was facing, in her own home, she found herself not staring at Damian Curtis at all, but at her brother, on that fateful night when he'd bludgeoned her and left her for dead. That night she'd been frozen to the spot, just like this. Panic, surprise, fear, all taking control and preventing her from properly defending herself.

She couldn't let that happen again.

Dani snapped into focus and launched herself forwards, roaring with determination as she did so. Curtis just stood there, a grin spreading across his bloodied face as he pulled the axe up above his head.

Dani was three yards from him when a shadow appeared in the kitchen behind Curtis. Jason. Covered in blood. He was coming forwards, towards Curtis, kitchen knife in his hand.

But Curtis must have sensed him. Or was it the movement in Dani's gaze which gave it away?

With the axe aloft, Curtis spun and drove down…

'No!' Dani screamed.

She barged into Curtis from behind and the stumble in his step meant the axe's blade jolted forwards and sliced across Jason's shoulder rather than bedding in. He yelped in pain, and his own momentum wavered as he drove forward the knife he was holding. It glanced across Curtis's side. Not even a groan of pain from him.

All three bodies collided haphazardly, and they fell to the ground in a tangled heap, both Curtis's axe and Jason's knife came free. Dani hit her head on the laminate floor. She was dazed, but not seriously hurt, but she also had no weapon. And Curtis was an animal. As Dani tried to find the strength to hit him and to pull away, Curtis bucked, spitting and growling as he threw out his fists and elbows at both Dani and Jason, who was barely mustering any response at all now. Dani took several blows as she scrambled backwards.

'Jason!' she screamed as she finally broke free.

In front of her, Jason was unmoving. He was covered in blood, head to toe, and it was impossible to tell what wounds he'd already suffered.

There was a bang on the front door behind Dani.

'Dani!' Easton shouted.

'Call back-up!'

'Fuck's sake, Dani! I'm coming in.'

There was an even louder thump this time, but the door didn't budge. Dani pushed herself another half yard back as Curtis got to his knees. The axe lay out of his reach in the kitchen. But the knife, the one Jason had wielded, was right there on the floor next to him.

Curtis, almost oblivious to Dani now, balled his fist and hammered it down onto Jason's exposed head.

'No!' Dani shouted.

Curtis smashed Jason's head again and again with his fist. Then he went for the knife.

'Get off him!'

Dani was back on her feet. She wasn't even thinking what she was doing now as she rushed forwards again. The knife was in Curtis's hand. He drove it into Jason's back. Once. Twice. Dani grimaced each time. The sound as the blade sliced into his flesh was horrific. Jason didn't even flinch.

Was he unconscious or dead?

Dani lifted her heel to smash it into Curtis's head. He pulled the knife out and turned. Slashed the blade across. Dani's foot connected with skull, but the blade sliced through her ankle. She gritted her teeth but tried to stay strong. The blow to Curtis's head didn't seem to deter him at all. He sprang upright as Dani tried in vain to adjust her stance and deliver another blow.

She simply couldn't outmanoeuvre him in time.

The uppercut from Curtis was a perfect contact and sent Dani's head spinning. Her legs abandoned her, and she plummeted to the floor.

'Dani!'

His voice was loud yet felt distant. Easton.

Another thud at the door. It still hadn't opened.

Dani's eyelids were heavy. She fought to stay awake as Curtis hovered over her. There was a snarl on his face, but he stared down at her almost with curious fascination. The blood-dripping knife was still in his hand, Dani realised. But she couldn't move. Curtis lifted his arm—

BANG

This time the door did open.

'Drop the knife!' came Easton's shout.

Dani was drifting, but she was sure she could hear the distant sound of sirens. Curtis didn't look in the least perturbed by his predicament. He lifted his hand and flung the knife. Dani didn't see where it landed, but the sound it made, and the sound Easton made, told her he'd been hit.

The next time Dani groggily closed then opened her eyes, Curtis was gone.

'Easton! Don't... let him get away!'

That was what Dani had thought at least, though she wasn't even sure if the words had passed her lips, and if they had, whether they'd been in any way intelligible given the state her brain was in.

A shadowy image of Easton hobbled over her, heading into the kitchen and after Curtis.

As hard as she fought it, moments later Dani finally succumbed, and her brain shut down.

Chapter Thirty-Five

'Dani.'

His voice was distant and weak.

'Dani, wake up.'

It was Jason. He was OK?

'Dani. Open your eyes.'

She felt his touch on her skin. It jolted her from darkness and her eyes sprang open as she lurched up gasping for air.

She expected to see Jason over her. She'd heard his voice so clearly, had felt his hand on her.

Yet she was simply staring up at the ceiling.

Sirens blared outside now. Blue light strobed across the hallway. She could hear footsteps rushing, getting louder by the second. Dani pushed herself up onto her elbows. Her head throbbed with pain and confusion.

'Jason!'

He was still lying on the floor across from her, in a heap, unmoving. No sign of Curtis or Easton.

How long had she been out for?

Dani dragged her body across the floor.

'Jason, please.'

She was sobbing by the time she reached him.

She put her arm on his shoulder. His T-shirt was thick with dark blood. In fact every inch of him was.

'Jason?'

She gently shook him, but there was no response. As carefully as she could, she moved him onto his back. His eyes were closed. There was no movement in his chest at all.

Dani heard shuffling up ahead, somewhere outside the open back door. Easton hobbled into view in the kitchen doorway, his face screwed in pain. His eyes met Dani's. He didn't even need to say it.

'I lost him,' he said. 'He's gone.'

And as Dani looked down to Jason, those exact same words took on a whole different meaning.

'Ma'am, let me see him.'

A calm, female voice. A paramedic rushed to Jason's side and dropped her weighty bag on to the floor next to him.

'Is he breathing?' the paramedic asked in a hurry as she felt around his neck for a pulse.

Dani looked to Jason's chest again. It remained flat and still, just like the rest of him. As tears flowed Dani said nothing, just slowly and abjectly shook her head.

But then she saw it. Just the tiniest of movements. Not in Jason's chest, but in the blood around his nostrils that pulsed ever so slightly in and out, the movement almost imperceptible.

Yet it was enough. Enough for hope. Curtis was gone. But Jason was alive.

Chapter Thirty-Six

Dani hated hospitals. Even before she'd lived in one for over a year following her brain injury, she'd never felt comfortable inside them. Her prerogative was always making sure she got out as speedily as she could. That was particularly the case this time. She, Easton and Jason had all been taken to A&E at nearby Queen Elizabeth Hospital, albeit Jason had been blue-lighted there and Dani hadn't seen him since. All she'd been told so far was that he'd been rushed straight into theatre.

That had been more than three hours ago.

Easton, with only a gash on his ankle from the knife Curtis had thrown, had already been discharged, but Dani was in a bed and had been through several series of tests already to try to determine the extent of her concussion, her previous history of brain damage meaning she was considered particularly high risk – even more so as she had a history of seizures, which she still took daily medication for, along with the raft of antidepressants.

'At least you got a bed,' Easton said as he pulled back the curtain around Dani's cramped space. He limped over.

'Take it if you want,' Dani said, before wincing in pain. The simple act of using her voice caused a tremor-like stabbing at the front of her head.

'Don't take this the wrong way, but you don't look too good,' Easton said.

'As good as I feel.'

Yet however poorly she felt, she couldn't think of anything worse than lying there.

'What news?' she asked.

'Nothing,' Easton said, hanging his head. 'Maybe if Curtis hadn't been some bloody knife-throwing circus freak aficionado I would have had a chance to catch up with him. He legged it over the fence, through the next garden onto Ivy Road. He carjacked some poor middle-aged woman.'

'I meant news on Jason,' Dani said.

'Oh. No, sorry.'

'But carry on.'

'They found the car just off Bristol Road, a couple of miles away, so he wasn't in it that long. From there, no one knows. He must have had another vehicle down there or something to have just disappeared like that.'

'So he's just vanished without a trace?'

Easton shook his head in despair. 'It seems that way. Obviously, we can try and track his movements as best we can on CCTV, but for now, we don't know where he is.' Easton paused for a few seconds, looking pensive. 'There's something else. His dad is missing.'

Dani shuffled up in her bed a little more. 'Go on.'

'We sent that request out to other forces earlier today... or was it yesterday? My brain's all screwed with the time now... what time is it?'

'Two a.m.'

'Yeah, anyway, he wasn't in his apartment at his place in the Peak District, but they found a lot of blood there.'

'So Curtis killed him but took the body? That doesn't match.'

'No. Like it didn't match that he killed Oscar who had nothing to do with his trial, and like it didn't match that he held Sophie hostage.'

And Dani still didn't like any of those apparent deviations from what otherwise appeared to be a simple case of vengeance. What was going on in Curtis's mind?

'I need to get out of here,' Dani said, raising herself from the bed. Easton reeled back, although he didn't look particularly surprised.

'I won't stop you,' he said. 'But are you really sure you're up to it? I mean, brain injuries and all that. You know more than anyone what it can do to you.'

'If my brain is more damaged now than before, then what can I do? They've given me all the medication they can. But Curtis is still out there, and I'm not going to lie in a bed while he carries on his killing spree.'

'I get that. But there are other coppers out there who can help to catch him too, you know.'

'So you're going to be taking a long holiday now, are you?'

'I didn't say that, but, Dani—'

'Easton, he was going to kill Jason. He could have killed both of us too.'

Easton said nothing to that. He stepped aside, and Dani pulled back the curtain and stumbled out into the ward. She took a few curious glances as she walked along with Easton, most likely because both of them had limps and bloodied clothes, but no one tried to stop them. But Dani wasn't leaving the hospital yet. She had to find Jason.

It took them nearly ten minutes of asking, with mostly unhelpful shrugs in response, before finally they found the post-op room he was being kept in. Under guard, Dani noted.

'In case you're wondering, we did have an escort too initially, but I sent them away,' Easton said as they headed along the corridor.

The uniformed officer sitting in the chair outside Jason's room stood up and held his ground as Dani and Easton approached. Dani explained who they were, and although reluctant, it seemed like he was about to let them through, until—

'Detectives, please.'

Dani turned to face the white-coated woman hurrying down the corridor towards them. When she reached them, Dani glanced to her name tag. Dr Ramachandran.

'He's only been out of theatre for an hour,' she said. 'He's not in any shape for you to see him.'

'Theatre for what?' Dani said.

Ramachandran sighed and looked as though she was building up to explain. 'A collapsed lung. Initially. The knife wound to his back went through the ribs and punctured his left lung. But we had complications too. While we were operating he suffered a cardiac arrest. Twice. There was a lot of internal bleeding as well, including on his brain. We had to operate immediately on that, or he would have suffered a fatal haemorrhage.'

Dani was lost for words. How the hell had Jason gone through all that and come out the other side alive? All the while she'd been sitting in a bed across the way while staff busied themselves about her damn cut leg.

'We've done what we can but he's too fragile for us to operate any more,' Ramachandran added.

Tears welled in Dani's eyes.

Easton put his hand to her shoulder. 'What are you saying?' he asked.

'He's in an induced coma, and on life support. But I have to be very clear, there's minimal brain activity and it's far too early to say if or when or how he'll recover. Right now we can't do anything more than wait and hope he improves sufficiently for us to be able to reassess next steps.'

'I want to see him,' Dani said, trying to block out the doom and gloom words.

'He won't be able to communicate with you at all, or even hear you. Please, I'll let you see him, but don't touch or disturb him. He's simply too fragile.'

Dani nodded, and Ramachandran stepped around and pushed open the door.

Blips and beeps and the whoosh and wheeze of the ventilator filled Dani's ears. It was an effort just to step inside the room, and she only managed one before she stopped as her eyes fell upon the figure in the bed in the darkened space. All that could be made out of Jason was one arm sticking out of the sheets – a catheter taped just above his wrist – and his neck and bottom half of his face, with his forehead and scalp covered in thick white bandages. His eyes were closed, and his face was puffy.

'I have to stay with him,' Dani said.

'Detective, it's really not going to help, I—'

'I'm staying with him. I can't go home and leave him here.'

Ramachandran huffed some but eventually relented and soon she was gone.

'Do you want me to stay too?' Easton asked.

'No,' Dani said. 'Go home and get some rest. You can pick me up in the morning.'

'Are you sure you'll be ready?'

'I need some sleep. We both do. And I'd rather be here with Jason than anywhere else tonight. But come tomorrow, we've still got a killer to catch.'

Easton said nothing. Dani didn't look at him. She'd made the position clear and she wasn't going to change her mind.

'OK,' Easton said after a few moments of silence. 'I'll see you in the morning.'

He turned and limped out of the room.

Chapter Thirty-Seven

The knife wound on my side hurt like hell a few hours ago, but with a few drugs in me the pain is all but gone now. I'm still enraged about it though. How fucking dare they do this to me?

I stitched and bandaged the gash myself. Perhaps not the best quality treatment one can get, but I know it's good enough, and I'm really not bothered about a bit of scarring if my needlework isn't up to scratch.

What I am bothered about is the fact that bastard stabbed me. And the fact he's still breathing.

Your mistakes are stacking up. I'm beginning to question if you're really up to this.

I'm up to it. And I'm adapting. That's all I can do.

First the bite: that has to be how they identified you so quickly. Then Sophie. Now this. Not just a mistake, but a failure.

It's not too late to make amends. And I will make amends.

I chose you because I thought you could handle this.

I can and I will handle this. In fact, I'm already planning my next move. And I'm still on top here, have no doubt about that. Look how easily I got away from them. And I'm not running. I'm staying right here to finish the job. I even did exactly what they would never have expected me to do. I dumped that little yellow car I'd stolen and then headed on foot all the way back to where I'd come from to collect my van. Just as I expected, they're not clever enough to spot me if I continually tweak my appearance. Act confident, act like you belong, that's a big part of it too, but even I'm surprised just how easy it was as I walked right past the house, right past the still milling ambulances and police cars, jumped into my van and drove off.

I get so much energy from being so close to them. Yes, I've had some pitfalls, but I feel I'm really perfecting this now, living like a ghost. They only know me, only see me, when I want them to. When I strike.

By which point it's too late.

Yes, the list should have shown one more tick tonight, there's nothing I can do about that now. It *will* come another day.

Day always follows night.

Death always follows life.

Tomorrow I start again. And there will be more blood.

Chapter Thirty-Eight

By Monday morning, Dani was at least feeling like the worst of her concussion had passed. Despite wanting to keep on the case twenty-four-seven, she'd spent many hours over Saturday and Sunday at the hospital, both to be with Jason, but also to continue her regimen of checks. The conclusion of the doctors, thankfully, was that her brain was fine. As fine as it could be anyway.

The same couldn't be said for Jason.

He remained in a coma, and the doctors were remaining tight-lipped as to when they were expecting to see any kind of improvement in his condition. Dani could literally do nothing but wait.

Yet the worst hours of the weekend weren't those spent uselessly by Jason's side, but those spent at home. The pain of being in *their* house, not just the place where she and Jason had made a life together, but the place where that life had been so violently interrupted, was both heartbreaking and harrowing.

Easton had offered to put Dani up, so too had Gemma. But Dani didn't want to run and hide. She would face this dark spell head-on, no holds barred, just like she had in the past.

McNair had insisted both Dani and Easton could take some time off to recuperate. The force with which Dani had rejected that idea had nearly caused a tremor across the whole West Midlands.

And so Monday morning rolled around and after a stuttering weekend it was time to get things moving again.

Top priority remained finding Damian Curtis, and an extensive team continued to work to that effect in the background at HQ and beyond, siphoning through whatever data they could get their hands on, knocking on doors here, there and everywhere. The police had also now been granted access to the Redfearnes' personal data, including phone, email and financial records, and a team were mobilising in HQ that morning to get started on analysing that data as it became available. The barrage of abuse from the Redfearnes' lawyers, Amanda Johansson in particular, had already started, but it was thankfully McNair's task to bat that back.

Dani and Easton had other places to be.

'Dani.'

The soft voice jolted Dani from her rumbling thoughts as she headed past her front gate towards her car. Naturally on edge, she'd already scoped out the street, looking up and down more than once as she'd walked down the drive, yet she'd not spotted the slim figure of Larissa Clarkson at all. Had she been hiding in wait?

Dani turned to face Larissa, who was all of five yards away on the pavement, but she also took a half-step back, so her hand was only an inch from her now open car door.

Larissa, head hunched down in a baggy hoody, was yet again bleary-eyed – the effect of continuous tears? Or was she now on something? As innocent a party as Larissa was in the horrific crimes of her father, Dani also knew Larissa had had a far from straightforward upbringing, had been something of a troublemaker, to put it lightly, and illicit drugs would certainly not be hard for her to come by given the people around her. Not that Dani could fault the young woman if she felt the need to turn to alcohol or drugs to get her through.

'Larissa, wh—?'

'I just wanted to say… I'm sorry… Sorry for turning up here the last time, surprising you.'

'Look…' Dani started, but she really didn't know what to say. The truth was she felt terrible for how she'd left Larissa in the lurch at court, and how she'd turned Larissa away from her home the last time; but then once again, Larissa being here, unannounced, just felt… wrong. 'It's just I've got so much going on. Please don't feel I've washed my hands of you now the trial's over. I still want to help you. If you want—'

'I only came to say goodbye.'

Dani paused. 'Oh?'

'That was it.'

'You're going somewhere?'

'I don't think I ever properly said thank you. For what you've done for me. So… thank you.'

'There's no—'

'Goodbye, Dani.'

Larissa turned on her heel and walked away. Dani was caught in the same quandary as before. Why did she feel so rattled all of a sudden, in the presence of this nervous and damaged seventeen-year-old?

Dani began to head on after Larissa. 'Wait.'

Larissa didn't let up.

'Larissa. Shall I buy you a coffee? We can talk.'

Dani increased her pace. But what was she going to do? Rugby tackle her if she didn't stop?

Then Larissa suddenly darted left, straight into the road. A black pick-up truck roared towards her. The horn blared, tyres screeched...

It missed Larissa by inches, but she just carried on, oblivious.

The driver gesticulated as he accelerated and headed on past. Dani took one step into the road to follow. Larissa, on the other side, turned to face Dani, causing her to pause once again.

Then Dani's phone rang.

She lifted it from her purse, barely taking her eyes off Larissa.

Easton.

But when she set her eyes back over to the other side of the road, Larissa had gone.

Dani shivered as she answered the phone.

'Easton?'

She realised how out of kilter she sounded.

'I'll be at yours in two minutes. Thought you'd appreciate a lift.'

Dani slumped. She'd been expecting something a bit more dramatic than that.

'I'll wait outside.'

—

An hour later Easton and Dani were left twiddling their thumbs in the reception area at Long Lartin prison, awaiting a chaperone. When the doors in front of them opened and Dani glanced over and saw the dull grey skirt and suit jacket of the person coming through, she immediately thought it was Deputy Governor Cartwright coming out to greet them, and she had to double-take when she saw the face attached to the clothes, and realised she was actually looking at Dr Collins, the psychiatrist.

The doctor seemed to do the exact same thing when she clocked Dani and Easton. She changed course to head over to them, though as she neared she looked about as comfortable as a cat in a swimming pool.

'Detectives, what a coincidence,' Collins said.

'Is it? If you ask me, the coincidence isn't you being here now, Dr Collins, but the fact that you're the psychiatrist for two killers who shared a cell. I'm still trying to figure that one out.'

Judging by the awkward look on Collins's face, she had no idea how to take that comment.

'I presume you've been here to see Ben?' Dani said. 'Unless you have a whole fleet of killers here under your watch.'

'And I presumed you were my two new security guards. You know I'm under twenty-four-hour watch now? There's an unmarked car sitting out there, some schmuck in there for my personal pleasure.'

'Under watch? He's there to protect you. You think it's a joke that Damian Curtis is out there getting his revenge on everyone involved in his trial? You should be glad we're taking this so seriously.'

'You think that's what Damian is doing? Seeking revenge?'

'Are you saying he's not?'

'Well, if that *is* what he's doing, I'd hardly be a target. I'm one of the few people who's helped him these last few years.'

'Then I'd be more than happy to ask my boss to remove any form of protection for you. If that's what you want?'

Collins was now glaring at Dani.

'Thought so,' Dani said. 'So you've just seen Ben, I presume?'

'A bit of an assumption on your part, but actually, yes. You're probably aware his legal team is continuing to work on his appeal.'

'And of course your input into that is going to be of the utmost importance, if they're ever going to get him off for the heinous crimes he committed.'

'*Get him off?* I'm really not sure what you're hinting at there, Detective. I don't dictate the laws of this land, and I do hope you're not bringing my professionalism into question. Again.'

'Of course not, Doctor.'

Dani realised Easton was squirming next to her, not sure whether or not to take part in the barbed conversation. He was better out of it, to be honest.

'I can only think that perhaps your rude and aggressive tone with me is related to your ongoing case, rather than my being here,' Collins said.

'My case?' Dani said. 'Curtis was *your* case, wasn't he?'

'He was my patient. Whatever happened to get him in, and out, of this place was outside my control and input.' Collins put her hands to her hips and huffed dramatically. 'You know, I only came over to say hello to you out of courtesy. I'm sorry for having done so.'

She went to move away.

'So what's your take now?' Dani asked.

Collins paused. 'On what?'

'On Ben? Is he sane or not?'

'It's not a simple question of insanity or otherwise.'

'But what's your verdict? You testified before that he wasn't in full control when he killed. When he tried to kill me. Is he in full control now? Is he no longer a threat to the public?'

'I haven't reached a full conclusion on that yet.'

'What about Curtis?'

Collins sighed. 'I haven't seen Curtis since his release; you know that already.'

'What would you have said about Curtis before his release? Was he no longer a threat to the public?'

'I can't deny the facts, and that for whatever reason it looks like he's seriously fallen off the rails.'

'You reckon?'

'I told you before, Curtis is very different to your brother. He's suffered mental health problems for much of his life.'

'Yet only now has he decided to become a homicidal psychopath. So why's that then?'

'Interesting choice of words, actually,' Collins said.

'What is?'

'Psychopath. You probably think you know what it means. You've seen plenty of movies, read books where there's a psycho on the loose. Someone who's mentally deranged and kills at will with no remorse.'

'You're saying that's not what a psychopath is?'

'Unfortunately not. There are a good many psychopaths who are exactly like that. The problem is, psychopaths are often the opposite of stupid.'

'Clever, would have been an easier way to put it,' Dani said, receiving a glower in response.

'Very funny,' Collins said. 'My point is, psychopaths aren't crazed lunatics, dribbling, speaking gibberish and rocking back and forth in a chair. Often they're charming, articulate, intelligent. They can come across as the most normal people in the world. But they simply don't think and don't feel like you or me. Love, even hate, fear, empathy, all of the human emotions most of us exhibit naturally, are simply traits they don't have. In fact they often learn to mimic emotions simply to allow them to *appear* normal. It's cold, and it's calculated.'

At those words Dani couldn't help but be reminded of her own mental misgivings. During her initial recovery from her TBI, she'd endured months of tests, scoring the lowest possible results for display of emotions. Her brain simply hadn't functioned like it had in the past. She still struggled now, though to a lesser extent. A lack of empathy, outbursts of anger that were uncontrolled even if they weren't exactly unprompted, were all signs of her ongoing less than perfect mental state. But had she really recovered from those initial dark days, or had she simply learned to mimic, just like Collins was suggesting psychopaths did?

'But remember,' Collins said, 'no psychopath sees themselves as such. They don't see themselves as bad, or for the monsters they are. In their own world, they are the hero.'

'So what you're saying,' Easton said, 'is that Curtis could have been a psycho all along, but he was pretending to be OK? Well, kind of OK, but not really... you know what I mean. Don't you?'

'Not really,' Collins said before she checked her watch. 'And I never said I was talking about Curtis, did I? Sorry, detectives, I really do have to leave.'

She turned and walked away, leaving Dani to ponder those unsettling words.

Chapter Thirty-Nine

A prison guard Dani hadn't met before arrived shortly after Collins had left, and led Dani and Easton through. When the guard opened the interview room door, Dani spied inside and saw Ben and his lawyer, Gregory Daley, sitting the other side of the table, nattering to each other quietly. They quickly stopped their discussion and looked expectantly to the new arrivals. Dani stepped in first but then stopped, partially blocking the doorway.

'Actually, Mr Daley, you're not needed today,' Dani said, matter-of-factly.

Daley looked perplexed, his nose twitched with indignation. 'Good morning to you too,' he said. 'I'm sorry, Detective, but that's really not your call to—'

'Ben. Tell him,' Dani said. 'Just you and me today. DS Easton and Mr Daley can keep each other company for a while.'

Ben sniffed as though he wasn't sure whether he was impressed or annoyed by Dani's blunt demand. Dani turned to Easton who looked a little bemused – she hadn't pre-warned him this was her plan – but she was confident he wouldn't go against her. Not now. Not after what had happened to her and Jason. She was doing things her way from now on. McNair would surely understand that too, even if she'd previously forbidden Dani from seeing her brother on his own. In a policing capacity at least.

'Ben?' Dani said, facing back to him.

Ben turned to his lawyer and mumbled something. Daley grumbled in response and started to shuffle the papers in front of him.

'Very well, we'll go along with your little game for now,' he said to Dani. 'But I'll be in the room next door, listening and watching.'

'Actually, no you won't,' Dani said. 'Easton will take you for a coffee. Courtesy of the public purse, unless you offer otherwise.'

Daley glared at Dani.

'It's fine, Gregory, really,' Ben said.

Daley said nothing more. He packed up his things and was soon heading towards Dani.

'Whatever you're playing at…'

He lost his train of thought, or perhaps just thought better about whatever threat he was about to deliver. He stomped past Dani and he and Easton disappeared. The guard shrugged before he closed and locked the door.

'I love it when you show your bitchy side,' Ben said, with a childish smirk on his face.

'Shut up, Ben,' Dani said. 'You and your lawyer might think this is a game, but I really don't.'

She took one of the seats opposite her brother.

'I knew you'd be back,' he said.

'Of course you did. You made sure of that by withholding relevant information the last two times I was here.'

He shook his head. 'I'm not a bad person, D—'

'Not a bad person? You're a fucking murderer!'

300

His eyes pinched with disdain. Any amusement she'd seen earlier was now entirely gone. 'That's not what I meant,' he said.

'I really don't give a damn what you meant. You know why I'm here. And this time I'm not taking no for an answer. Tell me what you know about Curtis.'

Ben didn't answer straight away. He held Dani's eye. Neither broke the contact. 'I think I made myself clear last time. I'll give you what I know when—'

'Damn it, Ben, people are dying! Don't you realise that? Don't you care? Innocent people who were just doing their jobs, who are going about their everyday lives, are dying horrible deaths because Curtis is on some insane mission.' Dani's words became more and more choked as she went on. She tried hard to push back the tears that were welling. 'He attacked Jason. Me too. I was there. I tried to save him… I don't even know if he's going to make it.'

No, it was no use. She wanted to be strong but there was too much raw emotion and tears were flowing. She didn't even attempt to wipe them away as they cascaded down her cheeks.

Ben said nothing.

Dani reached into her bag and took out her phone. She scrolled to the picture of Jason in the bed at the hospital. She could barely look at it. She pushed the phone across the desk.

'He's in a coma. On life support,' she said. Ben's eyes were still fixed on her. 'Look at him! Look at what Curtis did!'

Ben's gaze finally moved down to the phone. He only looked for a couple of seconds, before his eyes moved up again and he let out a big sigh.

'I'm sorry,' he said.

Sorry? Dani wondered. Sorry for what Curtis did? Or sorry for not talking and helping when he could?

'I had no idea you and Jason would become involved,' Ben said, shaking his head with what Dani took as genuine dismay. Or perhaps he was just a good actor.

What was it Collins had said about mimicry?

'But what do you know?' Dani said. 'You have to tell me. Do you really want more people to die?'

'Of course I don't! But I gave you the choice before, Dani. That was days ago. I gave you the choice and you showed your true colours. You don't give a shit about me.'

'That's not fair. I'm doing my job as best I can. I'm trying to save lives. I'm trying to catch a killer. You think I wanted to be in this position? With you? With Curtis?'

'Like I said, I had no idea you would become involved.'

'It doesn't even matter any more. What matters is that we find him. Can you help us or not?'

'I'm sorry, Dani. I honestly can't help with that.'

'Then what was the point of all this?'

Ben pondered that for a few seconds. 'I'm nothing like Curtis. You see me as some sort of monster; I can tell by the way you look at me, the way you talk to me. But I'm not. Curtis. He's a monster.'

'Yet you said he was never violent towards you, or anyone else here? So what do you mean?'

'I could always tell what lay beneath. You must have found out his background by now? He's had bloody voices in his head for years. He would sit on his bunk jabbering away like it was completely normal.'

'Saying what?'

'Just crap. Nothing sinister, but he was seriously messed up. But...'

'But what?'

'I always got the impression that before he was just talking to himself. If that makes sense.'

'Not really. You said he was hearing voices?'

'Yeah. That's what he told me. But when I listened to him talking, it was more like he was just chatting to different versions of himself. Like good conscience, bad conscience or something.' He must have noticed the perplexed look on Dani's face because his own expression turned sour. 'Look, I'm not a bloody trained psychiatrist. I don't know the ins and outs of these things or what any of it means. I'm just trying to explain what I saw and heard.'

'That's fine, I'm listening. I'm just trying to figure this out, same as you. You said that was what he was doing before, like there was a change?'

'Yeah there was a change. Maybe again, it's just the way I'm interpreting it, but... he started to talk to someone else.'

'Someone else?'

'Like not him. A real person. A she.'

'A she?'

'Are you a parrot or something?'

'Something.'

Ben tried to hold back a smile, Dani did too. This wasn't a time for joking, and inside she admonished herself for even attempting it, especially here, with this man.

'But he didn't want her in his head,' Ben said.

'How do you mean?'

'Well it was pretty damn obvious from what he said. "What are you doing here? Get out. Get out, you can't be here. You can't do this to me, go away." That sort of crap. I mean, at first, a couple of times I really thought there was someone else in the room with us. Hearing that sort of thing in the night when it's pitch-black, I even doubted myself a few times as to whether we were really alone. And he certainly thought we weren't.'

'Did she have a name?'

'Fuck knows. I wasn't ever about to try and join in the bloody conversation. Normally I'd shrink into my bed and hope he'd forget I was even here.'

'You're not messing with me?'

'No, Dani, I'm not.'

Dani thought about what Ben was saying. In truth, it didn't make a whole lot of sense to her. Except Ben was sure there had been some sort of change in Curtis's psychosis. But when exactly had that happened, and more importantly, what had caused it?

Really though, when she thought about it, did any of this even help in any way? Unless Ben could help them find Curtis now, what was the point?

'Seriously, Ben. Is this all you had?' she said, sounding as unimpressed as she felt. 'Your interpretation of a madman who talked to multiple people in his head?'

Ben looked pissed off now.

'Of course he's batshit crazy,' Dani said, sounding agitated and determined to push Ben's buttons. 'Look at what he's doing! You've waited all this time, while people are getting slaughtered, and this is all I get? Some

304

half-baked story about Curtis rambling to his alter ego. This is fucking pathetic.'

Dani went to stand up.

'You want more?' Ben said, practically baring his teeth like a dog. He was angry. Inside, Dani was pleased. An angry Ben was far more likely to give up what he knew. 'How about this? He killed them that night.'

He looked pleased with himself now, though the anger was clearly still there.

'Who?' Dani said.

'Who do you think? His girlfriend and her son.'

'Yeah, and that's why he was sent here. What's your point?'

'No. He was sent here for manslaughter. But he killed them.'

'He crashed the car deliberately, you mean?'

Now Ben looked impressed with himself. As though this was the moment he'd been waiting for.

'No. The crash didn't kill them. He did. He stepped from that mangled wreck and finished them both off with his hands.'

'He told you this?'

Ben nodded. 'He was drunk and high that night. He was in a rage; he wanted them dead. That's what he told me. Whether or not or how he was going to do it, who knows. But after the accident, he saw the opportunity.'

'Jesus, Ben. You knew this and you held on to it?'

'No. I offered it to you before. You refused.'

'That's not how it was.'

'That's how I saw it. And I'm telling you now because I realise you'd never come through for me. You couldn't care less about me. But I'm doing the right thing.'

Dani shook her head in disbelief. Though was it at Ben for his actions, or at what Ben was saying about Curtis?

'But you still said it was an accident,' Dani said. 'So he hadn't crashed deliberately to try to kill them?'

'An accident, yeah. He was pushed off the road.'

Dani's brain whirred now as she tried to recall the details of the reports she'd read from that night.

'There weren't any other cars involved in the crash,' she said.

'He crashed headlong into a parked van,' Ben said. 'But it was the other car that caused it to happen.'

'What other car? There was no other car.'

Ben turned his palms over and shrugged. 'I'm just telling you what he told me. The other car caused that crash, nothing to do with him. As far as he's concerned, everything bad in his life stems from that moment. And he's been waiting for his chance to get his revenge ever since.'

Chapter Forty

'Why don't we get a psychiatrist to help us here?' Easton said as they drove along the A435 back towards Birmingham. 'Like... Cracker or whatever he was called?'

Memories flashed in Dani's mind at the mention of the name. She'd loved that TV series when she was younger. As teenagers she and Ben had sat watching it together on the sofa at home, back when life had been so simple. In fact she'd loved anything detective or mystery related, always trying to get one step ahead as the plot unfolded on screen or on the page. It perhaps explained why she'd been so bent on joining the police herself.

She pushed the fond childhood memories away.

'For what purpose?' Dani said.

'To figure out what the hell is going on with Curtis.'

'Firstly, we don't have access to Curtis.'

'Not directly. But we have Dr Collins?'

Dani thought about that one for a moment. Ben had talked about Curtis's psychosis, the voices in his head.

A thought struck her. Dani reached for her phone.

'Dr Collins?' she said when the doctor eventually answered, sounding a little flustered. Background noise suggested she was driving. 'It's DI Stephens again.'

'Detective. Everything OK?'

'Are you busy? We'd really like to speak with you again.'

Collins, sitting back in her office chair, once again looked put out by Dani and Easton's presence. Was she like this with everyone? Perhaps it was because Collins saw Dani as her natural opponent, given that she continued to be part of Ben's defence team.

But was that all she was?

'Curtis is psychotic, yes?' Dani said.

Collins frowned and fidgeted in her seat. 'It depends; exactly what do you mean by that term?'

'You're the trained psychiatrist. You know what it means. He's been suffering psychosis for years, right? Hearing voices. Communicating with voices.'

Collins nodded. 'That's correct.'

'So where do these voices come from?'

Collins sighed and looked to Easton then back to Dani. 'That's such an open-ended question it's almost impossible to answer.'

'Pretend you're on the witness stand,' Easton said.

'I'd say exactly what I just said.'

'You can do better than that,' Dani said.

'If you were more specific, perhaps I could—'

'Who is Curtis communicating with?' Dani said. 'In his head. You analysed him. So who are these people?'

Collins sighed again. 'To put it simply, they're figments of his imagination.'

'Does he take instruction from these people? Do they affect his behaviour?'

'In a roundabout way, yes. In a legal sense, no.'

'Meaning?'

'Meaning there's a significant difference between psychosis, which Curtis exhibits, and dissociative identity disorder. Are you familiar with that?'

'Humour us,' Dani said.

'Very well. The latter, or "split personalities" as you might have heard it referred to, is where a person exhibits multiple distinct personalities that inhabit the same body and mind but at different points. These distinct identities rarely, and sometimes never, communicate with each other. DID can lead to extreme cases because some of these personalities genuinely have no knowledge of the actions of the other. So what if one of the identities commits a crime? Who do you punish?' Collins paused for a few moments as if to let her words sink in. 'But regardless, that's not Curtis at all. There is only one *identity* at the fore. His. All of his actions are carried out consciously by him. Yet it's true that he might have felt compelled to act in a certain manner because of the voices he hears.'

'Then what about this new voice?' Easton said.

Collins paused again. Her eyes narrowed.

'What new voice?'

'Ben told me there was a new voice,' Dani said. 'Curtis was talking to a woman, in his head. Someone he was battling with, who wasn't there before.'

Collins sighed. 'There was more than one woman he heard. His mother was the loudest—'

'No. Not his mother. I imagine she would have been long-standing, correct?'

'Correct.'

'I'm talking about someone new.'

Collins sat back in her chair, a ponderous look on her face. 'Yes, I think I know who you mean. Curtis did mention her to me.' Another pause. Another sigh, as though Collins was struggling to figure out how to explain it. Or just to figure out what she was prepared to tell. 'Honestly, I know very little. You need to understand I never got to view footage of him in his cell on a day-to-day basis, so I rarely ever got to see him talking to any of these people for any length of time. I was only able to help him with what, who, he opened up to me about.'

'But you're saying he did talk to you about *her*,' Easton said.

'I was aware of her, yes.'

'And?'

'And I don't know what to say. There's no name. There's no identity or personality as such. I already said this isn't a case of DID. In reality, it's little more than an echo. But I knew she, this new voice, was becoming more dominant, by which I mean he was hearing it more often, and that he personally didn't like her.'

'In what way?'

'She aggravated him, put him down. There was nothing sinister about it, about her, though. At least no more than any of the other voices he'd heard for years.'

'Could she have caused him to kill?' Easton asked.

Collins shook her head forcibly. 'I really can't say, I've not—'

'Just a simple yes or no,' Dani said. 'Could this voice, or any of the other voices, have forced, coerced, or cajoled Curtis into killing?'

'You're asking for—'

'I'm asking for a yes or no. That's it.'

'Yes! The answer is yes. Of course a voice in his head can have an influence on his actions, so yes.'

'Do you believe that's what's happened here, with Curtis?'

'I can't answer that.'

'I'm sure you could.'

'But I'm not going to, based on the little direct evidence I have.'

'Then how about this one. Again, a simple yes or no, then I promise we'll get out of your hair. Is it possible that someone, a real person, introduced that voice into Curtis's head?'

The silence that followed seemed to go on for an age. Collins didn't blink the whole time, her hard glare fixed on Dani.

'Dr Collins?'

'Yes. It's possible.'

Dani's mind brimming with thoughts and half-baked theories, she and Easton were soon heading on foot back from Collins's office to HQ.

'Where are you going with this?' Easton said as they strolled along Colmore Row, past St Philips Cathedral. A cluster of pigeons shot up from the grass beyond the fence and Dani, still on edge, jumped at the sudden noise of dozens of flapping wings.

'Maybe I'm reaching here, but what if that voice is the answer?' she said.

'To Curtis killing?'

'He wasn't a killer before, he——'

'Actually, according to your brother, he *was* a killer before he went to jail.'

A fair point actually, and they really needed to get to the bottom of Ben's claims.

'Yet the man who came out of prison is still a different, more violent beast to the one that went in,' Dani said. 'What if it wasn't prison that changed Curtis, but *someone*?'

'Collins? You think she introduced that voice into his head? Is that where you're going with this? Why the hell would she do that?'

'Which is exactly what we need to find out.'

–

Once back in the office, Dani first called to update McNair on both the morning meeting with Ben, and the subsequent meeting at Collins's office. Thoughts tumbling in her head, she and Easton were soon headed to the newly set-up project room to brief the team and catch up on progress. Easton was left to delve into the forensics findings, while Dani sought out Grayling and Constable who were sitting next to one another in the far corner.

'I need you to take a look in HOLMES for any files relating to Curtis's manslaughter case,' Dani said to Grayling.

'You have those already, don't you?'

'I think so, but can you double-check, make sure there's nothing we've not picked up? Maybe there's something that's been misfiled, so set up a keyword search.'

'Is there something wrong?'

'Very possibly.'

Dani briefly explained what Ben had said about Curtis, and the need to figure out as much as they could about the circumstances of the crash that he'd been jailed for. She also explained about the meeting with Collins, the voices in Curtis's head. Easton headed over to join in.

'One major issue I still have is how the Redfearnes became involved here,' Dani said. 'Curtis is out for revenge: that makes some sense, but Oscar had nothing to do with Curtis or the trial from what we can see.'

'Nor does anyone else have anything to gain from Curtis's killing spree,' Easton said.

'What?'

'You were suggesting someone put that voice in his head to cause him to change into this deranged killer, that it might even have been Collins who did that. But what's the motive? What does she, or anyone else gain from these deaths?'

Which was a great question. And one that Dani had no answer to at all.

'We'll search through everything to find the answer,' she said. 'We have access to the Redfearnes' records now, so we need to identify any reference to Curtis or Collins, however small or seemingly insignificant.'

Easton didn't seem satisfied, but Dani turned away and moved over to Constable, who remained neck-deep in CCTV searches, his task widening exponentially each time Curtis struck.

'What have you got?' Dani asked.

'Plenty of images that could be Curtis at various points,' he said, 'though I'm not altogether sure what to do with it all.'

He flicked around various windows for a few seconds.

'So in Winson Green,' he said, 'I've managed to track the moments around when Sophie escaped. We can see her coming onto Butler Street here.'

Dani watched the jumpy image as the young woman, grimy and jittery, came into view, shuffling along the street, looking nervously over her shoulder every other step.

'And we have her from this angle too,' Constable said, switching to another view showing Sophie from the back. 'I've been going out from this time bit by bit, both before and after, to see if I can pick out Curtis. I've not yet come across him prior to Sophie's escape, but then I found this.'

He scrambled around for a few more seconds before opening another file. He hit play. It was the same camera as before, which had showed Sophie's back.

'This was about twenty minutes after Sophie was found. She'd already been taken to hospital by this point, and the police first responders were still on the scene.'

Dani stared at the screen. The marked police car in the near distance, outside the grocery store, was clear enough. She glanced down to the timestamp. She and Easton hadn't arrived until sometime after, not until Sophie had been identified and the alert passed to them.

'Across the other side of the road, there,' Constable said, pointing to a dark figure on the screen.

Dani kept her eyes on the figure. Wearing dark jeans, a black T-shirt and with a baseball cap pulled over his head, he was pretty innocuous and certainly not easily identifiable.

'You can see him glancing at the police car a couple of times. Then when he's past it he crosses the street...' Constable hit pause. 'This is about the best shot we've got of his face.'

Was it Curtis? Dani didn't really know.

'Then if we move to the next camera, we see him heading down Malvern Road towards the warehouse, the same way Sophie had come from.'

Dani shook her head.

'He walked right past the police,' Dani said.

'He may not even have had an idea at that point why they were there.'

'We were only minutes away from getting him.'

If Sophie had been identified by the first responders sooner would it have made a difference?

'Can you trace where he came from?'

'Unfortunately not. There are too many dark spots once you get past the shops.'

Dani supposed it was an interesting enough find, further evidence pinning Curtis to a crime scene, but it really didn't help much in actually tracking him down.

'But,' Constable said. He typed away, opening and closing windows. 'On your street…'

Dani gulped as images of Friday night flashed in her mind.

'I've done a lot of work trying to trace his movements after he dumped that stolen car, and I'm pretty sure this is him.'

Dani's eyes narrowed as she focussed on the figure now on the screen. The clothes didn't quite match. Curtis had been in jeans and T-shirt in her house, but this figure had a jacket and a cap on. But the size and shape certainly fitted.

'Where is that?' Dani said.

'Argyle Road.'

Dani had thought so, but that meant… 'He's coming up the hill towards Ivy Road.' She glanced down to the timestamp again. This was over an hour after he'd scarpered from her house.

'I know,' Constable said. 'And I lose him soon after, and there aren't any cameras on your street, but it looks like—'

'He was returning to the scene.' But why? Then she got it. 'He had a vehicle?'

'I reckon so, yeah. And I've done a bit of digging, and don't ask me how I got here, because I really don't know, but I've managed to tie the same van, on different occasions, either in Harborne, near your street, or in Winson Green, near that warehouse.'

Constable brought up another file, scrolled through the video and hit pause. A blue Ford Transit van, facing towards a camera. The driver's head was obscured by the glare on the windscreen, but the number plate was clear enough.

'Do you have any clearer than that?'

'Not really. But it's either a big coincidence, or I think this van could be him.'

'You've run the registration?'

'It's a fake. Not registered.'

'Shit.' That really didn't get them anywhere, other than perhaps adding weight to this being Curtis.

'How many blue Ford Transit vans in this city?' Dani asked.

'Hundreds probably. Thousands even. What do you want to do?'

Dani thought for a few seconds. She knew one thing. They couldn't take risks now. 'Get an alert out for that reg. As wide as you can. And after that keep digging. Trace that van's movements as much as you can from what you have access to. If you map out its most common routes, we should be able to narrow down where it's coming from, and where Curtis is at. At the very least it should point us to the right area.

Dani's thoughts turned back to her meeting with Ben, and what he'd said about the crash. Why had Curtis never mentioned in his police interviews that there was another car that night? And why had whoever had been in that car never come forward as a witness?

She had a thought and turned back to Grayling.

'The road the crash happened on... Clement Hill, right?' Grayling nodded. Dani turned back to Constable. 'Are there cameras on Clement Hill?'

'Give me a second.'

Constable took more than a second, but he was still pretty damn quick.

'No. Never been any. But there is a tower on Shortland, not far from the junction with Clement.'

'How long's it been there for?'

'No idea. Not all the records are readily accessible.'

'OK, then please find out. Try and pinpoint Curtis's car that night, the Corsa I mean, and any other vehicles that were in the area immediately after, heading away from Clement Hill.'

'But what exactly is it you're looking for?' Grayling asked.

'The ones who got away. And very possibly the whole reason why Damian Curtis is now out for revenge.'

Chapter Forty-One

The house in Rugeley, Staffordshire was large and modern and bland, much like all of those on the small estate of new-builds. Dani wasn't massively familiar with the area, though judging by the deluge of BMWs and Mercedes and Audis parked outside the houses, it was distinctly middle-class. She pulled up behind the police patrol car that was sitting outside number twelve, and was about to get out when her phone rang. It was Constable.

'You found something?' Dani said hopefully.

'You were right. There was another car.'

'You got it on CCTV?'

'Yeah. There's no other explanation. At the least, it had to have passed by the crash site, certainly before any police or paramedics were there. The timing works exactly.'

'Was the registration visible?'

'It was, and I've already run it.'

'And?'

Constable gave the name. Just as Dani had suspected. Finally much of the case was making a little more sense. Which was good, because it was confirmation that her decision to split up and send Easton off in the opposite direction was the right call.

Dani thanked Constable and asked him to continue digging before she ended the call and stepped out of her car. She had a brief chat with the police officer sitting in the car in front, who looked and sounded bored silly, before she headed up the short drive to the house. Three minutes later she was seated in the bright yet sparse open-plan kitchen-diner at the back of Oliver Waite's house, waiting for her machine coffee.

'I feel like a prisoner in here,' Waite said as the fancy-looking contraption on the sleek countertop gurgled away, steam rising up from the spout.

'The sooner we catch Curtis, the sooner your life can return to normal. And I don't think anyone said you can't leave.'

'Maybe they didn't, but what would you do in my position? Would you want to be out there while that madman is on the rampage?'

'Technically, that's exactly what I'm doing,' Dani said. 'And I don't want to alarm you further, but actually all of Curtis's victims so far have been attacked in and around their homes. Perhaps outside is safer after all.'

Waite shot Dani a look which was somewhere between fear and animosity. The machine finally stopped, and Waite grabbed the mug and splashed a little milk in before he headed over. Dressed in jeans and a baggy hoodie that did little to hide his obvious flabby bulk, Waite was unshaven with messy hair. Dani could scarcely believe this man was an experienced defence lawyer. She was sure she'd seen him before down at the courts in Birmingham; she'd certainly recognised his name at least, but seeing him today he was nothing like the man she'd expected.

'Your wife isn't home then?' Dani said, glancing to a picture of a blonde woman caked in thick make-up. Waite took a seat at the opposite side of the glass dining table to Dani.

'She doesn't live here any more,' he said. He didn't expand on that and Dani wasn't going to pry. Perhaps their divorce or separation or whatever it was partly explained Waite's new look.

'So what can I do for you, DI Stephens?'

'I need to talk to you about Damian Curtis.'

'I kind of gathered that.'

'You headed up his legal team.'

'I was assigned his case. He couldn't afford to pay for his own lawyer. I'm sure you understand how Legal Aid works.'

'So you're intimately familiar with his case and trial?'

Waite looked unsure about that question. 'You could say that.'

'One thing I struggle to understand is what happened?'

'What happened how?'

'With his case. I mean, looking back now, what you knew, the evidence you had from Dr Collins as to Curtis's mental health issues, why on earth did you settle for a voluntary manslaughter conviction?'

Waite looked agitated already, as though he felt Dani was challenging his professionalism. Which, in a way, she was.

'I think you're mischaracterising both how legal representation works, and also how a murder trial works.'

'I am?'

'Given the events leading up to that crash, the arguments he and his girlfriend had, the fact he was high on booze and drugs, Damian Curtis was charged with murder. That was nothing to do with me. You'd have to speak to the CPS about that, but it was quite clear to me that what happened that night was nothing but a tragic accident. He never intended them dead.'

'Is this you speaking in a personal capacity or as an advocate for Damian Curtis?'

'It's just me speaking. Curtis was entitled to representation, same as anyone else. I did what I felt was the best job I could for my client, backed up by a very respectable barrister.'

'Kenneth Feathers. Who's now dead.'

'I'm well aware of that, Detective.'

'And our theory, which is unfortunately playing out more times than we'd wish, is that Curtis is on some sort of mission of revenge. Which would itself suggest that perhaps Curtis doesn't quite agree that whatever you and Feathers and others did for him *was the best job*. From his perspective at least.'

'God knows what's going through his mind, but I honestly have no idea why he feels in any way compelled to try and punish Feathers, or me or anyone else who was trying to *help* him.'

'But why did you settle? You said yourself you didn't think he tried to kill them. So why not go for death by dangerous driving? Why not involuntary manslaughter, or voluntary manslaughter through diminished responsibility and have him in a hospital, where perhaps you'll agree now is where he belongs?'

Waite glared at Dani as she took a casual sip from her mug. It was a damn good coffee actually.

'I get the sense you're trying to get under my skin,' Waite said. 'Though I don't really know why.'

'Why? Because we have a man on the loose who is mentally deranged, who's killed multiple people in just a few days—'

'Allegedly.'

'Allegedly? Are you serious?'

'He's not been brought to trial for these crimes, has he? You might be happy to jump to a conclusion but it's not something I ever do.'

'OK, whatever. I've jumped. He's a murderer. He tried to kill *me*.' Waite squirmed a little at that. Had he not known? 'And I have to ask myself, why on earth was this man back on the streets?'

'Which again is not a question for me. That's a question for the parole board.'

'Except you were the one who put his case forward to the board.'

'I represented my client.'

'And look where that's got us.'

'If you're trying to suggest—'

'I'm not suggesting anything. I'm trying to understand why a man was convicted of voluntary manslaughter through loss of control when the evidence of his own legal team showed he was clearly mentally unstable.'

Waite sat back and let out a long sigh.

'I really don't know what you're trying to achieve here,' he said.

'I think you do. I think you just don't like how your actions have come back to bite you.'

He gritted his teeth. Dani could tell by the small pulse in his jaw.

'My client was facing a charge of murder,' Waite said. 'He didn't deserve that. Given the circumstances, it was a trumped-up charge, but the CPS were gunning for Curtis from the start, and I really don't know why.'

'Perhaps because he killed two people.'

'It was a road traffic accident. How many times are you aware of where the CPS has charged for murder after a road traffic accident?'

Dani didn't answer. She wasn't sure Waite really cared to know.

'The CPS set their stall out, and we had to pull them down,' Waite said. 'There was no denying that Curtis was present that night, so we couldn't move to acquit. I apologise if you know all this, but it seems like I need to set it straight for you. There are partial and complete defences to murder. An example of a complete defence would be self-defence, but that clearly wasn't applicable here. Diminished responsibility, on the other hand, is only a partial defence for murder, as is loss of control, and both lead to a sentence for voluntary manslaughter. The former refers to a defendant's underlying mental state, if you like, the latter to a moment in time when they... lost it.' Waite shrugged at his own apparent lack of eloquence. 'A severe provocation from a partner, for example, could be deemed loss of control based on the particular circumstances.'

'Which is essentially what Curtis was convicted of in the end, and it's a charge which carries a long custodial sentence, as opposed to him being placed in a mental health facility.'

'It was a position we negotiated with the CPS outside the courtroom. If we'd pushed through with the trial to conclusion would we, with Dr Collins's largely uncontested expert testimony, have persuaded the jury of diminished responsibility? It's possible. But Curtis could also have been convicted of murder and locked up for the best part of the rest of his life. We took what was offered, which we knew would see Curtis spend a few years behind bars.'

Dani shook her head at the matter-of-fact manner in which Waite was talking about the legal process, like it was all a game of chess, rather than a pursuit of justice.

'The only difference, as you pointed out, is if we'd succeeded with the diminished responsibility argument, Curtis would have likely spent his time in a mental health facility rather than in prison.'

'Which, wouldn't you say, given where we are now, was exactly what he needed?' Dani said.

Waite shrugged. 'That's really not for me to answer. I'm a defence lawyer, not a medical doctor, and he had plenty of oversight at Long Lartin.'

Yeah. From Dr Collins. What was the truth about her role in subsequent events?

'It's my job to give clients the best representation I can,' Waite said. 'And it's their right to have representation. My conscience is clear, in relation to this case, and every other I've been involved in.'

Though the way he said it made it sound as though it wasn't the case at all. Or was that just that he was now shit-scared that he might be on Curtis's kill list?

'And I'll state again,' Waite added, 'that Curtis received constant psychiatric assistance at Long Lartin, which was key to his parole application. It's not like he was locked up and the key chucked away.'

'Yeah but what good did it do?' Dani asked, kind of rhetorically.

'Who's to say we wouldn't have had this exact same outcome even if he had been in a mental hospital the last few years?' Waite said. 'The point is, Detective, the man out there killing now is not the same man I represented.'

Which was the most worrying part still to Dani. What the hell had happened? Where had this new voice in Curtis's head, and by extension the new Curtis, come from?

'Tell me about the other car,' Dani said.

The sudden change of course had the desired effect. Waite looked jittery, though was trying his best to contain it. Not a reaction of someone who had no clue what Dani had said, but of someone who felt they'd been rumbled.

'What car?' he said.

Dani took pause while she nonchalantly sipped her coffee, letting Waite stew, his agitation growing by the second.

'The night Curtis crashed,' Dani said, 'killing his girl-friend and his son, there was another car at the scene. Another car that Curtis claimed pushed him off the road.'

'I don't know where you've got that—'

'From Curtis himself actually.'

Waite's eyes narrowed as he stared at Dani.

'What I don't get is what happened to that evidence,' Dani said. 'Whether or not that car caused the crash, anybody in another vehicle in the vicinity that night was a potential witness. But your team called no one in that regard at trial, and there's certainly nothing in the police files about it.'

Still Waite didn't say a word. Dani felt he was about to shut the conversation down once and for all. Why was he so desperate to hide this?

'And I do recognise that you weren't assigned his case until a couple of days after his arrest,' Dani said, 'so likely you didn't get the process started of making that evidence go away. So who did?'

Waite shook his head. 'You've lost me.'

'I don't think I have. *Why* was that evidence buried? Did they pay you off? Is that it?'

Dani looked around the room now, in mock admiration.

'Probably not all to my taste,' she said, 'but this is a pretty damn nice house for a Legal Aid lawyer.'

'You f...'

Waite shook his head angrily, his body was tense. He looked like he wanted to explode.

'Is that all you've got to say for yourself?' Dani said.

'Get out of my house.'

'Let me put it for you this way. Screw legal privilege to your murderous client. Unless you convince me otherwise, I'm arresting you right now. Obstruction of justice for starters. But how about assisting an offender too? What else? I wonder even whether conspiracy to murder could fit, under the circumstances.'

'This is absolute nonsense. How dare you—'

'Curtis killed them, didn't he? After that car crash he throttled his girlfriend and her son to death.'

'Whatever you think you know, you're wrong. Everything I did was above board.'

'Then tell me what you did.'

Waite was silent again.

'On the one hand, making that evidence go away helped Curtis, right?' Dani said. 'He was convicted of manslaughter, not murder. You probably thought you'd done a great job for him, given you *knew* he killed them. But the biggest question I have was why did that witness not come forward themselves? What were *they* trying to hide? Though I can take a good guess as to *how* it was made to appear they were never there at all.'

'You've lost me now.'

'I don't think I have. Money. Money and political clout. Something which a family like the Redfearnes has in spades.' Dani paused as she waited, hoping, for a response. None came, though Waite looked anything but confident now. 'Henry Redfearne was the witness, wasn't he?'

Now Waite did look genuinely confused, and Dani stumbled slightly. What had she got wrong? She felt as though she'd had Waite the whole way there, right up until that last moment. She'd long wondered whether Oscar Redfearne was killed as a means of punishing his father, and that theory had been given great weight just a few minutes earlier when Constable had confirmed it was a Mercedes belonging to Henry Redfearne that had been at the crash scene that night.

'Henry Redfearne was the witness,' Dani said, trying to sound as convincing as she could. 'He caused that crash, but he also saw Curtis murder his girlfriend and her son right after. As far as he was concerned, Curtis deserved what he got, and Redfearne used his lawyers and his money to have his involvement buried. Because he couldn't bear the thought of having his name and reputation dragged through a court case, regardless of whether or not it was his fault.'

'I've never met Henry Redfearne in my life,' Waite said. 'I've had no dealings with that man whatsoever.'

He looked a little smug now, which really was quite something under the circumstances.

But then Dani got it. Waite wasn't lying. What had Pamela said about the true head of the family? Sometimes the most obvious explanation was the right one.

'Oscar Redfearne was the driver,' Dani said. 'That's why he was the target. Not punishment of his family, but because Oscar had caused that crash. 'But... he would have been, what? Fourteen? Fifteen?'

Waite chose the silent treatment again, though the confidence was draining from his face once more.

'And it was Caroline Redfearne, not her husband, who pulled the strings to get any reference of her son being there that night wiped away,' Dani said, thinking out loud.

Waite said nothing, though the answer was clear enough by the sunken look on his face.

Dani got to her feet.

'Oliver Waite, I'm arresting you on suspicion of obstruction of justice...'

–

Dani was back in her car five minutes later. She'd left the disgraced lawyer in the hands of the rather confused officer from the patrol car outside Waite's house. At least the policeman had something more interesting to do now than to sit in his car all day long. Dani would follow up with him, and with Waite, later. For now, she had a much bigger priority.

'Easton, are you still at Drifford House?' Dani asked when he finally answered his phone at the fourth time of her calling.

'Yeah, sorry about that. I was in with Henry. He's getting pretty arsey with me here. I think I've just about outstayed my welcome. What do you want me to do?'

Easton's intent had been to keep Henry busy long enough until Dani made the decision whether or not to arrest him, but more importantly because if Henry was the man involved in that crash, it would mean he remained a target for Curtis, and so far the Redfearnes hadn't been provided any police protection. But it wasn't Henry who needed to answer questions about that night, nor who needed protection.

'It's not Henry,' Dani said.

'What?'

'It wasn't Henry who buried his involvement in that crash.'

'So I don't need to be here then? I was actually quite looking forward to reading him his rights.'

'No, you are still needed there. It was Caroline Redfearne. At least I'm pretty sure it was. But it was Oscar driving that car.'

'Whoah, Dani, slow down. What are you talking about?'

'Oscar Redfearne was driving the car that sent Curtis off the road. He was a teenager, not even old enough to drive. I can only guess after the crash that he saw Curtis step from the wreck and kill his girlfriend and daughter. And then he panicked. He fled from there.'

'And Daddy and their lawyers helped clear up the mess for their son?'

'No. Not Daddy.'

'Shit. Caroline?'

'I think so. Make sure she doesn't leave. I'm on my way.'

'But… she's not here.'

'What? But—'

'She hasn't been here the whole time.'

'Then where the hell is she?'

'I haven't a clue.'

'Then you'd better go and find out.'

Chapter Forty-Two

I've been waiting a long time for this one. The main event, you could say. Nine days since I made my first move. I'd had in my mind back on that first night that I might have been able to kill two birds with one stone at Drifford House. Then Sophie had happened...

An unexpected deviation. A welcome one at first, yet one which has since turned rotten. Nothing I can do to change that now. But I'm back on track, in more ways than one, and I think this time I really will get the chance for a two for one.

I've followed the Bentley Continental all the way from her home. I've been keeping close over the last few days, and I know she's barely been outside. She's locked in grieving, or something like that. She's making a rare trip out today, though she isn't alone. The man driving the car is some sort of private security guard. I've no idea if he's a regular detail or if he's someone the family have employed simply in response to me, though I know she doesn't leave the house without him now. Does she know she's a target? Does she realise *why*?

She really should by now, but I'll be kind enough to explain it to her sooner rather than later.

I follow the Bentley all the way to central Birmingham. The traffic coming into the city in the early afternoon is light and I stay a few cars back to remain out of sight, having to use my intuition whenever I get stuck at a junction or at traffic lights. As we approach the city, I'm still within touching distance, and it's not long before we're heading off the A38 carriageway and onto the grid-like streets around the central business district.

The Bentley pulls to a stop outside an innocuous entrance to an underground car park. It's just a square hole cut into the wall of a Victorian office building, a metal roller door covering the entrance.

I drive on past and park the van in an on-street parking bay. There's a pay meter two cars away, and I have plenty of change in my pocket, but what I don't have is time. If my van gets a ticket then so be it. My main aim is simply to reach my quarry.

I grab my bag and get out and quickly stride for the car park entrance, where the Bentley has already disappeared inside, and the door is already rolling shut. It's three feet from the floor when I reach it, and I duck under as effortlessly as I can.

The door closes with a light thud. Beyond me there's a concrete ramp leading down. It sounds and smells strange in here. Enclosed. No natural light; it's muggy and dank. It reminds me of my time in confinement. Not a nice thing to be reminded of. Particularly not at such an important moment. I have to fight to keep my focus and the rats at bay as I begin to walk down.

You're so close now. Make it count.

Her kind words of encouragement help me feel relaxed, though I know when the moment comes I'll be anything but. She continues to offer advice as I walk. I wish it was always like this with her, it makes me feel almost... human.

I walk softly and as I reach the parking level I see the small space underneath the building has room enough for barely a dozen cars, and there's no one else about apart from the newcomers.

She's just getting out, the door held open for her by the black-suited man. He's taller than me. He's quite bulky too, though he's also a bit dim, or at least not very well trained for his newly appointed role. I know this because I'm only five yards from them when he finally seems to sense my presence, approaching him from behind.

I already have the wrench in my hand. It will work better than the blades for this particular part.

The guard first glances over his shoulder. Then he double-takes. Then he finally spins around when he realises this isn't a drill.

'Larry!' she screams as she too figures it out.

I'm already rushing forwards. The wrench is swinging ominously in an arc for the guard's head. He sees it coming. Probably thinks he's out-thought me. He lifts his forearm up and the thick metal smashes into it. The crack and his shout of pain suggests maybe I've shattered bone. I'm already spinning and moving down, aiming to take his legs, but he sees that coming too and manages to shift his weight and plant himself. It might not have been a problem if I was one hundred per cent, but I'm wounded still, from that bitch Dani Stephens and her bastard boyfriend. I don't get anywhere near enough power in the swipe. The guard wobbles but he's not going down, and as I right myself, his fist catches me in the side of the head.

It's me that's going down.

'Jesus, my phone! Where is it?'

It's her. Fumbling in her bag. I can't let her make that call. But Larry the goddamn lump is on top of me. He's punching me in the face. Big meaty fists with sausage fingers. Each strike is like being pounded with a mallet.

There's blood everywhere.

My blood.

It wasn't supposed to happen like this.

You can't fail now!

I can't fail now. But I'm losing consciousness. I don't know how to get out of this position. I've no weapon in reach. My arms are pinned, and his hefty weight is crushing my chest.

Then when I'm on the brink, he slows, then seems to take a moment's pause. He's panting, out of breath. All muscle, no stamina.

No, he's checking she's OK. But he's given me the glimmer of hope I needed.

I buck and he jolts, and I wrench an arm free. His fist flies forwards again and smacks me in the eye, but as he pulls back, I grab his wrist and pull up my head and sink my teeth into flesh. He yelps in pain. I grind down, twist and yank back and one of his thick digits snaps off in my mouth like the bone of a chicken wing.

I spit it out. He's roaring in pain and anger, but his impetus is gone. I grab his head and pull him down and the next moment my teeth are clasped around his neck.

Rinse and repeat.

I'm soon left with a lump of flesh and gristle and blood in my mouth. He's left with a golf-ball sized hole in his neck that's spewing thick blood all over the floor, and me.

I haul him off me and pull myself onto my feet as I grab the wrench.

'Put the phone down,' I demand as blood and spittle flies from my mouth.

She doesn't drop it, but she does pause as she looks over to me, petrified. I see a line of liquid running down her bare leg from underneath her floral summer dress.

'Put it down, now,' I say.

Her hands are trembling. She couldn't punch the numbers in even if she wanted to.

And she does nothing but scream in hellish terror as I launch forwards with the wrench.

Chapter Forty-Three

As emotional as she was, there were no tears from Dani this time. She was beyond that now. She was devastated, distraught, and mind-numbingly miserable. She was also ashamed. Once again she'd failed.

'Come on, Dani, do you want to get out of here?' Easton said as he came back into the reception area from Amanda Johansson's office, where the mutilated bodies of both Caroline Redfearne and the lawyer were being busily poked and prodded by the FSIs. Downstairs in the car park were the similarly mangled remains of Larry Denning, Caroline's personal bodyguard. The thin blood trail from the car, to the lifts, and through to the office suggested Caroline, too, had been attacked there, but then dragged up to the office before she was killed in typically gory fashion. Dani winced at the thoughts of what the three had gone through.

'No,' Dani said. 'We can still help here.'

'We can, but we don't need to. Forensics have got everything under control.'

'No,' Dani said, getting to her feet. 'I'm not leaving here until they're done. Until there's nothing more we can do. I'm not running away from this just because it's getting harder and harder to bear seeing Curtis's latest handiwork.'

'Of course. I wasn't suggesting otherwise. But don't you want a break at least? Five minutes of fresh air?'

'Easton, use your bloody ears. I said no. If you need a breather, go ahead. But I've got work to do here.'

She stomped past him, barging into his shoulder. Not that she was really angry with him, but at least if she channelled anger rather than the other conflicting and more defeatist emotions, she knew she'd have far more power and focus to see this through.

She carried on back into the office. Almost robotically she stepped over the bodies, the pools and spatters of blood and the white-suited FSIs, to Johansson's desk. She grabbed a paper evidence bag and began to sift through what she could find. Thumb drives. DVDs. Papers.

'Dani, what are you doing?' Easton said.

'Collecting evidence.'

'You can't do that.'

'I'm doing it.'

'We have to do this properly. Virtually everything in here is privileged.'

'Not any more.'

Easton came over and put his hand onto Dani's, pinning it to the desk.

'You know it doesn't work like that. Just because Johansson is dead doesn't alter her rights, or those of her clients.'

Dani snatched her hand and glared back at him.

'If there's a crime involved, perpetrated by Johansson, it does change those rights, and you know it. And just because these two are dead, and I really am fucking sorry we were too late to save them, it doesn't detract from the fact of what they did. If they covered up Oscar's involvement in that crash, and through illicit means—'

'You don't know they did that.'

'Which is why I'm doing this. We have to be sure.'

Dani turned and pulled open the top drawer of a filing cabinet. She rifled through. Everything was filed alphabetically. She found files labelled 'Redfearne' in the third drawer down. She took them all. She continued on, taking anything obviously related to the Redfearnes, leaving anything obviously not, and making a gut call on anything that she couldn't tell either way.

It only took her a few minutes. When she was finished she had several piles of files and paper bags ready to take. Easton remained standing, arms folded, staring at her.

'Now, I'm ready to go,' Dani said.

–

They headed on foot the short distance back to HQ, passing by the office building where Dr Collins worked. Dani paused for a moment by the steps outside. Yes they'd made some headway in figuring out the true nature of the crash that had led to Curtis's imprisonment, but the biggest question that remained for Dani was what – who – had set Curtis on his devastating killing spree? And why? She looked up and down the street. No sign of the car for Collins's protection. Dani pulled out her phone and called the number for the officer assigned to her.

'Where are you?' Dani asked.

'Visiting clients again today,' PC Oxley said. 'I've never seen so many prisons.'

'Don't let her out of your sight.'

'Well, I mean… she's inside right now. I'm in the car park, next to her car.'

'You know what I mean.'

Dani ended the call.

'Collins isn't going anywhere without us knowing,' Easton said. 'It's Curtis we need to find.'

Dani said nothing as she moved away.

–

Darkness had long descended, along with a vicious rain storm, later that night as Dani sat by the hospital bed in the gloomy room. The curtains remained open and Dani watched the trickles of water running down the pane. The sound of the rain pelting against the window did a good job of drowning out the whir of machinery and the blips of the monitors keeping watch over Jason's flimsy signs of life.

Dani stared at her boyfriend, as her brain rumbled with turmoil.

'People are dying,' she said, not much louder than a whisper. 'People are dying, and I can't help but blame myself.'

She got nothing in response. No movement in his face, his body. Not even an uptick from his monitors in some sort of subliminal Morse code.

'I just wish you could help me,' she said, fighting to keep herself from breaking down. 'I need you, Jason. I don't know how I can do *this* without you.'

Though she truly had no clue what she meant by *this*. The case? Her life? Both?

She leaned over and reached out and delicately tangled her fingers with his. She got nothing from him in return;

his hand was lifeless and cold to the touch. Yet she still gained an ounce of strength from the contact.

She rested her head on the edge of the mattress, pressed up against his side, and closed her eyes.

–

Dani had an abysmally sleepless night, a combination of the worries of the case, her trauma at Jason's ongoing physical frailty, and because of the seemingly constant toing and froing of nurses coming in and out of the room at all hours to check Jason's vital signs.

Yet bizarrely, come seven a.m. in the morning, when Dani finally gave up on trying to keep her eyes closed, she felt somewhat rejuvenated, at least mentally.

One thing she knew for sure: she couldn't sit by and wallow. As disturbed as she was by everything that had happened since Damian Curtis had first set out on his grim mission, she also felt as though she was one of the few people who could crack the case and bring him down.

She had no choice. She *had* to bring him down.

She put a twenty pence piece into the slot, selected extra strength and extra sugar and the machine rumbled away as the curiously brown/grey concoction that was supposedly coffee began to squirt out into the paper cup. She knew the machine coffee tasted like crap here, but at least the sugar would provide her brain with some fuel and the warm liquid would soothe her insides.

'Rough night?'

Dani turned to see Easton right there behind her looking not so bright and breezy – an awkward look on his face like he didn't know what to say.

'About as bad as yours I reckon,' Dani said.

He didn't seem to get that. Dani took her coffee. When she looked back up to Easton he was staring at her quizzically.

'There's something on your face,' he said.

Dani frowned and wiped at her left cheek where Easton had indicated. Her hand came back with a small red smear on it. Dani shivered when she realised what it was. When she'd left the crime scene the day before there'd been a large blotch of blood on the side of her trousers, whether from Caroline Redfearne or Amanda Johansson, she didn't know. She'd handed the trousers over as evidence, but had the blood somehow transferred to her skin during her getting changed? She'd not had the chance to shower since.

'I thought you might want a lift to the office,' Easton said.

'No, I'm not going to the office. Not yet. I need to freshen up first, but then… Well, you'll see.'

–

The weather remained seriously gloomy and strangely chilly for midsummer as Easton drove up the tree-lined drive, rain-drenched Drifford House in front of them. The whole experience on a day like this was far less climatic and impressive than on the previous occasions Dani had been, as though the bricks and mortar, too, were locked in grief the same as the house's remaining occupants.

As well as the police car by the front gates, there was another parked up on the gravel in front of the house: the protection the family should have had all along, if only Dani had known they remained targets of Curtis.

Yet it was the Redfearnes' deception which had sealed their downfall in a way, not that that made Dani feel any better for what had happened.

Pamela, dressed all in black – mourning, or was that just her normal attire? – showed them through to a lounge that Dani hadn't been in before. Like everything in Drifford House it was huge and ornate and in many respects tasteful, although the overarching mood was sombre and the man sunk into a sofa, staring out of the window, was downright miserable. Although smartly and immaculately dressed as always, with a tailored blue shirt and grey trousers, Henry Redfearne looked dishevelled and lost.

'Mr Redfearne?' Dani said, grabbing his attention. He turned to them but didn't make to get up.

Dani and Easton moved over and sat down on the sofa opposite.

'I'm very sorry for your loss,' Dani said.

Henry still said nothing.

'We won't take up much of your time today, but—'

'Where were you?' Henry said, finally catching Dani's eye. His tone was hard, and the clear accusation knocked Dani slightly.

'Sorry?' she said.

'You've been running around this city for days while that madman is out there killing at will. Where were you? My son... my wife... I've lost everything.'

With those final words, his initial bravado cracked. However strong and bullish Henry Redfearne was under normal circumstances, right now he was understandably dazed and broken, and Dani felt immensely sorry for him, even if she still didn't trust him or like him.

'I'm very sorry, Mr Redfearne,' Dani said, trying to sound as apologetic as she could. 'Believe me, we're doing everything we can—'

'Why was nobody watching her?' he said as a tear rolled down his face. He didn't attempt to wipe it away.

'We didn't know she was a target,' Easton said.

'We do have to ask you some questions, though—'

'Why?'

'Because we need answers,' Dani said. 'You lost your son eleven days ago and you've repeatedly said you have no idea why Damian Curtis would target him. Now Curtis has killed your wife too. Perhaps you're a target, even. We can only help if we know what we're dealing with.'

He said nothing to that, though Dani was sure a sliver of his old confident self was returning in his demeanour, as he no doubt got ready to batten down the hatches.

'Mr Redfearne, you can have someone here with you if you like,' Easton said. 'A friend or a lawyer?'

'A lawyer? Except she's dead too.'

'But that's one of the things I wanted to ask you about,' Dani said. 'Because, was she *your* lawyer, or your wife's?'

Henry glared at Dani now as he weighed up an answer. He didn't look anywhere near as broken as he had moments before. Dani was glad to have the real Henry in the room; she felt much happier challenging this man than the one who'd lost his wife and son.

'It's just that from the case files I've seen that Johansson kept, Caroline seems to be the main point of contact,' Dani said.

It was true, although Dani hadn't had nearly enough time yet to read through all of the files she'd taken from Johansson's office.

'Is that a problem?' Henry said.

'No, I'm just trying to figure out the dynamic.'

'Caroline had known Amanda for years. That's all.'

'How?'

'How?'

'How did they know each other?'

'Fuck knows. Who gives a flying crap? They knew each other. From getting their nails done or from the spa or something.'

'Would there have been any business between them that you weren't aware of?'

'*Business?*'

'Did your wife seek out legal advice from Johansson on a personal basis, as opposed to in relation to you two as a couple?'

'Well how the hell am I supposed to know the answer to that? You're asking me to confirm something that by the very definition I wouldn't know about.'

'I think DI Stephens is suggesting you could have been aware of the fact your wife was seeking advice in a personal capacity,' Easton said, 'even if you weren't aware of the details of that advice.'

Now it was Easton's turn to receive the glare.

'Mr Redfearne? Are you able to answer that?' Dani said.

'I don't know anything about their dealings together.'

'Were you aware that your son was involved in a road traffic accident when he was fourteen years old?' Dani asked.

No response.

'He was driving a car registered to you. A Mercedes S550.'

344

Still nothing.

'We have reason to believe on the night of the seventeenth of January 2016, while driving on Clement Hill, he caused another driver to leave the road. That car was being driven by Damian Curtis. His girlfriend and her son died that night. Damian Curtis was convicted of their manslaughter. Did you know about that?'

Henry was saying nothing.

'The thing is, there was no reference to your son being there that night in any official records.'

Henry looked away now, back out into the garden.

'Were you aware that your wife, together with Amanda Johansson, paid bribes to have your son's involvement in that crash wiped away?'

'How dare you bring these allegations against my wife?' Henry said, turning back to face Dani. 'I've not even identified her body, and you're trying to smear her integrity.'

'Is that a yes or a no?' Dani said. 'Because while I appreciate the sensitive timing of this, there's no getting away from the fact that this is a serious crime, nor from the fact that if you had anything to do with this, you could be next on Curtis's list.'

'Like you said, Johansson was my wife's lawyer. Not mine.'

'So that's a no?' Dani asked.

Henry didn't answer.

'Why was your wife going to see Johansson yesterday?' Easton asked.

'I've no idea.'

'Did you know that's where she was going?'

'No.'

'Can you think of a reason why they would be meeting?'

'No.'

Henry Redfearne abruptly got to his feet. He straightened out his trousers.

'I've really got nothing more to say to you two, about this, or about anything else. Good day, detectives. I'll get Pamela to show you out.'

With that he promptly walked out of the room. Easton and Dani glanced at each other, Dani as bemused as Easton looked.

'I guess we're done here then,' Dani said.

–

As they drove away from Drifford House, Dani really hoped she'd never have to set foot in that place again.

'It's a pretty convenient excuse he's got now,' Easton said.

'It is indeed. Wife dead, son dead, lawyer dead. Even if he was neck-deep in that scheme, he can claim ignorance to the whole event.'

'But we have got access to their personal and financial records, don't forget.'

'We have,' Dani said, 'but unless we find a direct instruction from him in relation to paying someone off, or in relation to his son's involvement in that crash, it won't be enough.'

'Perhaps, on this occasion, he really has suffered enough already,' Easton said. 'At worst, he paid a bribe to get his son off what might have been a pretty mild punishment for a minor crime. Oscar didn't cause those deaths. Now Henry's son and his wife have both been brutally murdered because of it all.'

'Perhaps he has suffered,' Dani said. 'But I'm not going to let him off the hook just yet. I want to know exactly why Caroline was going to meet Johansson yesterday.'

'You think it's significant?'

'A few days after her son was killed? Without her husband? And he's claiming ignorance about the whole thing? I'd say as far as things not smelling right, that pretty much stinks.'

'We'd better hope what you took from Johansson yesterday gives us the answers then, otherwise I'm not sure how we'll ever find out.'

Well he'd certainly changed his tune, Dani thought.

'You know what, Aaron? I'm beyond *hope* now. I'm simply going to get this finished, whatever it takes.' She looked over to him. 'You with me?'

'You're the boss,' he said. 'Whatever it takes.'

Chapter Forty-Four

As they drove back to HQ, Dani made yet another call to PC Oxley.

'You're still at the prison?' Dani asked.

'En route to Birmingham, I do believe,' Oxley said.

'To Collins's office?'

'Apparently so.'

'Good. Tell her I'll be coming to see her later.'

–

In keeping with Dani's own mood, the project room at HQ had a melancholy feel about it when Dani and Easton arrived. With a bit of cajoling and an update on the various strands of the investigation, Dani managed to lift the downbeat mood slightly, and the team were soon busily scouring for the answers Dani was seeking. DC Mutambe had been given the new task of leading the search through Johansson's case files, to add to his ongoing digging into the Redfearnes. Despite her brashness the day before, Dani wasn't asking for a gung-ho rampage through every facet of Johansson's professional life. The dead lawyer undoubtedly had numerous perfectly legitimate clients whose legal privilege remained intact, but any interaction between Johansson and the Redfearnes was fair game as far as Dani was concerned, and would be identified and filtered out for review.

Grayling had the task of trying to find a connection between Collins, the Redfearnes and Curtis's other victims. If they could identify any sort of motive for Collins in Curtis's rampage...

Meanwhile Constable was still busy leading on CCTV, busily pulling together every movement he could find related to Damian Curtis in the ongoing effort to pinpoint where he was so successfully hiding day in, day out.

Dani left Easton to follow up on forensics and the crime scene from the previous day, while she decided to take some time to roam through a bit of everything. Which she did largely to frustration after frustration for more than two hours, until Constable piped up.

'Boss, come and take a look at this.'

Dani headed over.

'We're still trying to piece together Curtis's movements in and around the crime scenes, and it's becoming clear that he's spending days scoping out each site beforehand.'

He pulled up a spreadsheet that was crammed with data: dates and locations, times and references to CCTV towers.

'If we look at Drifford House, for example,' Constable said, 'there were ten separate occasions over the four days before Oscar was attacked when Curtis's Transit van was picked up in and around the area.'

Constable pointed to the cluster of data on the spreadsheet all labelled as Drifford House.

'It's the same for the Deville murder, for Feathers in Edgbaston, for Rugeley, even for your street.'

Dani winced at that comment. 'So he's well planned,' Dani said, not really sure if she was missing something. 'I think we knew that already.'

'Yes, but I've done my best to trace his movements back, like you said, to figure where he's coming from and going to.'

'And?'

Constable pulled up an image of a map of the West Midlands, onto which several hundred red and blue dots and lines were superimposed.

'I've tried to separate direction of travel by red and blue. So red precedes blue on any particular day or trip. You can see it's not an exact science, but if you follow the colours, and the direction of the arrows, you can see patterns starting to emerge as to his most usual routes. The biggest cluster we have seems to be originating around here, south of the city.'

Constable used his finger on the screen to circle the area. It was probably a couple of miles wide, at least, around Northfield and King's Norton.

'That's a pretty big area,' Dani said, and Constable shrank a little in his seat as though his bubble had been burst.

'I know. I'm narrowing it down as best I can, but—'

'No, it's good. It's really good. Keep going... Wait a second. The arrows on there.'

Dani pointed to the cluster of dots and arrows right in the centre of the city.

'Yeah?'

'Show me that data on the spreadsheet.'

Constable nodded and pulled up the spreadsheet which in a couple of clicks he'd transferred to a pivot table.

He played with the data for a few seconds until he was showing all the entries around Birmingham city centre. Dani stared at the information, but she couldn't quite figure what she was trying to see.

'Can you email it to me?' she asked. 'I need to have a think about this.'

'Sure.'

Dani went back to her own seat and was soon delving into the data from Constable as her thoughts continued to take worrying shape. With links to the CCTV files all included in Constable's spreadsheet, it was a minefield of data and Dani's mind was soon flooded with information overload.

She frowned.

'Easton,' she called over, 'where did we get to with Curtis's movements yesterday?'

'It looks like he followed Caroline's car all the way from near Drifford House, so he must have been spying on her from there, waiting for the moment.'

Had he known Caroline was heading to see Johansson or was that just some sort of bonus? No, that wasn't what Dani was thinking about here. She shook her head to get back to the earlier thought.

'But after the attack? The van was still there, right? He abandoned it?'

'Van was there,' Easton said, 'on the street right outside the office block. Full sweep done by forensics before it was towed. Nothing much of interest found.'

'And we lost him where?'

'We have him on camera as he moved on foot towards Colmore Row, then nothing.'

'But that area has cameras everywhere.'

'It does. But this was basically rush hour, the busiest period of the day in the busiest part of the city with office workers everywhere. He could have got on a bus or headed to New Street or Snowhill station quite easily, and we've no idea if he somehow changed appearance. Slipped a jacket on or something. We have to assume he knows the cameras are there given the way he moves, so...'

Dani agreed on the last point, but she was heading in a different direction altogether on the rest of it. She went back and focussed on the series of CCTV captures around Northfield and King's Norton, where Constable had said he thought Curtis originated from.

'I've only got the clips here,' Dani said to Constable as she clicked into the links in unison. 'How do I see what came before and after these moments?'

Constable got up and came over and took control of the mouse.

'We've already been through the full files on each of these days; you won't find anything more of Curtis.'

'It's not Curtis I'm looking for.'

Constable looked at Dani curiously, but said nothing more and Dani was soon scrolling through the feed for a CCTV tower on Ryland Avenue in King's Norton. She went through a whole day in a matter of minutes, but saw nothing that took her eye. But then on the next file...

'Shit,' Dani said. Everyone in the room turned to look at her, but she barely noticed as she continued to scroll.

Sure enough, later that same day, she saw it again. Then again the next day. The same car each time. She knew exactly whose it was.

'It's not his starting point,' Dani said, loud enough for everyone to hear. She got up from her chair.

'What's not?' Constable asked.

'The area you circled for me. It's not his starting point; it's not where he's staying.'

'Then what?'

'Easton, you're coming with me.'

She turned and strode for the door without waiting for his response.

Chapter Forty-Five

The lift took an age to arrive. More than once Dani had to hold back the urge to race down the stairs instead.

Finally she and Easton were both inside, heading down.

'Are you going to explain?' Easton said, looking more than a little anxious.

'Curtis's routes into the city centre,' Dani said, trying to find the words to explain it succinctly, but her brain was still firing at warp speed. 'He took two different routes in. Sometimes coming up Newhall Street from near St Paul's Square, but other times he'd loop around Snowhill and come along Colmore Row.'

'And?'

'And why would he do that? If you're coming into the city from the same direction each time, to the same spot, why would you go two different ways?'

'Traffic?'

'No. It's because he was going to two different places. Two locations, for different purposes. Two locations, right around the corner from each other, but on different parts of the one-way system.'

The lift doors opened, and Dani had to hold herself back from sprinting out. As she strode for the exit, her mind once again flashed back to the day of the attack in her home. How she'd been gunning the car across the city to Harborne, Easton in the passenger seat telling her to be calm, telling her everything would be fine.

Everything hadn't been fine. If they'd arrived a minute earlier that day, would it have made a difference? What about thirty seconds earlier?

'Dr Collins's office is right off Colmore Row,' Dani said as she finally burst into a jog once they were outside, heading away from HQ towards nearby Snowhill station. Their destination was all of two hundred yards further away.

'Shit,' Easton said.

'She lied to us. Collins… she's been lying this whole time,' Dani said, her heavy breathing already making it difficult to talk. And she hadn't realised how tired and sluggish her body was today until now. 'On the CCTV… the cluster around Northfield… That's near where she lives. I even saw her car on the same cameras that picked up Curtis. She's been seeing him all this time. Perhaps even helping him to hide.'

'And last night…' Easton trailed off.

'Last night… maybe Curtis never even left the city centre,' Dani said, finishing what she thought he'd been about to say. 'After killing Caroline and Amanda… what if he went straight to Collins's office? He may have been there the whole time.'

'We need back-up for this,' Easton said.

And this time Dani wasn't going to say no to that. 'Call it in,' she said.

Easton already had his phone in his hand.

Bystanders, late arrivals to work, early shoppers, those out for morning coffee meetings, all stared over curiously as Dani and Easton ran along the street. Easton talked hurriedly and out of breath into his phone. By the time he was finished, the entrance to Collins's office building was almost in touching distance.

Strangely, the scene outside was serene and calm – except for the two red-cheeked coppers approaching.

And there was Oxley's car, right outside. No one inside.

'Where is he?' Dani shouted, the phone already to her ear.

'You did tell him not to let her out of your sight!'

Oxley didn't answer the phone.

'They're already inside,' Dani said.

Was Oxley already dead?

Or had Dani made a big mistake and Curtis wasn't even here at all?

Dani raced up to the intercom, trying to clear her head as she pressed on the buzzer.

'We don't have time for this,' Easton said.

He reached forwards and slammed his palm against every button. A second later a raspy voice came through the speaker from someone inside one of the other units.

'West Midlands Police. Let us in, now,' Easton said. The force of his demand was sufficient. A second later the door buzzed open.

Dani glanced to her right as she rushed inside. A couple of hundred yards away, blue lights were visible amongst the city centre taxis and buses. Help would be with them soon enough, but Dani wouldn't wait.

She took the stairs two at a time, Easton right behind her. When they arrived at the top of the stairs, Dani was sweaty and puffing heavily. The door to Collins's office was locked shut. Easton and Dani shared a questioning look, before Dani moved over and pressed the intercom buzzer and then knocked on the door. Through the frosted glass, Dani could make out little of the waiting area beyond. Though it looked empty in there, didn't it? She pushed her ear close to the glass. After barely two seconds of waiting, she'd had enough.

'Easton.'

He understood the request. She stepped to the side as Easton moved forwards. He lifted his knee and launched his heel to the door. The thumping contact echoed through the enclosed space. Easton hit the wood again and the force was sufficient to break the magnetic contact and the door swung open.

Dani raced in first.

'Oxley, you there?'

The words had barely passed Dani's lips when she saw the pool of blood on the floor, at the head of the corridor that led to Collins's office. As she traced the circle of red she found the thick-soled shoe of a downed figure, poking out.

Oxley.

Dani faltered in her step.

'Back-up will be here any second,' Easton said from behind her.

Then there was a bang and a scream from further down the corridor. Collins?

No, they didn't have time to wait for back-up, even if they were only thirty seconds away.

Dani reached over and grabbed a book from the reception desk. That was all. A big, hard-backed book. Better than nothing. She rushed for the corridor. There was another scream from through the open office door, though Dani couldn't yet see who or what lay beyond the threshold.

'Damian! This is the police,' Dani shouted out.

She slowed when she was three yards away. Easton was still right behind her.

'Dr Collins, are you in there?' Dani called.

'Help! Pl—'

Her cry became muffled. But Dani also thought she could pinpoint where in the nearby room the sound had come from.

Putting paid to better judgement, she rushed into the room.

It was like the scene from a horror movie. Blood spatters everywhere. Collins was on the floor by her desk. Her grey skirt and white blouse were both drenched in thick, dark blood. The gashes on her arms, her torso, were stark and gruesome, and Dani lost her breath as she stared.

Damian Curtis was standing over Collins, axe in his hand, held above his head. He turned to Dani, a snarl on his face.

Their eyes met.

A second later Easton lurched forward, swinging wildly with a glass weight he'd picked up from somewhere. Curtis jumped towards him and the men collided and went down in a heap.

Easton was dazed, and Curtis was soon back on his feet and with a battle cry of pure rage he raced towards Dani. Easton shot back up and he grabbed Curtis's shoulder. He tried to hit him again with the weight, but he was set all wrong and Curtis tugged him forwards. Easton swung and missed, and Curtis spun and slashed the axe across.

The blade glanced Easton's belly and he shouted in pain as he went down.

Curtis lifted the axe above his head once more. Dani was in pure survival mode now. There was nothing else for it. Fight back or die.

She lifted an arm to protect herself as the axe came down. She bent at the knees… then sprang up like a jack-in-the-box.

Her raised arm blocked Curtis's axe swing at his wrist. With her other hand she launched the book up, spine first, power and momentum coming from her body's upward movement.

The thick spine of the book crashed into Curtis's chin. His head snapped back. The axe clattered away. Perhaps Curtis would have fallen down from that perfectly planted blow, but the next moment, Easton jumped onto his back, and wrapped his arms around Curtis's neck.

Dani rushed forwards and barged into them both and all three of them crashed to the ground. Easton took the brunt of the fall as the bodies piled up on him. But he didn't let go. He wrapped his legs around Curtis as he tightened the grip around his neck.

Curtis coughed and spluttered. His cheeks were deep red, his eyes bulged.

'Get him on his side!' Dani shouted.

Easton managed to swivel. Dani tried to grab Curtis's wrists. But he was having none of it.

He lashed out and caught Dani in the eye. Then the next second he reached to his side and there was a blade in his hand.

Dani threw herself back just as the knife whooshed through the air, narrowly avoiding her neck. Curtis swung at her again, and again. He couldn't reach her. But unless she got closer, she couldn't cuff him either.

Then Curtis changed tactic. He twisted the knife around and sank the blade into Easton's side.

Easton grimaced and groaned, his strength seemed to waiver slightly. But Curtis's strike had at least given Dani an opportunity...

She flung herself forwards and grabbed Curtis's arm. She twisted it around as he withdrew the knife from Easton's flesh, blood dripping from the blade. As he fought against her, Dani forced Curtis's wrist back, almost to breaking point. The knife came free.

'Come on!' Easton said, the desperation in his voice clear. The power in his chokehold was quickly waning.

Dani clasped a cuff around Curtis's wrist, wrestled for his other hand and managed to squeeze it into place.

'He's done!' Dani shouted.

She immediately pulled back as Easton let go and shoved Curtis over so he was face first. Easton dug his knee into Curtis's back, and forced his face into the carpet with his hand.

'Damian Curtis...' Easton said before pausing, out of breath and gritting his teeth in pain, 'I'm arresting you on suspicion of murder...'

Dani stared from Curtis, to Collins, to Easton as her colleague read the madman his rights. Easton was out of breath. Blood was seeping through his clothes, both from the knife wound and the blow from the axe. He looked like he was about to pass out.

Dani heard the rush of footsteps from out in the corridor. One, two, three, uniformed officers burst into view.

'It's fine!' Dani shouted, dazed and out of breath. She looked to Collins. 'But get an ambulance. Now!'

Dani pulled herself over to Collins and knelt down beside her. Her eyes were wide but glassy. She was gurgling for breath. Dani really didn't know if there was anything anyone could do to save her, even if the paramedics arrived that second.

'Look what you've done,' Dani said. Collins's weary gaze met hers. 'You made him do this.'

Dani didn't know why, but despite her less than sympathetic words, she found herself reaching for Collins's hand. She grasped it and felt the faintest of squeezes back.

'Is... he... dead?' Collins said.

'No,' Dani said. She looked over to Curtis who was gibbering away as two burly policemen dragged him up onto his feet. Easton was hunched over, clutching his stomach in agony.

Dani looked back to Collins whose eyes appeared even more pained now.

'I'm... so... sorry,' Collins said.

'Just tell me why?'

'N-No.' Collins managed the slightest shake of her head. 'It... wasn't me. I... swear. Only... tried to help... him.'

They were the last words Dr Collins said before she went completely still.

Chapter Forty-Six

Dani hadn't wanted to make any more trips to Drifford House, but this one was worth it, even if Easton couldn't be there with her; he was still recuperating in hospital the day after the fight at Dr Collins's office. She'd tell him all about today soon enough.

She didn't bother to go inside the manor house though. The uniforms could do that. She only wanted to see his face.

Dani was hanging on her open car door when Henry Redfearne stepped out into the rain, flanked by two policemen, his wrists cuffed behind his back. Dani didn't move. She had nothing to say to him.

The policemen escorted him over to their car. Henry's gaze and his sullen pout was fixed on Dani the whole time, right until one of the coppers pushed his head down to ease him into the back seat. Dani waited until the police car was heading away down the drive before she moved. She was about to sit back in her car when Pamela appeared in the open doorway to the house.

Dani thought for a moment. Then walked over.

'Did you know?' Dani said.

'Know what?'

'About what Oscar did that night? The crash? The cover-up?'

Pamela said nothing. Dani would have to weigh up whether it was even worth pursuing now, given all the chaos and misery that had already flowed.

'I'll be in touch,' Dani said, before she turned and walked back to her car.

–

'I thought you might have come alone,' Ben said, when Dani walked into the prison interview room with Constable in tow.

Dani looked over to Daley, sitting next to her brother like the good little guard dog he was.

'Same to you,' she said. 'Are you too afraid to speak to us by yourself now this has all blown up?'

'Not in the slightest,' Ben said, pure nonchalance. 'So who's the new face?'

'DC Constable,' Constable said as he and Dani took their seats.

Daley and Ben shared a look but said nothing.

'You got him then,' Ben said to Dani.

'Curtis? Of course we did. We always do in the end. Take yourself for example.'

'Very clever.'

'But not as clever as you obviously think you are. And I'm also guessing by now that you've heard the news about Dr Collins?'

'The news that she's dead? Or that she might well have been the person who set Curtis up for all of this?'

'Well obviously you've heard both then,' Dani said. 'Though I do have to ask myself how the press found out about the latter, given the police haven't made any public statements about Collins's *alleged* involvement.'

Ben shrugged his shoulders. 'You're asking me?'

'You see, the problem any detective has, with any murder, is that to gain a conviction, it's vitally important, in virtually every single case, that we have a motive.'

'OK?'

'And my big problem with Dr Collins and this theory working through the tabloids that she somehow put Curtis up to all this by implanting a voice in his head… what's in it for her?'

'Once again, you're asking me?'

'Well I can't ask her. She's dead. So why not you?'

'Other than I'm locked up in here with virtually no access to the outside world?'

'Though you do have your crony here to do your dirty work outside these walls, right?'

Dani glanced to Daley.

'I beg your pardon?' he said, genuinely offended.

'Didn't the papers suggest Collins was having it off with Henry Redfearne?' Ben said. 'That the wife, Caroline, I think her name was, was going to smear him in the press pretty soon. Scandal, divorce, lots of money involved. The tabloids would have loved it. So maybe Collins did have motive.'

'You really are clued up,' Dani said.

'I have a lot of time on my hands.'

'Except it's all bullshit.'

'It is?' Ben said.

'So I ask myself again and again. If not Collins, then who else not only had a position of influence over Damian Curtis, but something to gain from his nasty mission of revenge?'

'Why does there have to be anyone else at all?'

'Let's just say there is.'

Ben shrugged. 'OK then. Another doctor, perhaps? Certainly, someone trained in psychiatry or something like that, wouldn't you say? I mean, where would you even start?'

'Sounds like you've already been thinking about this. Never have the answers slipped off your tongue so easily, Ben.'

He glared coldly at her now.

'Detectives, is there a point to this meeting?' Daley said. 'A particular question or questions you're looking for answers to from my client, relevant to your case?'

'I know it was you,' Dani said, her eyes narrowing as she focussed in on Ben. 'I know it was you. I don't know exactly how you did it, but I won't stop until I prove it.'

'There's nothing to prove,' Ben said, trying his best to look perplexed. He glanced over at Daley. 'Can you believe how ridiculous this is?'

Dani got to her feet, Constable followed. 'But you made one big mistake,' she said.

Ben looked at her quizzically.

'We've got Curtis now. And sooner or later he'll talk. He'll tell us exactly what you did.'

For a fleeting second Ben looked just a little bit unsure of himself, but the look was gone again in a flash.

When Dani reached the door, she looked back to her brother one last time.

'Happy hunting,' Ben said, with a sly wink.

–

It was getting late by the time Dani finally made it back to HQ. She'd deliberated whether to head straight to the hospital, to check on both Easton and Jason, but ultimately decided she wanted to go back to the office, given there was so much that she and McNair needed to catch up on.

'Quite a couple of days,' McNair said, standing behind her desk with her arms folded.

'You could say that,' Dani said.

Behind McNair the sun was just creeping down behind the shimmering multistorey office block across the road. The end of another hot day, though McNair's office was ice cold from air conditioning, and a wave of goose pimples rose across Dani's bare arms.

McNair remained standing, and Dani similarly didn't bother to take a seat. She couldn't read the look on McNair's face.

Was this good or bad?

'How's Easton?' McNair asked.

'Last I heard he's had quite a few stitches, and it'll be weeks before he can move about properly, but he was lucky. The knife didn't damage any organs. He should be absolutely fine.'

'And I'm certainly glad about that. But there's going to have to be some serious thinking about how all this played out, and why we've now got one PC dead, and another of our team in a serious condition in hospital.'

Dani nodded again, a lump in her throat at the thought of PC Oxley's death. She felt truly terrible about that, even though she was sure she wasn't at fault. Regardless, she understood how the bureaucracy worked, no point in fighting it unless she had to. There'd be an internal investigation not just into what had happened to Oxley and Easton, but about every aspect of the case.

'Where've you got to with the press leak?'

'I simply don't know where their information came from,' Dani said. 'It's a small team, and honestly? I trust them all. Maybe there isn't even a leak here. The team have crawled over the Redfearne data we have. There's nothing in there to suggest Collins even knew Henry Redfearne, let alone was having an affair with him that would give her a motive for wanting Caroline or anyone else dead.'

'Hmm,' was all McNair said to that.

'And… I really don't believe Collins put Curtis up to this. You didn't see the way she looked at me, or hear what she said. I believed her. She didn't make Curtis kill those people.'

'Which, according to you, leaves only your brother.'

Dani nodded.

'Except you have absolutely no evidence how he could have done this.'

'No,' Dani said, trying to keep her head held high, though it was a struggle. 'But that doesn't mean we shouldn't keep looking. He had access to Curtis, he had motive for this—'

'What motive?'

'All those games about the offer of information for leniency. He wanted Curtis to kill because the information would give him leverage.'

'Except he never gave us any useful information until it was too late.'

'No. But then there was the attack on me and Jason. Ben's own personal revenge. Plus, the fact his lawyer is now busy discrediting Collins for their own sick gain. It wouldn't surprise me at all if Daley had that story about Collins's involvement leaked, had the bogus story of Collins and Redfearne put out there too, just so they can claim her expert testimony is tarnished.'

'Quite some accusations, from where I'm standing.'

Dani sighed. 'That doesn't mean it isn't true.'

'No, it doesn't. But it does mean I have to consider very carefully what we do next here. We've already had a complaint from Henry Redfearne's lawyer.'

Dani tutted. 'Another one? He doesn't waste any time, does he?'

'No, he does not. But you know someone in Redfearne's position is going to fight hard against whatever we throw at him. We're going to need a watertight case against him.'

'Sexual harassment, obstruction of justice, what else do you want here?'

'Make your case then,' McNair said.

'What?'

'Explain it all to me. Convince me.'

Dani took a deep breath to compose her thoughts. 'OK. January 2016. Oscar Redfearne takes his dad's car for a joyride. He causes a crash, but he's fine. The occupants of the other car are Damian Curtis, his girlfriend and her son.'

'You can prove this?'

'We have plenty of corroborative CCTV evidence. My brother's testimony, if we can get it admitted. If we get Curtis talking, even better. We managed to get hold of evidence of the repair work carried out on Redfearne's car.'

'So the crash happened. You need to tie Henry Redfearne to it.'

'I'm trying. That night, Curtis was drunk, high on drugs and in a rage, and the car trip followed a blazing row. He confessed to my brother he wanted to kill his girlfriend because she was trying to leave him. But the crash didn't kill her. In fact, Oscar witnessed Curtis step from that car and choke his girlfriend and then her son to death. Then Oscar panicked. He fled. Told his mum. She and her lawyer, Johansson, did some dirty deals to make sure Oscar's presence that night never came out.'

'Again. Can you prove any of this?'

Now it was Dani who sighed. 'It's going to be hard, given most of the people involved in that aspect are dead. But we'll try. Following the money has to be the best way. It's possible Henry Redfearne was all part of this too.'

'Possible, but not very proveable. And then?'

Dani slumped a little, already sensing where McNair was going to come out of this. 'Curtis is sentenced to manslaughter, which he was disgruntled about to say the least. Dr Collins was assigned to assess him as part of the trial, and was holding sessions with him up to his release.'

'But not since his release? I thought I was told we saw Curtis's van in and around Collins's home and workplace multiple times over the last few weeks?'

'That's right. But I now believe Curtis was just watching her. Like he did all his victims.'

'But it's equally likely she was holding secret sessions with him. That if there was a master manipulator here, it was her. Is it not?'

Dani sighed again. She guessed McNair was right, evidentially at least, even if she didn't believe that to be the case. The one person who could corroborate her theory was Curtis. Would they ever get him to talk? Given his mental state, would his confession even be admissible evidence if he did?

'And these voices?' McNair said.

'We'll need professional help to explain this, but Curtis has a long history of psychosis. Basically, he has voices in his head. I don't know how, but I'm certain someone implanted a new voice in him. A voice that persuaded him to kill.'

McNair scoffed. Dani felt her cheeks flush a little. She knew it sounded outlandish, but she was absolutely sure that's exactly what had happened.

'And you think that was your brother. A fellow inmate at prison, with zero experience of psychiatry, as opposed to Dr Collins, a long-standing therapist?'

'Collins had nothing to gain. My brother does.'

'It's a hell of a story,' McNair said.

'And I wouldn't be standing here telling it if I didn't believe it one hundred per cent.'

McNair took the longest sigh that Dani had ever heard in her life, then sat down behind her desk.

'We have Curtis locked up,' McNair said. 'We'll push forward with the murder charges against him. I also think it's worth pursuing Henry Redfearne. Find a money trail that links him to knowing about the crash and the cover-up. But this voice in Curtis's head? The idea of someone using him like a puppet?'

Dani bit her lip.

'I'm sorry, Dani. Without something direct, a confession at the very least, then it's a no go. The CPS would never go for it, no jury would ever buy it. We have our killer, Curtis, behind bars. If Collins was the mastermind, she's already dead. If it's your brother, he's already locked up. I can't advocate wasting resources chasing the impossible. I suggest it's time to move on.'

Dani simply had nothing to say to that, but it felt like a hole had been punched right through her chest.

'Are we done?' McNair said.

Chapter Forty-Seven

Three Weeks Later

The sun was shining outside, its warm rays cascading into the room and bathing everything in lustrous light. It didn't help Jason much, nor was it helping Dani, who remained as low as ever, regardless of how much medication she took. One positive was that she'd heard today that Sophie Blackwood had returned home to her parents. Her physical wounds were still healing, her mental scars might never, but Sophie still had a chance for a life.

And Easton, he'd be back at work in no time.

As for Jason...

'I think we got Redfearne,' Dani said to him. 'He's still saying nothing, his lawyers barely let us get a word in, but everything around him is crumbling. We have nearly twenty witnesses now alleging sexual harassment. We think we might have a chance at hitting him with conspiracy to rape too. Our biggest breakthrough this week? We found the money trail. We can link him right back to what happened to Oscar that night, and the bribes paid in the aftermath.'

She took her hand back and stared at Jason's face. As ever there was no movement, no reaction to her talking to him, though she only hoped he could hear. His brain function was improving bit by bit, day by day, even if he remained in a coma. His condition made her wonder all the more about Curtis. About herself, even. About how incredible and complex the human brain is, but also how utterly vulnerable it is too.

Damian Curtis wasn't a good person. He hadn't been since the day he took his girlfriend's and her son's lives, perhaps even before that he was bad too. But Dani remained convinced that he was only the monster he'd since become because of expert manipulation.

In a way, Dani actually felt sorry for Curtis, even despite the fact that it was his hand that had led to Jason being here, and all those other people losing their lives.

'I just don't know how we're going to get him, Jason. I know it was Ben. It had to be. All this time, I questioned whether he just lost it all those years ago. But maybe he really has been a psychopath all this time. What does that say about me?'

Once again Collins's words about psychopaths, about the mimicking of emotion and 'normal' human behaviour, rattled in Dani's head. Were both she and Ben guilty of doing that?

'At least we've got Curtis,' she said. 'He'll spend the rest of his life in a mental hospital, I'm sure. It's something, even if I'm still tormented by all the other people who were hurt and killed… people that could have been saved if only we'd got him sooner.'

A tear rolled down Dani's cheek at those last words. Whatever words of encouragement she'd had from the force, she still felt responsible. Even if she'd apprehended Curtis that day in her home, it would have saved four more lives.

'But do you know the worst part?' Dani said. She picked the newspaper up and put it onto the bed, the headline facing up towards Jason, as if he was going to suddenly open his eyes and read it and give her comment and comfort.

'I saw this coming. Ever since the last time I went to the jail to see him. I knew Ben, and that bastard Daley, would find a way to play this for their own gain. Without trial, Dr Collins has been disgraced. They're asking for all of her work, *all* of it, to be thrown out. Several applications have already been made for mistrials in cases where she gave evidence. All because of little more than tabloid sensationalism, spurred on by Daley.'

Dani wiped at the tears now as she tried to pull herself together.

'I know it wasn't Collins. I just don't know what I can do to prove it.' She paused now as her eyes flicked over the newspaper's headline story, the call for Collins's lifetime of trial work to be disregarded. The threats of applications for mistrials. 'I've spoken to people in the know... It's possible, I mean, really possible, that if they succeed with this, that Ben actually has a chance of getting out. He could walk free, despite everything I know he did.'

Dani was trembling now, with fear and shame and something else she couldn't even describe.

She reached out and took the paper away and dropped it onto the floor. Then she held Jason's hand again. She squeezed.

'And I'm terrified,' she said. 'I'm terrified for me, I'm terrified for Gemma and for the kids. She's already talking about what protection the police could offer her.'

Dani closed her eyes and shook her head in despair.

'I need you for this, Jason. I really need you for this. I can't do it without you any more.'

What was that?

As the words had passed her lips, she was sure she felt a twitch in his hand.

She opened her eyes and stared down. She squeezed his hand a little harder, then relaxed her grip.

There it was again. Just one finger. Just the slightest of movements.

Had he heard her? Was he giving her a sign? A sign that she wasn't going to be alone. That he'd be right there by her side.

She looked up to his face, almost overcome with emotion.

'Jason?'

She waited. And waited.

And waited…

But there was nothing more from him.

Nothing at all.

Dani lay her head onto Jason's chest, as her tears continued to fall.

A Letter From Rob

Thank you so much for reading *The Rules of Murder*, I really hope you enjoyed reading it as much as I enjoyed writing it.

If you didn't know already, *The Rules of Murder* is the second book in the DI Dani Stephens crime thriller series (after *The Essence of Evil*), and she's a character that I've really developed a great affinity to over the last two books. A strong and complex character, and one whose backstory is as dark as it is incredible, I've rarely had such pleasure in taking a character on a journey as I have to date with Dani. I know I don't always make life easy for my protagonists, but you can always be sure that whatever I throw at Dani, she will fight to the bitter end, and have no doubt that there are plenty more of DI Dani Stephens's escapades to come yet!

One of the aspects of the series that I've found so fascinating thus far is the exploration of criminal psychology, and what it is that makes some people killers, which goes hand in hand with analysing psychopathy, sociopathy and the like. There's such a huge minefield of research, debate and case history out there that you can be sure that this is a theme that will continue to feature in future novels – as long as I don't get into too much trouble before then because of my increasingly unseemly Google search history...

I'm very grateful for reviews (as are all authors), so if you could spare a few minutes to write and post one online that would be hugely appreciated. I know many of my readers have followed me from my very first book, and I'm always happy to hear feedback, and to interact with readers online (and in person if you ever see me out and about!). You can reach me via my website (where you can also sign up to my newsletter), and on social media, links as follows:

Website: www.robsinclairauthor.com
Twitter: @rsinclairauthor
Facebook: fb.me/robsinclairauthor

All the best
Rob Sinclair

Books by Rob Sinclair

The Sleeper series:
Sleeper 13
Fugitive 13
Imposter 13

The Enemy series:
Dance with the Enemy
Rise of the Enemy
Hunt for the Enemy

The James Ryker series:
The Red Cobra
The Black Hornet
The Silver Wolf
The Green Viper
The White Scorpion

The Dani Stephens series:
The Essence of Evil

Others:
Dark Fragments